WRETCHED

SARA HAILSTONE

Running Wild

to the women of this family,
the ones who have crossed over,
to the living,
and to those unborn.

PROLOGUE

We were wretched.

This family was wretched.

Exiles. Outcasts. Strangers in our own homes. We assumed, because ego was that brilliant with her trickery, that we were victims of this state. This wretched country.

Linguistic roots we tongued in night-visions: wreccan, avenge, to drive out, punish.

Etymological currents. Internalized and lived along.

Vile and despicable.

We spoke to ourselves harshly.

Wrikan, to persecute, from the root of werg, to work, to do, from vergas, distress, or slave, or vragu, enemy, then urgere, to inflict or take vengeance.

We thought that we were born separate. Defined edges.

We assumed that we began, it was not so.

We were born into their lives. Attached. Hinged. Hooked in.

We chose to enter here. Rooted.

We chose here. Barbed. Blood-bound. Genetic rivers.

These eternal collisions and encounters. We chose them.

We overlapped. Time, geography, and energy. Bodies. Threaded biology with memory. Our mortality, ribboned-brazen-truths that haunted or ignited us. Fire set to ruins.

History was crucial because we were braiding perspective with language.

We existed in the horror of larger historical processes. Our tiny lives. Folds. Discrete sacred spirals. Trials.

Assumed linearity inside military labyrinths. Generations and geographies later.

Mazes.

Phases.

We were wretched.

This family was wretched.

STORYTELLER

"But I bring with me from the distant past five nights ago the time-traveller, the primaeval one who will have to learn, shape of a goldfish now in my belly, undergoing its watery changes. Word furrows potential already in its proto-brain, unravelled paths. No god and perhaps not real, even that is uncertain; I can't know yet, it's too early. But I assume it: if I die it dies, if I starve it starves with me. It might be the first one, the first true human; it must be born, allowed."

-Margaret Atwood, Surfacing

I have felt your death too many times now. Each month you flowed out of me. My womb cramped and you detached.

I think how you must not feel at home. I don't blame you. Those thunderous noises around you. Cavernous spaces you've consumed. I am sorry for the unyielding sense of relief surrounding your departures.

Your existence has been wretched, clapped full of comings and goings.

You have been a worry pressed blunt like an exclamation mark.

I have felt your tiny deaths. Again, and again. Especially during those brutal anxious years when I artificially ensured those tiny deaths. I relied on knowing that I could stop that internal murdering one day. I wanted to "Draw You Down" like I'd read other mothers do.

The Women of this family hungered. Hunger for knowing, also, hunger for ensuring safety. We often gravitated towards external reassurances assuming permanency. We wanted to touch invisible things.

'You are only three generations away from all this' and you must know what I know. I encountered this degree of separation that there were other Women I read of who went 'Away.' We risked going Away too.

Daughter, you risk being consumed by this hunger that throbs like a citrus heart. I think you are going to want to know too.

This throbbing citrus heart, splayed open like a lotus core, artichoke, well, we accelerate planetary exploration this way. Navigation. Our cosmic seas. Inside this citrus heart is another frontier.

Living is uncertainty, any certainty is a misconstrued falsity. The truth will often be intangible. You cannot place your own existence neatly within truth. It is not yours. It is free from possession, unlike post-War Men and Women.

Do not worry Child. You've got you.

Turn.

The ultrasound technician told me you were faceless. You lacked distinct human features. She compared you to a fertilized egg of a sea urchin. I did not know what a sea urchin was. I thought of tadpoles, plump, meaty, staring at me like globular moth-eyes, beady. You were nothing of the word 'beady.'

My little seahorse. Curved. Neon and pink. I see you.

You are not faceless. I have known what your face looks like, no matter what age you are. I knew your face the moment I came to be me. My knowing penetrates deeper than ultrasounds.

If I was handed a mallet and pointed chisel, presented with the most exquisite marble, I'd sculpt your Pieta contours. My intuition, a map inside. My citrus heart, a passionate signature carved across your chest. Michelangelo needed illegal autopsies to know this inside. Models in draining tubs. I need myself: this citrus heart.

I have flipped through pages of pictures of unborn babies. It is fascinating to witness this insideness.

Humans want to know.

They believe that knowing the physicality of something will be the finality of preparedness.

Yet, this insideness cannot be contained in scholarly reports, substantiated scientific analysis that Women were born knowing.

There was one book acclaimed for being the first to exhibit coloured pictures of an unborn child. Your grandmother owned it. I imagined how such a book changed knowing. I have seen the large gray primitive mouths gaping just above blood-red hearts.

I know how your face will form.

There are six separate peninsulas curving toward the center of your head where they meet and fuse to form delicate arches. You've got wide-open, black-ink eyes that stare straight into me. After twenty weeks those bulbous black fruits will grow over in order for the most intricate workings of your eyes to develop. I know all of this. The book showed me.

The book did not show that you are going to witness with those eyes. I want you to be strong and have no fear to testify. Daughter, we are not bystanders.

In scientific terms, you are a living organism that began from one single cell, my fertilized egg. You were a mere textured speck in your most original formations. I chose your Father, channeled direction and pulled him to us. Releasing chemoattractants, my egg signaled the direction of your Father working inwards. Push and pull. It took six hours, but when that encounter took place, it was the first time that he and I had truly met. You dug your way deep down then, completely submerging yourself in my uterine lining. We came home.

Conception is not a race. Conception is selection. Choice.

My cauldron womb is an internal sea, an inside terrestrial world of deep-beginnings. This womb shapes. This womb transforms. This womb, a snake, a head, and tail. She creates possibility.

My blood flows freely through a thick spongy layer of cells to you, and you absorb nourishment. I am your shelter. My body is your first home. As you grow into your own Woman one day, you sometimes will wish to be back inside this warmth. You could try and seek warmth in the exterior. Rock faces heated by summer sun. Warm bath water. Towels out of the dryer. The sweating underbelly of a thick porcelain mug of tea. Men. Partners. Relationships.

Float.

This biology is your mortality. I am your origin. Yet, you own you.

I feel you in your liquid glory floating. I could cradle your form in two of my outstretched fingers. Your bones would be soft, malleable. Your skin would tell the story of your insides, delicate and intricate. Shark-like, your bent spine blazes pink through rice paper skin.

Your bodily makeup is complicated. You're growing at an alarming rate. As early as three weeks you had developed such things as a nervous system.

The skin of your back thickened along a central line that formed a distinct groove from the front to the rear of you. This groove closed into a tube from the top swells of your body to form your brain. Your brain began smooth-surfaced before shallow curls began, your indentations. You became increasingly more complex. No fear, even in the most coiled arrivals, your maturation was orderly and predictable. This organ will be heaviest and you will need to hold it up high, do not let it drag, if only for a personal falter. Then, you know, it will be your citrus heart that is heaviest. That is okay for a short while.

Your face is turned to the winds and you are gulping air. You will arrive.

A spiritual maturation is meant to be slow, that is the deliberate hypothesis of prenatally.

Yes, you are complex and absolutely glowing in that amniotic oasis, but you are neurologically vulnerable.

Glow.

Do not equate this vulnerability with fragility. No, I will show you how to harvest strong sensitivity in this immense vulnerability.

My Mother's womb was an exposed globe. My insideness was rocked by surging tidal waves. Once his foot kicked and a wretched reel of her reaction quaked, I turned over immediately into Feminism. This Feminism evolved into Empowerment.

Turn.

Float.

I almost lost battling lifelong behavior patterns of consuming and draining energy stores. I thought back to my hands and knees pinned to my mattress in my bedroom. My child's body rocked me through insomnia.

I will watch your hands and what you do with them. My ears will perk with the strain of any incessant finger drumming. I will check if you wring and wring those beautiful hands.

Love them. Do incredible things with them. Hold your heart with them. Lift your eyes and let those fingertips touch and arch like confidant steeples.

The growth of your fingers is a morphologically observable event and I will continue to watch them after you come heaving into this dry place. My Girl, you are a developmental cascade and utterly unique in that flow. You are an evolutionary process of tripartite structure.

Turn. Float. Glow.

I will watch your fingers because they are small statues of survival. At day thirty-two those hands were plates, tiny paddles, and your digits were webbed, like an underwater being. Your fingers came to be from death, apoptosis, and this natural process is a microcosmic function of other compelling life patterns. There will be balance, as with life, we shoulder death too.

When those tiny hands were paddles they underwent their own death. A lysosome enzyme release and those striking digits then, came to be from a programmed cell death.

Just as I feel your movements in my lower abdomen, fragments of where you came from will gradually drift to the surface of your knowing. In night visions, within waves of intuition and from inside that throbbing citrus heart. These inside-risings will not always be pleasant.

You are turning and floating.

We are glowing.

You are perched in the throne of an under-water torture.

Drip. Drip. Drip.

The lessons of your life constantly falling and crashing like water droplets against your third eye, consistent and deliberate to try and break your composure.

The deeper you step into your rites as a Sacred Feminine, the closer you flow towards the Divine. There will be an opposing force testing you. Those leaky plot lines that confuse you, or leave you curved awkwardly around question marks.

You are the complex of tissue and bone turning and arching in a gaseous plane. Keep pumping your legs.

Once you come to know yourself, it will not be hard to doubt others that were put into your life to be conceived as the support beams of your house. Be your own support beam. You are your own house.

No, my Daughter, you are a temple and you are the priestess of that sacred space. Come home.

Nothing is ever what it appears to be. Certainty can only come from within. I was certain you were living right from the first breath after your Father and I connected as one. Double helix spiral. No medical practitioner had to tell me. No pregnancy tests.

Your heartbeat. The birth of a universe, right after the moment of cellular conception, your heartbeat began carving out space for you in this world with your unique rhythm. Soul print. The origin of miraculous electricity.

My Girl, remember that truth can be found inside things, not outside alone in the world because what needs protection and security digs its way inside and holds firm there.

The whisper of your ears curls slightly like shells buried in grains of sand. You're cradled in a sack of amniotic fluid that does not muddle noise like rippling salt water. I am conduit. There are also no muffling air cushions around your eardrums that would fracture the meaning of my words and your recognition of my voice. I absolutely know that you can hear my voice. My heartbeats steadily etch out time for you.

When the time is right, my Little One, you will claw your way into this place, eyes swollen, lungs heaving. My body will open to let you pass, and you'll emerge from me like a big sigh.

Please, if anything, be a fighter.

Cloudy water will put out fires too.

STORYTELLER

We think that we are born to count years, to track the linearity of mechanical time in an agonizing and deflating dance. We assume that we begin, it is not so.

We are born into their lives, detached, but bound by blood, an energetic ownership and eternal allegiance that we chose to enter into. These existences are eternal collisions, encounters, that when toxic, can erode the soul. We wanted to believe we were truly free, but our wings were clipped, we had clipped them ourselves.

We were not meant to fly.

They did not want us to soar, or feel the warmth of freedom, of true happiness, on the backs of our sunburnt necks. Instead, we were meant to be their human-pawns, manipulated to perpetuate their hatred of difference, waging their Wars, dying in their fights, and when the Men returned home from battle, and the traumatized and fearful Women were relocated, these survivors were punished for the minds that faltered when continuously exposed and coded to violence, to their capitalist and military bloodshed. Alienated through governmental policy and deliberate gaps in paper work, they applied terms like shell shock and mentally ill to cage them, the ones who came before. These terms are constructs. They grew up out of consequences.

We exist in the horror of larger historical processes; our tiny lives unfold generations later, in geographies far away.

We overlap.

Time. Terrain. Trajectory.

Threaded with biology and quaking with memory, our mortality is a brazen truth that either haunts or ignites us.

This family is "wretched," that is our way, a shockingly accurate self-perception.

We *are* wretched.

We behave and live against their traditional rural fears. This small town was fearful of my sharp-honest tongue. I would not let falsity pass, even if that new knowledge would take me out like a tidal wave, my Girl.

I am a strong swimmer.

STORYTELLER

I haven't been ready for you yet. I needed to explore the dark pits of my world and navigate my depths with space for mistakes to happen. Trial and error. I could not have you become a casualty of this fitting into myself, this learning, this growing.

I strove for the ether reaches of Truth. Gnawed on the sharp pit of knowledge until I tongued this serving into smoothness. Beach glass. I've been devouring and regurgitating. And, I'm sorry, but you couldn't be a part of this. Sometimes exclusion is kindness. Absence is protection.

But Daughter, you're a part of me, and you might have this hunger too.

I know you do.

I can sense it.

When It is time for you to learn difficult teachings, this narrative is here to help translate this brutal-beautiful story to you.

The Women of this family have always thirsted for warmth and security. They've gravitated towards men in order to grasp at such things. Self-manifested desire has been our undoing, but it is far deeper than desire, too. *You are only three generations away from all this and you must know what I know.* There were other

Women I read of who went *Away* amongst this chaos and fear, we didn't.

We remained in the masculine no-man's-land perpetuated as normative social clockwork. I must protect you. No, I have to provide you with some story, some flutter of transparency and knowledge I did not have. I want you to survive this.

You're going to want to know, the dark will lure. You're going to be enthralled by men, a naked shoulder blade, and a strong working hand. You will be turned briefly against the other women around you, and you will know what that fearful bitter taste of dis-empowerment feels like. You'll want to be able to hold the security of loving in the palm of your hand even though it is impossible.

Living is always an uncertainty.

Loving throws you into certainty.

Some certainty can be a misconstrued falsity.

Truth will never be tangible. You can never own it or place your own existence neatly within it. It is not yours. It is free from possession, unlike post-War men and Women.

But don't you worry Girl. I've got you.

STORYTELLER

They tell me again and again how faceless you are.

But I've held your face in my trembling hands. I've kissed it and rested my cheek against it. I've wiped tears from frightened eyes with dirty tissues. Even when I am gone, and it is your turn in this world to make something meaningful of it, I will still know how your face looks. Even as you age, I will always know you.

You are mine.

But, you will always be your own.

STORYTELLER

The growth of your fingers is a morphologically observable event and I will continue to watch them after you come heaving into this dry place. Remember, your beautiful body is an intricate and organic growing of gene expression and protein elucidation. My Girl, you are a developmental cascade and utterly unique in that flow. I warn you now before you charge through humanity with an arrogance of true individuality, you are organically an evolutionary process of tripartite structure. Ancient and primitive, those hands that I will be watching echo the Devonian Sarcopterygian fish, the Tiktaalik Roseae. The fossils of such a creature was discovered in our home geography, the Canadian arctic. This creature is considered three hundred and seventy-five millions years old. This ancient fish could walk on land. Remember, we assume that we begin, it is not so. We choose to start over, somewhere different that will work us into the soul we crave to be. You are an incredible individual of a beautiful organic collective.

Your fingers are small statues of survival.

I will observe how your fingers react to death, and I will prepare you to accept such processes. When those tiny hands were paddles they underwent their own death. A lysosome enzyme release and those striking digits then, came to be from a genetic mechanism and programmed cell death that those medical-clinical-tongues still cannot articulate. I know that this process is congruent to life in general. Learn now that death is natural and it happens when it needs to for other more strenuous and capable structures to come through. Do not challenge it because as soon as you resist the intrinsic patterns of life, you will shrivel and falter within that dissonance. We will address such hardship now and work through it spiritually, my Girl, because I want you to be free.

Shark-like, your bent spine blazes pink through rice paper skin. You will learn to master transparency because it is crucial for wellbeing. This narrative will teach you the hardship and haven of the sheer feminine power. We are powerful Women and it is time for us to embrace our feminine power. There are times when you will need to be open as a book, readable and yielding. However, I want you always to be able to protect that insideness despite the external warring. We are Women who do not hide our insides and the ones who fed the contortions of plotline and domestic fears caused trauma and pain. You will be strong for these contortions Child. I can show you a way to thrive but remain open. My Love, we value complexity and are not fearful of the changing face of contradiction because learning lives there. Change is freeing. We need change.

You must protect yourself first and foremost because you are your own fortress. Never forget that.

I will start at one beginning because our story has many beginnings, and that is okay.

Life is not linear therefore, your existence never will be.

I suffered from famine as an unborn. She was starved of safety; her womb an exposed globe, my insideness was rocked by surging tidal waves. Once foot kicked and a wretched reel of her reaction exploded. I turned over immediately into feminism.

The stories surrounding your birth will never be straightforward, as I've painfully learned. The lack of transparency I blamed on family, biology and my battles were a brutal cognitive dissonance, until I accepted that we were souls struggling to be happy in the ugly shadow of war. Just as I feel you now swimming in my lower abdomen, fragments of where you came from will gradually drift to the surface of your knowing, in night visions, within the beautiful waves of intuition.

You are turning.

You are floating.

We are glowing.

They, and I mean those who attempt to contrive and control astral planes, they will want to chip away at your self-acceptance as if you are perched in the throne of your life under water torture. Drip. Drip. Trip. Drip. The pieces of your life lined up like dominoes and the constant falling and crashing like water droplets against your third eye, consistent and deliberate to try and break your composure.

Listen. Do not let them take your soul away from you.

Listen. Do not let them take your mind from you.

Listen. Do not let them take your body from you.

Those leaky plot lines that confuse you, or leave you curved awkwardly around question marks, remember that if everything was straightforward and handed to you, this experience and moment would not be what you call life, this journey. Life is learning, you learning about yourself and how you tick. Watch for the ones who want to study you, study yourself. Those unanswered questions are opportunities for you to think up the answers to them yourself like magic. Then, only then, you will realize that those roller coaster plotlines are simply learning curves for you to enjoy, it's a ride. It's okay, though, if you do go off track. Your self-understanding will be wrapped in doubt and confusion, but that is okay, relax.

You are the complex of skin, tissue and bone turning and arching in a gaseous plane, an invisible ocean. Keep pumping your legs. Take in the way the winds rush through tree branches, liquid currents through corral groves and seaweed forests. Picture the planet upside down, your spine pressed firmly against the lungs of Earth and you are safe.

My Love, you are your own compass and that immensely

powerful organ pumping inside the bars of your ribs, pushing blood and oxygen throughout your human temple is the essence of living. Breathe. Listen to the way you pull in those winds that lift leaves and how your body was designed to transform those winds into the very substance that feeds the plants and pushes the clouds up higher into our atmosphere, know, please, just know, we are one and we are alive and living with this planet too. That is why we call nature our mother, she births us and she is powerful enough to sustain life . It is a gift that we dwell on the contours of her face and she is crying because for so long we have been taking everything out of her and pushing her to her very limit. We balance, us humans, we teeter and totter on the precipice of a very dangerous falling. Hush. Listen, you are your own compass and your body is directing you home.

Your insideness is your gift from this Mother. Imagine the first woman pregnant. I used to like to. Her gradually swelling body. Not knowing if she was healthy or diseased. Not knowing if she was living or dying. That first woman, growing full like the moon. Her bleeding stopped. In flux. What came out now grew up and around. Those first generations of birthing women, they were goddesses. Held between worlds. They ushered in the invisible to the material.

You are to listen to that little voice inside of you, if you follow and trust, if you give all of your essence and loyalty to this little voice because these inside currents, energetic tides have been taken from us for an eternity of human existence on this planet and it is time to reclaim it. That movement inside of you is invisible, but science is just starting to keep up to it now, neutrinos, we convert the essence of the sun and moon beams too and everything that we feel and emote, well, my Love, that is mass too and has weight. And, because it has weight it means that it is important and integral to our coming-to-know. Listen to that knowledge because in that listening you will own your conscience and you will naturally orient yourself to the tides and currents around you. You will become one with the planet. My little one, you will discover Gaia there, and she wants you to come home.

Yes, this coming-to-know will push you to the very essence of your psyche and essence, you risk losing complete control, you might also appear to have joined the walking dead, but you are given the opportunity to know that you can make your own choices.

You own your own soul.

You own your own mind.

You own your own body.

Once you come to know yourself, it will not be hard to doubt others that were put into your life to be conceived as the support beams of your house. You must be your own beam. Be your own support beam.

You are your own house. No, my Daughter, you are a temple and you are the priestess of that sacred space. Come home.

Most times it will feel like you are trapped in a dreamlike trance where the film over your eyes blurs your sight. Your feet will feel like they are lodged in thick cement, that is okay, relax.

You will sense when something ferocious will charge at you out of the darkness while you are vulnerable, but that is merely your intuition, your feminine power protecting you.

I am here to guide you through this fear.

Thoughts are powerful, they matter. Thoughts create your reality. Perspective. Your life is a journey of getting to know how you think, why you feel and in essence, to gain self-mastery of that beautiful raw insideness.

We only need to fear two things: great sudden things that cause physical attack, and your own insecurities. The rest, essentially, is meant to be by higher energies and we accept those adversities. The rest, they are constructs of the mind watered by the falls of oppressive and other external fearful structures. I reassure you, my Girl, you can love yourself and the world around you at the core of this chaos. That expression and commitment to your heart, in fact, is the point of this mortality.

My Girl, remember that truth can be found inside things,

never outside alone in the world because everything that needs protection and security digs its way inside and holds firm there.

There will always be some who are going to try and bring you down, turn you against yourself. Many will not want to see you shine. Sadly, jealousy and fear mark the faces of many from your past. Mostly these faces bleed tears of fear. Fear is a terrible state of being. Do not dwell in this toxic emotional realm. If you grasp the certainty within yourself, you can be your own fortress against their bullets.

They scorn my soft murmurs to you, but I know that you are listening. I know this because I know myself, this insideness, better than the outside. The outside does not know us, truly. I know you. I also know that humans have the potential to heal, to recover and that life is meant to bruise the knees in order to appreciate the sensation of a strong spine.

THE PRESENT

Nelle sinks lower in the hot water. Her dark hair mats in a net along her neck and fans seaweed across her shoulders. She glimpses the flash of olive skin under the surface and thinks of sunken wood, waterlogged. The water gently laps against the edges of her body, the ridge between liquid and skin immersed, presses her in like a firm cocoon. Metamorphosis. She feels hidden like a secret and inhales deeply filling her lungs.

Lifted, her full breasts protrude from the water's surface like otherworld-islands. Warm oily lavender wafts around her fish-form. Subtle curling steam settles around her, the landscape of fog-hugged-shores of these otherworld islands, and Nelle feels safe, a secluded lake. She flexes her spine against the porcelain tub bottom letting the lake envelope her throbbing body, the islands sink.

Nelle turns, floats, and glows.

She wanted the antique claw tub because her nanny had owned one. Her eyelids twitch, she sees the warm form bent beside the tub, altar arms suspended and tender fingers massaging the child's temples. Small hands wrapped tight around crossed legs, knees tucked under a child's chin, Nelle can hear singing, the arch of her young song filling the space. Her nanny was the one who wanted to hear her songs, let her little voice carry on into purple morning hours. She was not hushed or redirected away, pulled into the old woman's orb, kept alive there. She goes back to the memory of those baths, the soapy child, her kneeling nanny with a devout reverence throughout her adolescence. Such moments, escapist reprieves, tranquil intimacy the two females cherished away from chaos.

The Old World lovers found the tub abandoned to dirt, flaked with eyesore paint, fungal, and ridden by the vegetation, stinging nettle suffocated the basin.

"Look!" Her heels indented the earth, "I want that!" The sudden pitch in her voice startled him and he tensed. He shielded his eyes to the white slant of afternoon sun with a calloused palm and sighed.

"It's full of shit Nelle, it's an abandoned trough." His ears rang. He envisioned his body working around the tub, transforming it pristine, and the suns that would set along the path of his spine throughout the antique's rebirth. He secretly labeled these projects as distractions, his hobbies served him open skies and bodies of water and he wanted to be there instead, or lost amongst the clean smell of wood shavings and sawdust that coated his surfaces. He was not pulled to the ache of joints from stripping paint, or the patience needed for refinishing an antique. He kicked at the nettle, thick and twisting around the basin, and sighed.

"I know." She scrunched her nose. "But, we can clean it. I can help." She angled her face to the right and winked at him with those dark irises that saturated her pupils. She knew she was up to no good when her wants had pulled him from his other interests. He sighed again and shifted his weight between his feet. He arched his back and cracked his spine. His lower back ached, and he hunched forwards slightly eyeing the stubborn nettle that consumed the tub. He smirked and nodded.

Nelle coughs, pulling water into her nostrils. Suds slide down her body as she sits up rapidly blowing the water from her nose. She slouches, cups her nose with her palms and rests her elbows on the rim of the tub. She studies the veined-skin expanse of belly. Wrinkled hands cup the mound, breath fills her lungs slowly, and she squeezes her eyes tight, the memory of her relief at those nods, how she had felt ignited, celebrated, always threw herself in those arms. His sunburnt neck hid the shadow that had fleetingly crossed her face, a warning flutter like those from crow's wings.

She surprised him by pulling out her patterned gardening gloves from the bag at her side. She dove her hands urgently into them, cracked her neck loudly before digging around the base of the stalks. He studied her hands as she expertly worked the stubborn stalks free from the dirt, dropping them alongside her in a growing pile. He pursed his lips, shook his head and continued to observe her, arms bending and extending, the muscles twining her spine contracted in persistent rhythms.

They had crashed into each other young. The collision, a powerful synapse, they wove identities, ignited the lonely amongst their circles, stirred up envious and cautious dust clouds, the crowds could only shield their eyes from the immense light that they created together in the halo of their young love. They oriented fast in synchronous rotation, natural satellites, she assumed their love would surmount to a great pull, like the moon and Earth. He could not recall the moment of impact, but she could. The physicality of that conservative rural classroom, they were high school students, this encounter was not etched into his memory, branded to his soul like hers, she could have taken much from the history lessons on young love they learned together there. A Cleopatra and Antony narrative, Gilgamesh and Ishtar, unknowing, they were writing a wretched story together.

Her luster and youthful body captivated him. He resisted pooling into her consistently, but he fell hard into the aura inkjet black depths of her eyes. He faced his own truth there. She stripped him naked with her gaze. He loved her for this. He memorized her lithe frame and flawless olive complexion. Mornings lapsed into lazy afternoons while they lay intertwined on blankets in open summer fields, his strong fingers braided in the waves of her long ebony hair. She was his goddess, and from the moment they crashed into each other, she lost her soul to the one with Green Eyes.

Her shoulder blades rolled like wheels against her sundress and she swore under her breath as the tiny hairs of the nettle caught an exposure of skin while she tried to avoid touching the plant. He smiled and languished in the scene of her thrumming determined body. He had yearned for this moving body throughout the terrible solitude of his childhood. The sound of him clearing his throat was lost amongst the whirr of grasshopper noise.

He could not know what synoptic meteorology was or how it was translated for their love. Atmospheric processes and connections to weather, he would not conceive of that knowledge, how the sun haloed her in the crux of that tub. His eyesight was crystalline, yet, the young man was blind, completely blind. The winds picked up suddenly playing with the folds of her sundress, Nelle's dark hair lifted in the air like an underwater plant on free currents. She was a mermaid.

He wanted her to be his core crystal. Their bodies moved cautiously and unknowing around the contours of that tub, a baptismal basin, they could not know the holiness of their loving. Spinning in a watery pool of iron, their love was dense. Flags and mast markers, they could not know how many pivoted around their flaming light. They lived slowly, took their love in a rhythm unlike others on their conservative planes, getting married, making babies ruthlessly, these two knew to wait, and to go slow.

Yet, their love pulsed and rotated faster than the movements around them, pushing tectonic, if they could have heard the velocities of their sound, the pressures and rising temperatures building in the inner core, it would explain the perpetual anomaly of the final repel.

They could be ripped from each other. Lost in a magnetic field, tilted lines near a splitting equator. Nelle would be imprinted from a historic Canadian discovery later in life. The

Oak Island Stone resonated with an older pregnant woman floating in a refinished claw tub.

Hieroglyphs became her language, "The people shall not forget the lord, and to offset the hardships of winter, and the onset of plague the Arif, he shall pray to the lord. Holy Grail, Ark of Covenant."

The dust would settle and she would accept how everything was meant to be, how the loss was meant to play out.

The peaking nettle mound began to tip over beside her rubber boots. He wanted to keep walking, abandoning the tub to nature's havoc. He knew at this age not to pull her back and stop her from such an impulsive task. He honored his impatience with her silently, chewed on the edge of his tongue, wetted his teeth and spat onto the earth beside her. She was his gardener and she loved sinking her fingers into the soil enabling green to grow up and thrive, but he could not learn the art of patience, how the green things could not be suddenly rectified, but grew in their own facets amidst the order of their own timelines. She was stubborn too, like a weed. He knew it was difficult to budge a boulder, even worse, to rid a manicured lawn of dandelions.

"Here," he offered as he furrowed his eyebrows. He slid open the blade on his pocket knife, tested the edge against the pulp of his thumb. Leaning over, he worked the blade through the thicker stalks inwardly cursing the heat and itch of sweat glazing his shoulders and back. He labored alongside her silently, she dug out the roots and remaining bases of plants. He severed the stalks and threw them on the pile.

They cleared the basin while the sun moved closer to the ground. Nelle rubbed her palms together, gallantly beaming and climbed into the porcelain wreckage. The hem of her dress slid back against her thighs and she propped her knees against the rim of the tub. He crooned his neck and made no effort to conceal that he stared between the triangle of her thighs and hem.

Nelle tilted her head back and laughed into the winds. She

pulled her chin down and locked her gaze with his and they hovered along that edge for a second. His green eyes shone in the white light. Mischievously, he slipped his knife into the leather holder on his belt. His muscular hands pushed the sleeves of his button-down plaid shirt past his elbows and she studied the beautiful flex of muscles along his forearms.

"You're gorgeous."

His dimples deepened and he leaned forward playfully pinching the excess skin around her mouth. She laughed and swatted his hand away. He climbed into the tub with her and rested his cheek against the rise of her breasts. The width of his torso pushed her thighs wider and he settled into her corners as the soles of his work boots made slight circles in the air.

Nelle stretches her left foot beneath the bath water, her ankle cracks, and her calf flexes against the basin. She stretches out her right foot and arches her lower back letting a slow sigh dispel and ripple into the silence of the farmhouse. Far off in the back of the house she hears a slight pop, the house settling into the night and she wraps her hands around her stomach inhaling long and slow.

In the halo of that bath, the water swirling and holding her together, she could faintly smell the fresh grass, the heat of the sun baking the porcelain and the sheen of his green eyes against her breasts. Nelle sinks lower in the water letting the surface crease below her glistening eyes. Her chest rises and falls sharply. The water muffles the sob.

Curled fetal in her bathwater cocoon, Nelle hovers on the brink of entrances and exits, fixed at the center of a crossroads, she smells the overlap of spaces, old and new worlds.

Overwhelmed with the depth of juncture, she wants to disappear. She tips her chin against her chest and lets the water rise, she pushes her body lower, completely submerging her anxious form in the water against the hard tub basin. Eyes shut and body clasps tight around breath held in lungs.

Nelle pictures a closed purple lotus bud, green and lush, roots pulsing tentacles slowly rising from the depths into air. The lotus petals folded tight inside each other, worlds within worlds, tiny existences, double lives. Nelle bursts open, pushing her face above the surface sucking in a mouthful of air, propped up on altered elbows, she studies the currents of water rushing down her breasts, forking like rivers around the swell of her womb. Arched between dreams and reality, Nelle cannot pull her memory from the sunlight and two warm bodies in a paint-chipped claw tub. Solitary and hammocked into the bruising night, she cannot hinge on the form of a world she is meant to inhabit.

She shakes her head, sits up again, pinches the bridge of her nose, and wipes the excess water from the corners of her eyes. Her chest chokes, and she tightens her muscles suppressing another sob. Water has spilled over the rim of the tub soaking the wooden floor, seeping against the lines of the room, collecting slowly in corners.

The house is old. It slants.

Nelle lifts her left hand and lets her closed fist hover above her knees. She blinks several times as she unfurls her fingers in a petal motion, her palm transformed into a purpled-flesh lotus flower. Her crooked fingers remind her of triangles and she thinks of math class, algorithms, chalk against board, Pythagorean theorem, and, like notes released from her clarinet in music class, she thinks further of cherubs, children gods, Horus, strong women, Isis.

She grips her left wrist with her right hand forming a triangle with her arms above the triangle between her legs. She smiles.

Osiris.

Solar power.

Her mind is pulled back to the university lecture halls, the almond shaped Byzantium eyes, Hellenic traditions, and her cheeks burn red, suddenly like fire. She needs to go farther back to another geography.

It took years to understand what the act of meditation was. A mental train ride, she lets her insideness melt into the internal inferno, again, she dunks her body under the water letting time evaporate. Underwater her right hand touches her left breast, trails along the valley of her chest to press against her right breast, slowly, she lifts her fingers from the water to wet her mouth before falling back to her left breast. Triangles. Geometric lines. The reality of parabolas.

Nelle laughs underwater, air bubbles rise up and pop. The thought train pulls her farther inside, she sees three Women, a triptych. Crossed legged. Three vibrant lotus flowers. Aligned. Fertility Maiden. The Earth Mother. The Crone. She brings her hands together, clasped underwater like the reflection of a full moon on the surface of the ocean.

Her lungs burn, back arched, and the pressure of flexed facial muscles rock her out of her shell. Nelle shoots up suddenly again, ignoring the waterfall, the wet floor, the disappearing suds in the periphery, her braided hands pressing against the center of her chest. Her nostrils flare, she smells sulfur, that pungent boiled egg smell of hollowing out yokes for devilled-eggs. She breathes in the aroma, eyes closed, hands against her chest, Nelle unconsciously straightens her index fingers and presses the pads of her thumbs together forming the outline of an egg against the core of her chest.

She pulled her index fingers slightly apart, forming the shape of an inverted triangle. She smiles, opens her eyes, and separates her hands. Again, without dictating the train of thought, she watched as her right hand presses the space between her breasts, swoops lower to her womb pressing the highest tip of her bulge before falling again to the triangle between her legs, pressing intimately. She sucks in air, utters a prayer of thanks inside her mind before lifting her hand back to her womb, a slight press, and, finally, resting both hands on her heart.

She pictured masses crossing themselves in cathedrals, clothes and propped caricatures before stained glass. She laughs, imagining her claw tub suddenly sitting dead center of the altar, the collective gasp. She wipes the smirk from her mouth. She cannot suppress the laugh as her train of thought circumnavigates the holy mirage. Nelle is back under the blue sky with him, and both are intertwined and ignited in the curve of that claw tub. He had vowed, she recalled, shaking her head, that he would not spill the water onto the floor.

"See, we fit nicely." Her fingers wove into his blond hair and she massaged the curve of his skull, he savored her massaging and the heat of the sun against his back. He inhaled the smell of her skin, earth, and lavender. He could hear the lapping of water against their bodies and he saw himself in another image stepping into a doorway capturing the scene of her slender petite body gleaming in the water as she twisted like a seal. He suddenly grew hard against her. Her crystalline laughter rose above his head.

"I guess you like the tub," she joked, lifting his face up to hers. She leaned her face over him.

She rotates onto her side in the tub, falls hard out of memory, carefully cradling the swell of her stomach, and weeps into the night. The weight of the little life between her hands surges through her like a lightning bolt, and she wishes that two sets of hands were anchored to the growing mass inside her.

At twenty-two weeks pregnant, Nelle is impatient, and she is entombed in fear.

She knew she was pregnant before the doctor verified it, and she felt elated. Her body had been given passage into something miraculous. She had stepped into her Divine Right. But, her thunderous and worrisome thoughts lately had consumed her to the point of deflation.

She could be casually folding linen when a line from a book she was reading would sift forward. "Came into this world with the knife sticking into his heart." She'd shiver and hunch over with a jeering pain shooting straight through her abdomen. She envisioned little knives like the plastic ones in sandwiches and soft bloated bellies shadowed with the grip of a handle and the contortion of a blade in tiny chests.

There is a white noise ringing in her ears that grows to a high-pitch siren and Nelle covers her mouth with a clammy shaking hand. She thinks behind her eyes how knives become pulled in rather than stabbed.

Pulled in.

Pulled in.

She recalled things that are sucked inwards like anxious cheeks or frightened turtleheads and she would careen to the toilet locked in a criminal gag.

She's been imprisoned in the confusion of the physiological rejections to such thoughts. She thought she worked through all of this. Blaming the sudden fits on the pregnancy, the hormones, the altering bodies, she vomits, and waits for his ghost to suddenly appear behind her, holding her hair back and sliding strong worried palms along her back.

She'd seen that worry hang on his features and knew that he would not stay.

The water is lukewarm now, cold, and Nelle fingers the wrinkles webbing her heels and palms. She feels a chill creeping up her back. Parallel. They had become waterlogged like her hands and feet, lost their heat faster than bathwater, she could not have fathomed in the rise and collapse of their lovemaking that she would be pregnant in this tub, alone.

She released the instinctive cradle of her hands and flips onto her back. She's been turning again and again in this tub. Her teeth chatter slightly. Nelle shifts her bloated legs, letting them open and be comfortable. She pulls in petal-fists against her chest. Her eyes reflect her hands, neither fully open nor closed, and she floats. The chill blankets her shoulders, and she knows that soon she will have to get out of the tub.

She hears an older voice. "It is time to get out now."

The slight weight of her hands against her chest draws her lulled focus and she envisioned the web of veins rising like tunnels under her skin on the tops of her hands. She knows that her face is youthful and it deceives others, they assume she is much younger than she is, but, if only they looked at her hands, absorbed the stories of those wrinkled bulbous joints from relentless cracking, they'd know her true age and experiences.

She wouldn't have to utter a word, the physicality of her hands would convey enough and leave the things she was uncomfortable with, or afraid to speak of, dormant.

Again, she lifts her hands above her knee, this time letting her right hand unfurl in a purple lotus flower.

She remembers the moments of panic, she couldn't move, her feet fixed to one point, she'd wring her hands again and again. If only he had wanted to give attention to the wringing. She uttered a silent prayer. Verbal conversations always pulled too much out of her, the valley of her tongue she knew was a no-man's-land, and she willed her teeth to shred the words before they became ensnared and owned by him. His ears and mouth mutilated the word and regurgitated something else much more contorted.

She wiggles the middle finger of her right hand, nervously pressing the knuckle and short meadow of proximal phalange against the surface of the water. The thin scar running an inch and one quarter along the edge of this meadow shimmers like a waxy pine needle. Nelle recalls the memory of the rock's fall, the immense searing pain and the stitches. Seven stitches itched from that finger for several weeks, and she was thankful the falling stone hadn't broken bone or crushed ligament. She'd never broken a bone and upheld that accomplishment as a polished pearl amongst the stones of her hectic childhood.

The balanced rocks on the large boulders that flanked the Toronto Beaches were mesmerizing. An artist had stoically decorated the boulders by balancing rocks. She joked that they were drilled together and that nature could not possibly enable such a critical balance.

She now acknowledges from her claw tub cocoon that the balance was nature epitomized, and this was the summer she had upset her equilibrium.

Her left hand gripped the neck of a wine bottle and she pressed it expertly to her lips between pockets of slurred laughter, bodies wrapped in blankets and hope dotted the boulders, careening and balancing like the artist's display. Showing off in her drunken haze she tipped one of the stones and let it crash into the waves, the others laughed and she felt safe in their social halo. She cracked her neck to the left while recalling how she had gallantly stepped forward for a picture with the boulders.

Snap!

One successful picture of the others. She entered the frame.

Snap!

The flash of the camera-phone, and the simultaneous searing pain of the split in her finger from a falling stone, pushed a scream from the pit of her gut and the picture captured her face contorted and red, her right hand a bruised red blur.

Nature's lesson she knows now, she had paid the price dearly for disrespecting the balance. Pressing her brows together in a frown, she wishes she could have known earlier that this tremendous upsetting and imbalance was in fact occurring inside of her too, and the scar remained to remind her of her anxious callousness.

There are two more waxy, pine-needle scars glinting like fish scales below the bathwater surface. One severs a dominant writing callus on her right pointer finger and she'd become insecure to make her point in conversation after its appearance until the marks faded. The second scar swelled in a deformed lump on the right side of her pinky finger. She fans the right hand out flat under the water and blinks several times at its true misshapen vulgarity. There is a morsel of admiration, perhaps love, for the small resolute survival of each battle that hand had entered and exited.

Still coursing in oxygen and iron, she is thankful for her humanity.

Squeezing her eyes closed she sees the glint of scissor blades and the blotchiness of her hand curled angrily around the handles. She had stabbed at the garbage in a fit of panic when she couldn't face his hot non-verbal judgments of her abandonment of the domestic chores. She couldn't care anymore if they lived in filth or carnage. The debris in her mind remained, no matter how pristine the house became. She gave up without telling him. She'd let finger marks on surfaces go, sit overfilled garbage bags by the door, abandoned the film of the bathroom to mold. He didn't see, wasn't looking for it, and suddenly one day, he looked at her; no, he saw her, and the bags around her eyes, the severe grim frown. She had turned into a shell of herself.

The stabbing was a protest to the garbage, to the debris and chaos that accumulated and lined their nest like litter. Ribbons of fright seized him as she had stabbed and buried the blades into the garbage until her knuckles bled. Transfixed with shock, he rocked into movement at the sight of the blood. He twisted the scissors out of her grip almost angrily and wrapped the wounds in a dishcloth.

Nelle broke, collapsed over her knees, her torso racked with feral sobs. Panic seized her lungs, shallow constricting waves consumed her, and she began to hyperventilate. Nelle had learned in the hollows of those panicked grottos that she didn't have to go through this anxiety simply to show she needed help. That she was not okay with things. There were other ways, methods. Better communication. The attention and focus of those luminous green eyes. There had to be love there, for those green eyes to survey the extent of atrocity, not to be ignorant of it.

Stuck in their matrix, Nelle thought she wandered a love labyrinth.

The physicality of her hands bore their own stories, and she knew that these limb-ends breathed with their own tiny souls, survivors, they fought to be present too. The things her hands got her into as a child, throughout her unbridled adolescence, the discipline and reprimands bred wariness, the things she did with her hands, she became hyper-aware.

Nelle tapped them nervously, drummed them along edges and surfaces, clasped them white-knuckled, and squished them under her bum during circle time. They wanted her hands to be still, but they could not be stilled. She picked at lifting guitar calluses. She cracked her knuckles and played church and steeple with her fingers. Her nails were round like shells, not elegant like almond slivers she yearned for.

Her hands felt hefty, awkward. It took years of patience and accepting her imperfect hands to feel feminine and graceful. She learned eventually that her hands did not detract from her femininity, but complimented her unique mold. Nelle's tenacity, kindness, that quiet unconditional love she honed for, those lost in the throngs of barbarity, those more embedded characteristics, virtues, not the shape of her nails, or how expertly she manicured them, superficial physical attributes, it took expert mental training to love herself past those brutal intellectual constructs. She loved others with those hands. She created art with them and made things grow.

Nelle picked up a pen and began writing through tragedy with those hands. *Hamartia and I...*

She sighs, relinquishes the disfigurements in her hands to the depths of the tub, and closes her eyes.

The hands of her Women were thick with calluses from gripping that metallic chain. Enslaved to protocol, to performance and the associations to the movements and expectations of what those hands did, were intended to do, her Women hid their pain. They suffered, their joints burned and ached from arthritis, but they continued to heft that chain. The Sacred Feminine cried, wept to them from the inner recesses of their being to let go of that chain, drop it, let it fall away, admonish it, and rest, rest for a short while. But they could not hear this sacred voice.

Her Women were not ornamental. They were not soft but hardened and working. Their hands were roughened work hands, no showpieces. They sacrificed much with those hands, refraining from taking care of them first to keep the little bums dry, to pick stones from stubborn colonial fields, or to marinate the meat that the men expected on the tables when they arrived home after weathering their outside storms. They built lives with those hands while reefing on that chain. They built up respected matriarchies braided with a sacred maternal love that they coyly cradled to their hearts and whispered into the delicate curl of their ears.

But despite their potential power and holiness, Nelle's Women tripped over the aggressive cliffs of masculinity, became lost in the war zones they laid out, cut by the barbed-wire hell holes of their manly memory, the Women drowned under expectation and embedded societal violence. It simply is a history of humanity, the ugly linearity of civilization, the great masculine dominance, a universal human process that has forged walls between Mothers and Daughters, Grandmothers and Granddaughters, Sisters and Cousins, Nieces and Aunts.

Their hands faltered under the pressure of performance anxiety, but her Women were expert, they camouflaged that anxiety in an incessant domestic race to keep them steady, and the house pristine. The chain lengthened, curled steadily around them and tightened, pinning them to certain places so they were forced to plant roots there, fixed to trunks of pain that layered like bark through generations. Man-made and inorganic, her Women held on tight to those links passing the chain on to the younger Women for short breaks and tribulations they concealed as life lessons.

What they thought, they did.

The Women absently and deliberately fingered the steal links, each one a complex capsule of a story, of fears, of sacrifices, and bubbles of laughter, the chain raped and consumed them, but they carried on, loving and living with it.

She rocks shut like a shell and folds into the fetus position. Nelle holds her womb with her left hand and in this hunch she places her other hand along the column of her neck. She feels the weight of the chain coiled there, around her neck, waiting, digging down into her skin, she anticipated its settling like a living thing that she will grow into, become a part of. The chain clinks like angry teeth against the porcelain tub, she shudders. Nelle has seen this chain trailing between the Women of her family and she knows the sounds of its cold metallic body intimately. Generation after generation of dis-empowerment, fear, and self-doubt tightly bound around placated and calculated normalcy, she resents the chain as much as she feels comfortable with it.

Probing and releasing her fingers around her womb, she sees herself as a recluse child seeking out refuge in small-enclosed spaces. She felt safer inside things like truths, circular clothes rack her commercial fortresses, cardboard boxes, hulls of ships, and the dark spaces under beds, like a stowaway bent for sandier shores, she hid herself away, unseen.

Nelle knows now that she was acting like a refuge, someone wretched and outcast.

Her fantasies were expert at shielding her because Nelle's world was a make-up of storylines that her family could not place or align straightforwardly together for her, so she elaborated. This piecing together required many hours of strife and self-facing, a significant historical self-actualization. She learned words like *victim* and *perpetrator*, *mouth-bound bystanders*, and she learned how to search out these personalities in her rural world.

She did all this because they could not sit her down, explain it all to her. They simply could not clarify the process of family history, their microscopic little lives, but she knows that there was too much playing out that they could have changed before realistically letting themselves become powerless. And if they attempted to sit her down, explain it to her, she could not have listened because her truth did not resonate with the body of that story, the storytellers were too subjective, too subliminal, and she learned early about the selfish excluding hand of bias.

But the clinking was not so apparent there, in child storyline and make-believe, and that metallic scent not as imposing and dominant. The dark was a safe blanket from the labor of hefting that chain and like the haven of the womb, she yearned to be back there, inside.

A cusp of a worry clouds the water.

Can I be that soft warm place for her?

Home?

Most nights, like tonight, the darkness veins up around her like weeds breaking through concrete.

A Rose in Concrete.

She can only turn her face away and let history pin her to the mattress.

STORYTELLER

I will be the storyteller, but the story is not mine.

The democratic policy is taking them out one by one in a tidal wave of paper mazes with deliberate dead ends. It's policide. We lost the spiritual democracy when the white man came and kept coming, took, and kept taking. The systems that put on the headdress of The Way and cut The People away from Gaia, away from that life, animism, they enforced paper democracy when in reality they had enslaved it.

Cycle of ages.

Bodies ground through brutal negligent police gears, deflated balloons, isolating and excluding policies, and deliberate dead-ended and no-exit government paper mazes. An unfeeling face of process alienates them, death, death of the soul.

When the soul is taken, shells are left. Shallow graves. Then, they start taking themselves out, one by one, two by two, they cross into that false ark, paired and bleating. Herds of sheep walking directly towards the blade of the ax of a grim reaping slaughter. Degradation of the physical in a slow agonizing process.

Women are the pulp of the very trees of the paperwork. The Sacred Feminine is a movement, a wave, an awakening and an opening that has been stenciled over and kept hidden for centuries. Monotheistic religious systems, governmental hierarchies, and patriarchal monarchies have been laid over, carefully and often brutally. Mining and raping Gaia. Her earthen face. We forgot that Women are in essence trees, powerful sacred trees. Planted on earth. Branched in air. Spaces between the visible and the invisible. On the land we live, the paperwork that colonial systems serve us, enslave us, they place those stacks in shaking hands of the very trees that keep the human species going. Barred from access, illiteracy of their language, way of being. There were always *other* ways of being out there.

Daughter, our words are hieroglyphs. Instead of carving our stories into stone faces. We are laying texts, carving out cyberspace, which is just as important to human civilization. I called them #Techglyphs. And, this way of self-expression helped bring me to the space to tell this story to you. Parts of it exist elsewhere. Go find it. A heart pumping here, the veins and arteries reach out and extend beyond the perimeters of this text. Beating and visceral, our existence here is organic.

We evolve.

We unfold.

We branch out.

Trees.

Pineal.

Eye of Horus.

The legislation is naive, unsafe. It is too easy for the perpetrators to utilize this paperwork as their tool of removal and exclusion, social genocide, people are dying: Policide.

Those in power served the lines of policies, assimilation and exclusion portrayed as order and subservience to a greater power that is supposed to protect us.

One document, The Indian Act, affected us.

The oppressed have been left disturbed and unstable. A diagnosing culture of uneducated observers. With nothing but experiential and sensorial evidence, that is the beauty of the order of hearsay: it can do everything, or, it will do nothing.

From this order and because of the vulnerability of our legislation perpetrators can enter the system first for expensive protection, and they are saved, shielded and unharmed, this way.

Behavior becomes frontline resistance. Misconception is reinforced. Fear biting at heels, worry of the fault lines in their own processes and policies to be known, questioned.

The People will pull *other* knowledge up out of unbound secrets that have been kept hidden.

Words and actions in alignment existing freely in novels that will rock geography: only history can save them.

The other is sacred.

THE PAST

She pushed the small mass against her womb. The rectangular coffee tin made a shallow indent and Amélie heard the folded papers shift inside the container. She released her mouth slowly allowing her lungs to fill with air before she pulled her lips back inside her mouth in a private desperate line. Despite the cold winter air pummeling her weary frame and wet-snow blotting her face, a thick salty coating of sweat glazed her skin, and she trembled.

She halted yards away when she spotted the sign posted on the large wooden doors:

Halt! Qui dépasse cétte limite sera fusillé!
Stop! Anyone exceeding this limit will be shot!

The looming façade of the General Dossin de Saint Georges Barracks consumed several blocks in a rectangular hunch, white and angular. The Dossin boasted a large courtyard behind the thick wooden doors. Constructed in 1756, she knew that the large building now housed the prisoners to be shuttled to the death camps in Germany and Poland. The majestic façade felt like a sting, a mockery of protection. Amélie wondered if these people too had studied the large courtyard upon their arrival. She memorized the classic white walls lined with perfectly square windows. She knew without having to be amongst those embodied souls that arrived that this building had been the site to bear witness to brutality. She shifted her weight and closed her eyes. Her throat burned as she cleared it coarsely. She envisioned the prisoners' arrival to the camp, the lumbering army trucks, cubed uniformed shoulders and the glint of guns, pathetic mounds of suitcases littered the grounds, and the prisoners organized like cattle into squares of frightened huddles.

She shuddered. Her jaw line ached. Amélie opened her mouth slightly and expelled a hot cloud into the winter air.

Mechelen was a strategic city for the Germans in moving people from the country. The masses had not reacted to the environment and atmosphere of Fort Breendonk, another smaller heritage site outside the city, so they took the site of the Dossin in Mechelen as the war raged on. On July 15, 1942 General Harry von Craushaar, who was the deputy head of the German military administration, appointed Major Philipp Schmitt to oversee the Breendonk camp and organize a transit camp for the Jews in Mechelen. The first round of prisoners arrived by July 27, 1942.

Through hearsay, Amélie knew that the Wehrmacht guarded the camp, so she assumed there would be more cover around the larger site. Perhaps that exposure, the feeling of being stripped, made vulnerable, was intended. The Reich pressed down around the people of the city, and the people of the city hiccupped with the onslaught of violence and brutality. But, mouths continued to open and force out syllables of resistance.

Amélie felt a warning of collapse under the surging fear standing before the transit camp. She pressed the coffee tin against her womb harder, and the knowledge of the risk she took with the contents inside the tin buried itself with a forceful current inside her as she crossed her ankles and sagged under a severe physical buckle. Her torso swooned above her ankles. She raked the back of her hand horizontally across her brow line displacing tears and focused her attention on the image of a man, the one she had abandoned in her flat—the Romanian— with his angry naked body twisted grotesquely in her sheets, that redirection forced a hard swallow from her and she remained planted.

A deep cold tremble penetrated her abdomen and worked its way up her spine in a goose pimpled march. Angry-looking patches of blues, purples, and yellows wove together along her back, fanning up towards her neck like footprints.

Romanian eyes glared in her thoughts, with fists coming down on her quickly. She spat into the dirty snow at her feet. She heard again the sound of her cries while his hands rang out a deranged song against her ledges. She bore his anger with a bent graceful back, knowing her body was his only distraction from the fear of a world burning down around them.

Their Mother had brought her Romanian sons to Belgium after the death of their father, an engineer who perished under Stalin's terror in the east. Amélie never dreamt that when Eli, the man with brown eyes, became a constant presence in their plight, she would abandon his affection—his love—and marry the Romanian for the sake of protection from Hitler's violence. She had sought out people, her connections to find out where they would have taken Eli. She had gone to her family friends, the Romanians.

I wish I hadn't. J'aurais aimé ne pas l'avoir fait.

She looked at the grounds of the transit camp between the polished black iron bars and felt shame for the desperate contour of her survival. Snowflakes fell on her cheeks finding their demise with a subtle, yet magnified, crackling sound as they mixed with her thick tears.

She pushed her blonde hair away from her cheek bones. She felt small and vulnerable.

Mechelen's grounds were empty. Charred black leaves settled in sad piles around the perimeter of the square before spiraling

43

in the winds, lifting and tumbling, appearing like letters cast away to the air.

Amélie instead saw sheets of paper with blue pencil markings. She envisioned her fingers cradling the sheets like relics, a thick throbbing lump forming in her throat.

She had kept her back to the Romanian, waited until he had slumped over in the chair before she pulled the papers out, her heart bursting to consume the blue pencil markings.

The snoring Romanian did not see her reading the letters, taking in every lover's word, he did not see her delicately fold the papers and kiss the tattered edges before she slipped the small bundle into the dented coffee tin beside two sets of forged identification papers. He did not see her when she quietly slid the tin behind a line of books on a shelf.

The Romanian slept.

Eli had written to her with a blue pencil crayon in an unrecognizable urgent scratching from Mechelen. She thought, at first, her nephew had written to her from the Ardennes, but the form contained the letterhead of the internment camp, and she knew.

He had only known the putrid decay of Mechelen's dormitories. Over the past several months, in the lonely hours of his imprisonment, he thumbed a picture of a woman with blonde hair until the paper balled up. He rubbed away the ink of a photograph of Amelie's beautiful poised face. Eli's mind remained locked, fixed on the memory of two lithe bodies arcing and vital in the light.

Amélie couldn't let it go. She had memorized the address, the Boulevard du Midi. His urgent calligraphy branded her mind.

And she knew.

He was alive.

"*Bonjour à St. Martin*. Say hello to St. Martin." Her conscience turned the text over in her mind until a wringing pain beat steadily behind her right ear. He was writing to her in coded messages.

Amélie did not sleep that night. She lay unmoving, studying the slow takeover of darkness by the morning light. A wavering line shifted, casting a purple bruise across the room. Her body lay lifeless, still and silent, her spine locked along the expanse of mattress, eyes unblinking, she bore holes into the ceiling.

The next day, Amélie knew she needed to restrain her anxious reeling and hold tight to a forced calmness that would keep her quiet, silent enough that she could arrive and leave without notice. The sense of urgency surged in her chest and she shifted stiffly from the bed. Her mind pushed her body mechanically.

She dressed slowly, unrolled her winter stockings up the cold flesh of her legs ignoring the shards of glass that shone and chattered like teeth on the floorboards around her ankles. A thick grey moth fluttered against her vanity mirror, and she was caught, transfixed for a moment in its dim struggle. Shifting her attention away from the moth, she clamped a clammy hand down on her knee, and pressed down with meager weight in a futile attempt to make her leg stop shaking. The shaking increased intensity. She gritted her teeth and managed to slow her breath.

She felt outside of herself.

Amélie positioned her foot on the edge of a chair for balance, she studied the top of her hand enclosing her kneecap, the pale fingers were skeletal and gaunt like the exposed ribs of a dead fish washed up and baking in the sun. She smelled something she would later associate with August shorelines and lake algae, her nostrils flared around the sharp odour and she felt a shift in her focus that stilled her.

The emaciated hand lifted from her leg and smoothed the coarse pin skirt across the span of her thighs. Disembodied, she buttoned a cotton shirt over her chemise with ice-cold fingers and tucked the thick fabric into the skirt with redemption. The skin under her eyes pulled down into shadowed hollows. Instead of stiffening and growing cold, she cultivated the opposite and stayed warm, she surged out into the violence of the War as she had not done yet, and there her thoughts crashed into the Romanian.

The mirror had grown into virgin territory during this self-evading, and she stopped looking completely at herself in it. She'd name her reflection later in a new land beside the shimmering chasm of a lake. She'd open the surface of that lake swiftly with the breach of her body welded into a deliberate forward thrust. She would dive because it was easier than trying to identify the face she no longer recognized, those ice blue eyes that gaped open before her like caverns. Lost between nightmares and the deepening pits under her eyes, she writhed in pain for the one with brown eyes.

The reflection of her unsteady fingers played against imaginary piano keys on the vanity and wetted her eyes instantly. She remembered the music they made together, wherever they went instruments appeared, he would sing, she could accompany any song his voice etched out.

An urgent shout filtered up to her flat from the street, she pulled her hands apart and raised them to her scalp, dislodging her from dreaming. There was a frightening shiver of voice swimming through her sensitive head.

You'll give it away. Ne le donnez pas. Don't give it away.

Amélie braided the voice with the resolute dressing of her hair. The pins dropped like tiny nails against the vanity, thin perfectly shaped ringlets fell alongside her temples and chin.

She combed out the pin curls with deliberate meditative strokes. Gathering the blonde tresses into a tight bun at the nape of her neck, she admired the slight waves extending from her hairline to the ear like the sand ribs of the ocean floor. She wanted to fall into water and not get up. She winced as her hands brushed against the lifted purple bruises that trailed from behind her right ear beneath her collar. She pulled a knitted wool sweater over her head. The seconds slipped away, she sat in front of the mirror transfixed by the altered body she'd prepared to face this day, wondering. She admired the outline of her arranged self despite the tangled sheets looming in the background reflection.

She had turned twenty-two in February, but the deepening lines around her eyes suggested that she was several years older. Her cheekbones protruded beneath her crow's feet forcing the translucent skin taut across her face in a sickening grimace. Stony fingers blankly traced the river of dark veins that ascended her eyebrows and disappeared amongst her uneven hairline. The fingers hovered in the air, suspended for three consecutive painful thoughts and dropped to the sides of her skirt, she exhaled. Amélie measured time through these mournful movements. A body in flux through war.

Quel est l'âge, vraiment? What is age, really? She can hear her father, his comforting baritone voice speaking to her from the empty corners of the room.

"Un homme parmi les enfants sera longtemps un enfant, un enfant parmi les hommes sera bientôt un homme." A man among children will be long a child, a child among men will be soon a man. She spoke his wisdom quietly to the room and knew that only the walls would listen to her now. The only other voices she heard filtered through the speakers of the Fada radio. These voices began early in the 1930s, but she was too ignorant then, consumed by him to register the rising pitch of these voices, the dominating volume, or the frequency of their verbal lacerations.

He had sat upright in the night and cranked the dial. July 8,1941, she reworked memory while eyeing the Fada in the reflection of the mirror beyond her shoulders. Amélie dropped her right shoulder and recounted what they heard, *"Tous les Juifs doivent abandonner leurs radios."*

All Jews must surrender their radios.

Forbidden access to media and then no bank would accept further deposits from Jews.

She wondered in retrospect why they had not acted earlier, and paid attention to the signs. She ached thinking back through the atrocity of it all.

Her shrinking body hinged on a memory skipping stones

across surfaces she could sink back into between breaths and blinks. The Au Bon Vieux Temps, the café off the Rue du Marché Aux Herbes, just north of La Grande Place, these slanted places contained the fiber of her survival. She held onto the memory of Eli's sudden entrance, transfixed by his earthy smell and kind composure. His impression carried her beyond the images of the Romanian's fists coming down hard, and Eli's memory offered her reprieve.

She was drawn to the café because it was hidden. The narrow pedestrian impasse offered shelter from the market crowds. She wound north. The café was narrow, but lofty with a vaulted roof, hops and coffee aromas wafted above the wood of the tabletop, she rested her elbows and inhaled. Her corner felt safe, and she reached into her purse and pulled out her book. The owner placed a glass of dark brew in front of her, the right corner of his mouth pinched back protecting a smile.

He had let in a flurry of rain and wind as he entered. Her nostrils pricked up from the delicious scent of sweet ozone and she whipped around and faced the door nearly tipping her over. The young man's ebony hair matted in whirls around his crown, haloed and shining white, crow-like. His eyes, luxuriant and as rich as the malt of her draft, she quickly buried her shyness in the brew. She pushed slightly back into the shadows of the corner and covered her face with her book.

Eli moved towards the bar. He caught her in the corner of an unexpecting eye. Flashes. *A curve of spine. Fingers entangled in the waves of hair pulling that face towards his mouth suddenly.* He stilled briefly, swallowed. Something pulled him deeper.

The squat owner studied the young man as he stopped and shook the passion from his head before settling at the wood. The old man chuckled, turned, and began pouring a draft.

Eli hunched over the bar wood, his finger traced the rim of his glass. A decision was made. He smelled her from his seat, lavender and soap. It destabilized him. He knew that her skin would be soft, warm and giving against his hands. Her hair fanned across his chest would be a heavenly sight. He was transfixed. Against the typically reserved nature and shyness of his character, he got up from the bar and made his way to her dark corner.

"*J'adore la pluie.* I love the rain. Most people curse it, but I want to be out in it." Amélie turned away, embarrassed that she opened the conversation about the weather hiding again behind her book.

"I want to rub the wet from your hair." He surprised himself. Her irises widened, the skin of her eyelids narrowed. She did not anticipate the flush that consumed her, she was unaccustomed to such boldness, but his autonomy ignited her. Straightening, Amélie tipped the glass transparent and patted her mouth with a cloth napkin draped across her lap. She set her book down. A chill swept her neck and shoulders, the tiny hairs on her arms stood straight and hard. Eli leaned his mouth close to her neck. Her mug made a soft moist ring as it connected with the bar wood. The heat of his body flooded her and took her under.

She leaned towards him and let the man with the rain and winds take her soul in his hands.

The winds picked up, ice and snow pebbles beat down, Amélie pulled the ends of her scarf tighter, cupped her gloved hands around her bluing lips and coughed. The iron bars lined her view extending high and menacing into the wintry skies, she pushed her feet deeper into the sludge, planting down.

She held onto memory, the comforting aroma of earth from his skin, the softness of the skin of his lips tracing rivers of pleasures along her contours, she collapsed softly. Her eyes watered and stung, she blinked hard and coughed again pulling her shoulders up. The coffee tin slipped between her fingers and she fumbled, clasping the bundle again.

She felt exposed and small. Her ears rang out and high-pitched frequencies pierced the inside cavern of her skull. She feared buckling under the searing pressure. She saw her bed, her escape, she saw the tangled sheets, the devastating swell of Romanian fists protruding from the lines etched around her eyes. Painfully, she forced a modest survey of the grounds again.

There, in the snowdrifts collecting in corners, in the spiraling black leaves circulating freely amongst the square she could hear them at it again, the shrieks, the bloodied face, the fierce stabbing ache sculpted into his beautiful contours, Eli's brown eyes, she witnessed the light leave those eyes and glaze over.

She felt the burn of his pain in her own chest. Forced her heart to still, poised and statuesque, her lips opened and closed in desperate prayer as she hid.

Donne moi de la force. Give me strength. *S'il vous plait.* Please.

She walked out into the war with the tin, a suitcase and the clothes on her back. Her chest was tight and she found it difficult to breathe, she felt an incessant urgency to retaliate against the weight pressing in on her like a vice grip. The thunderous metallic scrapes from the trucks and revving engines propelled her into motion. Amélie jumped back from the fence and twisted her fearful body inside the shadow of a tree before anyone in the vehicles could spot her. The convoy of four trucks sped into the grounds and slid to an aggressive halt in the slush before the gate. She jumped, three sharp honks echoed through the camp. Her breath hung around her flaring nostrils, she waited. Soon she'd break open in a fatal retch.

A single shadowed outline lifted from inside a windowed office adjacent to the gate, expertly marching in a precise ninety-degree assignment towards the gate. Amélie's ears pricked as the officer turned the key in the lock. The gate split silently and two barred wings fanned open for the convoy. The trucks were parked in a line, the square filled with SS guards and officers. She bit down on her gloved-fist, tears brimmed her eyes. She swallowed a moan.

In the ugly spaces between white spiraling snowflakes, she spied the bodies that filtered from the convoy, she shuddered as fierce commands rode the winds, and her cheeks burned. She folded in and closed her eyes behind her collar. The trucks emptied. Officers and personnel filled the square forming tight angry huddles. A stern perimeter of armed guards filed forwards securing the square. Bags and suitcases littered the stones; her frightened ears grasped at the German utterances veining up around her. She struggled, twisting interpretation. The ferocity of their tone, the sheer volume of their voices, she knew the convoy triumphantly returned the ones who had escaped the night before. Keys were pulled out by surging adrenaline fists and forced into the locks on the backdoors. She braced herself for the bang. Doors careened back on the sides of the trucks, determined hands heaved bodies from the canvas-backed cells in a chaotic fury.

Her eyes rested on the entrance of a man in an officer's uniform. He held his shoulders high and straight, chin up, gaze downcast, his ice-blue eyes rolled dangerously between polarities as he shouldered through the crowds towards the prisoners, cuffed and bent before the guards. The winter light struck the hard lines of his eyebrows beneath the rim of his hat. Amélie shivered thinking of the scarecrows dotting the fields in the South of France. She envisioned the intensity of anger that those piercing shadowed eyes could administer. She curled back against the trunk of a tree.

Philip Schmitt crossed towards the prisoners. His left hand grasped the leather leash of a bared-fanged German shepherd. The animal's mouth split wide, white rabid salivation foamed at the corners of the animal's mouth. The beast bucked and strained against his collar, wheezing desperately, and growling to get close to the bodies bent over before the guards. Schmitt pulled violently back on the leash forcing the animal to bay against his side.

In the harrowing vignette of that hell, she could never have known the balance that would later be served to that man, the one with the scarecrow face and German shepherd. Shrunk and dilapidated between the tree and fence, she was consumed in raw emotion. He crossed the square, moving with the embodiment of Hitler's projections with intentions. He sought out resistance prisoners and delivered a Draconian code of ethics.

She almost gave it all away. Her gloved hand muffled the

fervent gasp as Schmitt approached a darkened form near one truck and pitched the form violently from the ground forcing the body straight and exposed. Amélie registered his face immediately and she keeled over.

Te voilà. There you are.

THE PAST

The winds whipped his crow curls around the arches of his thick brows. She yearned to trail her mouth beside those arches, curve down towards the corners of his lips. She studied the way he averted his eyes, gazing down at the ground, his authenticity pulled deep inside the core of a reeling man imprisoned before Schmitt's feral stare. He dipped heavily, letting his body become malleable to the ferocious grip of the officer. From his position, he did not see the sliver of a silhouette tucked between the shadow of wrought iron and wood.

But Schmitt saw the silhouette. His gaze caught the slight shift of shadow Amélie's form blacked out across the patterned bark. Rage had surged up from his essential core and shot angry currents like lightning bolts into the corners of him. His right hand pulsed against the leather dog leash as he surveyed the space. His left-hand bit into the meat of Eli's arm. He ground his teeth and squinted past Eli's right shoulder in concentration. Schmitt then caught the flash of blonde tendril which had been whipped from the shadow in the wind.

He knew instinctively that there was a woman, a particular woman, perhaps the very woman whose face had been rolled clean from the surface of a lonely, condemned man's photograph he had eyed. A deep grimace broke the officer's face, and Eli shirked slightly as he looked up and caught the man's blazing eyes probing him. The officer's gaze shifted above the line of Eli's right shoulder several times before he broke his hold on him, offered up the dog leash, and pushed Eli into the hands of another guard. Eli could not see the officer push off towards the camp entrance, the burn of revenge in his eyes.

Amélie gasped when she saw the officer push Eli to another soldier and turn towards the entrance. She collapsed heavily against the tree. A painful sensation throbbed in her abdomen, and she pushed off from the shadow of the tree and connected with the slush and snow, her heart beat rapidly between her ears.

She fled.

STORYTELLER

There will be more taking than giving. A desperate drag. It will weigh on you, a Woman, coded and translated to enter into this humanity as the giving and sacrificing Mother. It will weigh on you. And, the love you will know for your children, you will want to sacrifice everything for them, unconditionally.

Preparation to endure the taking will be rooted firmly in your relationship with Self.

We are our thoughts. There lies the freedom of our ownership and internal construct, master your mind and you will be strong.

The Women of this family grew around knives in their chests. Tree trunks. They were raw. They carried this rawness on their shoulders, yoked that "Damaged Goods" label which they passed on to the younger feminine generations, an aggressive bared-teeth tribute. As "Damaged Goods," our Women were shielded. They obeyed the crest of this shield, held it heavy between Self, between Self and The Other with a grim loyalty.

Language-cages can box you in. Break the language down, recreate, transform that gnarled tongue-talk that chokes and weighs heavy. Invent your own language. Forge new labels for Self.

Learn to love that knife protruding from your breast, own its invasion as you could a flower as you face this world. Appreciate its imperfections for the unique story that nests there, your being is not the knife, and you are not the wound. A tree growing around a barbed-wire fence.

Set down the shield, abandon it, the ugly thing is no family crest, but is only a heritage of self-inflicted worry and pain that attracts aggression. A depleting martyrdom. Violence thrives in there. Abandon it.

Please, honor that we are the Women who will grow around the chain, grow around that knife. We learned how to accept that intrusion and without that intrusion we would not be.

Let us tongue our own language as we reclaim it and acknowledge that we are not "Damaged Goods." We do not have to live with such constructs from our past, carrying them, hefting them around like heavy masculine weaponry into the future.

No, we do not. We won't.

Face the imperfections and fault lines in your legacy head on Child, grit your teeth, and lengthen your spine through this immense self-confronting. It is not easy. It is not always graceful.

Take grip, hold on. Pinch whatever strand of fabric you can anchor onto. Don't let go, we are unraveling from the fray, Little One. We are then, braiding memory with language. That braiding is the formation of a strong family moving forward.

"Damaged Goods."

Start with two definitions:

1) Items that were expected to be in good (if not brand new) condition, but were discovered eventually not to be.

2) Someone who was once healthy and/or normal, but isn't any more due to unfortunate, traumatic events in his/her life (i.e. physical abuse, emotional abuse, sexual abuse, drug abuse, etc.).

Do not let this language fool you Child, this language is only the hollow of stereotypes within certain contexts. Constructs.

Dictionary dust. Although it is embedded in society and it chokes us out and away from ourselves, this unwitting street-slang, becoming vernacular, pervading everything, setting us all up, especially how this language dictates how we perceive ourselves, do not lay still once you collide with these idiomatic pillars.

Get up! Keep moving! Kick your feet!

Turn. Float. Glow.

I assure you, Daughter, that this self-confronting does not have to be brutal or violent. We do not have to waste away, to sacrifice ourselves in this process of transformation. This self-reclamation, no, this re-configuring and owning does not have to be painful or aggressive like the war zones from which you were bred. Caterpillars quietly cocoon. Butterflies grow wings gently.

My Child, reclamation is not brutal. My Love, we can learn to be gentle too. We can be soft with our Selves. Be kind to Self, first, forgiving. It takes practice, like learning any new skill.

There is a gentle hand running along the bark of that tree, tracing the chain.

Your Great-Grandmother worked through her mistreatment silently and passively. The deepening lines on her face, testimony, the sunken eyes in their sockets witnessed, her voice harbored angry edges. Her rage expressed in slammed microwave doors. Deliberately dropped objects. Lies. Commands. Demands.

Her disconnect was profound, disorienting for others. Only the most intimate to her, absorbed vacillating put-downs, and they rotated in silent agony around her perturbed mass.

Translated pitilessly as a societal masquerade, a thin-lipped mouth projected abuse and neglect. Caged and gagged in an orb of anger, this family was lost for some time, consumed by lonely expanses of a severe societal misinterpretation. They built up the scaffolding of lives contrived from faulty fabrication.

Do not underestimate how far this anger has stretched and

from which cradles of geography your story is woven. Colonial ax gnashes in the trunk of that tree growing around a chain-link fence. There is Greek nationality married to a Russian masculine energy amidst the rising machinery of Stalinism. There was a Romanian engineer murdered in this regime leaving a widow and three angry sons. The widow took her sons from the threat of Stalin's violence and war, brought them to Brussels to study before Hitler's genocide. There is the feigned politeness of a British heritage crossbred with dark-pigmented Roman roots. The Dutch were there briefly, if not those that immigrated to the New World and rooted down in Pennsylvania. A poor honest Loyalist and a York family cemetery. There was also a Scot, an Irish Catholic, and, of course, the French war bride from Brussels.

Yet, there was something more.

Despite bloodlines, they will want to name you, to tattoo claim onto you, plant you in the soil of the New World with wondrous and enchanting fiction. Girl, do not let anyone tell you what you are not, despite yearning for the opportunity to be original.

Your great-grandmother married one of the Romanian sons and it lasted for two months during the war. Overlapping love, and let me tell you, she became caught up in a dangerous love triangle. The man she loved was taken. She replaced him with a Romanian with Greek blood and a ruthless Russian homeland, and he beat her for two months. She didn't say how he left, or when. Little One, it was all only for survival, in the chaos and terror of Hitler's iron reich.

Do not underestimate the depth of such angry roots, how long this anger has been carried, passed between the Women of this family in a misshapen ceremony of duty. We end owning this anger in our time, in our lives, and amongst the mundane every day.

We grow into the chain, we change. We grow into the blade.

I tasted the poison of this anger, too. It was terrifying to confront a lifetime of pretending that things were okay. The theatrics eventually choked me out. I was twenty-something. A lack of understanding and empathy fed anger. Any actual acknowledgement of the cold simplicity of the generational machinery of domestic violence, the hierarchy of abuse, and how it is served nearly took me out. Alienation and subversion of the Feminine planted a seed of abhorrence in me. Not until I reclaimed, embraced my Empowerment, stepped into my Divine Right as a Sacred Feminine, loved myself, was I free.

I grew to learn to love the chain.

I grew to learn to love the blade.

In a final drag between my soul and the lines of pretense, I tried to enter the bureaucratic paper mazes and compartmental-ized remedial hands of those systems, the shadow of those insti-tutions, and I felt degraded and alone. I abandoned my body there for some time. I was encased and saturated in an anger that nearly claimed my wild essence. I love you beyond the clutches of this crazed anger. I broke cycles. I prepared our environment for you. I want you to continue to do the same for the next seven generations.

I acknowledge that the system placed families in positions for the opportunity of ruin. War disrupts family. If we do not fix ourselves in our capacities, then, the system will claim us. The system, that government eye, pyramids, the masculine institu-tion, supported by the confining professional cage of confiden-tially, well, Little One, it simply is another mechanism to be perpetrated against us. Quietly. Unnoticed.

The documentation and paper applications. Data input, crunching numbers. The statistics of other souls alienated by the same system. Creating surplus, backup, that customer-care congestion, the same government-ink exterminated. Daughter, it persists, is neglectful, those paperwork labyrinths. I know it only as "policide." Coined it as that.

You risk perishing without thinking beyond it.

Their ink cannot acknowledge or trace this anger because

when they do, they must work back through the masculine story. Then, they would be required to own the plotline, to expose contributions to this anger, toxicity that stems beyond Stalin's hammer or Hitler's rejection, beyond the alienating process of immigration, the outcome of domestic abuse. Do not choke, they want you to stay professional, maintain banality, do not be fearful of appearing unprofessional. Sensitivity is powerful. Emotions and feelings matter. Intuition will protect you.

This family was let down by systems that enabled the birth of refugees, war-brides and adopting scoop. Process. Children to be adopted by alcoholics in shell-shocked shadows. Bred on lands of immigration and reservation, the sick were quarantined. Displaced. Legacies burned by the terrifying hands, the ghost and haunting of mental illness. "Policide" ravaged bloodlines, segmenting and segregating babies to geography and adoption breaches. More little ones were ruthlessly bred. Paperwork protected loveless marriages and divorces.

Our Women, they spent entire lives enduring grueling mistreatment, they have for centuries, as it has been set up as "their position." The ripples of that mistreatment are far and close. Micro and macro. There exists an extensiveness of this timeline of subordination. Our Women did not love until they were loved, no, they could not love because they were not permitted to love themselves, not until personal moments of significant confrontations. Loving our Selves was revolutionary.

We faced our wretchedness. We looked straight into the barrel of that wretchedness, spit in the eye of its self-manifestations and maintenance. When we wanted to be safe we really were exposing ourselves. But, once we realized that we could, we walked out into their wars without fear, we walked out into their wars and planted roots, walked out into their wars and found heart. We did survive. We survived because we realized that instead of carrying a chain, yoked and sweating, we were gracefully growing into it.

Be cautious, though. Move slowly. When your body reacts and wills you to move fast, think deeply, and reflect before you react. This is hard to do. You will learn it in time. Give yourself that time. Give your Self the space for error. Hold your chin up, pump, don't stop kicking, surface in their treacherous waters and smile through teeth that you want to bare, but let your lips relax, and hold your pain as gently as you can. *She* will come in time.

Let Grace return.

THE PAST

She sank like an anchor into his passion, settled on his ocean floor. His fingertips wrote an exquisite map along her skin. She rested inside the reprieve of those sensations as they pressed each other against brick walls on the way home.

Their bodies came together in embraces that blurred the lines of identity, and she knew from the way she swooned as he forged a path of heat with his mouth along her neck that she was his, he was hers now.

The hinges of their limbs and torsos, the gasping orifices and breath that slid lyrical between teeth, catapulted their passion and bodies together like bombs, and their love ignited flames against that kitchen table. The piece of furniture collapsed under that hungry collision. The building rattled. The landlady scowled scarlet from the basement.

He pulled the skirt from her while unknotting her hair. He fingered the blonde tendrils and he inhaled the lavender perfume of her skin. She gasped and fell into him frontwards, ripping his shirt open with ravenous claws. Abandoned to the floorboards long after they arched and took flight from the leveled tabletop, was a scattering of salt and pepper mills like tiny soldiers in the midst of their chaos.

She had no time to toss a pinch of salt over her shoulder and she did not notice that he had knocked over the broom.

Skins left on the floor. Naked bodies on the table.

An apple had flown off and rolled into the corner.

STORYTELLER

"Sanctuary established for ... the true woman who possesses exceeding wisdom, soothing ... and opening the mouth, always consulting a tablet of lapis lazuli, giving advice to all lands, the true woman, the holy potash plant, born of the stylus reed, applies the measure to heaven and places the measuring-rope on the earth—to Nisaba be praise!"

- Enheduanna, The Temple Hymns

Empowerment is an important word for me. The word is being thrown around a lot lately, spoken without spirit. The word became a trend. Please know, pure words begin in the heart visually and emotionally, then signal the mind. Pure thoughts are seeds, we can plant them, they can germinate, ideas sprout, actions align and roots dig deep, stories are written and perhaps something has changed. Pure as in with intention to move forward. Pure as infused with spirit. Something internal, untamed. Empowerment is more than a word for marketing. Empowerment is being. Spirit aligned with language. Language manifesting action. Empowerment can create existence.

Pay attention to the words around you because they are attached to being. Observe the mouths that hook language, deconstruct the ways they own that language, how they hold back, when they let go. Apply these currents to your own self-perception and you will know who you want to be.

We create our reality with the words we speak. We create our reality with the thoughts we think. We are creators. Creatrix.

To empower is to give someone authority to do something. To enable them to arrive at another state, to give capacity for transformation. Growth. Essentially, to empower, to have power over oneself, to realize and utilize that coursing energy from within that fuels and propels us.

Fill out Child, have courage to take up space. Carve out space. Honour Self. Acknowledge Self. Love Self. We are present, and we are also absent. You will be your own source of empowerment, my Girl.

We can be wretched and empowered simultaneously. Spirit is fluid. Flux and flow. We are lifted. We are also brought down. Hot air rising. Cool air falling. Beautiful captivating storms. Thunder and lightning. Inside the eye of that fluctuation, we can love ourselves.

Fear, sometimes, can push us to get things done. To propel. To succeed. Without that horn-rearing anxiety we would not know the capacity of our greatness. Courage. Fear and anxiety are integral layers. It will help us to respect and define our limitations. Then, when we are ready, we grow beyond them.

Daughter, you are an incredibly unique and powerful being. You are your own. There will only be you once.

I want you to enjoy your empowerment road. The pain, the struggle, the hardship, without adversity you would not awaken. Alchemical transformations. Pressure.

The hard parts of witnessing your human struggle will be to want to protect you and shield you from pain. I will sometimes see how unjust the way society can be, and how unfair the process is.

Know I will stay and I will help hold space for you through

that struggle. I cannot protect you always and I cannot shield you, but, I can help equip you with the skills and practice to cope and conquer when adversity rears its head. Adversity will be a part of your life, but how you face that adversity will be our job, together.

I am your Mother.

I am also a Woman.

I enjoyed discovering I am also more than a Woman.

Daughter, we are Goddesses, each one of us, divine and ethereal: The Sacred Feminine.

This society has been crafted by a consuming masculine energy. The manifested framework has written over the presence of the Sacred Feminine. The patriarchal grid laid down has birthed dysfunction, women barred from stepping into their Divine Rites. Women denied self-love. Empowerment.

Safety. Shelter. Clothing. Food.

Believe me, look around you and observe the fragmentation of the female body and mind. The masculine wedge existing as if it were organic and spontaneous, as if we are separate from earth and water and skies. The Mothers and Daughters war against each other in this system, in these patterns and designs. Sisterhood is subsidiary.

We are slaves.

We war against Self.

Show yourself the respect that you want them to give you.

Honour Self first. I am here to help model that self-love in the helix of my own humanity.

Flawed and flawless.

Perfect and imperfect.

The air in your lungs that flows in and out, feel the security and space inside and outside of you in that movement. The reality of that air entering and exiting, that is your essence, your humanity. You are one in your uniqueness. You are one with the universe.

What we breathe out, the trees take in. What the trees let out, we take in.

My Girl, you are born from a line of women who have been dis-empowered, this is not uncommon for our Women, "the subordinate sex."

Constructs, they fooled us from knowing ourselves.

No ...

We do not let his story write us out.

THE PAST

Eli and Amélie used old pantyhose as rectangular sachets for the loose-leaf tea. Silently working through their ultimate occupation, he sewed and she tucked the pouches stuffed with tea from the black market into paper packets. She studied the lines of text in the newsprint while she folded. Lost in the complicated military plotlines, she tore off bits of tape from the dispenser and slid the edge of her thumb carefully sealing the packets. The weeks progressed, and she noted the virulent shift of languages in the papers as the Germans entered and occupied, French to German, unlike the mouths that opened and closed around them, letting in and expelling panicked air, frightened words. Amélie and Eli worked quietly between words and inked lines. Thoughts pushing against the external war-talk, replacing the intimate conversations that could have taken place between them instead.

Blitzkrieg. Lightning war. Campaign. Air attacks. As they worked through the months of Occupation, the language became angrier.

May 28th, 1940, Der Verbannung, she folded the face of King Leopold III inside the tea packet, brought her fingers up to her mouth and tore a cuticle loose with her teeth. She huffed, pulled her lips inside her mouth and turned her work-hardened hands over in the candlelight studying the cuts.

Eli discreetly watched her between needle and thread. Dipping his eyes to her collarbone he envisioned his mouth there. Lost in the rhythm, he started a stitch and stared. The enticing bone distracted him from realizing the anger Amélie pulled in and hid with the firm set of her mouth, she swallowed a deeply etched snarl curling her lips. She did not want him to know just how much she resented helping make the tea bags. She wanted to hide away and work around the war in pretence, but the newspaper lines, their cramped confines, were a continuous non-verbal confrontation. She was spiraling out.

Eli blinked and his eyes returned to the pantyhose squares strung between his fingers. He smiled to emptiness. She continued tearing tape and pasting the translucent slivers to the newsprint, eyes averted, hopelessly wanting to ignore the text. Hinged on diminutive gesture, she pushed through by entering and remaining in a mental occupation. Bent over, curved and crooked, her hands working through a degrading cadence, she could only conceive of the world in front of her eyes, the war beyond their walls, she retched under its full weight, busying her unsteady hands instead, she resented and found reprieve in the same breath making tea bags. She strove relentlessly to pull her thoughts down, usher them in from that dangerous ledge as she worked alongside him.

"*Nous ne serons pas en faire.* We will not make it."

She turned a packet around in her palms, sighed, and set the piece to her right.

"*Pas maintenant avec eux ici.* Not now with them here."

Her thumb massaged the back of her fingers in nervous circles. A door opened and shut in the hallway upstairs, she drew her shoulders into herself, looked ceiling-ward and held her breath. She did not glance sideways as he dispelled his own breath and froze. Perfectly paced footsteps beat a marching anthem across the boards and down the stairwell adjacent to their apartment above their heads. Hands arched in midair, lungs held, they felt the tears pressing the corners of their eyes, but they remained motionless as the noise receded below them and disappeared outside.

Eli released, emptied his lungs, and wiped the wet from his face. A soft chuckle shook his frame and he set the tea down, the callous of his elbows cradled on his knees.

He laughed.

He wept.

He laughed.

Shaking hands retrieved the hose and scissors, Amélie jumped with each sharp slice of the blades. She studied the mounds of hose collecting around his feet.

Her body broke open, a deep chill winged across her shoulders and neck. She kept her hands full, cracked her neck discreetly and cleared her throat. An insipid light filtered into the room from beneath the curtains that remained closed now, Amélie yearned to pull the material down, let the sun and winds in again. Her nostrils flared, the subtle spiced notes from the tea were a reprieve. She hummed and tore tape.

Teeth gritted, white-knuckled, and brow-creased, Amélie attempted to work through the fear that rode the back of the echoing footsteps. The severe concentrating brows, fierce cubed shoulder blades and perfectly polished boots haunted her. She wiped her forehead. Beads of sweat collected on her upper lip. A chapped hand wiped away the fear.

The last time she broke out in such a sweat was that day, during that encounter. She could put a face to the sound of the footsteps and closing doors. The meeting was a significant turning of tables, Amélie felt the acidic bite of shame in the back of her throat. She shifted her body away from Eli, uncrossed her legs and continued working with the newsprint.

They ran into each other in the hallway, she had returned home from dropping off some orders. She didn't want to know where he had come from.

She could only script in her mind, unfocussed and becoming

crazed, ruminating the lies Amélie had begun weaving. She wanted to sleep, just sleep.

Eli coughed over the tea, and she jumped. He could not see how her eyes remained fixed on him in the sliver of light stealing into the room.

He did not know how she worked backward and forth through the memory of the encounter in the hall, between the woman hiding the man with the brown eyes and the man with cubed-shoulders, Aryan eyes.

"*Oui*. I live alone for now. Ma Tante is away selling her fashion pieces." The lie burned through her, she stopped herself from averting her eyes and shifting her weight from the heels to the balls of her feet. She stopped herself from the impulse to tug her earlobe and avert her eyes. She had cleared her throat and wished him well with a steady gaze as she shuffled away, sweat-glazed and heaving. She knew he knew there was something more that the woman with the curls and dishonest stare hid.

She peeled over. Thin arms circled her abdomen, she arched like a steeple, for once, and she began to pray internally. Amélie wiped her eyes hard. She swallowed and continued on her way.

Eli and she crowded the space in front of the Fada each night with their burning ears, not daring to turn up the volume for fear that the neighbours would hear. They grew desperately reclusive and servile in the past weeks, fear gripping their colons punching up their intestines with the news of the rising betrayals from the Belgians.

They understood the extent of the malice that the Nazis systematically implemented across Germany, Poland, and Czechoslovakia. Amélie visualized a map of Europe and the black-booted flooding of German troops into their territory. She waited with fear, anxiety, and with anger. Eli tapped his fingers against aching knees, painstakingly hiding the shudder in his heart so Amélie would not collapse with his slow deflation. He did not want to die. The one assurance the young man had cleverly grappled with was the anticipation of forged documentation that was delivered in the folds of a book from a good friend. Amélie did not know. Eli wanted to surprise her with survival.

He still assumed the movement between her beautiful chapped lips were prayers for him, for their love. She prayed for survival too, for a life in the future that they did not have to hide.

The Nazis arrived in their totalitarian physicality, and she continued rubbing the wood of the table while the black boots marched in the reflection of the windows.

They marched through the streets, their boots malevolently clicking against the cobble stones, their black uniforms casting dark shadows across the faces of the Belgian inhabitants. They shrank under the low thunder of determined heels as they filled La Grande Place.

She dropped her tea bag. The pain in her temples rooted to her tearing eyes and caused her hands to tremble so violently she heaved them into the nearest feeble chair. Eli came to her and lifted her up against him. They wept quietly, the loose leaf mounded politely on the floor.

She had silently observed the flags bearing the clawed arms of the Swastika. The Swastika both startled and repelled her. The blood-red background of the flag and the black symbol was a spider of death. Despite her agonizing fear of it, she watched it without blinking. She envisioned a large red spot atop the back of the Nazi symbol.

"Flies," she joked with Eli, "we're just food for the Black Widow." His eyes did not squint when she chuckled.

Within hours the Nazis had transformed her city.

The Germans were always watching, all consuming, ever-present. The people became perished and thin as they tried to not draw attention to themselves amongst the chaos of the boots. In their leisure time, the Germans would sit on sunny terraces, their gaze constantly pivoting amongst the hurrying shadows of people passing by. They missed nothing: mothers palming bruised tomatoes, children stomping through puddles and the sagged faces of beggars that starved on the street corners.

The entire city was starved, the Germans occupied the food and delicacies, and they professionally averted their eyes to gaping ribs while they remained focussed on picking out the hidden Jews and resistors in the dilapidating crowds.

She quit her work in the restaurants as soon as the Germans began frequenting the terraces. She could not face them for fear of her secret lodged inside. They would know. She did not want to die.

She had been absorbed in Eli's orb for months, and she felt like a moth picking amongst the lights in the dark, eyeing the others in her city. Bodies did not touch only to get around each other in a deliberate sidestepping. The bodies did not idle or line the streets with conversation. She twisted her ears to the stationary bodies and noted that they were silent, except for a burning cough or a muffled wheeze shielded by facial hair and the sides of a gaunt hand.

The people were hungry, their work clothes and coats draped around shrinking shoulders. Top hats fell crooked on skulls and the once-tailored suit dresses hung around breasts falling down-wards and in. Amélie was suddenly shocked at her blindness and her insolence to the state of her people.

The warmth of his hands, the edges of his lips were almost the shadows of a prison cell to her now, she shook her head tossing the dangerous dichotomy between her ears, a blessed distraction or a cursed ignorance that would risk her survival if she continued on living in its shadow.

It was easier to turn inward, live thinking only from the perimeter of their existence, and she found a meager position as a seamstress in a tiny shop around the corner of the flat. She worked and helped with the tea. She relished the hushed company of the other women there, inside, away from the clicking boots and evasive eyes. Together, they sewed and shook. They could not utter how Brussels was a changed city. They were changed also, did not really know this at the moment, but they began to speak and live in a different language too, that rotated language of the black spider, the violence perpetuated between

73

its arms, the Nazi teeth. She heard this language as it rose up around her, smothering the city and its people in fear and misery.

The Petite Rue Des Bouchers was crowded with pressing crowds and she almost fell into the streetlamp when a brusque dark coat shouldered her. Amélie leaned against the streetlamp for support and scanned the angles of the shifting crowds. The rhythm of the city moved around the pounding feet and sunken eyes, but the clockwork of the work-crowd disrupted by the anxious urgency of the depression years had been substituted for this crowd-behavior, fear—fear and the reality of death.

Her face looked grim, seeing herself in the reflection of the streetcar. It squealed to a halt in front of a line of listless bystanders. She had tiredly dropped her fare into the metre and fumbled into an aisle seat. The car lurched forward and the passengers jogged with the momentum, most sat with slits for eyes, neither looking at nor acknowledging the other forms around them, others blatantly stared. The communal chatter that had been characteristic of streetcar rides was nonexistent. An elderly woman leaned against the back of her seat and sighed, a young boy absently sucked his thumb leaning heavily into her collapsing frame. Another child shifted forward slightly and tried to pull the boy's thumb out of his mouth with a wave of innocent laughter, but her mother urgently hushed her and pulled the little sleeve back. Amélie smelled the fear, there was a communal inward retreat, and her temples began to throb with the awareness of the substituted noise and chaos inside of their heads instead.

She tried to distract herself from the fear and worry, she thought about the sparse potatoes that needed to be peeled and how she could add a pinch of salt and pepper that she'd bargained for to bring out the flavour of the wrinkled roots. She drew her lips inside of her mouth and ran her tongue along them discreetly, inside, in order that no one else in the car would pick her out. The rising wetness in her mouth shifted her thoughts and she saw his fingers and how the pads of his thumbs traced slow circles along her temples. She languished in the resonance of his voice as he would fall back and take the bags from her and begin to pull the items out ceremoniously to make the arrival lengthen. She closed her eyes and felt the warmth of him, how his skin was a furnace that burned the cold from her. His eyes exposed a kindred soul that immobilized her whenever she caught him staring from across the apartment. She could rest in his arms while the Nazis marched and ate Europe. A cough raked her feeble form, and Eli pressed closer.

At first, she didn't see the young woman who had gotten on the streetcar at the previous stop. The woman had ebony hair knotted at the crown of her head. The low sharp murmurs of the other passengers roused Amélie. The woman moved cautiously down the aisle, her eyes roving over the stiffening spines that she passed. Amélie noticed how the woman's eyes were dark like coal and shimmering with emotions like Eli's. She was not extraordinarily beautiful, but her slender frame and symmetrical face caused most of the riders leaning against the walls of the streetcar to follow her with a sparked gaze. The yellow star sewn to her tidy brown dress was a stain and because of it, she was faceless.

The Woman stopped close to Amélie, her eyes shifted to the empty seat near the wall of the car. Without thought Amélie slid over to let the woman sit down.

Instantly a man sitting behind them leaned forward and hissed, *"Amant Juif!"* Jew lover!—the slur bit into both women, they grew hot and sticky. The words stuck to her like burrs.

The slur was spoken with such intensity that Amélie could feel the hatred coiling around each syllable. She felt a clammy blush creep up her neck and spread itself over her body. She stole a quick glance but the dark-haired woman's face showed nothing of what she was thinking or how she felt. Amélie recognized that blankness. She stared each day into its depths, the ripples in mugs of tea, or mirrors in bedrooms, that blankness was inescapable. She rolled her shoulders in their sockets, reached up, and placed a palm against the middle of her chest as the air released out of her lungs.

The man's slur had unhinged something that had been carefully balanced inside of Amélie and she couldn't bear to be crammed in the humid streetcar any longer. She reached up and pulled down hard on the car's line. The streetcar glided to a stop at the next corner. Amélie stood in a shuttering mass of unease and flew from the car with a burning dread catching her chest, vice-grip.

His skin was hot and stuck to the insides of her arms and clung to her as she draped her bare leg across the line of his hips. He shifted his weight and repositioned them in the chair. Eli's breath, steady and even, etched out time and she curled into herself. Amélie pulled air in through her nose, pinching her lips and eyes, pushing air out, in and out. She wished the breathing would steady her.

She attempted to shake the man on the streetcar from her head, but his insult formed a dreadful echo caught inside of her. *"Amant Juif. Amant Juif."* She shuddered; Eli kissed her softly in the middle of her forehead.

The Woman appeared again in her memory, moved towards her while Eli held her and took Amélie's place in his arms. That Woman crossed her ankles politely and clasped her shaking hands in her lap, unlike Amélie's insecure posture. Poised perfection. Amélie ground her teeth. Orderly bodies. Amélie buried her face in Eli's armpit. She envisioned the ripple of angst that the brown-eyed woman had bit down hard on to hold back from breaking open, that fierce ball of white feminine light, it could explode from the depths of her in crystalline laughter, a melodious song, carefree unrestrained bodies, shifting and rotating in love, or it could propel her to turn around and drag the Man's face across the seat of the streetcar.

The Woman on the streetcar could lift off, hover above the ground, spread thick with hatred, and dance above their heads, her eyes shining and dark, and her hair sleek and divine. She could flow within the contours of her body, that feminine prism dividing light into rainbows, but Amélie saw the reality of the woman, boxed into hatred and she was shrinking away, sinking down, dying. The boots clicked and the lines of men moved past, shadows rising high on the walls, their military dressings glinting like newly unrolled barbed wire.

The people grew cold and small.

Amélie had suffered from insomnia for some time now, and the work taping the bags had grown like nettle in her eyes. In the hollows of the night, she'd roll onto her side, prop her face up with her hand, and let Eli's profile manifest in her line of vision. The rise and peak of his nose edged against the dark became fierce and apparent. She had never noticed. She pressed her nose against his, again and again, without ever taking in the peak, the profile, how they would translate him, what that nose was defined as, embodied and manifested in.

She ached, pressed her other hand back to the middle of her chest and sucked her lips into her mouth. She let the tears well up in the shadows and quietly run down her cheeks, journeying to the corners of her mouth as she sucked in her lips. They fell in magnitude drips from her chin onto the mattress. This moment was a severe letting go that she had not anticipated. She had never contemplated in the fragments of their physical and emotional connection that the notion of loving him was something wrong, something that she wasn't strong enough to take on.

She frowned in his arms, a distinct line along the middle of her forehead deepened, she reached up from her chest and rubbed her finger along its borderline.

Pourquoi aurait-il être épargné de ce traitement? Pourquoi avez-vous pensez que vous pourriez exister, en ignorant ce? Why would he be spared from that treatment? Why did you think you could exist, ignoring this?

They could only make so many tea bags to feed them. She could only wipe so many tables, mend so many war uniforms, leaving and picking up work elsewhere because staying too long anywhere was dangerous.

Soon, she knew, someone would wonder about the man in her apartment. There would be eyes following, searching her out, and tracing the movements of her life. The fear choked her out, and her body raked with spasms from the chair. He hushed her and ran a finger along the line of her jaw.

Most nights now the sheets were too hot and she kicked them to keep them from wrapping and tangling around her ankles. She felt suffocation, a fear of strangulation, and soon this paranoia evaded her everywhere. She remembered him in his sleep, and cherished that memory while she coughed. She had watched him, her cheek planted to the mattress. His back was beautiful, muscular, and like valleys and mountain bases she could lose herself there in his meadows. His map. His landscape. She could only hide him so long, she knew, and slowly came to accept it. There was a war building up around them, threatening to tear them down. She witnessed the searing arms of that black spider, felt the burn of those Nazi fangs. They were only food. Flies.

Existence was reduced to the confines of their apartment on the Rue du Marche. Eli remained at home cutting and sewing small squares of fabric for the loose-leaf tea. The work was tedious, mindless, but with each tea bag, Eli envisioned visas for them. He filled the rest of his afternoon writing, translating, and transcribing for other Jewish refugees arriving from the East. He wrote several pamphlets the people pressed about between their hands and hid against cold-chilled chests, but nothing he wrote was overly substantial, he had been an intellectual before the arrival of the Germans, before the Occupation, but now, he was isolated from what was going on around him and he grew hollow and restless. He resented his lack of connections. The flatness of his words on dead ears.

Amélie sold the teabags to the neighbors and the clients at work, switching from several jobs to maintain anonymity in the fearful city. There was the sewing and the roomful of women who did not ask her any questions or offer anything of them-selves. She stayed there longest. Eli grew agitated and cabin-fevered within the paper-thin walls of the apartment. He'd catch himself absently sitting and staring at the torn yellow wallpaper while clenching and releasing a white-knuckled fist, counting the minutes, waiting, always waiting for her to return home.

She'd arrive to the snarl on his lips, try and kiss it away, but it bit its way deep into her. Soon she came to simply ignore that snarl. They came together during these moments, before their growing apart, in a fit of knocking bones and sweat-glazed throats. They'd sink their teeth into each other's flesh and clench their fingers tightly in the fists of hair, branding their mouths along wet-tattoo-tongued skin. Amélie knew, could smell, she was aware of the cabin fever enveloping Eli. She wept privately about his confinement. She feared the changes in him. She feared for herself. Caged animal.

They moved around each other in the tight rooms of the apartment without speaking. Their only sounds, pencil scratching paper, sighs, and dishware clanking against ledges. They spoke to each other through the warm connection of their bodies. Their lovemaking hushed now and fretted over in the pact confines of the apartment building. The language from the streets absorbed them—the German language. They did not rehash what the outside Jews were going through because they were going through it too. They didn't verbalize plans for escape due to that enveloping fear, the walls could hear, those paper-thin walls, and the heels hammering up and down the steps, clicking and marching like those steady and determined German boots.

Sometimes it was difficult to tell them apart, the original inhabitants and the new ones, the hatred was a dangerous demographic homogeny.

They lived through each moment, each day's survival. They didn't want that outside war language that had spread throughout the city to consume them in private. Once the front door shut, the outside world was deliberately avoided. The remnants of fear and worry were pushed deep down inside to consume them in other ways, facets of their identity they thought were still apparent—coughing fits to hide other noises. The carnal simplicity of bodies coming together.

Touch.

That was what they had.

She dreamt of a man in the restless minutes of stolen sleep with a broad blond skull and blazing blue eyes. This man spoke to a little boy with dark hair and eyes. The air was different, warmer, the sunlight different, it filtered clearer, whiter against the back of her hair and she looked down to see that her hands were aged and rising with earthworm veins. The man spoke about a woman in the aftermath of the war, she had crooned to hear him speak about the life after occupation and she collapses amongst the lines of violence.

"They pulled a woman out into the square, those Europeans, someone brought out an axe, She screamed and kicked while they hooked her by the arms and dragged her through the crowds. I vomited twice and swallowed it right there, in the streets. I tell you, they did it, those civilized Europeans. Your French people. That axe, well they lifted it high up and when it came down they had sliced her down the middle. That's what you get, sleeping with one of them, the enemy. I left then, found a bar, and got hammered. It was disgusting. I hadn't seen that much violence throughout the war. Your French people."

She had shot awake drenched in the salt of her sweat, folded angrily into the grotto of a scream, her chest heaving. Eli had pulled her up into the warmth of his corners. She coughed.

It was the shrill-clipped cries of the black crow circling the rooftops that she eyed from their window that finally unraveled her. She did not know the animal's name, nor could she see it as clearly as it looked, perhaps like a phantom dark shadow catching light and dust in the air above them. Inexplicably, she felt that it was a crow, *la Corneille*, and she thought it must be the one creature left in this devastating city, a scavenger. They'd been reduced to scavenging, picking the meat off bones and circling frightened heads. She jumped and dropped the half-peeled potato on the cutting board when she first heard the bird's piercing cry. She felt monotonous, an opaque sky, an open hollow like the inside of an empty bowl and she dropped her torso onto her elbows.

She could hear them administer the system, the occupation of vacant military barracks, and the train cars they're gathering and pulling together in long brutal lines that consume the horizon. A chain-link fence. She could hear the sickening thud of the bodies hitting the tiled floors in showers pumped full with Hydrogen Cyanide. There were names knocking together inside her head, they pushed up against her skull leaving bruises, the Dossin Barracks, Mechelen station via Muizen which would bring him to Louvain or the railway crosses of Brussels and Cologne, to Germany, to that blood-stained landscape, a three day trip and they land him in Auschwitz-Birkenau or Heydebreck-Cosel. She ruptured and folded backwards.

Ils vont l'emmener. They're going to take him away.

The shrivelled potato rocked slightly, and *la Corneille*, the crow, cried and cried.

Storyteller
"I have been attacked most cruelly
Ashimbabbar has not spoken my verdict
But what matter, whether he spoke it or not!
I, accustomed to triumph, have been driven forth from (my) house,
Was forced to flee like the cote like a swallow, my life is devoured
Was made to walk among the mountain thorns
life-giving tirara of En-Ship was tekane from me,
Eunuchs were assigned to me."
–Enheduanna

Her story is the stone that they threw into the water, the one they cast out. She splashed when she landed, sunk the pad and lotus flower with her weight, and projected the first ripple.

She is the first known writer of world literature because she recorded her name. A princess from regions unified throughout Central and South Mesopotamia, her writing provided bridges for her Father's people, her ritual and ceremony reference and blueprint for the people. She wrote in Sumerian, the scholarly language while her father's royal inscriptions were recorded in Akkadian, the vernacular.

She was known as a high priestess. Respected as a mystic. Revered as the sacred scribe. Trusted as a teacher, and upheld as a scholar, her "womaness" was the pitfall of too much ambition in a secular military world. War disrupts family. She wrote two thousand years before Homer and more than eight hundred years before the "Epic of Gilgamesh." Dream diviner; the first writer. Let us honour her.

Enheduanna was the daughter of Sargon the Akkadian. Sargon came from Kish, one of the ancient states of Sumer. They say the King's Mother was a high priestess too. Sargon appointed Enheduanna, his daughter, the royal princess to be a priestess of the temple of the moon goddess, Nanna at Ur. Her ripples altered the fabric of the history of women and religion. I reclaimed these sacred roots. I only needed to retrace names in stones.

Enheduanna proved her father's trust and transcended her secular duties and scribal training. She affirmed herself in her own right as a poetess. Visionary heiress, Enheduanna's writings united the people of Sumer and Akkad.

Poetry that served the powers to keep lands together, lands conquered and forcibly united, the military masculine flooded the narrative of the Divine Feminine. Driven from her house, her story was also one of wretchedness. When her father died, Enheduanna was temporarily removed from her place as a high priestess.

Stay vocal through exile.

It did not take her until she became her own to understand that her writing was not intended to elevate her father or to unite his lands. She moved beyond the political and patriarchal lines. She did not need to write to ground her family's hold on Sumer and Akkad. Enheduanna understood that she wrote for the Lady of Love and War first, spiritual ambassadress, gifted writer, her texts mediated between the divine-essence in Ur.

Enheduanna depicts Inanna as disciplining mankind, Goddess of battle. Inanna unites the warlike Akkadian Ishtar qualities to those of the gentler Sumerian goddess of love and fecundity. Enheduanna's work as teacher and priestess offers a strong, powerful ethos. Her philosophy, wise woman and powerful priestess, she is released as an archetype. Inanna's power equals that of the gods. The feminine, then, is articulated in the tenet of Enheduanna as androgynous, necessary, and valuable in that particular worldview, the vessel of life, the circle, the hoop.

Plato steeped her memory in madness. Chaos, they wrote over her story, anchored the woman somewhere else, temporary-ribbed sponges of sand on tumultuous shorelines. Enheduanna received the writings with purpose, gifted with power and magic, her creative process is gold-foiled-divine-storytelling.

She prepared herself to receive the writings, the sacred inspiration. She heaps the coals in the fire and prepares to receive her greater self, her transcendent self, the Goddess. Her creative process, intimate interaction, spiritual union. She enters the organic matrix. For a time, in the middle of the night, they become one, and out of that union comes the song.

Enheduanna is both physical and supernatural: the rock, the water, the throw, the connection, the ripple. She is a professional, a high priestess, a first writer of rank and office and she carries the burdens, the responsibilities, the grief of that terrible role.

In one of the most powerful passages in ancient history, Enheduanna steps forward and speaks in the first person of her own composing process. She reflects on her written hymn. At midnight, she says, she has heaped the coals and given birth to the hymn fire. This writing process foreshadows the authors of the Old Testament, foreshadows those of Jehovah by a thousand years. Do not underestimate her. Do not assume that history has written her away, has verified her death and absence. We are awakening. Know that. We can reclaim.

Her story is important, Daughter, because we are also writers, creators, and we breathe existence into our own stories. These stories, my Love, well, they are our lives. Let us honour them.

You will know them by their eyes, the flash, the turn, the float of their mind, and the glow of their skin. They plant roots, those ones over here, in their ground, life trees, they pulse with the synergy of an organic compass that leads us home.

Turn.

Float.

Glow.

THE PAST

"Between August 15 and September 22, 1942, they organized five large-scale operations: four big round-ups were carried out in Antwerp (3,222 victims) and one in Brussels (641 victims)."

–Laurence Schram, The Transit Camp for Jews in Mechelen

"I wish we could disappear, fly away like birds," Amélie spoke softly, her face turned towards the wall away from him.

Eli was wrapped around the curve of her back. They had lain there for several hours. Not speaking, not moving, faces apart, watching the light play across the walls. The darkness of the night entered and lifted, the purple of the morning whispered and entered slowly. Her voice broke through the air. He had been waiting, rearranging language in his head, building it back up, wondering, how could he tell her coherently enough for it to come through for her.

There is a way for us.

"*J'ai essayé.* I've been trying." He cleared his throat. His voice was deeper, an early morning baritone that was almost lost amongst the heaviness of his teeth and tongue. He tried again before she could turn the language into something else entirely.

"*Il ya des documents.*" There are papers. Prolonged silence, she twisted slowly to meet his eyes. Her pupils were large, the edges of her irises expanded. Several seconds passed before she asked, "*Papiers? Qui?* Who?"

"Pascal, the bookkeeper. He delivered a book here yesterday. *Et il y a plus.* And there is more…"

"*Quoi?*" What? Her body stiffened, she had not felt anticipation in a very long time. She did not articulate that this sensation was hope. There was a flutter in her chest that knocked faintly against her ribs. She felt lifted.

"*Il existe des visas.*" There are visas. She blinked hard, blinked again, keeping her eyes closed for several seconds. He began to sweat looking down at her, wondering, then, her face broke into a smile. He wasn't expecting her to smile; he hadn't seen her smile in months. His lips covered her mouth and he traced tiny circles around the corners of that smile. Cocooned in the rising morning light they held on.

His lips travelled over her skin as vines of square light from the window grew high and the morning aged slowly. He explored contours of the inside of bent elbows and the silk skin at the back of knees. He traced short lines with his fingertips along the sensitive skin behind her ear and savored her feminine purring from his touch. Her fingers disappeared in the dark mass of hair on his head and she pressed her torso against his. She pulled his face close to hers cupping his jaw in her hands so that they could really see. He lay on top of her then. She looked straight along the line of his nose and kissed its bump and peak. He hid his face in the curve of her neck while gently traced her fingertips along his back. He folded into her and she cradled him like a wounded knee.

Afterwards, he remained tangled in sheets watching her dress. His eyes slid over the smooth line of her hips, stomach and breasts. He ran his tongue over his chapped lips as she bent to retrieve her stockings, and he leaned forward and gripped her around the waist pinning her back onto the bed. She laughed.

He helped her put her stockings on. She watched as he worked each stocking into a soft ring and then rolled it over her toes and past the arches of her feet. His eyes never left her legs. The stockings unraveled up her leg, and he carefully snapped each one into the garter at her thighs. He rested his head on her lap, and she sat motionless on the bed. She sensed something ceremonial this morning, perhaps a process of memorization. She shook her head, shifted her thoughts, and relinquished the worries there.

She stood abruptly and dressed the rest herself. He watched, waited, wanted to extend to her, pull her from her mind, but he knew instead to leave her alone, she was moving mechanically, and he knew that she was in fact ignoring the worrisome currents of raging rivers flowing in her mind.

"Au revoir." She kissed him on the lips and he reached up with his hand and cupped the back of her head holding her gently to him. They hovered in this connection, he held her there, transfixed and heaving. She traced the tip of her tongue along the canvas of his lips and lost herself in the corners of his mouth. He ran his hands along the stretch of her spine and framed her face with his fingers. He pulled her face back gently and looked into her eyes. Without a whisper she blinked away the wetness and slowly turned from him. He heard the muffled click of her key in the lock and the deadened shuffle of her feet down the hallway.

THE PRESENT

Nelle stands up from the rippling bathwater waterlogged and restless. She towels her body and meditatively rubs moisturizer into her spongy pores. Moisture beads the edges of her temples and nostrils. She feels hot and sticky, not cool or clean. Unsettled. The heat and bathroom steam tendrils around her bulging body in the vanity mirror pulling her down. Energy courses through the crown of her skull along the tunnel of her spine. She bends over the vanity counter and lets the salty river of tears well from her.

Fountain, she pictures the virgin mother cradling a grown man, his body fluid marble, contoured to her maternal embrace. She blinks, sees another mother embracing her child on an Egyptian throne. Further back, blink, she sees a mother embracing her child from a temple in Mesopotamia. Fountain. Mountainous spring. Nelle cries quietly. A healing cry she realizes after the currents subside. As the baby grows inside of her, Nelle can't deny that her own body is changing too.

Nelle scrolls through consciousness screenshots, thumbing past images and videos, those who had come before her. She hears rushing turbulent waters, an oceanic crossing. She smells wind-swept, auburn, northern fields and, in each moment, she recognizes an internal pounding of a blood-red tired heart. A Mother's heart.

There is the pungent smell of alcohol sweating from fibrous skin. Nelle closes her eyes to the mirror. That smell had evaded everything she attempted to move away from and into. She lifts her lids and studies the lines branching from the corners of her eyes like roots and it knocks her into the memories of the solemn surfaces of boulders, her perched lachrymose Mother, the fluttering pages of her Harlequin romance novels, and the black silhouette of that tree. There are black birds and blue pencil crayon scratchings. The inside metallic smell of a coffee tin with hints of coffee notes. There is laughter in an empty house, relief in rising snow drifts. She thumbs back through these spaces, a hint of knowing that she's moving forwards.

She shifts her weight in front of the mirror from one swollen ankle to the other. This stream of consciousness is tiring and new. An intellectual grind. A train of thought pulling her lately to that darkness again, disrupted emotional adolescent chambers. Her body is opening a healing that has been buried. Preparation before the baby moves from her inside to the outside.

Nelle ruminates over the pubescence nature of this train of thought. She does not feel yet the leaves of validation, recognition, affirmation, sought from the external that needs to first grow from the internal. The medicine ball of her reality is a pregnant body before a mirror in a house they built together.

Her globular torso brims with life. She assumed that she had grown from who she was, the behaviours she had hefted from childhood, consumed by conjecture, she did not want to become bitter. She wanted to become better.

She leans back from the mirror, relieving her arch over the vanity. Untucking the towel wrapped around her torso she pulls the cloth from either end across and down her back to her bum and around to wipe her arms and legs. She looks down and studies her new body, thinking.

There was a time during the renovations of this house that

her mind settled to the peaceful harmony of living in lightness. She felt weightless there and a love had been consumed. She did not like this disruption, the lack of focus and how that darkness crept up, lurked and veined in her mind. Instead, for the past five and a half months she'd relinquished and relived every hollow corner of her existence and how she'd relay a personal Empowerment road, legacy, a self-understanding that would nourish inspiration and hope for her Daughter.

She wants to lift her Daughter up and not weigh her down.

Nelle knows that this day rolls into her consciousness with swollen thunder clouds of thought and memory, ready to release, waiting to let go. Cleanse. She silently honours the milestone. It was this day, almost a decade ago, at the pit of her descent into the masculine behaviour cave of her ancestry, where her men lost themselves in pitch dark black rages, she had succumbed to their despair, to the loss of losing her Nanny, to losing her Self in that grind she spoke to her elder.

"Nanny, I've lost my hope. I'm sorry." Then, she felt a gentle loving warmth pool into her empty body filling her up so she could sit straight again, feeling assured that there was something else out there more encompassing than the mundanity and despair of her domestic troubles.

The blackout was illuminated, and she entered a beautiful rebirth transition of reworking learned anxious patterns. Days spent facing Self, flawed Self, and the alchemical configuration of century anger that Self no longer wanted to carry into Self— into Self-love. She wanted to rebuild her body because it had collapsed, her lungs lined with tar and resins, her sickly ribs protruded menacing like driftwood. She wanted to rebuild their love too. There was yoga and breath. Hours spent inside a gym and hours spent outside walking. Gardening. Writing. She learned how to differentiate between the inside and the outside, and above all, she carved out an identity for only her to fit into and fill up.

Nelle knew that her survivor Self remained hunched in her aching corners yet, ready, eyes blazing. Worried hands clutching bloody-bruised knees ready to shoot open again in flight. Scars on her body. Residue of the end of love. She knew it, but now, even with the voluminous consumption of her body in the bathroom air, rotating with life, a living ark. Nelle wasn't ready for that past Self to clench her teeth and take another stand.

She pushes her fingertips against the moist surface of the mirror. They squeak a line around the outside of the reflection of her face. She sighs at the outline and thinks of the sketch of the family tree consuming her desk in her study. A new project, one that's channelled from her writing. She wants this project to be a perfect heirloom for the Baby.

She knows too that she cannot deny that through her self-actualization there is an honouring of her creative potential as a writer, and in that act of esteem she knows her Self too. She knows who she is as a Woman, who she was, what she is capable of. Her potential and flaws. She wants to know who she is as a Mother and possibly a Grandmother one day. She wants to know, to live in this assuredness of authenticity, because, now she feels that diverse textile of elder-ancestral-Women souls, coming through. They take up residence in her body, braiding themselves into the veil of this reclaimed slippery knowing.

This knowing hinges her story to theirs. Raw authenticity and palpability. She shoulders the bravery to walk those foot-steps back and try to know the ones who accumulated to her. They are there still, speaking and breathing, willing a storyline—however imperfect—to manifest.

The People have forgotten the Sacred Feminine. A forgotten term. The People do not fully give credit to that capacity that the maternal, the Sacred Feminine has as a life-giver. Yet they show Nelle of the priestess who once kept a sacred flame lit, inhabited temples with spiritual authority and spoke to them about the ways of life. She was the teacher, the writer, the sacred oracle, and the People listened.

Nelle sees the mother again, Pieta. Her sacrifice and spiritual conception with the story of his crucifixion. Women no longer feel holy or virginal. They have been denied their sacredness. It has been lost for some time.

There is a memory of a female shaman who walks both sides. The dark. The light. She walks both sides of the moon. She comes too close to what has been ruined. She comes close with rage. She comes close with love and she grows it all back to life.

Nelle knows there are voiceless ones. There are dis-empowered ancestors, still haunted by the chain that had choked them out.

It is time for these voiceless souls to be heard, to be able to articulate breath from a molten sphere of collective memory, for a tongue to push that air into specific movements for the language to resurface, for the Sacred Feminine language to emerge.

Nelle hiccups in front of the mirror. She has not lost her breath in a long time. She muses that the tree is one quarter full, and this makes her anxious.

She is only sure of her Mother's side, the farming ancestry that extends from Tamworth. The family cemetery. The stories passed between generations was assurance, something tangible she could stand her feet on. There was a fence, linearity, and physicality in that storyline to reassure her of legacy. But then, there was the compelling narrative, the one that rang in her ears like a novel, and one plotline in which she couldn't put down an enigmatic character.

She had abided her time long enough to realize that she was listening to their delivery of information to suit them. She knew the answers would be riddled with lies and horror. Denial felt cold, but she had to delve in and attempt to articulate some form of truth, to achieve that ultimate extension outwards, to sacrifice her brief access to her family. Each thread of the story outlined for her Daughter. Threads of a web attached to their souls.

She resented universal narratives as a writer and Woman. She grew away from an objective eye of existence and any attempt at trying to fist absolute truth.

But, something has shifted inside of her now as her body opens and swells with this new life. Some semblance of linearity was wanted for this Little One.

Nelle can't have her wandering dream-lines, only one could be abandoned there.

RIPPLE

If there could be a conversation recorded
between Adam and Eve.

or,
The first story,

Lady of the Largest Heart,
Lady of the lake,

chalice,
a Goddess Womb.

Piece together the disc's fragments,
locate her poetry,

an ancient woman,
a sustaining matrix,
her body.

"I, I am Enheduanna," she says.
That moment, when,
out of the collective,

a new consciousness
was born,
self-definition,
self-worth.

Forward she goes
towards autonomy,

she tears mountains apart,
places upon them a throne,

she moves on her own,
and from the garden,

she know both
good and evil,
rage and calm,

she is wretched,
journeys through nature,

torn,
dust-covered,
"he eats away at my life,"

her pain
grows inside her womb,
and in the crux of the pain
swelling from her inner chamber,

she birthed a poem,
and,
she signed her name.

STORYTELLER

"She's a holy terror."

-Margaret Laurence, The Stone Angel

I will try to begin with your great-grandmother. She was enigmatic and because little was ever straightforward with her, I need to begin here. I think.

She was a paradox. Inconsistencies slid along her tongue and slipped from between her teeth into the air. She filled up the room with these inconsistencies, it was difficult to grow authentically without inhibitions there. I tried.

I was uncomfortable because I knew truth was something wet and forming to the container. I pictured myself as an underwater weed in her ocean striving to break the surface and touch the warm current of the sun. Just once. I can tell you that I knew her, and that I knew little of her. This knowing lasted blinks, and the sudden transformations were exhausting. My world, what it appeared to be, existed as a dicey flux contingent on what she could reveal of herself in how she felt in the moment.

Storylines changed each visit, and whichever comprehension

I had honed from narrative was completely levelled and built up differently each energy exchange. She was a master storyteller. My curiosity burned, but, as I grew into a young Woman, my wanting to know burned more, and I began noting that she left secrets concealed in her stories. There were many gaps, and other things could take shape. There was merit in what she would not say.

I strove for an enduring connection with her beyond situation. Although, Daughter, in the eye of storms, I appreciate that there was a unique bond between us that could be authentic despite an unreliable narrative. The fact that I sat and listened, as a Woman, it was enough to know her and know nothing of her.

Woman to Woman.

1. I grew up in the waves of processes. It took time to
   realize that this shifting was an Empowerment road.
   Until that understanding, I felt like a coiled fist in
   motion that missed the mark every thrust. I didn't
   want to feel like a fist, pushed together and sweating,
   it was painful. I wanted only to unfurl, open the
   hand, and clean the blood off. Stretch. Release.
   Unfold. I wanted only to cup my palms around
   warmth and lift it up to my lips like steaming tea.

This Woman was uprooted and dislocated. A war bride and survivor of war. She found refuge in spaces that translated her as a surviving victim because it was in the fabric of these constructs that she found any compassion or empathy for her situation. Your great-grandmother resented the translation of her body into that receiving society. The hard face of cultural comparison placed her in the centre, but also at the margins, yet, she clung to the perimeters that the war-terminologies set out for her and found solace in the rigidity of that living contrast. They were locals, the originals, and she was the other.

She was "other." The events leading up to her arrival in that small town were tongued and spoken, woven into an elusive narrative she carried safely in her post-war box. She lived there—a doll in a dollhouse. She picked up the roles, carried them, while she worked her hands and tongue to begin restructuring the storyline of the lives in that box. She worked them into her own shaping and forming, a narrative that fit her wants and met her needs.

She constructed the dolls and she outfitted the story of that dollhouse naturally. She picked up the stereotype of that box and held it up like a shield for protection, and in that shielding, she maintained self. She couldn't see though, Daughter, that in that maintenance of her past self, there was no bridge to her for us, only a shield that she might set down in rare nets of safety to let the perfect film of projection rest for a while. Then I glimpsed the vulnerable pulp of authenticity that she craftily hid behind that shield. I loved her there.

Girl, she was not born in Canada and she had carried this story of uprooting and dislocation in her thumbprint to the New World. A disruptive transplanting, the strain on the ties between language and culture, language and community, her dislocation between home. I lost her and found her here.

A sympathetic seed was planted in my conscience as I grew and became aware of a dollhouse life. To me it was a barbed-wire confined house, full of lost connections, slipping comprehensions, and her strained hooked conversations that tired us out. Or ignited us. I came back after resting and tried again. I went away propelled to see reality differently.

I knew even through child eyes that my Grandmother missed out on the conventions of language that enabled access to her, to us, and this loss of social normalcy isolated her. Her social position was completely altered with immigration, and she needed to survive holding her place amongst her new social hierarchy.

Home is rooted in language. Without the free-flowing syntaxes of those precious linguistic rivers, your Great-Grandmother swam against currents, fitted her fists through the links of that barbed-wire confinement growing hard from the fierce pushback. A tree growing into a chain-linked fence.

You will not know the slight melodious curls of her accent, petalled French language, the resolve of a blossoming bud. Raining petals from climbing a crabapple tree. Despite their beauty, I slipped and fell on those scattered moist petals.

Language, Child, is context. Language is not specifically word order. Etymology. Diction. The ways in which words are placed beside one another, vocabulary and grammar, fluctuating linguistic rules. Language is not the air and breath of a soul fraught to convey itself from the inside to the outside. To have it heard, no, to be acknowledged.

I knew there was much lost. I knew I truly did not know what she harboured on the inside. For some time, I assumed it was an accident, unintentional and bred from the unfortunate organic circumstances of the language barrier.

No, my Girl, that was not always the way. Sometimes, what can make us different and alienates us from others can also be latched onto and used for survival, a deliberate safety net, or more so, a shield from our own selves and others. Your Great-Grandmother poured herself into that Old World mould and stayed there, for survival, for protection that tipped into isolation and she did not acknowledge that she was saved and damned in the same reckoning.

Her behaviour, which was courageous, but obscure, full of perpetual social mistranslations, dreaded linguistic breakdowns —they caught up with us. They knotted tightly, and she skirted for the duration of her New World life, the expected processes of assimilation this way. Child, she liked being an outlier.

I flattened language with the butt of my tongue, pushed it up and out the top slit of my mouth, and I lost her. My slang, rushed sentences, spliced and run on, were slowed immediately and broken down altogether to something else, something more text-book. Something more proper and politer laying intricate brick-work over my expressions—my rural essence. I felt walls close in tightly, ugly yellowed wallpapered walls that peeled away familiarity with myself, my behavioural cues worn like beautiful flawed habits were non-existent for that blank canvas, those whitewashed walls, nothing to be lost in the breakdown when she built things up.

And, this wallpapering only happened with her immediate family. She made herself accessible to others, but to family, she was handicapped.

Don't be fooled, Child, when the situation appears before you, look behind it to see through it. Pay attention to bodies, how they move and take up space in situations, you will glean many cues from the physicality of a situation so you are aware what is being laid over truth, lattice-like. Pay attention to those moments when this work is done, you will feel a guttural sinking —honour that sinking and stand your ground, despite the social etiquette, you will halt and come crashing down with this stoppage. Peel back the layers and lay it out before you so you'll know what is truth and what is false. There will be a little voice there speaking with you, that is truth, listen to it, your conscience. There are ears you will encounter, those that cannot absorb sound as readily, but also those that move against the air deliberately. Don't be fooled by their pretence, you must listen to hear.

Speak. Push words out or let them go. Ego wants to express, to testify, but know, to own too.

She was a name-changer. Insertions and avoidances for the sake of the name game leaks into storytelling, the leaves of memory and identity roots. She could manifest a whole existence that way, or an event that never happened, or something that happened beyond the context she interpreted. She built a mannered and gleaming structure of boxes with names—she slid through hallways of rooms carrying different names.

I wondered, was she hiding or walking away from other Women who lived before and during war that she wanted to abandon and forget? Questions hooked me, pulled me in directions of disbelief and guilt. In anticipation, the unknown chased her, nipping at names yet unused. Then there was her position during the Occupation, names used as masks for survival. With Liberation, there was another hiding altogether, another name change, a transformation, from the woman who survived the war, to another new woman who would survive immigration and settlement in the New World.

She offered glimpses of narrative. Necessity of a name-changer. Glimpses of Self melt away from places like writing in sand, or stones laid in a pattern on a rough shore. Riddles. I felt fractured, strained to hear her narratives before they transformed. To place facts. No, to lay words she presented, in place, in some semblance of order for my own knowing. I couldn't see it then, but she had me shingling out entire lifetimes that overlapped and brimmed into my spaces this way. I followed storytelling as if it was presented perfectly with covers and pages. Do not underestimate the flaw of narrative despite perfect presentation.

So, let it be told, your great-grandmother perfected the craft of storytelling in the same brevity that she dismantled the tradition of it. She is setting, her story is embedded in the richness of setting, with characters. She creates characters, depicts them, but then, then she presents the complications, the thing that gets the ball rolling, and it's lost there, her narrative, run-on and repetitive. She doesn't strive for further process, a responding to, or a more significant resolution of plotline. There are no resolutions, only the grip of actuality in the process of events falling around her, and there is no recovery, no.

And, Daughter, there is no closure.

We need closure. We want closure. We want to heal.

Our first storyteller, she is a part of you and she is not a part of you. The past and the stories it holds—remembers—happened. They are not occurring now, they are not your reality, and they do not need to be. Be careful how long you let your mind rest here. Reliving the past is a refusal to evolve with natural life changes. There is comfort of familiarity in repetition, refuge in self-victimization. There is the avoidance of true transformation, a foregoing chance of becoming a better self for habitual selves that only want to get by. No, it is not your reality, but layers of your existence. How you consider and acknowledge these layers will give you a good life or drudgery.

Your great-grandmother transgressed seas and cultures. She endured the dark. Survived. But, she was a Woman that could push the truth of things inside and live falsely outside for survival. Name-changer and storyteller. I can tell you that she was all of those things and she was not. Do not assume that you know, because if there is one thing I have learned, we do not know.

You see, your great-grandmother is not of our blood.

Our origins are a split trunk, still smoldering after a light-ning-bolt shot straight through.

I do not truly know where we came from.

THE PAST

Eli heard the thundering polished boots on the hallway floorboards. He stepped once towards the door when the first rain of footsteps echoed up the stairwell onto their floor, but quickly stepped back, simultaneously knocking his other foot out from under his trembling form. He needed to hide, and there was no time to lock the door and pretend no one was there.

He cursed the back of his hands as they pushed his weight back up from his knees to his feet again, blood rushed down his neck pooling like lava in his lobes. His eyes burned as they brimmed with ferocious tears. A skin-crawling fear began to lock down his body and a rancid anger surged in his limbs at the stupidity of the moment. She had locked the door, he only opened it once for no reason other than to see the light filtering into the apartment building from a different barred window.

Eli washed his tears to the corners of his eyes and hissed while he wiped the wet from his fingers onto his shirt. His hands twisted violently around him, he pushed them under his armpits in a pathetic attempt to appear calm.

Three identical loud knocks boomed throughout the apartment. He jumped with each one.

"Ouvrir!"

Three more heart-punching claps, *"Vite! Vite!"*

Eli froze. His loins tightened into knots, he helplessly scanned the space for one last second for a hiding place, and he knew that it was useless. They'd find him anyway. He let his hands fall to his sides and he held his body steady and balanced between his feet. The final muffled sound of Eli clearing his throat was interrupted by a brawny voice.

"Ouvrir maintenant!" The tongue of the German accent was apparent in the resounding delivery of the French. The almost perfect utterance of that French was too streamlined and exact for a Frenchman. It was too clean, too efficient, crisp.

He shivered.

His thoughts raced and he became weak in his chest while he strained to remain composed. Lies lit inside his mouth like wildfires but he knew they'd burn themselves out first before they could save him from those footsteps and knocks. Sweat beaded along the back of his neck and shoulders until they became rivers flowing down his back. He flicked the wet from his eyes one more time before he decided to simply open the door. He slowly cracked it open.

Three uniformed men consumed the light of the wedge with glaring eyes. They were not impressed with the delay in this welcoming and came forward instantly when it was clear Eli would not open the door further. The tallest man, the one in the middle, spoke to Eli in a frighteningly calm tone. The man placed his right hand on the face of the door and pushed it in, exposing Eli's face and upper body. Eli shrank back.

"Nous recherchons pour Amélie Cyncad." We are looking for Amélie Cyncad. "There has been a report received that she's maintained very close interactions with some Jews."

Eli attempted to keep his eyes dry. He hid his shaking hands behind his back and tilted to the left slowly to conceal his body behind the door. There was no sense in answering directly. He knew that they knew who he was.

He took the time to clear his throat and focused on the edge of a uniformed shoulder to steal his eye contact away from the men before he spoke.

"*Je suis désolé.*" I'm sorry, he paused, "*elle n'est pas ici en ce moment.*" She is not here at the moment. There was no delay in their response.

"What is your relationship to Miss Cyncad?"

"*Je...,*" he could see the slight flicker of his eyes that gave the lie away, "I am her Brother, Pascal." He let the lie fall off of his tongue and waited, perhaps it could distract enough for more time. The rumours accentuated their cold professionalism, they knew everything and everyone. Eli doubted by the unchanging intensity of their stare that this lie would follow through and he sucked his cheeks in. The rivers of sweat had dribbled into dark ponds against his lower back. He wanted to sit down.

"We know that Madame's Brother has been dead for several years. *Qui es-tu?*" Who are you?

Eli forced himself to not wince at their reaction, but continued unravelling the material of the uniformed shoulder with his eyes. He inhaled slowly and wished for more time, if anything, to just feel her against him. He could barely recognize the hollow in the tone of his voice as he replied.

"*Je ne suis pas Pascal.*" I am not Pascal. He lowered his eyes and let them gaze on the perfectly polished toes of those black boots. They had openly caught him lying, and even if he hadn't been Jewish, they would punish him regardless because of the circumstances.

"*Je suis Eli.*" I'm Eli, he whispered under his breath and continued staring at the boots, refusing to meet their eyes. The man in the middle stepped past the door and forced it completely open.

"*Vous n'êtes rien mais un rat couché, Eli.*" You are nothing but a lying rat, Eli. The tallest man moved forward forcing Eli back. The front door gnashed open, gaping like a wailing mouth.

"*Nous savons que vous êtes un Juif.*" We know you are a Jew. "You are having intimate relations with the woman of this apartment. We will not let these disgusting acts against the State carry on."

Strong cold hands clamped down hard on Eli's arms and he jerked. His muscles tightened reflexively, and he flailed his head two times, but his strength crumbled when the third man forced him to the floor.

They discreetly beat him into delirium inside the apartment. He felt the blows to his body loosen the tissues and he pictured biting into an overripe peach, the bruised yellow and purple fibres splitting around his teeth, he lurched with the powerful stench of rotten pulp. His eyes swelled shut. The quick snap was a soft sound, but the brevity of the snapping carried to the depths of his gut, he felt his teeth pushed back, he felt the tenderness of his gums bleed. His stomach emptied when one of the men's black leather boots hammered into his side, crunching ribs.

They kicked Eli until he was unconscious, then they dragged him out. They dragged his body down the creaking hallway leaving a smear of blood on the wood. They didn't carry him down the three flights of stairs, but pulled him along instead, his head thumped grotesquely against the steps, his jaw smacked, and his teeth violently clicked with each brutal connection.

Eli began to come to as his body bent around each stair. The huddle emerged from the apartment building and the uniforms propped Eli up between them. Eli could only push ragged breaths through his swollen nostrils. He sagged brutally between the men. Through a filter of blood and pain he saw them open the doors at the back of a van. With one final swoop the uniforms lifted the bloodied body into the van and calmly shut the back doors.

There were many shadows lining the street when the group emerged from the apartment building and pushed Eli into the van. Shadows with eyes that pressed back into darkness becoming unseen. They knew.

They knew.

They knew that they were not him, just shadows coming and going.

A black bird picked up a pebble and flicked it. The creature stepped towards the pebble again and snatched it with a sharp beak. It flicked the pebble again and shrieked before lifting off.

STORYTELLER

"Nobody knows oneself until he has suffered. It's the hard law, but a supreme law as old as the world and sadly...we have to receive the price of this unhappiness and have to pay dearly to get it."

– Alfred de Musset

We can manifest love ourselves. We do not wait for it to be bestowed on us. We accept what love we are offered. We accept what we feel is good enough for us. We have a choice of the behaviour we tolerate around us. We can only control ourselves.

But, we found it easier to manifest how we were tortured, and we stayed there for lifetimes.

Grandmother tucked a quote in an envelope when I went away once. *Nobody knows oneself until...* She tried to reinforce our suffering through this quote, for us to connect and seek Sisterhood through this suffering, this human burden. The quote showed me that we were to formulate our identities based on this notion of perpetual pain.

I don't want to live that way.

Yes, we must be empowered to speak authentically and openly, without fear of our pain. But, in the extent of that releasing, which risks upsetting those souls around us, love and light have already started to fill in the void.

If that was your intention—to truly heal.

If not, the constant release of pain only disrupts balance and perpetuates the exact mechanism of domestic violence onto those around you.

We become chained slaves to our pain. DNA chains. Lineage. Bloodlines. Intergenerational anchors.

No. "I dropped the chain of pain." A dropped lizard's tail.

Yes. "I dropped the chain of pain" and focussed elsewhere because life blessed me with the knowledge that there is choice. There is warmth just as there is coldness.

Fists and peace signs.

Fists and lotus flowers.

I looked for love, battled with the darkness long enough and eventually chose love.

There was suffering, there was loss and death, but there was also love. This sensitive and resilient love was polished and held close to wombs and hearts, pressed between skins and flowed heavenly from singing lips. We protected it, watched over it, because this love was something that the masculinized society translated as weak, as something we needed to overcome, and we pushed through that mentality. No, this love is paramount right now and is honoured.

This sensitivity is power.

Our vulnerability is power.

We did not let them keep us fearful of who we were as Women, as people, as humans.

We are not victims or dysfunctional, our sensitivity is a gift, our sonar and radar, our survival skills. Sensitivity empowers us. Do not become ensnared in the current ideologies of victimization, because then you risk hardening, becoming insensitive, and essentially becoming alienated by your femininity.

We can choose to not suffer. Yes, I learned who I was

because of suffering and pain. But, the process can eventually become gentle. We can let ourselves heal. We can choose to have power.

We can love ourselves with pain present.

I wanted to tell her that.

I wanted her to embody that.

Ripple
she wondered what to do
when all seemed so blue,
eyes-closed-wide-awake-dreaming,
lips moved and ears listened:
flip your hands skyward, open, unfurl,
find peace in your palmed storyline,
eye your fingers and pray.
left thumb tells you to love and
know yourself, first,
pointer speaks of respect for your elders,
don't flip the bird in the middle,
but help the boy with the broken glasses,
rings on fingers made for love,
love your parents and honour their-human-story,
pinkies are small, but not pigs,
love your sisters and brothers then.
place the right pointer and middle ground
against stone and listen to the winds,
right pointer is to direct the Little Ones
and love them first because they are learning,
growing, planting roots, learning to hold space,
simply help them with patience, love, empathy.
those words are important for them
because they can grow into organic things
beyond language where love can thrive again.
the right middle is The Way,
honour Mother Earth before money and objects,
respect the laws of nature and organic forces,

don't toil with them because humans can't know,
and won't win: that is okay, that is the point.
she felt good, but she asked what to do and how
to keep her feet and hands moving.
she balled her left hand and studied the fist,
she curled the remaining three fingers on her right:
Fists and Peace Signs she sang out,
she knew which one she wanted to deliver,
which one would help if she offered,
when and how and why and where.

THE PRESENT

The shuffle is memorized. Ritual. She picks sleep from her eyes. The tip of her nose nearly touches the mirror as she examines her face, yawns.

Navigating the walls and doorways of that house with palms and memorized footsteps, some pieces never move, the furniture is consistent, security in the familiarity. She breathes past with fingertip antennae. She knows the textures of the house intimately. The slight edge where carpet ends and the hardwood meets. She knows that line with the pads of her feet, she knows rooms are ending and she's in another space.

Nelle fills up a glass of water with her index finger pressed against the inside of the glass. The water quenches, the coldness is a comfort. She sets the empty glass in the sink. The shuffle is now a careful tiptoe.

Marks on the walls and on the trim, to her they are the fingerprints of living, she knows each of them here, their living memory, and she carries them confidently in the cradle of memory. She fears closed doors and steel stairwells. Toes and fingers guide her through this fear, and she knows, truly, she shouldn't fear any falls, only the deepest darkest body of waters, she doesn't have to see to keep her head afloat. She has to want to keep her head afloat.

Her eyes burn and she winces in the mirror as she pulls her bottom eyelid down and away from her eye. She's peeled back both lids on the capsules of the contact lenses, and they rock against the bathroom counter like shells. The whites of her eyes are blushed, ringed in red, and they water. The continued veins vining up toward her irises, she wonders if they will ever touch and what will happen then. She overwears her contacts. Air hits the exposed pupils as she primes her lids. She pulls them and pinches them in places pushing air around. Her breath held, shoulders pulled up, chin jutting out, she takes position, the lens sits like a bubble on her other fingertip, and she blinks hard when her finger connects with the open socket. She holds her eyes closed longer than normal and she curses in pain and frustration. There is a hair or piece of dust on the lens and it burns, it's a small excruciating pain that can easily level her. She can't rub the eye and risk scratching the cornea. She tears up, a private sob rattles her slightly. She waits, curls her upper lip. Pinches the corners of her eyes and sighs.

She sees herself shuffling down a long dark hallway, trying locked doors, looking for an open one. Her eyes are closed and the panic of blindness has set in. Nelle is frightened, breath hangs around her, she's cold. The long high siren of her child's cry rings out from somewhere in one of the locked rooms, and she begins to hyperventilate. She sees the keys slipping in her hands and she hears them clinking menacingly against each other. The desperate drag through the hallway, picking through the keys like broken sticks, she's weeping and moaning, blinded.

There is no breath. The baby cries and hiccups. Nelle knows her little body is retching against the bed and she cringes, smells the salt in the baby's tears, and feels them hot and scathing on burning pink cheeks. The keys drop and she loses sight of her hands feeling for them in the shadows, fingers probing desperately, the dark swells unnaturally. She balls and spreads her hands open at her sides, jerks, hovers, and pulses open. Nelle slowly opens her eyes. The pain is gone.

There is no baby cry.

Not yet.

The house is hushed. He is gone now, she can't expect him. She tiptoes through the lifting dark. She goes out from the shadows, fingers stretched, on her own. Light filters through the Eastern windows, twilight indigo and cobalt ribbons escape to corners.

Nelle breathes in and pulls her robe tighter around her shoulders. There is a pot of tea on the counter. She sees her mug set beside the still steaming pot. A bran muffin is set out on a small ceramic plate. An ache pushes against the inside of her chest. Nelle sees the corner of the paper slipped under her plate, a love-note, after all this time, little ways he had shown her his admiration, she thought. But he is actually gone and she is only remembering.

Remembering the vice-grip, fists and palms over mouths and nostrils, suffocation. She took a breath. Hands came up and softly circle the curve of neck and jawline. She knows the pain is still raw, and she is healing.

She brews her own tea and tries to brush the shadow of a ghost from the surfaces in the kitchen. The stream of tea hisses and collects in her mug as she pours, a low soft hum escapes her lips. She cups the steaming mug to the middle of her chest and sighs blinking several times and holds her eyes shut for a long moment. There is a hooked feeling, it pulls inside her. She feels alone. The flutter in her womb lifts and unhooks. She turns.

The road signs flash past, she thinks of party banners, ribbons, balloons that float high up, high up. Blurred and streaming into one another, Nelle can't see just how hard she squints to follow the flurry of signs around the sharp corner as the van crests the highway's edge.

"What does that sign say?" His voice enters, falls into her silence like a skipped rock. She darts a look towards her father, but returns her stare to the reflection of her own face in the glass.

"It's an arrow." She doesn't want to admit it, from the pit of her gut she bites down hard against it, but she knows she can't see. She wrings her hands. She remembers the firm edges of things before her eyesight went. Until he asked her what was on the road sign, she never put much thought into her vision. She hadn't been able to see for a long time. She didn't want them to know. She feared glasses. She pops one knuckle at a time and squeezes the tears back into her head. A final swallow, her stomach cradles the lump. She absolutely fears glasses.

She resents the rush of adrenaline that pinches the edges of her face and spins her. Thoughts surface rapidly, consuming, she spirals and holds fists to her lips.

Sometimes, when a child has bad eyesight, there is something going on at home. There is something that these young eyes do not want to see. There is something that this young mind does not want to know. There is something that this new heart does not want to face.

Children are young and small, lower on the ladder of the hierarchy of domestic violence. There isn't much that they can change there. In the centre of that violence it is easy to fall into mirroring behaviours, but the cultivation of the opposite, that natural law alone can save them. In the helix of that domestic machinery, bodies change instead, a forced mutation, young and new. Regardless, the body copes, physiological protection, diffused eyesight. Just so they do not have to see whatever it is going on at home so clearly. The eyes go blind because they don't want to see.

Glasses on faces, there is weakness there, something that can be removed and broken.

Glasses on faces, there is vulnerability there.

They are showing you a story of something else broken, unbearable to see. That is where they sometimes carry their pain. Accentuated with fingers pushing frames up the bridges of noses. Sometimes, they rest the truth there.

She needed glasses.

Her father needed glasses.

THE PAST

She stiffened the moment she saw the bird fall. The animal stopped mid-flight and plummeted. Her head jerked to either side. She wondered if they also saw. Amélie squinted towards the roofline where the black body disappeared. White cold fingers pinched the bridge of her nose, but she couldn't steady herself.

Her feet clipped against the cobblestones as she tore through the crowds and streets towards the point of roofline where the bird had disappeared.

After an hour of weaving through alleys, with leaking eyes and a throbbing jaw, her torso swooned over her heels and she collapsed slowly to the cobblestones. Amélie fanned her fingers out on the ground and inhaled slowly. It was as if the crowd had eaten him with their very feet, consuming the animal before its body collided with the earth. She closed her eyes and exhaled. Behind her lids she could trace the outline of a shattered feathered body. She hissed and stood in one swoop.

Something is wrong.

And then she ran.

The slammed door shook the entire apartment complex. The terrified shriek that accompanied the slammed door turned every ear and lifted hair. Amélie slid down the surface of the closed door and collapsed against the floorboards. Her eyes remained fixed, unblinking, on the blood marks on the floor and door. The smell was overpowering, forcing her nostrils to flare and she inhaled the sickening iron scent in terror. Amélie broke open into a soft crow-cackle that gave way to a deep nasal-weep.

There is a rag under the sink and she wants to grab it. Use it to wipe it all up. Clean it up. Make it go away. Bring him back. She wants to pull her body out into the hallway and down the stairs letting the door stand open longer for the rest of them to see his blood. She'd go with the rag and wipe up the trail he left. The trail she spotted right away and followed with an emptying cavity up to her shredded front door that stood open like a wound. She'd wipe it up for him, his pride and dignity. She'd wipe it up for her, too so she wouldn't have to trace the ugliness of that memory.

The legs of a black widow spider that stepped straight down the center of their story.

STORYTELLER

Do not let the story trip you. I know how easy it is to fall into plotlines without questioning. We trip when our eyes do not see where we are stepping, but, my Child, we also trip with our ears on verbalizations when we are only hearing, not listening too.

We are the vibrations we put out. We are the frequencies we tap into, pick up on, honour, acknowledge, stay loyal to. We find refuge in the divine this way, intuitive waves—we are rafts in oceans and emptied cocoons after butterflies take flight. Learn to see the world from the lens of your third eye. We are the butterflies.

Do not allow the story to make you comfortable in the breadth of untruth. Rationality is compromised for comfort. Water flows in the path of least resistance. Story begins to tell lies, yes, and even family can alter the narrative.

Do not let the story fool you. Life is not pretend or make-believe when the polemic of the game is to tolerate and enable untruth to take up residence in our minds. Pretend and make-believe should be the luster of childhood, innocence, and creative-play. You will be deceived when the untruths are given the virtue of loyalty and the truth is feared. When the truth is feared it is covered up, hidden—avoided.

Listen, my Child, for the gaps in narrative, those moments of pause when the story needs to rest or be stopped, to formulate new untruths, story herself is tripping then, she just does not want you to notice an unreliable narrator.

THE PAST

Their shaved beards collected in mournful mounds around worn leather shoes, holed and unraveling at the seams, exposed skin, the men shook with emotion. Light glinted like a menacing smile from the straight blades, catching the Eagle and Swastika emblems as the guards planted the steel against throats and jaw lines, publicly stripping the men of their dignity. The SS men worked without speaking, their limbs lifting and arcing around the caving torsos of the religious men. With backs positioned to the looming white façade of the Dossin, the Germans forced the religious men to face their people. Men who had once held positions of respect and sacredness of the Hasidim, now held their heads high for pride in the cavity of that religious shaming, their chins shook privately, the only glimpse of shame and anger that the guards picked up on and exploited by deliberately working slowly and carefully. There was no need to rush.

Eli pushed his way from the rear of the crowd facing the men until he stood directly across from the shaming. The detainees had been herded from the dormitories, and the work lines and fields surrounding the grounds to witness the humility of the shaming. Officer Phillip Schmitt paced slowly between the line of shaming and the volume of prisoners with his feared German shepherd. Eli despised the man, his arrogance, the brutal aggression, and how he harassed the prisoners. Eli swallowed his anger with building pride. Schmitt was far taller than Eli by several feet and thicker in build. The man's pedigree was impeccable and he stared through his victims with controlled blue eyes.

Eli studied the backs of the guards and the professionalism they exuded while shaving. Perfectly lined limbs bent light beams over cavities, the light following the curve of bone to the pit of the dark stare of the religious men. The crowds recoiled as the bald-faced religious figures were ordered to strip their robes and garments. They shook, eyes cast downward as they sank inwards freeing their pained bodies from the security of the religious materials.

Eli's eyes stayed locked on the protruding slivers of rib and vertebrae, his body burned with a fury he had not known before. The drag down the stairs, his forced departure from her— memories convoluted in a painful fist of anger. Eli's dark eyes narrowed into lethal slits. He contained himself amongst the crowd's borders. The guards ceremoniously folded their straight blades, tucked them into their leather cases and clipped them to their belts while several other guards carried brushes and pots of black paint into the square.

Schmitt's face broke into a fanged snarl and his teeth, white and bared, consumed his features. The crowd of prisoners shrank. The German shepherd pulled on his collar wheezing and whining, his claws dug graves between the stones. The animal bared its fangs and snapped its teeth while releasing a flurry of gut-tightening barks. Eli remained planted, his teeth ground hard inside his skull while the others contracted in a collective gasp.

He couldn't believe that they'd dip the brushes in those pots and graffiti the proud chests of those men with the ugly arms of that black spider. Eli balled his fists against his sides while he looked at the grotesque theatricality. The men stiffened and sucked the empty cavity of their stomachs in and shamefully attempted to keep their shoulders rolled back and straight.

Stoned-faced, they stared through the guards. The brushes lowered and rose between lines of power. Eli missed no movement, kept his stare steady. They did not stop until each religious chest was pulled taut in a canvas of angry swastikas, a tattoo of shame for these men, and for the few who would survive, they would carry this humiliation with them into death.

The guards abandoned the pots and brushes and pushed the line of men closer to the prisoners. Once the shamed bodies flooded and constricted the space, the guards forced them to dance. Eli swallowed angry tears as he watched the elders, their naked arms arched ugly in the air pirouetting slowly to the tune of a dying woman's song. He sucked in air almost erupting in a malnourished hiccup while the men burned up in fear and humiliation.

Schmitt registered the looks of disgust on the prisoners and in reaction to this outward show of contempt, he stepped through the spiraling figures towards them. An angry black-leathered hand reached into the crowds pulling prisoners out into the square. Schmitt flicked his hand and guards came forward immediately slamming bodies together into incensed dancing pairs. Eli closed his eyes once against the lunacy, but then kept them open to the suffering spinning shadows despite the searing burn of his pain and fury. He pursed his mouth, crossed his arms, and widened his stance.

Eli could not anticipate the extent of Schmitt's fury, and this lack of preparedness against his evil unhinged him. Schmitt forced a frightened prisoner named Bernard into the centre of the chaos. The dancers continued to sorrowfully circle Schmitt and Bernard, Eli twitched angrily, memories of his conversations with the man in his mind.

Bernard Vander Ham was a mixed Belgian, forty-nine years of age, husband and father to four young children, slender and timid. He was the smallest prisoner, his thoughts spun, slid comprehension together and he curled his upper lip at the extent of Schmitt's cowardly and juvenile perpetuation of an unnerving schematic under the guise of political objectives. He observed

Schmitt pull out his straight blade, the golden emblem of the Swastika caught the light across the square and Eli scowled. Schmitt shaved Bernard of his beard and cut open the buttons of his prisoner's uniform with the edge of the razorblade.

Bernard shook violently in the wind, his nakedness an eyesore for the fading men mechanically winding around each other. They yearned to cease the torture, to breathe, to sit down and rest, to still their mind, but they forced their minds and souls to detach and continued moving their bodies. Bernard cast his eyes down at the ground and kept his head bowed as Schmitt came close to him sternly. He raised two fingers and arrogantly smoothed his mustache boasting a calculated grimace that spiked Bernard's heart rate.

Eli studied the map of Bernard's exposed chest in the funnel of light cast from the parked trucks. The circle of white haloed his form. Eli inhaled sharply as he watched Schmitt pull Bernard up off of his knees by the back of his neck, baring the man's upper body completely. Schmitt waited, teeth-bared, the wind played lightly with the material of his pants, he smoothed the material with his free hand and cleared his throat. Eli noticed the men emerge from the Dossin hefting a large vat of kitchen grease. Curls of steam snaked from the top of the vat, Eli froze.

Bernard's scream was branded in the hearts of the crowd as the men poured the grease from the vat onto his skin. The crowd of prisoners had surged and reeled internally. Eli could not determine the time he opened up from the body of the crowd and transgressed the square. He could not determine the moment he reefed the straight blade from Schmitt's belt and pressed it into the man's throat. Blood beaded up from the line of steel, Eli watched the smooth pulp of Adam's apple dent under the pressure of his grip.

They had kicked him mercilessly and smashed his fingers around the handle of that short blade. He remembered, his head turned sideways, battered cheek cemented to the ground, the thick of a black military sole connected with his hand, and he shrieked. He could hear the echo of that shriek still, and he pulled the course blanket around his chin. He wept silently. He sees Bernard, features contorted mid scream, the skin melting from his bones, the burning scent of grease fogging up the court-yard. Eli wept. His lungs burned.

Eli forgot about the photograph he hid in his chest pocket when he stepped from the crowd and put the straight blade to Schmitt's throat. He could not contemplate the severity of that discovery beyond the halo of the man suffering in the beam of truck headlights. The guards came between him and Schmitt with expert tactics that continued to baffle the prisoner in the shadows of the bunk. He knows that they would have killed him if it had not been for the photograph that fluttered from his chest as they pinned him to the ground.

"Halt!" Schmitt raised a black-leathered glove, his German shepherd growled long and deep. The dog pulled against the leash and Schmitt held him at bay. He turned the photograph around between his fingers as the lines circling his mouth deep-ened and grew drawn. His eyes shifted between the alluring feminine features and curve of skull of the man prostrated on the ground.

"Nicht jetzt. Ich werde diese zu retten." Not yet. I will save this one. Eli's ears piqued and he sensed the seed of revenge that had been planted. He knew Schmitt wasn't like the others, the ones that shot them point blank with one bullet. Eli had witnessed the man before there was a time when the officer had come across a mouse in the barracks. Eli remembered, recalled, the man's smile, as he slowly pressed down hard on the creature until it popped.

THE PAST

Amélie's arms were angled like bridges across the table. She eyed the lid, waited to pry it open. She attempted to steady her breath and ran her tongue along her chapped lips. She reached up and pulled skin away, winced. The post rested beside her, she dropped her eyes to the envelope and shivered.

She didn't want to wake him. Guilt burned from the back of her throat, she attempted to clear it without making noise. His eyes, those flaring irises, dilated, she had memorized the red rims, the crow's feet and then the searing pain of a fist coming down hard. Shoulders pinched and pushed up against the wall, Amélie searched the room again, turned away from the memory of their writhing bodies in the corner and lifted the envelope from the table. A thick hairy leg extended from the bed, she pulled back, let her eyes follow the limb, anxious trek, took in the width of arm, outstretched palm, innocent in sleep. The sleeping mound was real and she had let him in. She felt the room shift under her.

She shook her head, studied the light that filtered under the curtains, the windows had been blocked for months. Amélie missed the full light. Their world had become so small, downcast eyes, tunnel-visioned, quick walks through an occupied city, barred windows and curfews, she wanted to rip the covers down, let the city back in, to look up, simply to expand her arms and stare straight into the sun.

The post was from Mechelen. She let go, the paper settled against her steepled elbows. She cupped her face and pressed the wet into her palms, she dared not be heard, to wake him, risk being found. She inhaled long and slow, picked the paper up off the table, checked her view. The Romanian, incoherent and docile slept on.

The shame burned her up, anger seethed, she chewed on the side of her tongue, raw tears stung her eyes, and she wished for release. A gasp. A sharp cry. Something loud. The effort to keep quiet smothered. Her blue eyes flashed, crimson lids hinted of her shame. Amélie could not imagine that only months before, from the cocoon of that café corner, before the man with the winds and rains stepped into her space, she would one day sit at the table they made love on, another in her bed, while she scanned a letter he desperately penned to her from his imprisonment at the internment camp.

The single leaf of paper was a form Eli had filled out in blue pencil crayon. The handwriting was his. Amélie held the paper against her bowed forehead. She wept quietly. His handwriting was shaky, long jagged stick letters.

"*Poudre de talc, une valise, pantalon, contre de moustique, pain, boissons et une petite cuillerée à café.*"

Breath held, she lifted the paper up and smelled it gently. The list, lifeless, void of his essence, his touch, his voice, she yearned to go to him.

Her eyes shifted across the lines, following the format of the document. Suddenly, she let go of the paper, clapped a hand over her mouth. Rocked shut and folded her arms around her shaking form. The post fluttered, like a feather, a dry leaf. It settled by her heel.

Bien le bonjour cirque de St. Martin.

He was brave.

Te voilà. There you are.

The line branded behind her closed eyes, repeated the words, over and over again, her heart thundered in her chest.

St. Martin, a name, code, reference to the false documentation that he had hidden with the bookkeeper.

He wants them.

She dropped her head into the cradle of her arms.

He is going to try and escape.

She counted her heartbeats.

THE PRESENT

"I want to show you these." She speaks carefully while spreading two sheets of yellowing paper on the table. These papers are not average letters but forms filled out in bright blue pencil crayon. The instructions are in both French and German, the ink faded.

"This is what I have left of him, aside from a photograph," the words, enunciated with deliberate slowness. Nelle carefully pulls one of the sheets closer to her and examines the letters like a primary document that she would have used for one of her undergraduate essays. Disbelief. Her eyebrows come together. Lines form in her face as she tightens knowing that these sheets are a Jew's last hope for the outside world, for a life that he would never have. For pure survival. Escape.

"He was my love, you know," she lifts up her left hand, sighs, folds her hands gently together on the table. She continues, "I imagine that we would have married if he hadn't been taken by the Germans." She looks up from her hands, Nelle sees her grandmother's eyes discretely dampen and she blinks hard. Remorse and sympathy knock heavy in the middle of her chest. Her Grandmother keeps speaking slowly without interruptions.

"I don't know why, but I've kept these letters from him all of these years. I guess because they were the only reminders I have of him. Though I have a picture of him too." She pushes herself up from the table and disappears down the hallway.

Nelle pulls the second page close.

I was not expecting this.

The pages with blue pencil scratching, her eyes roving over the script. Throughout her historical studies at the University of Guelph and Queen's University she encountered many historical documents from the Second World War, but these letters hit her differently. They were her grandmother's, sent to her from her lover. The history was not distanced from Nelle. She could feel the energy of these two young peoples' hardship and love pulsating at the core of her own growing pain.

This man could have been her grandfather, someone who would have propped her up on his knee and told her stories about the war.

If he survived, I wouldn't be here. She wouldn't have come to Canada.

It hit her then that this man was never meant to be a part of her direct existence. She was served a broken family line and Eli's story was very much a part of it.

Nelle felt subtle currents of comprehension lock into place about who she was, how integrated and webbed life stories are, as she examined the texts. The emptiness she felt deep inside her that she swallowed and cried through alone at night, the vortex of a web, a fly cocooned as prey by the spider. Emery was gone. Eli was gone. She slowly started filling up.

I have so much respect for her. She's hidden so much.

Nelle notes that Eli had used many names when addressing her grandmother. One of the names from a letter dated July 28th 1943 was severely smudged. Tiny balls of paper particles clung to the letter and were stained blue.

Tears. Tea. Salvation.

A deliberate hiding.

Someone had blotted the page from the dampness and carefully muddled the name.

Nelle delicately ran her fingers over the numerous balls

sensing the pain and fear there. The smudge blatantly indicated that her grandmother did not want the name on the letter known, recorded, unless tears had coincidentally fallen. The light-blue smudge epitomized Nelle's complete understanding of her grandmother. She was a curious woman, successfully hidden in a self-constructed prism of lies, of secret identities. Nothing was ever straightforward.

Nelle realized that her grandmother would never be completely open with her and because of that she'd never know who this woman really was. The thoughts coalesced as an ache deeper than the swelling of loneliness she harboured each night. Nelle scrutinized the remaining names in Eli's letters.

Amélie Cyncad, Nelle's grandmother's real name. A name that never belonged to Nelle. Amélie Cyncad was the name of a young woman who attempted to take a stance against the oppression of the Nazis. She thinks. Amélie was now lost in the pale skin and hunched shoulders of the aged woman who slept with her back to walls and mouth open to doors.

Sophie Anoukas, another name pencilled into the lines of the Nazi document. This name seemed to be a partial truth to Nelle, a white lie. Theatricality or sorrow. Sophie was a name very familiar to Nelle. Grandma Sophie was the name she had taken for granted her entire life to be the true existence of her Belgian grandmother. Nelle was naive about people actually going by their real names, that there was any other way of living was not a component of her childlike innocence. She wondered if her grandmother ever cringed when she was addressed by the wrong name while Nelle and her older brother were growing up. She wondered if the name was like a slap in the face, a constant reminder that Amélie Cyncad was gone, Sophie the woman who prevailed. Nelle could never have fathomed as a child that portions of her family history were falsities, secrets. Nelle's past was ridden with them.

Amélie returns from the bedroom with a large framed portrait of a dark-haired young man.

"Here he is," she hands her granddaughter the picture. Nelle looks up and smiles sheepishly. Sophie settles back down in her chair. She sips her tea.

The photo was clearly taken years ago. It was a color touch-up of a black-and-white picture. The man's lips are unnaturally red and his skin-tone too much of a pale peachy shade. He looks like a made-up corpse haunting the family of the deceased at an over-perfumed funeral. Nelle immediately recognizes the photo that has sat on a table in her grandmother's painting studio.

The man didn't look like her Papa who was a massive fair-haired man, the man that had brought Sophie to the New World. This man had lips that spoke of tragedy, eyes falling together at the outside corners forming lines of sadness. Nelle had imagined that the man was sad when the photo was taken. He was handsome, regardless.

"This is the only picture I have of him." She folds her hands again and looks over Nelle's right shoulder. Perhaps she saw another world and reality beyond the confines of that kitchen table in a Canadian brick home. The exterior, so simple, yet the Women inside, so complex. Sophie breathes in and her eyes shift back to Nelle's face. Nelle readjusts, uncomfortable wishing that she could reach out and touch Sophie, hold her like she would her other grandmother and her own Mother. She remains still and distant.

"My life would be completely different if Eli had lived." Sophie struggles with the word lived. Nelle, determined, keeps her eyes on her grandmother's.

She swallows and softly speaks, "he died, didn't he?"

"Yes." Silence. Stillness.

"After the war I ran into his sister on a streetcar. I asked her about Eli and she just stared back at me, blank. I felt rude." Sophie pauses for a second and blinks strongly.

"She didn't have to tell me anything. I should have known that the camps got him. My Eli. I never received official word that he perished, why would I? You know. I was young, living in a fantasy for some time after liberation that Eli had survived and would try to come back to me, that he'd find me. Running into his sister ended that fantasy." Sophie pauses to sip her tea, her face blank and controlled. Nelle stares at her intertwined fingers sweating in her lap.

"I didn't even say goodbye to her. We were both holding onto the handrails for life, you know, those cars moved so fast. It was all too overwhelming." She tilts her head and eyes the corner of the ceiling.

"If drowning is anything like the feeling I had that day, then, I'd rather be burned alive." Sophie leans heavily on her elbows and stares into the depths of her teacup with the weight of her story. Nelle stretches, opens her mouth to speak and is interrupted.

"I stepped down off the car at the next stop and just stood in the middle of the sidewalk while the car moved on. I never once looked back. I knew that Eli was gone. I think then was when I accepted it." Nelle blinks as a laugh builds deep inside Sophie and splits from her carefully controlled demeanour. Her mouth opens and she grins, Nelle is frightened, not humoured.

"I swear that as I stumbled around the next street corner I bumped into your grandfather." Sophie's laugh gleans into a high wheeze and her eyes start to water. She appears feral almost, and unhinged. Nelle narrows her gaze and places a hand over her heart then her mouth. Sophie suddenly brings her open hand down hard on the tabletop in a violent outburst.

"It was just like that! *Bang!* And then it all started and it was all over at the same time." Sophie's laugh lilts and breaks. An open-mouthed-silent laugh. Her neck folds and her skull rolls back. Nelle is horrified by the noiseless gaping mouth.

She's screaming.

Nelle bends forward as her soul hiccups.

THE PAST

"The Belgian Jewish underground, assisted by the Belgian resistance, derailed several trains carrying Jews from the camp to Auschwitz during 1942-1943. Though most of these people were soon put on the next transports, about 500 Jewish prisoners did manage to escape. During an attempted escape on 19 April 1943, resistance fighters stopped the 20th transport near the train station of Boortmeerbeek, 10 kilometers south-east of Mechelen. 231 prisoners managed to flee although 90 were eventually recaptured and 26 were shot by train escort guards."

–The Transit Camp for Jews in Mechelen, Laurence Schram

Eli's boot broke through the rotted plank catching him off balance. His arms wavered as he centered himself, he shot a look at the snapped rail ties, the shattered wreck edged grotesquely in the moonlight disappearing around a dramatic bend. The voices carried to him what their eyes could not determine in the dark. Sabotage, a truck on the tracks. Salvation. The planks had been pulled up and the steel line severed. Eli looked skyward, his cracked lips and lined face cupped moonlight, he prayed.

Pivoting away from the carnage he envisioned his form weaving through long grasses far from the blood and death. He closed his eyes, watched his body grow smaller, vaporize, and he is suddenly making his way down her street, bounding up her stairs, throwing open her door. Sanctuary. Then, he'd get the papers. Then, they would flee.

He balled his hands and stepped forward into the night. His breath caught air, clouded. His limping form, an injured ant under a heavy starless sky, he collapsed often, heaved up, retched, cradled his arms close and pushed forward. Jaw-clenched, meditating from inside his terrified skull, his teeth ground, sweat burned his eyes like acid. The currents of adrenaline that flooded through him picked him up, again and again. The image of his boot kicking, the gaping hole, how he planted it on the upturned sidewall of the rail car and he escaped.

The cattle car had careened through the dark, a banshee shadow carrying them to a deliberate death, they knew, and they did not deny that the people in the cars never returned.

But, something else peculiar altogether fogged up this night and Eli was quite unaware of the magic working in his favor. His train crashed.

They heaved their damaged bodies, abandoned the wreckage after the cars had spiraled from the track. Some bodies remained still, the violence on their faces dropped many men, but Eli forced his body to stay up. Eli gritted his teeth, wiped the beads of sweat from his forehead and, instead of waiting, smashed his boot through three more rotted planks. The other men in the car crowded around him, fists raised in the shadows, a silent cheer rang through their ears. As he broke through the planks, hands surged forward removing the wood. The men stood around the gap, bewilderment stained their features and an unnerving calm settled over them for a moment.

A single voice broke the quiet and passed between the men like a handshake. "The Lord is your guardian. The Lord is your protective shade at your right hand. The sun will not harm you by day, nor the moon by night. The Lord will guard you from all evil. He will guard your soul. The Lord will guard your going and your coming from now and for all time."

Eli bowed his head, sucked in his breath and searched through the slabs of boards studying the haze of countryside beyond the train wreck. Eli looked once at the Men staring in wonder at him, emptied his lungs and was the first to leap.

The hush of the night and darkness blanketed him. He let his feet carry him over creeks and mud holes forgetting the others that attempted to stay with him for a short time. They were not driven by the same magic, his speed and agility through the dark soon lost all of them. Eli did not notice. He only knew how his hands gripped bark and stone fence, navigated him through landscape, he tripped, fell, stumbled, wept, let his tears wet the soil, he pushed through, a heartache, throbbing, fear of abandonment shrieked warnings in the columns of his ears and he continued on, not stopping to rest too long.

The sight of her rooftop in his skyline quickened his pace and he tripped. Eli looked up from his hands and knees, the image of his boot penetrating rotted board kicked him, he smelled the wet leaves and grasses, tasted the bitter surge of fear. He almost collapsed under the weight of memory, how he needed to shrink from the other figures, fall to the face of earth uttering prayers between his ears as they passed by him. Fear enveloped him. He did not want to risk her, but he had to have her, one more time. He locked his eyes on her roofline, set his jaw and heaved up, tripped forwards in a fit, bucked into the night clinging to hope's slippery grasp. Eyes closed, swinging.

He knew the broken window at the rear of the building. It pulled him close. The sheer force entry wetted his eyes and he disappeared up an alley. The stench of cat urine and human rot clung to him and he held his breath. The window, a black shallow he wanted to rest in. His hands found the sill and he let out his breath. Eli worked his fingers to the hinges and carefully pulled free two metal pins. The window frame lifted out easily and he buckled slightly under the sudden weight. He wheezed, suppressed a cough with pain and slowly leaned the glass against the brick wall.

A sudden commotion exploded high up in the building and he sensed immediately that the noise came from her flat. Without hesitation, he idled up through the hole and fell into the dark pit of his old home.

The familiar smells accosted him and he resisted that tug of comfort that wanted to pull him into a false safety net, Mechelen had reconfigured him. Lost innocence. Nowhere was truly safe anymore, not even inside. His feet missed steps. His heart hammered against his ribs and he focused on keeping his movement light, noiseless. He crept in.

Her door was locked. The wood vibrated and pulsed against the frame, Eli burned up fast. He felt the current of anger behind that door. His nerves surged and his mind went momentarily blank. Energy coursed through his body. Letting himself hover only seconds on the brink of total collapse before he sprung. Somewhere from the corners of his mind he thought of the idea of order, order in chaos, he threw everything into the face of faith. He pushed, the roof jutted out into the dark, vast black ocean.

In the openness of sky and fresh air, the noises of a man screaming and hurling furniture scorched through the clay tiles. Eli crept amongst the clay shingles, contempt spread over him in a fierce sweat, stiffened the hairs on his body, he bared his teeth and hunched lower, locking in his balance. He counted the length of his steps, seven catlike arches, and he knew he was directly above the flat. A frantic pitch, her frightened cry, cast him over the edge and through a window.

Amélie felt her world halt when the window gave and jewels of glass rained down on her and the angry Romanian's shoulders. The drunk cried out, hands flailing, red-faced and fuming, swatting glass diamonds, he pivoted clumsily and collided with Eli's fist.

Amélie shrank to the floor, she wailed, her hands broken crowns against her open mouth. The Romanian crumpled to the floor and the sound of the blow was a domestic thunder clap. Eli smelled the liqueur on them. The man's fingers curled into his palms like a dying insect's legs. Eli wanted to spit.

Her eyes took in the greasy mass of hair spread out on the floor. His contorted swelling features and bulge of stomach. She felt the shame. It licked like flames up her ankles. Cupped her pelvis. Broke in waves up and around her shoulders. Broken wings.

Her eyes lifted from the crown of the Romanian's head and caught Eli standing in a halo of candlelight painfully shaking out his hand. His other hand, bloodied too, protectively held the busted knuckles and swelling of the other. Broken bird. He fought back tears, forced his shoulders blades up and down, and looked down at her with heavy dark eyes.

She heard him exhale, long and hard, lifted her chin slightly in anticipation for him, but lowered it down to her chest and averted her gaze. She knew and hunched her shoulders in shame, letting her wounded wings fall. Betrayal burned. She mortally betrayed him, everything they had built a story upon, she had soaked it in gasoline and lit the flame, tossed it. Survival. His bewildered stare remained fixed and questioning. The naïve burn of trust and loyalty glinting and broken like the shards of the windowpane amongst the wood.

Amélie would not forget that sick feeling that grew from the core of her chest and veined out into her extremities like poison. That feeling, she wore it like a shadow. That sinking heavy feeling, tidal wave and mammoth, the surge of being swept off feet into air, she would soak the pebble of that memory in her mouth during her great rumination in her elder years. She would recall the severity of his eyes, the quickly dying dullness.

She imploded. A little girl running through the sun and fields in the south of France, the one that fell into anger when her parents went away, that little girl stood up and took over.

"I didn't think you'd come back!" She hurled the words out helplessly between them.

"I don't want to die!" She saw him sink and something shift

inside him, his eyes grew darker and he angrily wiped tears from the corners of his eyes. His grief pushed her further.

"*Il est plus difficile, en tant que femme.*" It's harder, as a woman.

"*Vous ne savez pas.*" You wouldn't know. His face transformed, she heard the sound of breaking branches, smelled the murk of lake, swamp-existence, and dropped to her knees. She rose up when he moved closer, a flurry of fists battered his chest. He stepped back in horror and looked away while she came undone on the floor.

She punched the floor and pulled at her hair. He winced. The crack of palm against the curve of skull embarrassed him. Eli felt the shift between them, irrevocable and binding, and he turned away from her wretchedness.

He looked squarely at the unconscious form shining in diamond shards, and thought of money. He spit near the sole of the Man's boot, and locked his jaw. He knew that he needed to leave without looking back, without letting an opportunity of forgiveness to surface, not after what he had sacrificed, how he felt to come back to her.

Eli couldn't risk bending down over her and pulling her into his arms, not now. He knew exactly what death looked like, the operations within Mechelen were successful in demonstrating that, he couldn't deny that he smelled death and betrayal all over her now and it terrified him. He battled with himself, hovered, shifted between the balls of his feet, envisioned stepping out of line, going to her, the final sacrifice, lifting her against him and falling into death here. He broke open.

"*Je ai été pris par eux.*" I was taken by them. *Don't tell me that I wouldn't know.* "*Je suis venu vers vous.*" I came back to you. She dropped her face. He turned away.

The siren set into motion a chain of events that determined the course of the rest of their lives. Eli knew the siren was sounded because of the derailment, each body in that derailment was coded and property of their violence. They'd find him before the sun rose if he stayed there.

For the second time in their story he was gone and her door stood open. Amélie left it like that, abysmal and exposed. She eventually got up off her knees and began straightening the apartment.

She left the man with the black and blue face on the floor, did not dare disturb him. Instead, she retrieved a broom from the corner. The handle slipped in her sweaty palms and the jewels of glass canvassed her skin in dotted red lines. She felt relief. The blood budding her skin, reminded her of something she had forgotten. Blood flowing inside bodies, nourishing, healing. Keeping things alive.

RIPPLE

Sometimes, after carnage, it is the diminutive
fragments of our lives that keep us living.

Loose-leaf tea.
Nylons.

Papers in coffee tins.
"Bonjour à St. Martin."

Spider webs.
Salt shakers.

An apple
Elbowed in a corner.
Domestic residue.

STORYTELLER

Daughter, those diminutive domestic fragments that we polish and hold so close, like they were breathing, no, as if we gave them breath, they will become our demise if we hold too tight. In that holding, the mundane, the complex, the surreal bleeds through, is braided together. We are sweet grass, we lift up, and if we are open, conduit for spirit, we are then blessed.

Let me tell you this story now from spirals, spheres, with the bonfire in the middle, the Baby, you. Let me tell you in a different tone. I am sitting, bundled between two worlds. The fire is warm, it licks the contours of my face, casts shadows, masks. The task ahead is to get it out to you.

I am here, still, sitting cross-legged between sunrises and sunsets, my back to the face of forest. The night wants to blanket me, take me in, but I am here, and I will tell you about them.

We burned this bonfire beside the river. Piled the dry logs up, stoked the flames high, and I sat down here, cross-legged, on the precipice, waiting for you.

Let me tell you, Little One, a story is born by character. In telling of the character's lives, a storyteller exists. Characters, their trials and tribulations, successes and evolution. Characters own dips, valleys and crescents of the plot lines of story.

Storyteller can speak character and story into living too. Story is alive. Story is alive in those spaces.

Those character spaces, if we were to be cold and plot them on a graph, transform them to the second dimension, those lines, many laid out perfectly like Freytag's triangle, those are lives. Our lives. Those lines represent the lives that helped you understand your own story, yourself, and brought you to where you are today. We can self-actualize together. We come to know ourselves in contrast. We balance that reclamation with isolation, the archaic, almost holy quest to know. In that knowing, we are living. In that knowing, we are alive.

We are one with the collective.

We are one with ourselves.

There is the Threshold Guardian, divine and wise, collective and individual. Man and Woman. That space between actuality and psyche, hate and love, she dwells there, open and throbbing, arched and testing. Her knowledge, how she pushes it up against you, forces you to contrast your own worthiness against it, she will either permit or prevent you from moving forward. Go with the flow. He is in her too. Listen to that little voice inside of you, that is her speaking, honour that voice. She's singing from the threshold, fire and ice, sun and moon, orbits.

I find you there in conversation.

It's an Orion story. It's the relationship with Inanna. She is slippery, and like water, I tell you, she will take the path of least resistance most times. But that high road is lonely like a labyrinth, so she will not fear to face you, to turn direction, orient her sky for you. Her currents could carry you along, or, you could find yourself swimming upstream, gasping for air. She can keep going. Pull the sky down like a blanket and walk away, wrapped in a robe, alone.

Pass the tests. Work through levels, that working through is an empowerment process. Awakening. You will find your paradise, but know that you will get there by honouring what pushes and pulls you. On your own, despite feeling that at times you were abandoned. You weren't, Spirit was there.

Push through the shadows when they haunt you. Remember, you are ethereal and luscious in your Womaness—your Femininity. Your pulp and weight will pull you through, you will arrive on the other side stronger, more defined. A Baby in a womb. Birth is transcendence. Conception is the successful transference of consciousness. That divine moment when something else enters all together and the first electric pulse surges and your life is then formed. You are holy.

If I were to hand you the shadows cast upon my body, I would say that they were only friends of the fire. Plato's cave. We cast our own shadows. Villain or antagonist, the ripples we make here, they accentuate the worst and the best in us. But, our obligations, as empowered Women, are to strive to honour our inner truth, each time.

Listen to Mother.

Listen to Father.

Honour Husband.

Respect Wife.

Respect Elder.

Protect Sister.

Love Brother.

Know yourself.

Family, they are the characters of our lives.

We are here to heal, to be healed, to reclaim and to pass on the flame of our divinity, together and separate. We want healing.

The Priestess returns. We hear the words of the Wise Woman, we are safe to be Lovers.

Archetypes, we are the sculptors of our own masterpieces, these little ant lives, love them.

We are blessed by the Mentor, pay attention, the Shape Shifter is everywhere and nowhere. Perspective. When you realize the beauty of this magic, you will become accountable, enlightened. My Radiant Supernova, you're a firework, light up their skies.

Do not assume permanence. Attachment is painful. Helpers

become takers. Takers become helpers. Cross over, she will herald you. Roles change. You might start out as the other. You could become the friend. It depends on your truth and if you honour it.

Aspire for happiness.

Be your own best friend, first.

Triple Goddess. Warrioress. Lover.

You will be checked, know, keep watching. They will be wanting to know how good you truly are, those tricksters. They enter and exit your life, leaving you cursed or blessed, depending on your truth.

They say the Devil is in the details. The Devil exposes truth, whether we want to accept it or not.

Warrior Lover. Adversity is only the necessary process of polishing. You are a pearl, Girl, swim, dive, don't rely on treading water.

Turn. Float. Glow.

Trickster takes you with a hand over your mouth. Perhaps one over your eyes. Keep your hand over your heart. Left with the carnal scent of fear and anger, that trickster will pull you back into the pit of your own self-betrayals of who you want to become. You could get killed. But, understand you risk death each day. You are lucky to be alive, celebrate. Sometimes it's comic relief, we were wretched here, we laughed, it's medicine.

There are worlds outside of our fire pit, beyond the face of forest and stone. Multiple worlds in co-existence, levels and layers, onions, golden corn orbs. Do not underestimate what you cannot see, or hear, smell, or touch.

Our Women endured worlds in which the power to orient through these layers and levels was forbidden. Witches, heretics, whores, psych-ward-girls: we put them there, built walls and fences around them, separated ourselves from them, blocked them out, locked them in. We punished the Archetypes. We punished them through "policide."

I will take you back to a beginning. The ending of other ways and life patterns. A starting point for our story, for now.

The systematic and legislative colonial invasion of Old World indigenous cultures through "policide," Written out of stories and their own language, the arriving white faces assumed all was their own, their home, land. Language and land. Culture. Behaviour.

Let me take you back to an understanding of those worlds beyond the fire most intimate to us. Let me show you that the suffering of others impacts us today. Empathy and compassion are muscles, like the brain, and the heart. The mockery of history ensnares us or sets us free. I think, yes, I feel that it is our responsibility, for some time, while scales balance to acknowledge this suffering and carry it forward to help heal in our community. We are evolving and there is a cycle of ages, Daughter. We are growing into a Transformational Community. There is a great weighing happening.

Bodies of water, rivers.

They consumed the core of our stories, villages, hamlets, creek-logged-houses, we grew up out of forest.

The Stone Age was animism.

The Neolithic Period, domestication, we as hunter and gatherers stilled. We settled. The shaman was religion and the people oriented inside animism.

Then, the city-state and polytheism became a layer. Mesopotamia. The peak of the Sumerians. Animism and the cosmos. Ethereal hierarchies. Gods and Goddesses.

Spirit was not only a process but fragments of psyche and natural forces.

Then, Daughter, came monotheism. Judaism. Christianity. Islam. A single masculine God, YHWH, Jehovah, and Allah. Spirit was taken from inside of us and put outside of us.

Next, with the fragmentation of religious institutions from the state, humanity witnessed the rise of corporatism, science and intellectualism. Secularism.

Now, my Love, we are moving into another cycle, spiritualism. The Transformational Community. A Global Village.

Stepping across the Canadian Shield, Precambrian, nature holds. Let me take you back to Canada, our home.

Our roots dig deep, push against the story of others who left their breath where we would later rest our heads.

We forged their rivers.

Entered their shores.

Blanketed geography with cartographers, foot trails transformed to the muddy wagon wheel ruts. Invaded and conquered, we created a planked-road-world.

Land surveyors pushed inwards, organized and rewrote the interior.

The extent of physical altercations, topsoil, eggshell thick, encasing a more vulnerable reshaping.

We assume that we own the land once we conform it to our needs. No, this is misconstrued domination, not progress. The focus on external change shifted us away from knowing the deeper detriment to the cultural invasions. Lost the internal way.

Habits changed. The hands that weaved became still. The Way, assimilated, acted over. Hunting routes. Paths that the ancestors had navigated, signed over to paper mazes. Renamed. The animals left, abandoned the tribes to logged-dusted lands, exacerbated, wasted. Once the First Peoples lost ownership of ceremonial ritual they looked up and saw the lands scattered with the dead buffalo.

Story threads far, 1000 A.D. we sit down again with "the Keeper of the Wampum." Let me stoke the coals of the Council Fire, pretend that the scroll I inked between my muscle-twined hands would whisper again. Reassure them of ceremonial recitations, sound out repetition. My lips moving in front of the flames, reading, heads nodding and fingers-pressed against reprieve. Prayers and dance. Reclamation.

Somewhere deep in me I feel a dormant seed of reclamation waking. Whispering.

Find me. Wake me up. Water me.

A secret.

Circles and hoops. Parliament. Spiritual democracy. Court room. The home and hearth. Town Hall. Let me stoke the embers. Come close to the heat, I will continue reading. Come Daughter, there is a seat for you upon the deis.

There are laws to recite. Traditions to keep living. The next seven generations are coming.

The beads work between my fingers, I absorb story.

They wrote over the poet's story. Abandoned the glyphs. Despite, Poets remained pure from influence, grew with the pressure. Tight wampum strings, narrative choked. Woman held the bow.

Poets kept the bow flexed.

That incorruptible pride.

Hands cup earlobes.

I do not wait for the noise of the Prompters. I embrace their voices, because then, well, then I know that they were there and we are safe.

It's come to it, voices converge with urgency, deviation from recital is tolerated, and they understand now how to build it up together instead of breaking it down. Additions are authorized because entrances are earned now. Respect has arrived.

They pushed the stone canoe from shore, crossed the river. My Child, do not fear the movement of Manitou. Like us, they, they come out of the stones when heated. What first appears fearful, tempers and anger, is truth speaking loudly. Manitou will help to confront and grow.

We are poets. We are rebels.

We are braiding story with memory.

Come with me, I choose to walk the trail back to humanity and philosophy of Oneness.

We are one. We are one. One is we.

The Bay of Quinte, we renamed it from the original, Kentio, or Kente. The French arrived, priests and missionaries, and Ursuline nuns. Kneading instructions like bread in their hands, eyes cast and fingers counting rosary beads, their chapped lips, prayers. The Cayuga nation, members of the Iroquois confederacy, had established the village of Kentio in 1665, after having sought out the north shore from the south of Lake Ontario. The Cayuga nation had suffered warring by the Andaste, Susquehannock groups throughout the south.

Let us go farther back, before war, before the lands became splayed and roped by longitude and latitude. 1615, Samuel de Champlain invaded, came down on an Iroquoian party, sabotaged, fragmented. He sent the Huron to bid on his violence. Georgian Bay, Lake Simcoe, Rice Lake, Trent River, Bay of Quinte: drops of water seek the ocean.

Story thickens.

Champlain was wounded. He healed with the Algonquins and the Wendat, or Hurons, in the north country. The warring and reaping, that chaos subsided in 1649 in the disintegration of the Huron confederacy. The tribes dispersed.

File and shelve the overlaid language.

"Francisation," the under haul and overhaul of cultures. Assimilation. Conversion. Colonialism. Attempted legislative extinction.

Wheat and barley, instead of corn.

Cows, chickens, and pigs.

French rags.

Thrown furs.

French tongue.

Hearths and chimneys.

Trades and occupations.

Bibles and pulpits.

Ursuline nuns. Missionaries.

Signed lines and land documents.

Baptism and wedding rings.

A new people grew from these woods. *Coureurs de bois*, forest dwellers, they crossed boundaries, immersion, consumed and assumed the interior frontiers. Out went the missionaries, gone. Runners of the woods.

Kentio was abandoned in 1680. Ravaged lands. The shield

grew under, iceberg. A trickster of potential harvest, they needed to eat, they moved with the food.

Entropic movements. Composites of these organic processes. Archetypes. Learn quick, go with the flow.

The United Empire Loyalists later replaced these groupings.

Warring storms. I exhale, release the inner clouds with gratitude, we've trekked through such violence, hold space for peace.

War pushes people. Displacement.

The American Revolution pushed refugees up and away. Neighbour fearing neighbour. Divided bloodlines, estates and ancestries. They came north, hoping to maintain the shallow indent of their foothold with the British Crown.

The people press against each other, floating sticks, bind together, drift apart, and become pulled into each other's ripples. We look for the heroes and the divine. We avoid, confront, or abandon villain, murderer, criminal.

No fear.

I weave in a sacred strand. Braided. I will not abandon you to the oppressor's pen. The ones who wrote the Old-World-History from the top down. The story of war and conquest, invasion and sabotage. No, let me set fires in the night of your imagination.

Take flight.

Turn. Float. Glow.

Let's go.

I take you to her, the Sacred Feminine. A linguistic reclamation. Intellectual attuning.

She carries names. She resides in places, with other faces. Their stories attempt to own her, but know, oh Daughter, know that she resides in each of us.

I will help you stay grounded. Centering will be difficult when you enter the euphoria of the language of the archetypes, that spiritual scripture. Careful, you could stay away, up, up, up, let me help you come down. Ground. That grounded wire.

Balance is crucial. You will keep diving, climbing up out of surfaces, forging new cliffs and plunge. Don't tread too long.

The Divine Feminine.

The Divine Masculine.

Creator and Creatrix.

They break through the latticework. Lift up. Blueprints. Layers. Reconfigure the carefully crafted maps. Ancient and eternal. Knowledge is power—powerful. Ignition. Revolution. It brings back lost worlds. Evolution.

The Creatrix is unfathomable. Let me use these words, Daughter. Wise, Intuitive, Untraceable, Evolving. She ignites Cupid, a feminine vital force. She represents the mystery of the unknown. When life stagnates, her power resurfaces, she ensures the green things grow up and thrive.

Clothed with the sun. The moon under her feet, stars like altars above her eyes. She serves us, a bridge, enter her shores open and sensitive, conduit, vessel. You will bow down with her, rest your face against cool clay earth. Watch her. She will guide you up, up, up. Away. You both will be blessed.

She will guard you.

She will protect the Sacred Union.

Women are portals. Intuition protects husbands, honours family, serves community.

The oppressed, the poor, the marginalized can lift off from the grimy surfaces they've been instructed to consume. The subjugated will sit up straighter, smile. The abused, those under patriarchy, they will rise up and laugh openly, sing, dance, and make love in her presence. Dropped veils. Empowerment is the fourth wave of feminism. We are crashing beautifully into each other, unveiled.

Our stories flow with the turning of the moon. We wax up, young maidens, become full, mature, and wane away, like the rain, old crones. Life phases, moon sketches, we are one with our oceans and rivers. They course through us, collect, pool up and overflow.

Emotions. Hormones. Metabolism. Digestion. Pheromones.

Know Self. Learn from Self. Learn with Self.

Test. Love. Stay open. Hurt. Heal. Reframe. Move with the ripples.

Go with the flow.

Turn. Float. Glow.

Let me be honest. Pull down the walls, the barriers of inclusivity, and let me move this forward. Baby Girl, we have much to reclaim. One hundred years ago, they would deduce my language as the construct of severe mental illness, feminine derangement, this degradation and denial is persistent today, but one hundred years ago, it would be a Bell Jar Story. The Yellow Wallpaper. I don't know if I would have come out with Self intact, able to love, to stay open, to lift up. My light snapped out fast with electroshock therapy, my poor pineal gland, lobotomy, water torture, bars, strait jackets, prison cells. I don't think I could beat the block. My Love, appreciate the society and timing of your birth, there have been many who have sacrificed their lives before us, so that we might be able to move it forward now, keep reclaiming. So many have perished unjustly. I live with the conviction to honour them.

Watch them, those ones, they will try and take your light.

Five hundred years ago I would be tried as a witch for speaking this way to you. The Inquisition would torture the teachings from me, splice the knowledge of the Sacred Feminine with demonic narrative, procreation with Satan. I'd have carried a broom, there would be an examination of my markings, the Devil's stamp, and they would degrade the very essence of my Womaness.

A Woman's Genocide.

We are locked in stories. Cast out from every paradise, every Edens and every Utopias. They took the God and Goddesses from inside us and exiled them, we then came to conceptualize energies as objective, distant, and removed from the very temples of our little ant bodies. They cast the higher energies into a Masculine mold. The Feminine was then abandoned and lost.

Have no fear. The snake can still bite its tail. Living is not linear or chronological, circles and hoops, spirals, or a double helix chain. Infinite regression. It is only a matter of shifting perspective from the mechanical to the natural. I reclaim my cauldron-womb. I am a witch. I am not a witch. Perspective. Language constructs.

I am a wild one. I am a snake, head and tail. Watch me work my magic. Witness the light and synergy. Liberate your skeletal carcass. Cast away your old skin. Know, my Little One, life is cyclical and we are self-birthing. Shedding skins. It's art and cooking: remixes, reshaping, transforms the stagnate into flex and flux, giving birth to new creations, ideas and ways of orienting to Earth rhythms.

Creator and Creatrix.

My Love, we are self-maintaining and self-destroying. We navigate the threshold, the crossroads between the spiritual and physical. Navigating the final frontier, the internal and conceptual. We are 21st century explorers seeking to reclaim what colonialism and imperialism pillaged from us. Metaphysical realities are our spells and poisons. We rub our palms together, keep the energy coursing, press our lips together and set our eyebrows in the arch of determination to get it out, rolled sleeves, hiked socks and boots, we're walking.

It's a re-envisioning. 21st century constructs. The Renaissance of the Divine Feminine and Divine Masculine. We will help move humanity into healing: emotionally, psychologically, spiritually, and physically. It's a rebalancing, acknowledging the Masculine and Feminine in each one of us, androgynous in moral and spiritual characteristics. Our very fibers, interwoven. It is our obligation to ground and center these contrasting and complimentary energies.

Now, my Child, let me re-imagine our people. Pass a peace pipe, prepare it, honour the directions and energies, release the sacred breath, give blessings, and stay open with me. Let me talk us through the archetypes.

The Divine Queen is authority, guardian of the present she moves and carries the bloodline on, caregiver, protectress of progeny. The biblical story of the Fall rendered our Queen subjugated, she ate the apple, cast the sacred couple from paradise. Originating from the rib, she was isolated to shuffling behind him, as punishment. But the rib was intended as a sharing to help build bodies designed to carry the bloodline on, to enable her bone structure to open and carry that throbbing life force, the cosmic womb, she creates life in that cauldron. She carries that life from the wet to the dry, from marsupial dependence to self-sustaining independence. The Queen is absolute in her selflessness.

Monotheism and patriarchy, the immense-masculine-stamp on each chained the archetypes, imprisoned them, and we became wretched. We've lost the Priestess, the lady of the intuitive domain, her awareness and insight trivialized in an insensitive age. The occult feared, knocked down and translated as evil. We lost the Divine this way. Murdered and pushed out of this living space, the Women in this family risked their lives to carry on the sacred flame.

We have a magical connection to mystery, pregnant voids, we are source energy. Do not let them take this light from you. We facilitate energies between the material and the spiritual. Mediators, we work to navigate the psychological and emotional energies, ambassadress. Except that our nations are not military-minded, seeking to conquer land—no, our kingdom is a matter of balancing the conscious and unconscious awareness.

Let us make it safe and open for the Priestess to return and conduct her spiritual work. She wants to reclaim ritual. Her magic, power, and knowledge can no longer be denied. She is Master of spiritual and material realities. Let her be confident, she knows—oh yes, she knows, do not question her intuition because even if she is inaccurate, she will be humble and acknowledge unknowing when the energies shift radically.

Remember, we cannot know the directions of the winds.

Remember, we cannot grasp a stream of water.

Let her be confident in her bearing. The competition has drug us out, decapitated us, and rendered our Women grotesque dilapidations. Know that she is able to call forth, from powerful spiritual storehouses, her mastery, her crafting synergy, transmutation, transduction, and transformation.

Let us empower our Priestesses, watch for risk of the Fall, let us build her up instead of pulling her down. Let us honour her thoughtfulness, acknowledge her depth of presence and intellect. Honour her because our unhealthy society needs her, it is time for healing. She is powerful, able to detach from inner and outer storms, she can connect deep inner truths and resources with her grounded and centered life perspective.

Oracle. Sensitivity is a gift. Emotions and feelings matter.

Attuned hearing, she picks up trajectories, she resonates, and she is not influenced by impermanent tendencies, fads, or impulses. We have become hypnotized to robotic cultures of two-dimensional cookie-cutter Men and Women. Enough, no more, we need the Priestess, her confidence, she brings a royal bearing to difficult situations. She can change this world. She can usher in culture shifts.

If we lose our heads, we have lost our spines, and we can no longer stand for anything. Remember, we fall for everything that way. You come from a line of strong Women. We celebrate them, they are in us, each moment, every second, and we harbor each archetype.

The Warrioress archetype empowers us in action. Watch her in her decisiveness and clarity of thought. She humbly serves with smiles and laughter, her experiential knowing, her courageous seed, she does what is right, even if her person does not benefit, because, for her, she wants to see the maintenance of established systems without conservative rigidity. She is loyal to a great good, watch her in flight. She makes us feel safe without oppression or threat.

The Male Gaze, fueled by voyeurism, reinforced by supreme objectification has imprisoned the lover. We've lost touch. Men have lost touch with their heart and spirit. Our Women, the Women of this family, we help our Men to help them reclaim. Sex has become pornographic versus a spiritual and sacred act. I fear that the spiritual power of sex has been taken further to be manipulated by other energetic powers to turn the sexes against themselves and each other. We have reduced ourselves to objects, the flesh and blood coursing through us—well, we've lost the magic. The Lover unites and bonds.

Our Magician, she is organic, our Alchemist, she possesses the power to infuse the spirit with flesh and desire. She is passion and well-being. Let her eat. Let her harvest her bounty without shame and guilt. Let her play. Stop making her into a whore, let her love her body, let her love you. Let her become empowered and plant roots. Let her be grounded. Let her find balance. It is time to appreciate and uphold our bodies, not to let them be constructed against us, or forced into a gladiator pit of shame. Release pain. Release guilt. We let violence exist openly outside of us and push love down deep inside of us like secrets. Get ready for the reverse, my Daughter, we are actors, not participants, in this reclamation, the beautiful societal regurgitation. We will craft our love in the open, with purity, with conviction, with empowerment.

We will use the old terms again without ridicule and the threat of the guillotine. The Shaman returns. She gifts us with practicality of magic, 21st century technology bridging the matrix and our computerized robotic societies. We've lost touch with the organic and occult. We unite in the invisible, and there, away from brutality and political control, we reclaim. The Wise Woman speaks again to us. She mines the fathomless intuitive wisdom. We need her miracles, solutions, and applications that will be the remedy for our unhealthy societies. She brings medicine and her teachings will transgress opposites. Challenge and disparate circumstances are her workplace, do not provide her with any barriers to the success of completing the task at hand.

Bullies, the Shaman will not hide or shrink away anymore. Just know, beat it out on the skin of a drum now, her success and prominence will ensure the survival of the clan, community, family, and human species. We risk extinction. We risk annihilation. She will save us.

Believe and dream, let the warm seed of hope grow within

you. The fourth wave is different, empowerment, this time we call on both Men and Women. Accountability, self-propriety, self-actualization, and proactive versus reactive behaviours. Time to take responsibility despite our outward differentiations.

Let us celebrate and usher in the Divine Masculine archetypes too. He is synergistically connected to all. Do not condemn him with hubris, he is meant to be confident in these connections. We need our Men to have balance, we've warred long enough. We let the beast run rampant, eating whole civilizations. It is time to return home. The Divine Masculine is spiritually grounded. He is in touch with his heart. He is not cold or callous—no he is not, he embodies unconditional love. He is steeped into the fullness of his Divine rights. He is inclusive, open, welcoming, heart-centered, focused, supportive, and inspirational.

Let us proclaim the archaic and not be fearful of such power constructs. The politicians and corporate bigots have run us off course. Our King, he is benevolent and fertile. He inspires and unites. Supporter and nurturer, his well-being and support builds up the next seven generations. He does not murder, he will not cut us down. We've lost our stabilizing men, those calming ones. Potent and viral, we've become accustomed to this corrupt conception of the leading tyrant and dictator.

The Warrior has lost his mystique and chivalrous shield. We've witnessed the disciplined leader and protector lead us into barbed-wire hellholes, no-man's-lands. But, the true Warrior maintains his compassion and heart during war, especially when in the midst of violence—engaged within the gladiator pit. He will fight the just fight. We want him to choose non-violence and peace. He 'knows himself,' and he will work with us, not murder us.

Storyteller is speaking, relaying again. You have hard things to do in your life. It is especially hard for the next seven generations. Let them know, each one of them, the Masculine and Feminine, we are each Divine and Sacred. Just know, without you there would be no people, the women carry on the next seven generations, spread the teachings, navigate the spiritual and material. The Men protect us in these processes. Fist and lotus flower.

We pass on our stories to the next seven generations.

Know then, our story will endure.

RIPPLE

"Duke Redbird's poem, 'Old Woman,'
'turning up' but not included in *Survival*.

Speaking to the Old Woman,
"How close you are to the earth
How low you've bent."

"And what of you
Will you sink below the surface
Of my perception/
And slip away from my understanding
And stand in the darkness."

This Old Woman risks extinction.
Is she a metaphor
of what colonialism has done
to the Native woman?

Is she our missing
and concealed
Canadian literary Venus
before colonialism

bent her low and
risking slipping beyond
our perception?

"Old woman,"
"I know who you are
I know this barren waste land
Upon which I stand
Was once a forest.
And you old woman
Had life and beauty

Energy and passion
Love and abundance
Freedom and
chatter with the gods."

A victim folded
inside a larger
national process
of extermination.

"Did they leave you with anything at all
Except pain and misery and hunger
What last word,
before you give up
Your spirit to eternity
Did they leave you even that
One word, one thought
To take with you to the last hunting ground
Love?"

A settler society,
Nationalists,
who would create texts like thematic guides.
There is no 'one word, one thought,'

just an appendix
at the end of a chapter
on the disparate treatment of Native figures
in Canadian literature historically.

I wonder if Atwood intended for anyone
to actually read these 'non-fictive' titles
she listed as a 'preview,'
or how much thought and consideration went
into addressing a readership
who would be interested in them
later on.

THE PAST

Their two bodies, violently writhing against the base of that tree. It haunted her.

Tattooed and branded, a traumatic-rooting, it bit and burned.

Their two bodies—she had searched the contour of sky, yearned for transcendence.

She turns the memory of her screams, outside of her own ribcage, the ricochet, skin crawling, over.

Searches back through.

Papers hidden against her chest.

The hollow in the tree. A coded reply. A bird in a nest.

Fear, the risk of discovery.

Smokescreen.

She crept in, water in the desert, apparition.

He saw her dip back behind the tree. Recognized her from the photograph that fell from the Jew's clothing. Rage. Reactive. He came at her. Pulled her down at the base of that tree. Crushed her bones into mud and pulled her shrieking into isolation.

"*Veuillez, monsieur, ne pas faire cela.*" Please. Please. Please. She hummed mantras while his fingers colonized her, exposing her to air. Breath, ragged, forced. She felt the rough concrete and his intrusion.

She could see the gates looming in her periphery. She heaved.

He repositioned family lines and stories that had not even been born yet.

The tree loomed large casting shade on the sprawling man who consumed bodies leaving ruins of bones and flesh and nightmares.

Movement at the bases of trees, planting roots, breaking sticks. Air and Earth. The space between. The lightning bolt shot straight through, leaving scars and wet-caked-ashes.

She let the chill creep up from the earth, course up her spine and she tasted blood when she bit down hard. Pain, sharp piercing purple pain absorbed her and thrummed along her like electrons in wire. She remembered his departure through the branches. Shuddered.

She was never the same
was never the same
never the same
same sane
again.

THE PAST

When Amélie eventually regained her consciousness she ceremoniously rubbed down the blood and tears until she glistened.

The wind howled, rain coated her. She trembled, rocked from her knees, the cold surged through her. Lightning-bolt. She feared that she would buckle and steadied herself against the trunk of a tree. The rain stuck to her cheeks and forehead, gleaming with her blood and tears. War-paint. Her loins, caked in dried blood, burned raw.

She wept, openly, the tears burning acidic rivers under her eyes. Time evaded her, the flat grey sky closed in. She had no idea how long she had laid there in the cold mud and wet snow. Light-headed, she steadied herself against the tree and rose up from the ground.

Teeth clicked. The winds picked up. Her sobs shook her shoulders. She flattened out her tongue to stop the shaking and clenched her jaw. The rain glossed over her skin, a baptismal shield. She lowered her face to the sharp indents in the mud at the base of the tree. Eyes flicked, the turning and twisting branded against the inside of her eyelids. Vomit filled her mouth and she retched uncomfortably. She arched and released everything out onto the earth.

Amélie eventually left that tree.
An altered Woman, empty.
A broken Woman.
A barren Woman.

STORYTELLER

People, especially Women, dwell in places unseen.

I took it for granted as a child that the idea of everything existing outside in the world was the finality of reality. I was misunderstood. We are wavelengths. Microcosms of the macrocosm, stardust. Vitamins and minerals. Nucleotides.

We either repel each other or are magnetic, we imprint. Don't be fooled either, sometimes what you assume to be apparent is non-existent.

The way you see things, how you are looking, must penetrate deeper than appearances, learn to function beyond the physical. Perspective. Feeling.

Inside each person is another world that they retreat to. There, they reside, retreat, escape to internal realities, emotions are vascular and rivers of coursing memories. Our women could easily return to this internal cosmic sea if an adverse outside pushed them there. The inward trek to find them when they turn in, to root and lovingly pull them out of themselves is learning how to love.

Love is process.

Spirit is process.

Love is Spirit.

Turn. Float. Glow.

Empowerment is self-love.

They are up, up, up, Away, which is paradise and utopic in essence. But we can't thrive just there, in those spiritual dimensions, the ethereal matrix. Our bodies need water, sun, air, and food. We need to play and to laugh, to dance and to sing. My Child, we need to honour the physical matrix, disconnecting between planes is insanity, or genius. Perspective.

We navigate between the unconscious and conscious worlds —sacrifice the children inside ourselves. Know that our Women have taken up residence there for survival. Inside and Away, they could keep their soul and divinity intact.

I would catch our Women disappearing through the invisible locked doors of the unconscious. We had many inside places. Spaces carefully hollowed out to lay down quietly in. We bore witness to atrocity, we needed somewhere to lay these burdens down privately.

Watch for the glazed-over eyes that moisten and lose focus. She will fall away into the contours of her mind. A place where the chain originated from out of a sense of security and stability. This chain bound itself to the very coils most intimate to us.

Her presence in turn is absence. The internal retreat barricades them from us, and keeps us from holding and loving them. We yearn for intimacy, recognition, that sense of knowing them, of understanding the Women who sit archly in covered armchairs. Poised.

Perhaps her retreats conjured up the shadow of a man breathing heavily at her throat. We don't always know. A knuckled fist gripping a torn skirt, sobs, and chest-heaves. The haunting memory of metallic cold, knife-blade invasions. Or, these outside memories could have pushed them inwards where residue of those encounters could not exist and it was safe inside, then. I didn't know. I couldn't know until they carried on her story; not even if she had offered it to me herself, or if I experienced the process for myself.

I would catch her in certain moments. Her hand would unconsciously glide to her empty womb. She was persistently ill.

Who really knew what upset her, energy low, a sinkhole, she'd take all of the love from you and she would remain a gaping void. I want to say that I never gave up trying to fill that void even though the behaviour of that constant filling drained me. I want to say that I acknowledged that I didn't have to. Regardless of the wisdom of my own self-care, I still attempted to build a bridge to her.

I'd ask her if she was feeling fine, and she would nonchalantly blame the sheets of rain drumming against the windows, primly unfold from her armchair and then retreat to the privacy of her bedroom. I was left alone, staring at clasped hands.

She received hugs. She did not give hugs.

She lived in a routine which kept her alive. She'd wake, prepare meals, watch TV, and, when she was younger, check her email. I knew if she was angry by the intensity of how she closed the microwave door, or how persistently she walked the upstairs rooms. Circling. She would sigh. Drop something on purpose to see if I would come. She would turn the thermostat off, but ask for help to turn it back on. Overall, she was detached from it all.

She held babies with locked arms. Did not know names or mannerisms of her loved ones. Each conversation with her was new. Her outward cold behavior, the way she stiffened her shoulders during an embrace, or the fish-flat ebb of her hand dispassionately circling my back. I only wanted to find a connection. I had to learn that she had been so hurt that her maternal love showed her the way, not what I expected that love would surface as. I loved her in her own way despite the pain. I loved her in my way and I know that most times, that way wasn't good enough for her.

When the flame of the Divine Feminine is stamped out, we lose each. Disconnect.

Clarity and dislocation depended on her disposition. Daughter, please know, there were good moments too.

We are not empowered then to be the Mothers we want to be. We cannot be the Sisters and Daughters we would like to be, either. Abandoned in the straights and narrows of a societal idealization, we lose each other.

We, essentially, are not the Women we want to be.

This is my interpretation. There is bias.

What I know I have learned my way. Despite the permanency of my words, my narrative, it is always up to you to live your way, learn for you, not for them.

Nothing is ever completely as it is projected to be, appears to be. Seeing is believing, is feeling, is turning assumptions over again. Feeling is believing, is connecting. Living is trial and error.

Do not fear to go inside and bring them back out. Sometimes they want you to, to find them there.

THE PAST

He restructured her body. She could not recognize the skeletal shell that encased her secrets, how she felt in it, the new noises it made, and what little she pinched of it in her fists.

She brought another body home.

The blood had dried and washed away easily.

Torn skin closed up and puckered over. That took more time, more shouldered slouches and winces from straining, but it sealed eventually.

Bruises faded. There was deeper damage and she stalked around this knowledge with claws and bared wolf-white fangs. Pretenses—she became an actress. Amélie sensed the mutilated monster that he had left behind. Her efforts to live away from memory in vain, the monster had taken root, her new shadow. Fingers to the womb, she wept, held the hollow inside her. She was changed.

Amélie lived a routine, counted breaths. It was simple. Nights spent wide-eyed and panic-stricken. She'd deep breathe into sleep. Sweat-stained rings marked her sheets. She hallucinated, saw blood. She ruminated over money, the rent—gulped and rotated on the mattress. She worried about food, imagined herself pressing fistfuls of it in her dry mouth. She glanced up, heard the sharp snip of her scissors. She relied on routine, a pretense of structure. She counted breaths, birds in the city. It was complex.

Eli was in each sound, each face. She was consumed with a hidden worry. She searched him out in the crowds. Face over her shoulders, she ached from it. His absence, a new presence to her, it consumed and burnt. Silent hysteria, delirium.

She dusted the debris from her surfaces discreetly. Crept low. Savored the scraps of food she could find, hunched in corners consuming, working out new networks.

Bite, chew, and swallow.

Bite. Chew. Swallow.

Everyone crept low and faced the thunderous sky of war. She blended in easily, a single thread in the fray.

It was not that easy, or simple, no matter the delivery of narrative.

No, it was never the same.

She expected the Romanian to consume her doorway when she returned broken and empty from Mechelen. The apartment was silent. The form in the bed remained tangled and still, she shuffled in and eased her body into a chair with a glass of water, studying the way the blankets rose and fell. Wet snow thrummed the windows, Amélie nestled in, let the storm surround her. Her thoughts lifted and hissed with the winds.

She did not ask questions when the form stirred and the blankets fell away. The angry masculine gone, cast away, replaced. Her eyes took in the blond hair, blue eyes, and slender arms. Curved rose lips, the woman in the bed opened, lotus, and gently whispered from the corner of the room.

Bonjour, Amélie.

Bonjour, Amy.

It occurs in highly detailed places, realistic settings, an invasion, much like the spider and the flags, the marching boots and planes. Amy was a childhood friend imagined into being by loneliness and never quite put away as Amélie grew older. Amy was always close, but often distant. There, but not there. Imagined into reality; brought real into imagination. And she knew what Amélie knew.

She knew the Romanian too. An invasion of the obscure and strange, it's unbelievable.

The Germans had taken a sound beating on the Western front. There was some seed of hope planted with the news of the allies gain on the Eastern bloc. Her mind flashed, she cradled the forms at the base of the tree and quaked. Rivers of water dampened her wrist. She emptied the glass.

The Soviets had been losing control for weeks now, and it remained a disappointment that Germany was not shrinking on all sides. She coughed, looked down, took in the stained torn material, her bruised skin and nervous blood pumping beneath it all, and almost let go. Amélie curved around the radio, cranked the dial, the news broadcaster's voice rose in pitch, she hiccupped. The Americans had joined the war now, something surely should change.

There was minimal physical change to the apartment, but what could not be outwardly seen was the magnitude shift between Amélie and Amy. Inside the walls of that apartment, the Women began to circle each other in ways opposite to the rhythm of those outside.

The days stacked and divided and the months cycled through slowly. Bombings pierced their nights, the Women trembled and leaned against door frames praying that their street would not be targeted.

She relived the horror beneath the tree, in her sleep, haunted; it gave her away. When she lived alone she did not know of the cries that punctured her bedroom and that sent her sweating into dawn. She awoke in pain, sleep in her eyes and a rasp at the back of her throat that burned. She confused this internal pain and what was done to her body with the war. Everyone was suffering and enduring their own pain. Her pain was no different.

She did not remember her nightmares. Unknowing, she thrashed violently calling out for Eli. Her fingers gripped the mattress and her back arched sharply. The night possessed and owned her, until Amy decided to come to her.

The first night Amy heard her friend's cries she sat upright in a bolt of movement. Amy yearned to go to Amélie, but feared invasion. She listened and rolled back into her blankets and covered her ears. She did this, again and again, until it became unbearable and urgent.

It took months for the night to crush Amy, to force her from her tabletop-bed and into the dark. The dark was a guide and she fingered her way to the edge of Amélie's bed. She could make out her friend's silhouette. She fell into the bed and pressed herself against Amélie pushing through the anxiety of the sight of her friend twisting.

Amélie's face and throat shone with sweat, her white night-gown stuck to her like skin. With shaking fingers Amy peeled back the blankets and pulled the hair from her friend's mouth.

The night cast shadows across Amélie's chest and stomach, rising and falling with the ragged breaths. When Amélie thrashed, Amy pressed her weight against her heaving torso. Amy held her there suspended, rubbing the wet from her friend's face.

The storm surged and showed no signs of abating. They locked eyes in the flashing light, both stared iris-wide and gaping. Amélie felt the sweat and realized that she was in the fit of a nightmare and that Amy was there to break it.

Amélie remembers the softness of Amy's hands and how they ran along her scars without ownership or questioning. She released unquestioning into this touch.

RIPPLE

"Last transport left on 31 July 1944, but allied forces couldn't
stop it before its destination was reached. When the allies
approached the camp by 3 September, 1944, the Germans fled
the Dossin camp, leaving behind 527 remaining prisoners."

Storyteller found a wormhole
of survival,
rabbit hole,

Slips and loops
In narrative,

Opportunity to create
lifelines that were wanted.

THE PAST

She did not know how to contemplate 1944. The year burst into their lives in a fit of cold, and they huddled together in blankets and fogged breath hoping to stay alive.

Amélie and Amy endured the bitter winter months with gestures and secrets. They had stopped working at the shop months before. There was no money after all to be made from the business.

War had levelled Brussels, and the people feared annihilation. They spent their time seeking to trade for food. They traded cloth for bread, devouring the mass without recoiling. Amélie discovered an array of herbs and the two women became experts trading through the black market. One day, they landed a trade for chocolate. They savored the melting nutty aromas. They tasted in anticipated gleefulness, fingertips coated and dripping, they giggled at the loud noises they made pulling the chocolate off their hands with their tongues. They could almost forget that a war raged all around them.

The women could not know yet that allied troops were pushing back the German front to the north of Normandy, forcing their exhausted mud-faces into Belgium borders. Reprieve. Some villages were empty of the Germans when the Canadians got to them, most times the men encountered skirmishes in the villages heaving under Hitler's final hold. The allies persevered. Large portions of western Belgium were swiftly liberated, though in other locations, the Germans held.

Amélie knew nothing of the fight for the Ghent Canal. The Canadians established a bridgehead after extraneous efforts. The allies conquered again, but the battle was difficult and bloody. They heard through word-of-mouth that the Germans were losing ground and that made them rejoice, feed hope. Amélie lost herself in distraction.

Events far away and close reworked her world like clockwork, and yet, Amélie chose to remain deliberatively reactive to her environment. Sensitively dependent, change was coming for her.

If only she could maintain the resolve to know the events of the world stage, if she had been directed to focus on events unfolding across the ocean in the New World. Saved by foreshadowing, she would teach the other women of the family from the crux of a retrospective gaze. Language shifts became echoes, showers, tidal waves. Ears missing terms, land parceling, veteran, acts, departments, and war-bride, she could have learned, prepared herself, fortified the soft stretches of her heart.

She did not know how to contemplate 1944.

Language evolved to house the diaspora. Survivors. The homeless. Geography uprooted. Obliterated bloodlines. These words restructured the systems and processes that washed up in waves into her isolated apartment hiding.

Geography exploded.

Displacement of dislocated people.

Post-war saw the planet's largest demographic shifts.

"Veteran," a person who at any time during the war declared by His Majesty on the 10th day of September 1939 against the German Reich and subsequently against other powers, has been therein engaged on active services in naval, army or air force of Canada, or of any of His Majesty's forces if at the time of his enlistment he was ordinarily domiciled or resident in Canada, and A)

whose service has involved duties required to be performed outside of the Western Hemisphere.

Land parceling war vets: Veterans Land Act R.C. 1952: "property," includes land and goods, chattels, real and personal, and personal or movable property, and all rights or interests in, or over, or arising out of, and all charges upon, property.

Farther back in the database.

1921 Ontario passed the Adoption Act. This Act introduced restrictive guidelines for disclosing any information about the adoption in general. Further changes occurred in 1927 and records pertaining to adoption were to be sealed and kept under jurisdiction of the Registrar General. Passed at a time when secrecy, shame and misunderstanding prevailed about adoption. Adoptive parents were told that the emphasis of the environment would shape their child's personality, and that genetics were hardly important. For adoptees it was thought that the need to know about their roots would never be of importance.

Knowledge, awareness, adeptness dictated. Resourcefulness would have saved her resolve.

The Piron Brigade arrived in the city on the fourth of September. The people rubbed the wartime sleep from their eyes and opened their mouths to cheer. The Liberation Front spanned outwards searching houses for Nazis and their collaborators, while the people flew to the streets in celebration.

The war had served the city an iron fist. The people became inhumanly quiet. The urban center strewn with beggars and policed by Nazis, life shriveled. The brilliant glow of the allied soldiers from Canada, Luxemburg, and Belgium filled the city. Women, children, and returning Belgian soldiers crowded the cobblestones, happily jumping and spinning with the sight of their liberators.

Amélie's world had been knocked open exposing her to a light so bright it burned holes in her caved body. For years she had spoken lightly, communicated through gestures that were calculated, spontaneous. A hand cracking back the spine of a book, the press of her soles to the embroidered rug, she knew the world through touch and was imploding quietly from the ravenous language that lifted from the streets through her open windows.

Amy had pushed the curtains aside with a magnificent sweep of her thin arm, struggling with the latch while gleaming with excitement as the panes creaked open into the air.

No more curfews.

No more fear.

The noise from the crowds below swept through the apartment. Amélie steadied herself against the wall, the ocean pulling her under, her face ashen, she shielded it from the windows pulling her body downwards in and around itself in an arched fetus stance.

Amy turned and gasped, *"As-tu d'accord?"* Are you okay? Why are you not happy? *"Pourquoi n'as-tu pas heureux?"* This is what we've been waiting for, hoped for it. It's over, Amélie, it's all over.

Amy saw the shadow of a dark bird caressing the bridge of Amélie's nose and recoiled then. The shadow swooped along the rise of her eyebrows disappearing behind her eyes. Amy shook the shadow from her head and envisioned the silhouette of a spider suspended from a web. Birds don't fly inside.

The women lifted their faces up and put on hats that had not been worn in years and wandered out to the streets to join the noise. They encountered a parade, rich with cheering and peals of laughter. The women clasped hands and wove their way towards the center of the city. Amélie had forgotten what happiness looked like and was affronted by it.

Horror.

The stretched mouths on the faces of children haunted instead of delighting. Menacing and open, she resisted the flood of emotions around her. Vulnerable, her sensitivity left her open. She attempted to lock tightly like a shell and push through numbness.

Perhaps, it was shock, or the changes that war instilled in the soul, but Amélie could not shake the remorse and darkness chaining her heart to ribcage. She placed her hand against her chest and pushed in, her pulse comforted in the sea of chaos.

She remained guarded and tight-lipped while Amy took to the noise like a sparrow released from a cage, flitting against the smiles of comrade soldiers. Amy was alive again, happy again, free again. She did not notice her wretched friend, trailing behind forging memories like the hard blows of a hammer that linked them to a chain of the darkest defeat.

THE PAST

She pressed her fingers against the glass, pulled them back and examined the oiled prints left behind. She sighed.

Wishes had become whispers.

Eyelashes on cheeks.

Faint stars above rooflines.

She traced the arch of the house across the street against the glass, noting the drabness of the wood, how it sagged over the years and darkened. The windows were shadows and still, she imagined the house to be abandoned, or else anyone inside to be sinking down and inside.

"You don't speak to me. I thought with the end of the war you'd open up, but you're worse. I don't get it. *Je ne comprends pas.*" Amy had left behind a slammed door. Amélie pressed the tip of her tongue to the back of her teeth blocking her mouth and relished in the disruption of the small "'clap.'"

She could not change the currents projecting around them now, splitting and wedging. Trajectories. Amélie could not envision her future.

Stolen directions. The war had consumed them. Stolen lives, identities, old innocent selves pushed deep long ago in a tree in Mechelen. She had not been with a man since Eli. New beginnings usually demanded explanations of old endings. She wanted to dwell on boundary lines thick and personal. Private and impenetrable. She dared not venture either way.

Brussels began to stir again from liberation, slowly piecing lives together and clearing the rubble that the Nazis had rained down for years as destruction had spread its face, menacing and fierce across the cobbled streets and under anxious feet. Amélie stayed behind glass watching the world from a distance.

She saw children screeching happily and rummaging through piles. One boy cheered when he located a pair of shoes in the rubble. Another boy ran and snatched the shoes midair kicking off a cloud of dust behind him while the other boy trailed bleating. She took in these scenes with a hand wrapped around weak tea and through eyes sharp and blue.

These eyes wept one morning when the grim lines of ragged men stepped into the window frame. Their bodies were emancipated, bones jutting underneath thin rags. Their eyes were black, absent of irises, blotted pupils of vexation. They walked slowly, with precision, heads bent, memorizing pavement. Amélie leaned forward and gripped the windowsill. Her gaze roved over each face, pleading, pleading.

Please, let him come back. Let him have lived. *Qu'il ont vécu.*

The line of survivors continued on and turned a corner. Their abrupt departure rocked her and she sagged turning from the window. She shuffled to the table. There was her hand, palm-up, curling in the air. His laugh. She smelled sweat and heard the muffled presses of beginnings. She shook her head and saw her sleeping, the soft line of her hips pushing against the wool blanket. Bliss. There was once happiness.

The memories overlapped and culminated in a white noise siren pitch in her head. Amélie gasped and sank to the floor. She wept there, alone, splayed beneath the table, body shuddering. She saw the glint of light pass over the glass between sobs. Her hand scraped along the floor extending towards the light. She pressed further and felt the cool glass encircled in her fingers. She pulled hard and fell back with the saltshaker in her palm.

The saltshaker, thrown from the table in a fit of need, of engrossing magnetism and here it was, quietly gleaming from shadow.

Impossible.

Her hand cradled the shaker against the middle of her chest releasing a flood of agony. She smelled his hand that swept it from the table, branded by the fire in his eyes while the shaker rolled and disappeared. Amélie crossed her arms over her chest and gasped. Her pain lulled her into an in-between sleep under that table. She remained there, transfixed and cracking when Amy, recalled out of need, sailed through the front door.

Amy almost missed her, but sank down in alarm when she spied Amélie under the table. She covered herself over Amélie, waking her out of that in between pained state. They rocked together, pulsing and exhaling. They could hear the cries outside from the streets, the cheering, the laughter. These sounds accosted Amélie, pushed her back into the webbed silence of her apartment, while they coursed through Amy, igniting a fire in her that she hadn't known for years. Divided, but welded together in gesture, Amy wrapped her arms around Amélie and held her until her shoulders stilled and fell. Amy pulled her hair away from her face and pulled back on her heels. With her hands curled around Amélie's arms, she looked into her friend's sunken face.

"You must stop this, this weeping. *Vous devez arrêter cela, ces pleurs.* I don't know what you've lost. Who was taken from you, but you can't go on living like this." Amy waited, anticipating a response.

The sun shifted, splitting Amélie's face in half and emblazing the room in a fiery orange. Amy watched Amélie's eyes glaze over and then she noticed that her friend was clutching something glinting to her chest. Amy said nothing and slowly pried Amélie's grasp on the saltshaker. Confused, Amy wiped the wet from her friend's face and with gentle fingers, she reached out and tried to take the shaker away. Amélie sank back and pushed herself up and out from under the table.

She did not wait for Amy to rise, but crossed the room with long slow steps and stood before the window holding the shaker to her chest. She stayed there with her back to the room, her face to the outside, waiting. Amélie did not jump when the front door slammed, she had almost anticipated it.

Realities reconfigured. She works back through internally. The shaker making slow unconscious rotations in her hands. The Romanian, he had replaced Eli, then Amy, figments of childhood loneliness and solitudes pieced together to form a friend—a vital, necessary friend—yet, Amy was chalk easily wiped from a school blackboard.

Amélie could not know then that her spirit had stopped balancing and grounding. She risked looming stagnation, ironically, rigidity that would carry her through a New World Hades.

She feared not being alone.

She feared her Self with other people.

Amélie cupped her ear around the noise of the shaker falling to the floor. It spiraled around itself two times then rocked back and forth ever so slightly until stillness. The empty room pressed against her, pushing her forwards out the window.

THE PAST

She was numbed, enduring days and nights inside a safe, self-constructed, private tunnel. Eventually, she stopped looking around her, no longer absorbing her surroundings. The chaos became too painful to entertain, the strangers, the survivors. Their pale skin and protruding bones told a story far too menacing, and Amélie would not conceive that he had been there. Those who returned.

Instead, she set her focus inside that tunnel and pushed forward, swallowing a shriek. She missed so much this way. The man with tuberculosis, the haggard woman with five young children, a young man smashing windows, and a girl with dark brown hair with fingers splayed on table tops. Amélie was looking for a way out, this was all her eyes searched for. There was also a quiet hope she nourished that he might return and find her.

The city noise hurt. Brussels had changed within hours from silent fear to chaotic celebrations. She was relieved the war was over, but it was difficult to flow into the change that was unfolding around her. She discreetly weaved her way through crowds.

Music filtered through the air, settling on the bottoms of feet, and these liberated souls danced around Amélie. She pushed with elbows as her wide eyes were relieved when she stepped onto the Rue du Marché Aux Herbes. She had not been to this street in years and the sight of it liberated was comforting, yet unsettling. She ran her hand along the iron railing of the bakery, savoring the smell of rising bread. Music and bread, almost foreign to her senses. She rubbed her fingers against the gothic statue of a lion that stood in front of the next building. She remembered that large window that overlooked the street. She had once held his hand and imagined them pressed against that window, fingers lost in reflected hair. She inhaled and placed her quivering hands under her crossed arms and pushed forward. She turned off of the street and up the alleyway that led to the café. Her heart lurched when the doorway came into view, the same brown mahogany.

The door was heavy, but she leaned against it and disappeared into the café. It was cool and dark, not yet hosting any customers. The walls and floor were the same, dark green and wood, but much of the furniture was missing and the bar was sparse with bottles. Amélie heard a low whistling coming from the back of the room and followed the sound. She tried to control her nervousness, biting at her lip to stop shaking, but she moved forward.

She saw the old man before he spotted her and watched his back as he bent to retrieve a box. Sweat gleamed on the back of his neck. She felt a tug inside her as soon as she recognized him, the blushing barrister. She cleared her throat discretely before he could heft the box, and he spun around with a pained startled look. He pulled out a handkerchief and wiped the back of his neck. The man studied her. He smiled suddenly and his eyes lit up in recognition.

"*Vous êtes en vie!*" You're alive. He exclaimed stepping towards her.

"*Oui, vous aussi.*" You also. She replied. The man smiled a half-crooked grin and looked down at his aged hands.

"*Nous avons de la chance.*" We are in luck. Everyone is gone.
"*Tout le monde est parti.*" His face fell, his blue eyes darkened to

grey. Amélie was sick of war talk, how no one could carry on a proper conversation without Hitler being there. She hated Hitler. The war left everyone sharp-edged and dry-mouthed.

She couldn't deny it either, the room was making her sick, Eli was everywhere. The barstools, the draft lines, that mahogany bar-wood smell. It all came crashing back. She hesitated for a moment but asked him.

"Have you seen him? You remember him, the man with the black hair? *L'homme aux cheveux noirs?*" Her gentle prodding was met with a blank stare. She added, "This place was special. *Cet endroit est spécial.* Maybe he..." she trailed off.

C'est stupide.

He twisted his fingers uncomfortably.

"No, I have not seen him. I will keep my eyes out for him." She closed her eyes, a prayer threaded through her.

Please, let him come to me. *Se il vous plaît, qu'il vienne à moi.*

She faced the man and smiled.

"Thank you. I am sorry to have bothered you." She raised her eyes. He offered her a sympathetic look and raised his hands in prayer.

In the alleyway, she stood still for a moment to collect herself. She pinched her cheeks, straightened her skirt and patted down her blonde hair. She set her teeth together, determined not to cry.

She knew, she had to embrace change and try to piece a life back together. She knew, even more so, she had to run. There was really no time to wait for him or anticipate that he'd return, again.

Amélie emerged on the Rue du Marché Aux Herbes and headed towards the streetcar disappearing in a throng of people. The sun let down rays, her forehead glistened. She wiped it gingerly, anxious with the heat of the day. The city felt crowded.

Once the survivors began to trickle back they began to pour into the city. It was unnerving for the Belgians. Those inhabitants who had condemned the Jews and now faced them again on equal ground stood ashen and unable to reckon something unhinged within themselves. Their faces said it. Shame. Anger. Guilt. While others continued to embody and live the ideologies of difference and separation that was served to them dogmatically—across centuries.

Guilt plagued them and they hammered through the crowds with their faces bent and their hands shoved in pockets. There were also many allied soldiers from various countries consuming the streets and filling concert halls.

With liberation came music again, which entailed dancing and late-night celebrating. Lured out and accompanied by Amy's frivolity, Amélie went several times to these dances and watched the soldiers and Belgian women dance. She was attracted to the gaiety of the dances, but felt an unceasing anxiety swell within her, while amongst the crowds, something darker lurked that everyone avoided facing. She swallowed the pain and feigned a smile because she knew that Amy was tired of her weeping—she was tired of weeping.

The streetcar pulled up with a hiss and people began filing in. Amélie anticipated dropping her money in the slot and braced herself for the lost weight in her palm. She placed each coin in one at a time, annoying others around her, but she concentrated on the loss of the money, how desperately she needed to get out of that country or find work. When the last coin fell with an agitated clink she worked her way to the nearest open space. The seats were full and the cars were jammed, so she weaved awkwardly to the back car. She passed men twisted around newspapers, scanning headlines. Mothers handed broken off bits of croissant to abate their children's restlessness on the ride. Young girls laughed loudly and then, Amélie spotted Amy.

She could not miss the chocolate brown hair or the laugh that reminded her of clear running water rushed through the car. Amy was turned away from her and did not see Amélie approaching. Amy nodded her head and erupted in another gestation of laughter, Amélie froze. She saw the large muscular arm draped around Amy's slender shoulders. She could smell the musk of the soldier and swatted the scent from her nostrils. She studied his hand and broad fingers as they twirled strands of Amy's hair around them. He dug his other hand beneath the folds of her dress.

Amélie almost gasped when Amy leaned forward and kissed the man. She embraced him with a longing Amélie had never seen, how her body caved into the man and seemed to melt from his heat. Her eyes were closed, her eyelashes fanned across her cheeks. She looked beautiful and happy.

Amélie felt the anger pumping through her veins and turned abruptly. She did not want Amy to see her, to register the anger and jealousy on her face. She had to distance herself from Amy, but yearned for her—all that Amy represented—to be near, to come back.

Amélie knew Amy had survived the war, and had come back. Before returning, the loss was overwhelming. Now her return was overwhelming. Amelie pinched the bridge of her nose hoping to stop the tears that lifted her eyelids. She scrunched her mouth in a wrinkled pit and dug her feet into the soles of her shoes.

I am tired of living like this.

"Je suis fatigué."

Amy smiled.

The thoughts cut and she began to shake. Heat rose up behind her face and she felt sweat trailing along her things sticking to her skirt. She moved to the middle of the streetcar and waited impatiently.

The cars screeched to a stop and Amélie nearly knocked people over as she fled from the car. She could hear her shoes angrily clicking against the cobblestones, felt the rush of air around her, but she didn't pause until the streetcar was gone.

Once far enough away, she stopped and placed her hands on her knees and bent over panting. She let the despair out, anticipating the torrent of tears that rolled along her cheekbones and dotted the sidewalk. Her bottom lip shook and a long moan escaped her.

She did not see the man watching her from across the street. He witnessed her flight from the streetcar and was instantly attracted to her energy. He followed her two blocks and watched as she leaned over about to vomit. He took out a cigarette and lit it, rolling it around between his lips. He studied the line of her back and the slight swell of her buttocks, appreciating the fullness of her, he followed the curve of her shoulders along her arms and felt an incessant desire to take her hands and place them on him. He could not see her face and this perturbed him.

He needed to see her face. She heaved and sputtered, almost falling to the pavement. He flew across the street, grasped her by the elbows, and pulled her upright. She was startled and felt the pinch of his grip around her like claws. She looked up into his face and gasped.

Phillip was a fair-haired Canadian. He was massive, with thick fingers and feral blue eyes, he radiated physical prowess, of a furtive desire to conquer and possess whatever he desired. He worked as a mechanic for the Royal Canadian Air Force. He was a Sergeant and fuselage mechanic. He repaired any damaged planes that came back from battle. He'd weld new plates for gutted hulls, fixed the gears in the plane's engine, or pieced together new machines from the other fallen planes. He would tell his son one day about the scenes he and his men faced when they arrived at empty battlefields days after the fighting had moved on. Phillip scourged the sites for anything that could provide him with tools or parts in fixing the airplanes. He tediously stepped over the fallen soldiers, cautiously rifle through tanks and planes; he even stripped the dead of their weaponry.

He had kept four Nazi rifles and would smuggle them back to Canada. One of these guns would be passed down to his grandson. The same gun that had killed many Canadians and other allies would be used to bring down a twelve-point buck in the interior of an Ontario forest.

Phillip memorized each fallen face that he had to step over in his search for plane parts but kept this to himself. Their gaping wounds and the unceasing red stain of blood shifted something inside of him and he was never the same again. Living amongst a landscape of death would bring out savagery. Unhealed wounds. He would breathe with lungs filled with the silent voices of those he walked over.

Just as Amélie shuffled through war-torn spaces in a state of numbness, Phillip too would live with half of him dead. Simultaneously living a life between being and non-existence would attract Amélie and Phillip to each other, magnetic forces.

She felt wounded in his arms and shocked. The day had turned so unexpectedly. She began with hope, jaw aligned in determination to muster some semblance of normality from before the war. She wanted strong warm arms enveloping her, to brush back dark curls. She just did not know it would be him, this stranger. But, there he was, fiery and penetrating.

"What is your name?" His English was blunted by a northern draw. She did not know this until much later. He spoke from a straight line, the corners of his mouth angular, pulling the last word of the question out, prolonging semantic, his tongue knocking against teeth, white and sharp.

She swallowed and thought of nothing but water, how it rippled against her protruding knees and flung outwards against a porcelain tub, a metal bucket, or a ship? She shivered.

"Sophie, Sophie Jeanne Cyncad."

The Present

She loops the letters carefully, the tip of her pen arcing and cresting along the valley of canvas. Nelle presses the curve of syllables into the highest branches on the tree and works her way down the trunk.

The letters are lives. She feels the weight of each name as she writes, each story, and as she perseveres, she realizes the trauma embedded behind. Deeper narratives that letters alone cannot convey. She feels pleasure there too as each letter connects names to each other.

The tip of her tongue protrudes pink between her teeth. She steadies herself, pauses for several seconds. Her eyebrows come together and there is a deep line she works out gently with her pointer finger. Inhale. A decision is made. Nelle records for her Daughter her surname, a maiden name. Belonging to her by name, she knows, not blood. An adopted name. But, she connects with. It was the name that she proudly spoke to those who tried to change it, to rename her and turn her into someone else altogether.

She would not use the names written in scrawling blue pencil crayon, they did not belong to her. They were not hers, but his, and she did not want to invade. She used the name that connected her through men, through time cresting marriages and bowed heads before bedroom mirrors. A shared name, made it their own in small facets despite adoption. She writes the name as a signature at the top of the canvas.

Nelle always drew the last letter up, striking through the entire name for authenticity. They could not steal her name this way. Her grandmother projected the name to carve out bloodlines, pathways for inhabitants of the small town to know where they belonged. She was the matriarch with a son jet black who birthed the two Grandchildren and great Grandchildren. A lineage was born, replaced another. A new tree planted.

She slowly leans back and reads over the names. Her grandmother's place was high up on the left side, an empty space beside her and many more falling above and below her. She wishes that it was easier to extend higher, to use her grandmother as leverage to climb the oldest branches and know exactly where they originated from. Her head tilts right, she thinks. Hovers on the edge of epiphany and lets her hand arc forward and rotate the entire sheet of canvas so that branches become roots and the newer lives extend into the sky.

She observes the branches spread out, roots digging deep, she exhales and feels the heat of embarrassment gloss her forehead for attempting to present her child with such a meager family tree. This knowing pulls her down into submission, but she resigns not to twist the tree back around. She'd leave them upside down then, adding in new names opposite to those who had once existed. Those whose footsteps left impenetrable paths, stencil overlays, beyond everything arbitrary and solitary about this upside-down tree.

It's us.

They forgot about the sacred breath, trekking lightly, respecting ground, she needed to go out and hear their stories in the winds before writing their names down. She needed to conceptualize the branches drifting in a gaseous oceanic sphere, underwater and rotating, all was drowning, and yet all was afloat.

Nelle pushes out air and rolls the pen between her fingers. She's hunched, but straightens and adjusts her posture immediately when the baby turns. Nelle feels her insides gently contour the form, opening and folding the baby in a deep embrace. She shields the protruding mass with a forearm.

The baby settles, stillness. The ache gone, that movement that she confused with indigestion. A life speaking.

Nelle sips slow and long from her mug and places the pen to the paper again. She stands back from the canvas and studies the outline of the tree on the page. Epiphany. *Trompe l'oeil.*

It looks like a woman.

She takes another sip, keeps working. It was easy to write him into the tree. He provided pattern, a generational lineage of initialed identities. Her Mother spoke to her once of the history of the family surname.

"The men carry the same initials, T.E.S. They've done this for generations. When I was pregnant with your brother, I anticipated breaking from this pattern, but that was not allowed. I couldn't, but I was happy to end up with your brother's name. He has a beautiful name. A Prime Minister's name."

The story is served.

Nelle felt removed from tradition because it didn't matter what initials consisted of the daughters' names. As a girl, she shook the pressure from her head and continued on. Trekking over grass barefoot, writing another world in her head, befriending dragonflies with large eyes and understanding that there was more to life than the passing down of letters. More to life that she could hear in the simplicity of winds.

Essentially, she was a girl and could not be a part of the name game. Then it was a curse, now, as a woman ballooning with life, she honours the relief pressing blunt into her that she is untouchable and able to write her own destiny.

Self-propriety. She could step into entire unfelt perimeters of the Sacred Feminine. Freedom. She wraps her mind around that seed in utopic glory. She can write the destiny of the Women differently from here on out. She just needs to write it down.

She finishes recording the names, plugging in the birth dates that her Mother had made for her in her own tree. Her tree was contained in a scrapbook given to her during her thirteenth year.

Her mother's family was carefully recorded: names, dates, deaths and births. The pattern reassuring. She knew that she came from a long line of farmers on her mother's side, those men that hunched over the earth picking stones. She remembers the stone fences framing her childhood journeys. She used to run along the boulders on Nanny and Papa's farm near Tamworth. There is a cemetery there of ancestors dating back to the early 1800s, Nelle pauses, adds to her list of things to complete before the child is born to visit this place and record those names too. She wonders why she focuses so much on the incomplete and clouded story on her father's side when she could easily fall into a sound and outlined family history from the Loyalist farmlands. Nelle essentially grew up on farmland, was raised under their sun in a barnyard shaped by the hands of settling ancestors. She wonders why her identity is not chained there, but is pulled back to the harrowing realities of her grandmother's immigration from the Old World to the New, her adopted grandmother at that.

What is hooking me here?

She would watch her Papa as a child count the herd and lovingly coax a cow while birthing. She remembers one evening coming across a large heaving cow in the back pasture. The animal's eyes bulged from their sockets and she eyed Nelle with flaring nostrils. She approached the cow and placed her palm slowly against the heaving side willing the animal to calm. The cow smelled of wet grass and manure. Nelle rubbed her hand across the vexed cow in slow large circles. The rhythm calmed the animal and the cow closed her eyes. A deep groan let out from the cow's slit mouth, Nelle felt the agonizing pain in the cry. She instantly smelled iron, a rich rusty scent that could only be blood. She ran to the rear of the cow and gasped.

Blood coursed from the cow's backside clotting with the dirt. Nelle knew instantly she must run and fetch her Papa. She ran to the front of the cow and traced her fingertips around the porous wet nose.

I will help you.

Nelle flew through the fields alight on the backs of fireflies. The dusk filtered through her long brown hair that whipped against her cheeks. She burst through the garage door in a fury rousing Nanny and Papa. They were perched at the kitchen table, the smell of boiled peas and popping steak from the stove warming Papa's leather cheeks. It was a tranquil scene, a space that Nelle would always remember later on, but that night, she could only hear the drawn-out cry of the fallen cow. Her grandparents took her seriously.

She followed him up the laneway to the barnyard. His silver hair cast a white glow in the purple light that travelled down his shoulders and arms. Papa always wore the same faded beige work shirt, rolled precisely to his elbows, and beige work pants. His towering frame was severed by the glint of a belt buckle, one encrusted with a beaming Captain Morgan. He walked slowly, but with direction.

His shoulders bent forward and his arms hanging straight by his sides. He had lost the middle finger on his left hand while changing a tire one day when the tire burst. Nelle secretly memorized the crests and valleys of his worn work hands. She would stare ashen when he would hand her his work gloves to wear with one finger sewn shut. He knew that the glove was altered. He knew that Nelle did not have the courage to call him out on it. As he walked she could see how he curled his left hand around itself to cradle the space of the missing finger. His pointer finger had moved into the middle space over the years and Nelle knew that many people overlooked the missing finger because of this.

She understood how they would not see the ghost digit that her Papa carefully tucked away. She focused on the small things, Papa's finger, the cow's curling nostril, and the wing of a swallow, which completely removed her from the world, placing her inside her own head. Nelle tripped on a rock and fell onto her knees before the cow and Papa. He called her trouble, "here comes Trouble," and he was right. But this night, Nelle had come to Papa with important information.

She watched him push the rolled-up sleeves higher on his bicep, his skin curled outwards in waves, a severe line punctuating the darkness between his tanned skin and the parts of him that the beige outfit shielded. He pulled off his gold watch, the one he meticulously set each morning in order that he was not off by a hair of a second, and tucked it into his pants pocket. He stepped towards the cow speaking to her in a relaxing low tone.

The cow responded instantly and heaved, sending one of her back hoofs into the air. He was not afraid but steadily pushed on her hind quarters and she lowered to the ground. She moaned and jerked her head while he placed a hand on the flesh in front of her tail and slowly leaned before her.

"Here, take this," he asked her, handing her his gold wristwatch. Nelle observed with large eyes as he pulled up the cow's tail and pressed first his fingers, fist, then an entire arm up to his elbow into her.

Nelle had never seen such an intrusion before, especially from Papa, and she turned her face away in embarrassment. Papa pulled out his arm and wiped the wet on his red handkerchief. He sighed and walked around the length of the cow. He pressed against her side and the cow cried and butted. He came around to face her and cradled her head in his hands. Papa was a very reserved man. He was passionate about morality and honesty, but he was not one to reveal his inner feelings to anyone but her Nanny. Nelle felt like an intruder when he began speaking to the cow in a hushed voice.

He told her not to worry, that she would not have pain. He was sorry and wished that she had not fallen. He understood that she was not calving and that she had fallen on the rocks. The blood was an internal injury that would not heal. Nelle shifted uncomfortably as her Papa wiped private wet tears from below his eyes and balled his nose in his fist. He pressed his fore-head against the animal and fell into a blanket of silence. The tenderness was overwhelming. Nelle felt a warm sensation clench the middle of her chest.

She wanted to walk towards him so that he would tuck her into his aura of servitude to the animal. She did not like standing on the perimeters, her fingers nervously plucking the dandelion bracelet in her pocket.

Suddenly he turned to her. She could see the dampness on his cheeks and knew that he was not ashamed. She almost missed the whisper that fell from his lips.

"Thank you, Nelle. It is good that I know whenever you find a cow has fallen." Nelle was euphoric and glided to his side in a rush of rubber heels and mosquito bites.

Papa placed his calloused fingers on the crown of her head and pinched hard. She wheeled away in a fit of pained laughter and he chuckled. The sensitive soul she'd seen moments before tucked inside the jokester. She handed him his watch and he slipped it into his pants pocket.

Nelle sighs and rubs her temples. She misses Papa and Nanny. They had passed years ago but the ache for them never left. Acceptance that those who had been such a strong presence for her, had given her such structure, were gone, took time. She cherishes memory.

She feels the pockets of space surrounding her and sinks into her chair. She needs to clear her head. Awkwardly, she rises again and carefully places the sheet of paper on the highest shelf of her bookcase and cracks her back to the empty room.

Light filters through the open window threading long ribbons across the hardwood floor. She watches the curtains dance across the ribbons, and catches the sweet taste of lilacs on the breeze. Her mouth waters for the outside air and a pillow of lilacs against her nose. She follows her impulses and leaves.

She drives north, cresting the igneous and metamorphic rocks of the Precambrian Canadian Shield. She learned of the Shield in school, but truly felt the resonances of the crustal barricade from the furrowed brows of farmers, of the maps she studied in school geography texts. These were the men that came to grow things from the soil but found rock instead. Nelle dwelled in the tragedy of their story, fearful of the shield beneath their feet. It dominated and dictated livelihoods. She resented anything that hindered *survival.* She did not know as a child that she was born into a landscape of severe lines and jutting boundaries.

Her tiny feet pounded against a shield that could run to nearly 4 kms deep of stubborn rock that sank beneath sedimentary cover. She walked roads that straddled contact between glacial and volcanic layers, which erupted in an intrusive fault system of dene rock millions of years old. She assumed the story of her roots was new, several decades new, so she did not smell the tremendous shaping of that land until much later.

That day she follows a road that crests farmers' fields lined with crumbling stone fences. She eyes sagging, barns peeling under the coming heat of summer. She glimpses cows huddled in the shadows of trees, pressing their noses into the new grass. She salutes each car that she passes with the farmer's nod, a slight bow of the head that was quick as a whip. She knows that she could also lift her two fingers from the wheel and that gesture would be the same, I know you. They waved. Cultural gestures, rural, and she appreciates the uniqueness of these exchanges now as an adult. She borrows the gesture from the farmers around her. She likes how they acknowledge each other.

The road begins to cut sharp corners around magnificent faces of boulders. She imagines how the settlers sweated while clearing the land for these roads. First, there was the beaten trail made by leathered soles and backs slung with hunting bows. The white man came lumbering with knives and persistence. They pushed the trail outwards by severing trees and dancing on logs. The horses and drawn wagons dug muddy ruts in the ground, squandering the early spring brush that grew up under tumultuous showers. The immigrants drowned in mud whenever they needed to go somewhere. The wet itch from the flooded paths inspired them to build the plank roads. Next, they ran rail lines through.

They extended north, pushing colonization into the jungle of trees and riverbanks.

Survival.

Nelle can hear the crashing blows of dynamite that exploded the rocks, sending clouds of powdered mineral into the immigrants' nostrils. She was not there, but she could search out their story in the face of a stone. She drums her fingers against the wheel and cranks the volume in the car. The windows are down pulling a wind tunnel through her hair. She revels in the lightness, swept away from the hunched spine of an Irish settler.

Nelle returns to this land each time she feels the pull. A vibration of collision, encounter, that shaped the land that she did not thumb from a book. The richness of minerals in the land came from an acid volcanic vent that bled sulphur to the iron rich host rock that produced the famous pyrite. A deposit of eruption and merging, this was land that kept her alive.

She was born into domesticity and stung from its sharp tongue. She washed her Mother's calves in tears and clutched her ankles under silk. She glorified the day her Mother stamped her foot and pushed the entire contents of her dresser into bags. They were leaving and she was allowed to go.

Her Mother held her hand and eventually their journey brought them to Queensborough. Nelle tasted the iron in the rock and became hypnotized by dark water that coursed through the village reeking of sulphur. She fell in love with the Black River and told no one because they would not understand. The river soothed her nerves with its steady pace. It shone black but sank deep in orange when the sun broke the surface. It was never what it appeared to be and because of this, the river demanded nothing from her.

Nelle senses the ripples of survival and endurance. She met the loggers that submerged themselves deep in the Northern underbrush hauling fallen trees to the shores of Lingham Lake. She envisioned them floating by thundering against the water, crashing together. They bobbed like corks, transcending the river into a shifting current of rolling wood. The Quebec loggers were like a balancing act, dancing from log to log prying them with their cant hooks and long pike poles in order to steer them down the river towards Moira Lake. Nelle could hear the throngs of excited onlookers who had gathered along the riverbank. They knew the journey from Lingham, past Queensborough along the Moira River to Belleville. She envisioned the loggers' muscled arms, wrapped tightly from the wet cotton of their shirts. Nelle admired the courage they had to risk falling into the water and becoming trapped under the logs. The water was exceptionally cold most times, and she could imagine the icy prison that flowed beneath.

The lumbering and mining industries fed the town and helped to make Queensborough become the bustling community it was in the late eighteenth century. Nelle heard the name of Daniel Thompson who had purchased the mill from Job Lingham in 1850. She could also hear the roaring whistle of the trains that lumbered into Queensborough from the Bay of Quinte Railway. The early inhabitants possessed large dreams for the hamlet. Even Sir John A. Macdonald owned eleven lots in the town between 1868 and 1870, and some again in 1886. The myth, or history, dictates that he sold the lots, or lost them to the Merchant's Bank for a vast sum of sixty-six hundred dollars.

The river told her this, and took her farther back than others dared to know. Nelle delighted in the native sounds of a place called Cooksokie, and those who lived on water and fish. She smelled smoke in the long hair of women who tanned hides and sucked marrow from bones. She heard their song drift amongst the rising steam of the river at daybreak and yearned to turn around and become lost in their time. A life before colonialism shook its fist and demanded names in their language. The mail would not be sent to a place called Cooksokie, no, the mail must be sent to Queensborough, a memory of Ireland, and the last fragment Daniel eyed from the shore as his boat sailed for Liverpool, reminiscent of the old world, labeled in the new world as legacy, an artificial naming legacy of European dominance. Nelle was happy that prosperity flickered for a few decades in the town, but burned out once industry stopped. Now she could enjoy the river voice alone and undisturbed.

She leaves her car unlocked in the middle of town and walks with her face towards the river. The sky is overcast sketching grey shadows across the road. Nelle strides along Water Street listening to the current and stops to watch it disappear and emerge under the bridge. She keeps walking in meditation.

She is sweating and hot when she steps into the Cedarwood Cemetery on the outskirts of town. There was no place to bury the dead when the immigrants came. Instead, this cemetery was a gift to the inhabitants of Queensborough. There was a farmer, John Moore, Sr., who set out one morning and eyed land in between trees that could cradle the dead. The Anglican minister only wanted those souls to rest there, but John Moore was persistent, this was a final home for all residents. The cemetery was born in 1893, through gesture and morality. Nelle had not expected to journey there, had not planned anything, but let the vibrations of her feet steer her. She was tired.

The place is blissfully quiet except for several territorial Blue Jay calls from the forest periphery as she floats past lines of headstones. The grass hums with a grasshopper symphony. The afternoon heat holds her and her baby. Nelle weaves through headstone plots reading in silence. Her hands massage her hip lines and edge of stomach. The baby is stretching and pushing against her hips and spine. The movement is not painful, but solace. Nelle stumbles across them this way, enjoying her body and the baby, their names, blanketed in a reverie of the swoops of a red winged blackbird and dragonflies. She inhales sharply and lowers to her knees running her fingers along the names.

The first name is a woman, Martha Stone. She was born in 1843 and died in 1915. Nelle swallows hard. Bewilderment absorbs her, the baby lurches. She winces and grits her teeth pushing down on her stomach to still the baby. Nelle never expected to find her name in stone.

Is this my family?

The second name is a man: W.M. Stone. He was born in July of 1857 and died in December of 1924. Her mind races and traces thoughts to a past riddled with holes.

She knew nothing of them, had never heard them mentioned. Sweat runs along her left temple and she wipes at it, hard, irritated. Nelle is tired of the gaps in her own life story. Ancestors sketched into stone, but cobwebbed in grass and unspoken existences. She wonders if it is meant to be this way. She grew up in the same locality as ancestors bearing the same surname. Irony. She feels alone, isolated from knowing lineage. Imposter. Counterfeit. She is not blood to these names, yet, she yearns for deeper knowing.

The crow shakes her to the core. The animal had landed on a gravestone a few steps away and began shrieking in the graying light. Nelle turns instantly and catches the animal with her voice. The emotions explode from her in a cloud of fury and she rises before the animal in a haze of rage. The bird recoils and snaps its beak. Nelle resents the intrusion, the dominating cackle of the wretched bird, how it lives on dead things. Her teachings have begun. She doesn't know.

Somehow, she senses that the crow understands the tremble in her back when her face was bent over the stones. The crow knew her vulnerability. She bends and sifts through the grass while the animal stares with glass marble eyes. It shifts from one foot to the other, eyeing her desperate hands. She nearly fools the bird when she rises in a flash and hurls a stone at it. The stone crests angrily through the pocket of air left behind by the crow. The animal ascends wildly and expertly with a skin-crawling shriek. The stone knocks over a plastic flower basket on the next gravestone.

Blood pulses sharply through Nelle's veins and she folds her arms around her stomach. The baby spirals with excitement pushing hard up against Nelle's diaphragm. With short breaths, Nelle turns back to the stones and slowly kneels against the ground. She dares not look at the shrinking black dot circling above cawing. Instead, she waits for the baby to still and allows the returning thrum of the grasshoppers to soothe her temper. The clouds split and light streams down on top of Nelle's head. She remains bent, her hands braced against the stones. She can feel the pen pressed inside her purse and smells the clean surface of the pad of paper. She drives her hand into her purse clamping down hard on the pen and paper. Nelle pulls them out and writes down the names.

Storyteller

Her isolation was solitude, for some time.

They took her seat upon the deis. They took her life-giving tiara away. Stomped out the sacred fire and pulled the sharpened reed from her hand.

Drove her out to wander wild mountains. She cut her feet on thorns. Outcast. Worn.

"He eats away at my life."

She cradled her anguish. Wrapped against her heart, infant. Expelled this torment from her innermost chamber in sacred breath.

She learned to channel rage, the anger that furnaced within her because of how they had treated her.

There were full-moon cries. Midnight crescendos. The beautiful Woman out under the moon, fingers gripped Mother Earth. She called out to Inanna. Aligned to Earth rhythms, Gaia.

Looked into the sun for a moment. Nucleotide. Flowed with the moon. Bowed down, rose and surmised. Her abdomen sponged bone. Her pained heart beat wings against a bird-cage.

Instinctively she cupped womb while walking. Closed her eyes and listened. Awakened that way, her anguish made her ready. Polished her down, those unforgiving sand storms. Exclusion was painful, but exclusion also gave her time, gifted her the opportunity to transform. Metamorphosis. She carved out space.

She was open then, coursing, able to receive her teachings.

Generational trauma. The subordination of Women. Her coming-to-know could have gone different ways. She could have perished under pressure, or she could learn to bend, and, in that bending, she could evolve. An oracle pearl, diamond.

Some Women give birth to babies.

She birthed you and this poem.

Thoughts are tangible. Feelings matter.

Her words built temples.

The poem orients her to learn about the world.

She's crafted cosmic perfection that heals. Medicine.

The clan is carried forward.

She comes home.

High priestess. Empowered.

She is then, *beloved.*

RIPPLE

Oh, je voudais tant que tu te souviennes
Des jours heureux où nous étions amis
En ce temps-là la vie était plus belle
Et le soleil plus brûlant qu'aujourd'hui.

Les feuilles mortes se ramassent à la pelle
Tu vois, je n'ai pas oublié
Les feuilles mortes se ramassent à la pelle
Les souvenirs et les regrets aussi.

Et le vent du Nord les emporte,
Dans la nuit froide de l'oubli.
Tu vois je n'ai pas oublié,
La chanson que tu me chantais...

Les feuilles mortes se ramassent à la pelle
Les souvenirs et les regrets aussi,
Mais mon amour silencieux et fidèle
Sourit toujours et remercie la vie.

Je t'aimais tant, tu étais si jolie,
Comment veux-tu que je t'oublie?

En ce temps-là la vie était plus belle
Et le soleil plus brûlant qu'aujourd'hui.

Tu étais ma plus douce amie
Mais je n'ai que faire des regrets.
Et la chanson que tu chantais,
Toujours, toujours je l'entendrai.

C'est une chanson qui nous ressemble,
Toi tu m'aimais, moi je t'aimais
Et nous vivions, tous deux ensemble,
Toi qui m'aimais, moi qui t'aimais.

Mais la vie sépare ceux qui s'aiment,
Tout doucement, sans faire de bruit
Et la mer efface sur le sable
Les pas des amants désunis.

C'est une chanson qui nous ressemble,
Toi tu m'aimais et je t'aimais
Et nous vivions tous deux ensemble,
Toi qui m'aimais, moi qui t'aimais.

Mais la vie sépare ceux qui s'aiment,
Tout doucement, sans faire de bruit
Et la mer efface sur le sable
Les pas des amants désunis.

THE PAST

Sophie unrolled the tiny black tube and spread a thick layer of crimson red lipstick on her lips. She puckered in the mirror and raised one dainty finger smudging the hard line of red outlining her mouth. She had transformed again.

She hummed softly to herself keeping her lips blotted. "But life separates lovers, pretty slowly, noiselessly, and the sea erases on the sand, the separated lovers' footprints." She tries to forget the songs that played from that Fada radio during the long hours of their waiting.

The humming grew persistent and incessant. "Fallen leaves can be picked up by the shovelful, so can memories and regrets. And the north wind takes them into the cold night of oblivion. You see, I have not forgotten the song you used to sing me." She conjured up the complex face of the Romanian, his hard lines and pictured his body shredded and drifting around her like dry dead leaves. She could hear Amy's laugh ringing through the corridor of her thoughts, envisioned the curve of hip, the striking smile and pushed memory deep down, ashamed. She's left with hard pressed lines, a mouth that does not turn up at the corners. The war, she wonders if those who survived it can still smile.

A pale hand placed the lid back on the tube with a sharp

click and began unrolling the pins from her hair. The humming faded in and out like a radio connection. Blonde tendrils fell against her shoulders and curled around her jaw. She feigned beauty. She eyed the woman in the mirror. Weeks earlier she had sat in the same space, wretched and ragged. Her aura poured forth now, stained with fear and war secrets, she embraced the harlequin façade. It kept her alive. She just wanted to be alive because she had accepted a long time ago that she had died inside.

The royal blue dress he had purchased for her earlier that afternoon was carefully draped over a chair in the corner. She ran her fingers through her hair pulling the curls apart. Pushing herself up from the mirror she drifted across the room.

Sophie sat with a sigh on the metal-framed bed and fingered the cream boat neckline. He had bought her this dress.

A flash of brown eyes, black curls, and she burned with shame.

He had also bought the red lipstick that bruised her mouth. She caved, her insides peeled away from the skeleton that housed them and the guilt was heavy. An anchor around her shoulders.

Yoked.

She rocked.

The Canadian was angular and hard. When he pressed his lips to hers she could not swallow the tremble that she felt rise up from him. She braced and pushed through, startled-deter-mined-bird. He needed someone who could absorb and trans-form the tremble. An alchemist.

She did not know yet that she could be a magician. She only knew that she was barren, that she needed to get out of the country as fast as possible. They were axing Nazi collaborators. She feared for her life.

From the words that rolled off his tongue late at night during his whiskey sweats, she gathered that he came from wilderness, a northern jungle. Lost in translation, her broken English could not build bridges to him. He did not let down ladders for her to climb either. They were lost between the languages and names of the homes they desperately wanted to help crystallize and convey for the other.

Sophie curved her tongue around the names of places he riddled off in the dark like a song.

Madoc, with its long "a" and "c" click, Sophie would sing softly this new language to herself when he was not there. She loved the name Moira. She thought it was beautiful and a word she had not heard before.

Sophie envisioned naming her daughter Moira. Melodic, it sang against her tongue. She hummed the name under her breath.

Sophie does not know the term Schryver Hill—isn't aware of Belden's Country Atlas of 1878. "Pleasantly situated at the base of a large hill which shelters it from the west winds and is the most important village in the township," Sophie does not know the literature of her New World home.

Moira comes from the Town of Moira in Deven, Ireland. Francis Rawdon was born at Moira, December 9, 1754. He is remembered for the American Revolutionary War, Rawdon fought for the British and was created Earl of Moira in recognition of his services. The disconnect of language and reality resonates in the simple act of her humming a fantasy of a child's name, imagining. Because, Francis Rawdon never visited Canada and never saw the county and three townships which echo his family and birthplace names. He does not know of the River Moira, Madoc, or Moira Lake. His right-hand personae was his wife and when he died in 1826 he had requested that his right hand be cut off and preserved until the death of his wife, the Marchioness of Hastings to be interred in her coffin. Sophie, in the war zone of domestic violence on the shores of Moira Lake and Schryver Hill would not know the immense love that the language hinged on. The irony is meant to cut deep.

Sophie could not pronounce Marmora. She tripped on the "o," pulling it out longer from her lips ending up with a word that sounded like "aura." Phillip laughed at her learning, but made no effort to speak French. He was repelled and absorbed by her otherness. She did not have access to his.

The insecurities were erased temporarily with whatever Phillip placed in her hands. A mask of bribes and distractions held out, gifted. Handmaid lace lingerie, leather shoes, and real silk stockings, she'd bundle the luxury in a fist, adorn the empty spaces in her room with these unspeaking things. She fingered the petals of the bouquets he brought her in ornamental painted vases. Despite the reality that Europe was a skeleton of what it once was before the bombings and devastation, the shops filled up with luxury goods and the black market boomed. Phillip's gestures hinted to her of an unspoken, but understood, destination of a Promised Land across the Atlantic Ocean waiting for them, The New World. She wanted out of the Old One as fast as the post-war complications would enable her. Each day she remained in Brussels her insides retched of the fear of discovery from those hunting down Nazi collaborators.

Language evolved again to meet the needs of the inhabitants of liberated Brussels and survivors across Europe. The survivors were called refugees, and their very presence in the streets forced Belgians to stop denying what they knew happened in the camps.

Sophie watched these souls return with blinking eyes, the guilt and shame built up inside of her brimming with threat of breakdown. She held her hand over her mouth and let her tears disappear into the folds of her fingers and palms. She knew they might only be twenty-something, but the skeletal frames inflamed with dysentery and hollow eyes of those souls shuffling back into the metropolis appeared elderly, sixty or seventy. Sophie wept privately about their fate.

She wondered how such bodies and minds could transition back into a reality that had murdered them, genocide. It was hard for her to face what the Belgians tolerated to happen in their spaces, murder, bloodshed and in the pit of war, survival was the only thought—who could think of how to help save millions of lives from Hitler's murdering matrix? Refugee camps and shelters shot up everywhere, and still, the Belgians felt. for the most part, distanced and separate from those horrid zones. Sophie looked for Eli in every refugee's face.

For years the people had avoided each other emotionally—family lineage was murdered and torn down. Mortality trumped legacy because the people saw just how quickly death evaded everything. They had cast their gazes to the cobblestones, repelled by any spiritual and emotional connections with others for fear of any accusation of assisting the Nazi crimes—accusation would mean their death.

Sophie noticed now how most had lifted their eyes from the ground, their shaking hands reached out again, and fixed them into eyes, lips, mouths, and bodies. Emotional touch had returned. She would bump into lovers embracing on street corners and blush. She watched women cradle chins and brush hair from children's eyes. Young people were laughing, their fingers intertwined. She would jump from men who had met and trapped their friends in a fierce embrace, hands clapping against skeletal backs and the laughter that would spill over beer mugs. She tried this language with Phillip, and found that it was best to wait until the night had settled and he swam with a slurred tongue. Touch. He would encase her hips in his hands and pull her against him roughly. They could not connect through language or daylight. Instead, they let the blur of the night engulf them.

She would only live in the moment with him, publicly on dance floors and in the wrought iron privacy of bedroom mattresses at night. Distraction and escape, she prayed that soon she could leave Belgium.

The Officer's Mess, a converted hotel lounge, a public dance floor. Voices and music. Phillip and Sophie made their way through the entrance. Phillip curled her hand around his arm and pushed her forwards into the throng of dancing couples. She could not recognize any of the blushing faces and fixated all of her attention on him. He wore his uniform, which was common amongst the men. She found that he emanated strength—pure masculinity—and she felt safe in this aura. Nothing was slender about him, not his body, nor his language or mannerisms. She felt reassured by his prowess, he would let no one take her, she was safe, she was sure. His nationality kept her safe. They entered through the arch of marble and he drowned his blue eyes in beer glasses. She soaked her lips in wine.

They drunkenly tripped out of the hall. Sophie inhaled the cooling autumn air. She felt the damp wet slicken the cobblestones and checked her steps in her high heels. Phillip leaned on her and pulled her against his broad side. He reached around and grabbed her from behind. She squealed. His laughter peeled through the street, bouncing off windows and locked doors.

They walked several blocks before he sank into the darkness and unzipped his pants. She was shamed by the sound of his urinating and crossed the street. She stood before a woman's dress store and noticed her reflection in the white lace and purple blockade. Sophie pulled the lipstick from her clutch and reapplied her lips in the glass. She jumped when she glimpsed the shadow of a man across the street fade into the darkness of an alleyway. The man's frame was too slender to be Phillip's, his height a few feet shorter. She turned sharply and sighed. She saw nothing but shadows and swirling litter.

Phillip suddenly clasped her around the waist and hauled her to him aggressively in a bruising kiss. She gasped and let his mouth crush her. She gripped his shoulders with red lacquered nails and felt a wave of heat burst from the pit of her stomach and settle in her groin. She was taken aback by the sudden rush. Sophie splayed both hands against his chest and pushed him backwards. She looked up into his eyes and swallowed hard. They were rimmed red.

He looked down at her from his icy blue stare, his eyes roving over her body. He licked his lips. A gust of cold air blew up around them and Sophie pulled her coat tighter. Phillip rolled back on his heels and then rocked forwards knocking into her.

"I'm sorry, pardon." His voice was husky and low.

"*C'est d'accord.* It is okay. Taxi?" She shivered, goosebumps hardened along her arms and neck, and she wanted to be wrapped in bed out of the cold.

He blinked, clearing his vision and nodded his head. Phillip smelled snow and missed home. She studied him, he squinted and sucked in his lips, and then heaved a long sigh.

"Let's get married." He slurred. Bewilderment webbed her skull and her face itched.

The abruptness of it all shot her straight into Eli, the inside curve of his elbow and the deep laugh that resonated throughout rooms, his dark eyes. She heard him turning the pages of a book, how he would lick the pad of his finger and turn the paper carefully, a small flutter like a butterfly wing. She wetted her lips in the dark. She could smell lavender rich and pungent. She felt fingers in curls dark and thick. She closed her eyes and listened as warm hands roved over her stomach and thighs. The heat puckered and burst within her and she stared down at Phillip with balling fists. She bit her lip hard and waited, fighting back nausea and hot tears.

"Will you?" He asked her simply and waited. She hovered in question marks that etched insanity into her mind. She felt the silence and knew that this doorway would only stay open for so long.

Projection. Her alone knitting before a window waiting. Her hair had grown silver, laced with a bathrobe and poor hearing. She felt the decades creep by. She feared this projection.

The woman's gnarled bloody body sprawled angular on the ground rose up in her memory. Nazi collaborators axed apart on cobblestone. She couldn't even wait for him, survival. She was still trapped in the crushing war cloud, she needed to run.

"*Oui.* I am yours." His mouth split bearing tiny white teeth, they glowed in the dark. He pulled her under his coat and walked on waiting for a taxi to wave down.

They could not see the eyes weeping in the shadows. How the eyes, dark as chocolate, traced the outline of the soldier and her. A gaunt hand emerged from the dark and angrily forced the tears back, pushing his skin back. He could not endure the pain that split his guts and itched in every one of his fingers. He wanted to throw his head back and scream. He could hear the scream between his ears, how his mouth stretched wide and the blood seared his vision and filled his ears. He lurched backwards and scrambled onto his feet—feral.

The couple did not see the shadow pull itself away into the labyrinth of the city. She could not feel the wet cold of the street as he laid his cheek down and gripped his fingers around the streetcar rails and waited. The curve of skull reflecting street lights, head shaved, the ebony curls she raked her fingers through, gone. She could smell the musk of a Canadian soldier in the dark cocoon of his coat and hear the waves crashing against the boat that would take her to the shores of his New World.

RIPPLE

"for women who are 'difficult' to love"

-Warsan Shire

"you are a horse running alone
and he tries to tame you
compares you to an impossible highway
to a burning house
says you are blinding him
that he could never leave you
forget you
want anything but you
you dizzy him, you are unbearable
every woman before or after you
is doused in your name
you fill his mouth
his teeth ache with memory of taste
his body just a long shadow seeking yours
but you are always too intense
frightening in the way you want him

unashamed and sacrificial
he tells you that no man can live up to the one who
lives in your head
and you tried to change didn't you?
closed your mouth more
tried to be softer
prettier
less volatile, less awake
but even when sleeping you could feel
him travelling away from you in his dreams
so what did you want to do, love,
split his head open?
you can't make homes out of human beings
someone should have already told you that
and if he wants to leave
then let him leave
you are terrifying
and strange and beautiful
something not everyone knows how to love."

STORYTELLER

So much depends on her. She's the hub holding a spinning wheel and she keeps the wagon careening forward with magic.

We lost her, she remained resilient, but the secret of what he took from her that day at Mechelen disrupted our bloodline. Rape is a mechanism of control.

The memory of the tree and what she left behind, sinking into the earth around the base of the trunk, a wheel stopped spinning. Thrown off and left broken, we lost the magic for some time and she carried the guilt and shame stoically.

So much depends on her.

We got lost in the story of the Woman who ate from the Tree of Knowledge, but this is a story about the Tree of Life. We are the Tree of Life.

Hold close. Hold fast. Hold tight.

I reclaim. Pack the pipe. Clear the air. Offerings. Sacred breath. Prayers and blessings. Acknowledge the directions and thank our ancestors, spirit guides, and power animals. We are taking story home.

The tree roots deep. Branches knot with the codes of our DNA, the matrix of creation, each helix strand. No one is alone in this. The magic lies in showing us the ethereal beauty of existence amongst chaos and disorder. The animals are listening and waiting for us to awaken. The plants and rivers are listening and waiting. The winds want you to hear again. She anchors, buds open in pentagram, inverted, we can go home.

We shifted away from what remained. The religious tongues brought perspective of objectivity, positioned humanity outside of Mother Nature, when we were always one.

Gaia Rhythms, the cosmic flow, trees became silent and existed only outside of us, we believed. Knowledge was written over with paper and currency. Societies stopped orienting to the lunar calendar, Mother Earth vibrations. The cycles ran deep, veined within our internal webs, our organic compass. We honoured Gaia in secret.

We circle the Earth—glowing moons, not ants. No, organic satellites. We are drawn to one another, our hues and hearts pulse. Dig deep. Open and awaken. We are Mother root. When we feel each other, when we connect. My Love, we are aquatic honeycombs, lattice-woven and webbed, pyramids. We are one. We are our own.

She drums with reproductive cycles, sings with the life fluid in plants, speaks with animals. She can influence the underground currents, mood swings, emotions. She sends out waves, ripples, she's spinning and weaving divinely.

She returns home, the way water flows.

She pulls on the ocean's tides.

Water seeks home.

She breathes with weather.

She plants light seeds, waters them with sacred tears.

We confused weeping with weakness. Self-victimization. She was cooking, making things grow and transform, a sacred alchemist, leaves from the tree. She showed us grace in her vulnerability, rainbow warrior. Healing wounds, letting spirit through.

We witnessed her exile. Lone spiritual warrior.

She recognized her soul and broke free from the False Matrix.

The winds have changed. They have stayed the same. I hear voices between the branches and stones.

The Goddess story. The Sacred Feminine sings her isolation pain.

Christ Sophia.

Lady of the Lake.

High Priestess.

Lotus and Lily.

Mermaids and Melusine.

The Holy Grail.

Chalice. The Goddess Womb.

Names, they help us reclaim. Words, they help us take back ownership.

We witnessed her face the flames of a generational rage. We carried this rage together for some time.

Daughter, this is not a harsh story. Breathe, fall back, turn, float and glow.

Reclamation can be gentle. We do not have to struggle. Have no fear, hone your essence, and practice patience.

Grace is here.

RIPPLE

"Inside me it is growing, they take what they require, if I don't feed it it will absorb my teeth, bones, my hair will thin, come out in handfuls. But I put it there, I invoked it, the fur god with tail and horns, already forming. The mothers of gods, how do they feel, voices and light glaring from the belly, do they feel sick, dizzy? Pain squeezes my stomach, I bend, head pressed against knees."

-Margaret Atwood, Surfacing

Stencils and residue,
We imprint,
Lovemaking
Tattoos the souls of unborn children,
They are there, karmic patterns,
Spiritual, lovemaking writes
The story of the children you
Have not brought into physicality yet.

Women cradle cosmic wombs in warm hands,

One hand over her heart.
Men dig in and plant a seed that
Becomes an entire family tree.

The vulva, cosmic gateway, the vagina, a passageway,
The egg, microcosm.
More than a fluid exchange,
Consciousness activates the egg,
Soul food, our love feeds the next seven generations.
Waves, we are intimate as oceans and shorelines, beaches,

Assumed for some time that we were defined separations,
Exits and entrances, no, holographic,
Blowing orgiastic bubbles, wasting,
Suds that penetrate and do not pop, blended,
We are one with our lover, we are.
Look into the snake's mouth,
She looks like the intimate
Spaces of women,

When a snake is sick,
It blows bubbles.

We let each other in,
Passion and ecstasy, union and spiral,
Giving and receiving, a relinquishing,
Micros of the macro, we spin galaxies together,
Spiders, our love can hold planets close, our bodies.

Love is designed
To activate souls and spirits through dimensions,
We connect on astral planes, those holy encounters,
We heal each other, because we are born broken.

Empowerment, yes, we teach our minds to be whole,
But we are only surviving that way, without love, well,

We are not alive, just living.

Your spiritual child visits you and wants you to know
Energetic fields are reality, not fantasy,
And we are not primarily physicality.
A Darwinian reduction, deactivated hearts,
Stolen knowledge, our children want us,
They yearn for us.

They choose us, don't underestimate
That if you yearn for a child, that hush of need
Signifies the premeditation of your child
Wanting to come to you, wanting to become.

Sacred unions are birthrights,
Stolen,
Economics, politics, war, religion, patriarchy,
We couldn't comprehend Divine Timing,
Delays can be protection,
Meaningful desire, important,
Conversations with the universe,
From our heart, shapes us,
Choices—that writes our lives.

The child is not physically conceived
Until spirit is ready to incarnate,
When the environment is conducive
To this new life,
When vibrations match,
This story shows you what happens
When we do not honour our vibrations.

THE PAST

The looming façade and breadth of the Gothic building consumed her vision. Sophie craned her neck and tilted her face back, her eyes travelling up the tower. Three hundred and ten feet of brick stacked above. She saw black branches scratching a grey sky. Sophie shook her head and clenched her hands at her sides.

The day was overcast and she was grateful that the sun was not letting any rays down. She approached the stone steps with a stone face. Sophie tilted her face upwards, again. Her gaze rested on the tip of the spire and she swallowed. She could make out the figure of the archangel Michael, a 5-meter-high gilt metal statue.

Michael was the patron saint of Brussels. She remembered her father sitting with her each evening to tell stories and strands of histories. He spoke of Michael with such conviction and holiness.

"The angel Michael had led the army of God against the Devil." He animated the spectacular battle with the swing of his arm and the crashing metal of their swords. Sophie would lean in close to her father's mouth to hear exactly everything he would say about Michael because he spoke softly.

"Michael rose up against the Devil and conquered. He's

remembered as the patron saint of chivalry. *La Chevalerie.*" She did not know what chivalry was. She would not learn or know of chivalry. That opportunity of knowing lost in the grit of teeth of a man in pain staggering under moonlight to get to her, of a man who kicked through the bottom of a cattle car and laid himself down to rest on street rail ties.

Sophie could not remove her eyes from the statue. Phillip discussed arrangements with the car driver. He was unaware of Sophie's upturned face. He could not fathom that she felt Michael's statue gaze upon them, crying. That she was transfixed between layers and far away from him. She could hear her father's voice, smell his aftershave, but could not pull out the courage to connect the narratives, the metaphor and irony. Instead, she stood, flushed, rolled her shoulders backwards and drifted up the stone steps with a stone face after cracking her neck.

Aside from the grey-haired judge and Phillip's Canadian comrade, Robert, and Sophie's landlady, Jean, there were no other witnesses of the ceremony. Jean had found Sophie a simple white dress with long-sleeves and endless buttons punctuated down her back like a gunshot trail. She helped Sophie dress that morning in Sophie's empty apartment. On the same floorboards that Eli had helped Sophie with her stocking's years before, Jean rigidly did up each button lining Sophie's spine. The two women were silent. They really had nothing to say to each other. Their relationship was falsely bound with feigned trust and betrayal.

Sophie's carefully set shoulders, hid the scowling lines webbing Jean's puckered mouth. Perhaps she was silently gloating that Sophie never married the Jew, or that she was gloating over having helped shape this new direction on a road that Sophie was diving head-first into. She needed to run, Jean knew, she was also not safe. When Jean finished buttoning the dress she turned away from Sophie and slid one hand discreetly into her purse. Sophie stood transfixed on those floorboards, absently gazing at herself in the bureau mirror. She wanted to believe that that woman was gone, the one who loved Eli, but she pushed her far down inside, replaced by a white dress and hollow blue eyes, it was life or death and she wanted to live. She let out a gasp of surprise when Jean placed a tiny gold chain around her throat.

"Quel est ce?" What is this for?

"A token of friendship. *L'amitié*. A farewell gift from me," Jean responded while fastening the chain.

Bonjour á St. Martin.

She continued, "Every bride should have something gold."

She turned and embraced Jean. They hugged briefly and let go.

She can only remember the moth flying inside of the caverns of the city hall and she does not know why this flying—the mindless bumping and flapping of it—triggered her.

"I do."

"I do."

A ceremony of strangers. Phillip thought that it was almost not real. When they left the city hall, she saw the black bird again. But, this time, the poor thing, it was rattled. One wing unnaturally back, dilapidated. Broken, it cried out to her as she walked by with a stone face.

RIPPLE

"We have travelled far with ourselves
and our names have lengthened;
we have carried ourselves
on our backs, like canoes
in a strange portage, over trails…
seeking the edge, the end,
the coastlines of this land."
-Gwen MacEwen, The Portage

Military protocol, he was to return first,
She was to follow: apple trees, branches, and ribs.

When he left the Old World,
He came home.

He took the wedding ring off
Because it felt like a game.

He didn't expect her
To survive the Canadian portage.

THE PAST

The army plane rocked, the turbulence lifted Sophie from her seat, pushing her against her seatbelt. She gulped. Anxiety and fear lit her nerves afire, and she closed her eyes, keeping her tears private. The plane was relatively small, seating twenty people. Sophie boarded the plane swallowing an anxious knot, she'd never ridden in an airplane before.

She was directed to sit beside a tight-faced woman in an army-green uniform. Sophie assumed that the woman worked for the air force. She timidly smiled at the woman who stared stonily back at her. Sophie turned away embarrassed and gazed around the interior of the plane. She knew that look and knew not to push the woman. Panic rose up in her throat.

Il n'y a pas de parachutes. Flustered, she turned to the woman.

"Où sont nos parachutes?" Where are our parachutes? She asked, her voice small. The uniformed Woman chuckled and shook her head with humour. Sophie felt like a fool for asking and burned up with embarrassment.

She turned her face to the window and remained huddled against the interior, not daring to even look at the woman throughout the remainder of the flight.

The engines gunned to life. White knuckled fingers clenched

the armrests. She couldn't fathom the speed of the craft as it lifted up into the air after shooting down the runway like a bullet. The trajectory and incline, she vomited in her mouth and the fear of looking weak in front of that woman forced her into a guttural swallow.

Je vais mourir. I'm going to die.

She fixed her eyes on the shrinking landscape and clamped her jaw shut in order to silence her gasps of fear. When the plane settled in the air and continued on at a stable angle, she could study the green fields behind her and expanse of grey water below her.

When I return now, I will be a visitor. *Je vais être un visiteur.*

She cried. But, she couldn't forget the image of that woman axed and dead. She cried harder and sucked in her moans.

London was an island misted, wet like the ocean filling her insides and leaking out. The rain continued to beat down on the city the entire week that Sophie was there. She was constantly affronted with the sounds, the smells and tastes of that city. London seemed louder, crowded, and bustling.

Sophie remained inside the hotel that had been converted into a house for war-brides. The hotel was beautiful, extravagant in furnishings and fixtures. She hadn't seen such wealth since before the war had started. When her car first pulled up in front of the magnificent building, Sophie hid her appeal in fear that she'd betray her homeland. Although the architecture was grand, Sophie soon realized that the women dwelling within such a gleaming exterior were poverty-ridden.

After one week, the brides were taken by train to Liverpool. In Liverpool, she boarded a large steamer, the *Mauritania*. She cupped a moment of relief—the first since the plane ride.

No plane. Relief.

She stood with cold hands locked on the rail and gazed out at the unbreakable horizon subtly dividing a grey ocean and sky. The bustle behind her faded while she studied the water. White-capped waves rolled towards her, consistent, rising and cresting while falling back into the expanse of ocean. Disappearing for a moment then rising again. Lines. Parallel lines moving without connection.

She saw people, their bodies rolling in those waves. The ones who came before. Hands entangled with tiny fingers of reaching babies, Mothers dragged out to sea and those that sank into the depths. She saw soldiers, their blood coursing and inking the salt-water red. All sorts of bodies with different skin. She shivered and pulled her shawl tighter. A long mineral wind blew across the surface of the water blotting Sophie's eyes. She squinted and inhaled deeply. The air tasted like pungent sweat, of a man turning in sheets stained and tangled. Sophie lifted her hands from the railing allowing her palms to splay pale in front of her eyes. She studied the lines and swell of skin.

She remembered her father, that gentle man who had believed in things extraordinary. He read to Sophie, his voice plucking the words from imaginary pages, enthralling the watery-eyed child. Once he set the book down and picked up her hands.

"Did you know that your hands say so much, Sophie?" He began tracing his fingertips along the lines of her palms.

"This is your lifeline, see how long it is, that is good, look how it extends around the side of your hand, and mine reaches just past the curve of my thumb. You will live long Sophie." His thumb caressed the line.

"You see these lines, the ones that border your fingers. These are your love lines." He met her confused gaze with warm eyes and a smile. His mustache pulled upwards revealing a full bottom lip and curling chin. Sophie giggled while pinching her toes and pressing her feet against each other.

"This one is the deepest and it is the first line. You will love fiercely the first time—that is usually how it goes." His eyes suddenly clouded and lowered. He tucked her hands under the covers.

She traced the lines of her palm on the deck, the waves lapped against the hull of the ship. She noticed how deep the one line crossed her palm and then was suddenly severed. A hairline breadth from the first line began another line less noticeable, but very crooked. She knew then what her Father had realized all those years ago, that her life would be caught up in something large and fierce, that she would love the first time, but then this love would be cut off abruptly and another would enter and render her unstable. She almost smiled. She looked out onto the ocean and curved her chest around the wind.

The waves remained consistent, rising and falling, and this reassured her. She did not gasp when she saw her own body rolling along the surface. Her hair fanned out around her face, a glowing halo. Her lips, blue and purple. Eyes, open and gaping. She looked into the hazel rings and knew that there were many stories braided into the tiny bands. She felt relieved in a way that she was with the other bodies in the sea, a community of the wet soaked souls that the Atlantic consumed. She was not alone.

The woman in the water rolled face first in the current. Her dress opened like an umbrella, and Sophie saw that clasped to her back was a tiny baby. The baby's hair was dark and matted, the small oval face frozen in a serene stare. She knew he would have dark curls. The bodies continuously spiraled in the waves, a gentle cycle that revealed both the hazel eyes and delicate furled arms of the newborn. Sophie was transfixed and she stood motionless on the ship. Her eyes shifted from side to side as she locked onto the rolling mother and child. They bobbed and folded with the current, eventually disappearing beyond the horizon.

She felt at peace, no fear, no sense of loss or deep regret because they were there, she knew now, they were there. They existed.

Instead she wetted her lips and tasted salt in the air. She ran her fingers through her hair pulling back her hands draped in seaweed. She laughed and threw the green strands over the edge. She smoothed her dress and pressed her fingers into her pockets.

She was not surprised when grains of sand cascaded across the deck when she pulled her hands back out. She slowly unfurled her fist and smiled at the white of a shell nestled in her palm. She was calm and bewildered in the same breath because rolled into the curve of the shell was a red leaf with pointed edges. She did not know it was a Maple leaf, she twirled the leaf between her fingers letting the silk of the leaf brush her throat. She leaned far over the railing and with a sudden arc let the leaf fall into the air. It looped and circled before laying down on the water's surface. She stayed there, eyes roving, the leaf floated away.

STORYTELLER

Our story is migration. Shadows of our character and identity. Self-conceptualization vibrates with the events and communities formed on, around, in, above, and beyond the Atlantic.

We are collective. We are individual.

As Women, we carry emotional and spiritual shells of our relationships that are inhabited and dug deep down into the earth beneath water.

The war-bride narrative is owned nationally, but, in that owning, our Women became spliced between two separate worlds. Child, let me show you how these Women could meet in the middle and find love there. I have had enough of this story about war disrupting families, that Women take care of the victims of war, that they perpetrate its vicious cycle further, that they are also bystanders of their own lives. Reclaim.

She came from across the ocean, alone, trembling into a world unlike one she had ever dreamt of before. Imagine the sense of separation, the pounding of the waves against the hull of a ship in which she endured sleepless nights filled with frightful imaginings. The steamer steadily disappearing into the fog, dragging her along, powerless to stop it. I imagine that she held herself motionless in darkened corners, remaining composed. Stoic in small cabins cramped with other young

Women, most with shrieking sick infants. She must have wept over the stricken departure from home privately. The abrupt line that was drawn between here and there forever etched in her consciousness. She hovered in departures that split identity. She lived between ideas so she could tell me the world from either side, perhaps this was how she found home again.

Aside from the troubles vining up inside her head, your Great-Grandmother was stricken with hunger. Food had been sparse for so long; their bodies had shrunk. She remembers a time when starvation was reality and these bodies could not take in food that came with liberation. Everyone aboard the ship was stricken with hunger, hunger to survive, to endure a New World, and leave behind the war-torn sorrows of the last.

Your Great-Grandmother traveled through her own doorway of no return, much like the robbed souls who entered through an invisible doorway on the throbbing shores of Goree Island. Be wary and cautious of comparison, we risk hypocrisy and unethical analysis. Especially when they tell us later that the door did not exist, that the door was a garbage shoot. Regardless of the flaw in the story—unreliable narrators. Slavery cannot be compared to migrating white war-brides.

Yet, what about that one story, the Women story? What about it?

The ocean is complex. So are our Women. So are our Men. The feminine, her story, it was also colonized, subordinated, cast out, and we have lost the power of a beautiful love for ourselves and truly upholding the capacity of our bodies. Before monotheism, we were connected directly to spirit. We were the portal that birthed between the spiritual and the physical. We are a diaspora of ourselves. Woman.

We connect emotions to our historical narratives and past identities and our concept of the perimeter and chronology of an event. Everything is emplotment. Nothing is original because we are one and we are creating together for one, for all, for ourselves. The story is always changing, it breathes and lives. The reception and spread of knowledge. If anything, we can only hold on to our memories, pockets of our existence to inform the present. Balance and grounding: we can learn not to let plot dictate love and our lives. Learn how to let it go.

The ocean, a shared space of lost humanity. If there was ever separation. Yet, we do not remain a part of it and stay alive that way. She arrived in Canada with a tired soul, or a soul brimming to the point she dare not speak any of it or else it would come crashing out of her. A fearful soul. Paranoia. No, she was a cookie-cutter, she'd face the rest of her life spitting out perfectly shaped candied-emotions that could make a mouth ache. Survival.

She arrived in 1946 to the sight of jutting cliffs and clouds swollen with thunder and lightning. The shores of Halifax were the tumultuous arms that would cradle her into the new world.

Pier 21, her name remains inscribed there. I think. Maybe we will journey to Halifax one day to try and find her name listed among the thousands. We can run our fingers over the letters. Maybe we will be able to know her differently, then, to pluck the absence in her story right out from underneath her.

What is left out is what is important.

Just like Ellis Island in New York, Pier 21 was also the primary landing spot for all immigrants in Canada. Originally called the deep-water terminal, Pier 21 was damaged by the fateful Halifax explosion in 1917. Devastation. Chaos. Carnage. Looting. 1924 ushered in the Pier's rebirth, facilities adjoining the south end railway station in a luminous and spacious structure. A complex of connected buildings, these services, Immigration Services, Customs, Health and Welfare, Agriculture, the Red Cross, kitchen, dining room, supplies canteen, nursery, hospital, detention center, dormitories, and airing gallery.

It was an entrance for thousands of immigrants during the Second World War, as well as a trembling exit for those leaving.

History is of comings and goings. Of the permanency and temporary residue of family lines. I've tried to carve them into a tree, but the bark has grown thick. Trees also grow around barbed-wire.

Here is a story.

494,874 service personnel embarked from these shores for a war-torn European landscape. 50,000 would not live to return home. The Pier also saw the arrival of 3,000 British children who had been living in the most heavily-bombed areas of Britain as part of the Children's Overseas Reception Board. And the war had come close, not only returning to us in the stencils of shell shock shaking bodies running back home. To those traumatized arriving with open dead eyes. The German U-Boats lurked our coastlines like sharks, picking off supplies. Halifax was a blackout city. Your great-grandfather, the farmer, he told me as a little girl that if the war had continued for even a matter of weeks more, we could have lost. Imagine. What would the world look like today? Daughter, how much different or similar would it be? The victory call came on May 8th, 1945, Halifax was taken over for twenty-four hours of mob rule and looting.

Her arrival was a blur: officials, papers, government stamps, raised eyebrows, and tight, controlled mouths, and row upon row of solitary women who either sat or raggedly stood with frozen faces. Respect and acknowledge that she was not sprayed green like the Jewish survivors who arrived. After navigating through the bureaucratic Canadian maze your great-grand-mother arrived three days later at the train station in Belleville, Ontario.

She told me this. Your great-grandfather met her at the station and took her out for a light breakfast. The streets along the way were crowded with cheering crowds. The entire city was celebrating the return of the soldiers of the Hastings and Prince Edward counties. People thronged the streets of Bridge and Pinnacle, waving to the marching soldiers. Many streets were closed off which gave her an otherworldly first-impression of Belleville. Unlike the simple bustle of a pre-war Belleville, the immense noise and unceasing crowds convinced your great-grandmother that Belleville was very similar to the thriving rhythm of La Grande Place. She was disoriented thinking that this BayShore city would be her new home, she had been mistaken.

Envision her eyes, how the pupils would dilate, or become pinpricks with the tangle of landscape beyond the car's windows. She found herself suddenly inside this culture while being apart from it. Imagine, unable to speak English comfortably, your great-grandmother was unable to participate.

Pay attention to silence—to what is not said. The story cannot always roll around in our mouths, we must tell it with our eyes and ears too. Our bodies. We must feel it first. You see, she absorbed the landscape through sounds and textures, the milk-underbelly of a frog, or the muffled cry of a train away in the distance. Her inability to speak, to express and understand, dropped her into a world of strangers, even in her most intimate spaces. She clamped her mouth shut and opened her eyes and fingertips to her alien world.

After a breakfast of bitter coffee and stale croissants, your great-grandfather drove her farther north in his spacious Cadillac. Her north trek, journey, kidnapping, quite figuratively, could be conceived as a literal tipping over an edge, a border of a civilization from a world she knew to the unforgiving rock underbelly and the peoples who could survive the Canadian Shield. She vocalized it many times to me, she wanted to go back, she didn't want to stay in Madoc and start over, she wanted back and she rejected fully enmeshing or accepting this new life.

She was Canadian.

She would always be Belgian first.

I tried to show her the family that she had created and the lives she brought into the world here. But, she was trapped in a cinematic loop of her life during the war. When she boarded that boat, before that, when she followed his blood up the stairs and collapsed on the inside of her door, or knocked into the Canadian, before her father orphaned her and her Mother perished, she was always managing severe trauma. A pain that manifested like an underwater rock ocean bottom that nothing in her control could grow on.

Daughter, don't misconstrue it either, The Canadian Shield is not an edge, it is a zone, and just as the forest will reclaim the abandoned and forgotten barn, that northern jungle will completely consume it.

He lived in a wooden house on Russel Street in a mining village. Russel Street was not Brussels. Imagine that you were her, you've moved from one of the biggest European cities in the world, to land in a town you could miss if you merely blinked at the wrong moment. The displacement must have been defeating. The complete sense of loneliness must have consumed her. Locked loops, not sacred spirals or hoops.

Perhaps you'd abandon your native culture and assimilate, but she did not. Her story is slippery as a Black River stone riverbed. She is a wild frontier. You cannot sleep with a man to survive that wilderness. You also cannot own a wild frontier Woman like you cannot own the Canadian Shield.

The Women that led to you, they were strong, and they were their own army. Warriors. She remained the Belgian in Madoc for the duration of her life. A middle ground was unattainable. Stopping the loop would be like venturing into a bloodied no-man's-land.

War disrupts family. War disrupts Self.

The dislocation your great-grandmother felt transcended bloodlines. It clung to pain. You must prepare for when their memories will clasp your hands tightly and pull you forward. Because, our Women, they survive too.

RIPPLE

amongst the tangled sumac,
the waxy-leafed poison ivy,
on top the Moira Lake hill,
there was an old fire pit.

the stones circled a blanket
of moss, a fossilized social
gathering.

invisible communities,
as natural as the ritual of a name,
mapped lives,
birthmarks led them to names, they will
remember your vibration,
the next seven generations
will hold them.

tree trunks
whisper to
stones, oral histories,
written from colonial drudgery,
until she awakened to vibrations,

non-verbal language, spirit,
until she let it in,
even in this land,
culture is living, story is alive,

especially here,
the wind sweeps up,
blades rush, moon crests
and faces a setting sun, a nocturnal
sigh, fireflies, the faded circle abrupt,
assimilated.

Crow plays, Crow cries.
if we know how to listen, practice patience,
"take care," she screeches, "take care,"
Crow flies between, around,
ladders and treetops, skyscraper cuts,
watch Crow circle, come down,

dips left to an underground trickle,
talking, walking, coming-to-know,
Knower and Known,
awake, she's in your neighborhood,
listen to the echo of her repertoire.

STORYTELLER

"Listening, I feel like it is more than I could now reasonably have expected out of life, for he has spoken with such anger and such tenderness."

-Margaret Laurence, The Stone Angel

Before I take you to her, I mean, before I show you her new life in the New World, I think, you must know of deeper layers. The memory of contact between the settler man and the indigenous peoples. The People walking in balance. These encounters, however distant temporally and culturally, comprise the tongued buds of your geographical palate. Fisted crackling leaves pushed them into the crevices of thoughts. The connections, pool deep, a clavicle of memories that vibrate pain. Travelling through the very marrow of your bones, rubbing the story raw because there is so much death.

They existed on the land, nomadic formations that bore them ears that cupped migratory winds, footprints in mud that smelled of the strongest hunger. They followed the smells with song, a long low thrum that swept beneath the wings of birds.

The originals, the People, they existed as a Divine order, sacred and organic, one with the land we walk on now. Dynasty was the rings of trees of histories and families, bloodlines. They hunted the woods with respect, leaving prayers and love from what they took, fishing rivers clear and magnificent. They forged the hills with weapons made from stone, leather, and wood. These projectiles and spearheads were granite rock, then they glistened quartzite, and finally were made of slate. You will find one of these spearheads protruding from sand on top of that hill with the fire pit. That is how you will know they were there, and that land was not always yours, or his, or hers. You will bend down, pull the weapon from the ground in magenta rhapsody, you will pocket survival and endure.

These remnants, life pillars not corroded or broken down by water and wind, came from the quarries of the Sagonaska. Yes, my Daughter, tongue the names and sing the lines of change, of domination. What I want you to know, to hear from the inner thrumming from my soul to you is that you should not take your location for granted. You must turn around, shake your head, and scribe the changing names into one Mason jar of legacy. This river is the veined existence of our Women, it penetrates beyond rock and ash, before the white man filled it with toxins, before it was over-fished and saturating the edges of daydreams, of dreamtime, of generations of Women who stood planted on that hill and eyed water through the branches and wanted to go home.

Sagonaska was tongued by Loyalist settlers who habited lands north of the border during the Civil War. The Mississauga natives, the ones who were before, knew of the river as Sagonashkokan. Can you see how names are not innate, are not only contingent on evolution? Rather, they are the outcome of domination, pulleys and gears of manipulation rotating by dominating hands. You will know this river as Moira, in Ojibwe, "tipped canoe," a life or death portage, a beautiful female sound that captivated your Great-Grandmother. I know this river as a feminine spirit, not the artificial identity of Singleton's River or

Meyer's Creek. The River Moira belongs to the Women of this family whose souls drained into her shallow belly. There were only so many tears that could be spilled there.

Yes, the first peoples that walked this land were coined Mississauga by historians. As members of the Chippewa Tribes, their presence stretched from the shores of the Bay of Quinte north of Moira Lake. It was very difficult for me to try and show you their voice, which is important. Instead, I met them in Moodie's colonial pages, embossed in literary genius that was appallingly contradicting to me. She found these peoples to be "small of stature, with very coarse and repulsive features."

They had names for us, the settlers, as well. There is a story of the name-changing of Moira Lake that is an unbridled tale of encounter. A band of Iroquois natives renamed the lake, Hog Lake. The white man had come and fished the waters of Moira for the golden dore pickerel. They came during the spawning season, indiscriminately fishing and depleting the shallow lake of pickerel. They scooped the fish from the rapids of the creeks and rivers emptying into Moira and carted the fish away by the oxcart full. The Iroquois were angered and robbed, the pickerel having been given to them from the Great Spirit of the Manitou, the settler fishers did not care, and they belittled the peoples while anticipating only a cooked dinner and money in their pockets.

This conflict could possibly have demanded the first game protection law in Upper Canada, but this is also story. To protect the rapidly dwindling stocks of fish, the game law was enacted to prohibit overfishing. The government appointed a squad of fish policemen with firearms, all European, to prevent their fellow settlers from taking the fish on the spawning beds.

Daughter, this led to favouritism. The policemen ruled the waters, exercising their hegemony to take the fish for themselves, for their friends.

The Iroquois lost their right to a sacred means of livelihood and this destabilized the people.

Yes, this is the language that grew up in the underbrush of

the New World that your Great-Grandmother was pushed into. Do not be fooled that such language, what I learned in the dusty lecture halls, was the linguistic seed of eugenics, but was not isolated only within the Old World. It is essential for you to know how encounters actually looked, because this thread is sewn into your collective existence and how your family grew out of this soil.

Humans were seen from the outside, analyzed like bacteria under the microscope. Moodie noted their "low foreheads" which could only be fathomed as an equivalent of their intellectual faculties, of their capabilities within a land so rugged that the European man cupped malefic hands in front of iron stoves while the indigenous man pressed his blade into the deer's hide and prayed inwards for nourishment and respect. Do not let these narratives wire your understanding of where you came from, you are much more than that.

You, like me, like the other Women who came before us, will feel souls beneath faces. You will listen to the story that was glazed over by the dominant pen. I want you to know exactly how our story came to be written from these lands, and what these lands meant to others.

Most do not know, or if they do, have rendered these origins myth, that the very four corners we drove through every day of our rural lives in Madoc, was originally an indigenous encampment. The core of that mining village grew from a native dwelling at the downtown spectre, today, the intersection of Durham and St. Lawrence streets with that red-flashing-light.

Legend has it that a battle took place between the Mohawks and the Mississauga Natives here. Now, the tires relentlessly press down, cementing existence with automotive tunnels. There is no knowledge for the first souls that survived in this space, of this land. Sacred breath.

Where they kept a fire lit. Where she dried the fish not two feet away, smoking the dried meat on wooden racks tied together with animal hide. He cannot envision such beginnings, how his shadow covers peeling scales and carved bone used as a needle for sewing. How there was a small lake where Deer Creek now crashes over rock.

They knew the land differently than the colonials, and now, what we know of the land today. They smelled soil and knew which way to find water. They forged the woodland interior with canoes, birch bark pieces waterproofed and built with wise fingers. When the herds and animals left, they followed them, memorizing the imprints of their migrations, the fleshy end of a bent limb, and the moist scent of upturned moss. They knew each change intimately.

It is crucial, my Girl, that I am honest with you. As best as I can be. We are the takers and not the givers. You must live with this legacy and seek to braid every conscious strand of your existence into this narrative with respect for their origins. For their suffering. Acknowledging that there was a genocide in the New World of the indigenous peoples. Scales need to balance for some time.

I need you to be an open mind with a critical eye to revert stereotypes, to dig truthfulness from the crustaceans of lies that have grown up fern-like over the centuries.

Let me pull your attention to a story that is ancient, our New World Babylon, no, farther. I go back to Mesopotamia in research and writing. No, farther back. We were here too. There are petroglyphs in Peterborough, our backyard, Kinoomaage-wapkong, "The Teaching Rocks," and they will reveal knowing of the future. The New World is the Old World.

Create-or-perish, the sculpting hand, busy against mortal fear, callous-grips-gneiss-hammer, Peterborough Petroglyphs, abraded into solid crystalline face. Five to nine thousand years ago. Nine hundred figures: zoomorphic, anthropomorphic, geomorphic, celestial, turtles, snakes, birds, human figures.

Others perched, majestic, on boats.

We grew up on holy ground.

The sun carved shadow puppets against sculptor's spine, wondered if they would read between the aesthetic order of that language, hollows, crevices, seams of the rock itself, the telling hung between, ears-cup-drip-below, underworld entrance, symbolic womb, words are magic, what they say happens, the journey of water, women in cycle, men in harvest, sculptor shaves Thunderbirds, horned-serpent-Mishipeshu-creeps, sculptor fears not because all is as it is. Petroglyphs teach, turn back to forest, crack neck bones, keep scraping, it's for the future, this story.

Hieroglyphics. Petroglyphs. Ancient maps.

We did not realize how old this land was. We did not know the people who lived here before we invaded.

Our people came and they mapped this land, stenciling over another civilization. Worlds existing in parallel. There was a spiritual democracy in place and a political governing system amongst nations that maintained peace. Think of a map, my Daughter, their purpose and creation. Maps are charted by the powerful. They are visual narratives of a conquering and possessive mentality. The borders and radiuses that pound unrealistic straight lines into this land were drawn by a hand that forgot The People. The hand ignored the pull of a conscience, in how the swoop of a wrist erased where they gathered and told stories. How the bend of the river was needed for maneuvering the hunting party and that the linear border severed ancient formations.

At first, they kept the indigenous names, let them exist on the first maps. Moodie wrote about The People and how they regarded these maps. She saw delight in their faces, to see the landmarks and waterways they knew like the back of their hand splayed across the paper. She looked from a position of textual literacy, that her people had drawn the map, had taken the minutiae pains to record each detail with precision.

Daughter, be wary of those that try to own on the page. Do not be fooled, the page is not life, is not the air that you inhale or the salt tears that pour from your eyes. Do not let paper own you. There is a difference between words, and thoughts, and feelings, and actions. When all align and are braided harmoniously, authentically with your essence, Child, then, you are magic and you are making magic.

What you think, your world becomes.

What you are is what you attract.

What you say becomes what is.

I want you to learn from those who behaved out of sync with essence and became lost in the aggressive juxtaposition.

I want you to know exactly what happened before our family arrived. What this land was we grew up on. We do not deny our imperfections, the Women of this family, no, instead, we can relate to impoverishment and dominance. So, can the men. They are tired. The bruise on the cheek, heart, and spirit risk fading, but, when the name-changers slide invisible into knowledge, emit that oracle-shriek, that banshee wail, show them your Fleur-fanged-grimace, and rewrite, reclaim.

They attempt to own, to place themselves as the winner. No one wins when one is suffering and one is in pain. No one gets left behind and every single one is wanted on the voyage.

Remember that on May 31st, 1819 there was a provisional surrender by the Mississauga Natives of the claims to their land in the townships of Marmora, Madoc, Elzevir, Grimsthorpe, Tudor Lake, Wollaston, Limerick and Cashel. I will not let you be ignorant my Child, their surrender altered your lifeline, too.

RIPPLE

There is a tree, it suspends me.

A portrait, a moor, the first pomegranate tree, lost innocence, a turning, a lightning bolt that shot right through and
split it open.

From earth, back to earth.

Without ending, without beginning,

Circles and hoops, sacred spirals.

As above, so below.

I continue, charcoal seared fibers, others tried to carve
history into it, her story, she forgot that healing would not
happen until she extended, spoke story beyond the lightning
storm, gave future generations of backs leaning against the tree a
language of planting roots, of grounding, clasped hands against
wombs, intertwined destinies.

The Tree of Life. Bloodlines. Infinite Regression.

The thunderous clap. Power outage. A searing that lifted
nostrils. Forced them outside to look for the one that was hit.

Eyes roving tumultuous skies. They find her struck, split
straight down the center. Learning curves, lengthening, shortening, or replacing names, like the snake shedding her skin,
memory can be as simple as a leaf falling, or the gnash that the
entire entity grows around.

She was.
She will.
She is
the same sane woman.
Women.
A tree grows through and around barbed wire fences.

THE PRESENT

There was no stone, no marking, or indication. She could not possibly have conceived that under that tree, there was a burial.

The soil had sponged the bones clean decades earlier, sinking the corpse deep in roots and nitrogen. Settled.

She did not know this.

Packed down in violence of the most oppressive nature, the bones, like a crystal, contained a painful song emitting vibrations, signals, and ripples. Dead light. Cold, a wet bonfire.

Only nature could remember, show memory. The grass would not grow over. Worms would not forge the grave with tunnels and decay. Not this one. Not here. The mound, the hill, and the tree encased the story. Only the soil would clean.

Nelle was little then with long caramel coloured hair braided down her back. She never wanted her hair down, falling thickly against the curve of her spine, because it felt heavy, it got in her way. She could not play. She could not run. Others would not leave it alone with their braiding and combing. She wanted space.

Each morning she willed her mother to brush the sheet of brown hair until her scalp glistened and burned. Then, her mother would grip her hair at the base of her neck and pull her head backwards, chin hovering below the ceiling, Nelle's eyes watered as her mother folded the long strands together in an excruciating tight braid that pulled Nelle's temples high, displacing cheek bones.

She then thundered from the house only to return at dusk with a frayed and dishevelled braid. With raw skinned knees and a fiery spirit, Nelle roamed that hill with an eye that remembered and owned.

She accepted that the hill was not her beginning, though she had resisted it at first. Her family had built a house in town when she was three, one with stairs and rooms to play in. There she had a close circle of friends that she would run along with, transforming the street into a hockey arena, the woods their underworld village, until her father relocated the family to the hill. In a frenzied cloud of renovation and further isolation that had fogged the quiet streets of the village on moving day, Nelle's family cupped the stillness of the hill in their ears.

The remoteness of the hill was bleak, and Nelle had to become accustomed to playing alone. This was when she learned that she could disappear, magician-like. She spent hours amongst the long grasses that broke in shaded torrents across her bemused face, spine sunken into the soft earth, she slept in air, and licked crushed berries from her fingers. This was how she spent summer, proudly waterlogged in her swimming suit, outside, the heat and chlorine snaking the silk from her skin. She would awaken, eat, and run.

On this day, she was bored, jaded from the games that only she could participate in, make-believe skits with her mute dolls and plastic Fisher Price kitchen set. She would not play pretend today or run barefoot across sticky pine needled forest floors. She was tired of cleaning the relentless sap from her soles stickering the tiled floors of the bungalow. Her natural concoctions of sumac and snake berries that she spoon-fed to painted mouths were not entertaining either.

Rather, today Nelle was determined to construct a fort by herself in the woods. The anticipation of her own secret space pulsed delirium through her veins. The sun baked the back of her neck red while she sat and sketched the outline of her fort with a blue pencil crayon. The paper wrinkled and began to crease brown where her hands pressed down hard. The pencil crayon began to slip between her fingers, wet from sweat, scratching the page with dysfunctional and random lines. Nelle furrowed her eyebrows in concentration, not noticing her tongue glistening and bitten tight by her teeth. She would occasionally throw her long braid behind her back; spread her tiny hands over the page and check to see if she was alone.

She rolled her drawing up and slid it into her purple book bag. Nelle slung the sack onto her back and made her way towards the garage. A warm breeze lifted several stray hairs around her face and she pushed them away with her palms. The long rings of a tree frog pierced from the branches overhead and she stopped instantly crooning her face upwards towards the green canopy.

She envisioned the tiny green body. The transparent membrane of the frog's vocal sac is expanding and contracting like a balloon. Astounded how such a small body could project a gripping shriek that halts the forest of flurry into remission, Nelle reached up and dragged her fingers across the hard ridges of her esophagus. She sighed.

The garage was moist and reeked of mildew and gasoline. She relished the damp air, how it clung to her neck and temples. Her ears rang within the sudden transition from the thrumming air to the hollow of the garage and she tried to shake the white noise from her head. Nelle found her dad's hammer and a box of nails. The nails were thick and difficult to strike into the bark. She did not know to look for thinner nails. She did not know how to grip the hammer, how to bring it down in a solid crack on the nail's head. Instead, she pinched her thumb while feathering the hammer over the nail's head in a rhythm of rapid weak strikes.

Nelle will not build a fort today. It has already been built, and she only needs to stumble upon it.

She tramped through the long grass behind the house

following the deer trails that had been there since before she became aware that they were trails. She assumed her brother's large feet pressed the grass down, or her father's work boots. She did not listen close enough to the soft thud of deer hide connecting with soil, and how it took many trips of stepping feet to carve out the trails. She can only see sneakers and work boots at the front door and assumes that those would be the only soles transforming the landscape there.

There is a rusted wire fence that severs the trail. Nelle knew that the best place to hop the fence was several meters to the left where someone placed an old bed box frame against the fence causing it to sag and eventually flatten. Nelle leaped up onto the box frame pumping her legs making the fence squeak and bounce. She howled with laughter and bounded into the air and landed with a resounding thud on the other side.

Pushing cobwebs from her face and trying her best to ignore the stinging nettle scrapes along her hands and wrists, she migrated through the long grasses and tangled sumac trees, then reached the clearing at the crest of the hill and spread her arms wide like a bird in flight. She circled the boulder that rested in the center of the clearing and abruptly stilled. Then she could see her Mother.

The woman wore a long black skirt and flowing crimson blouse that wavered delicately in the breeze. Her blonde hair pulled back in a white banana clip emphasized her cheekbones and the blush crept down her neck. She was beautiful, a blonde Madonna. She whispered into her mother's ear, "I don't like you sitting here."

Her mother was embarrassed and shifted on the boulder attempting to hide her tear-streaked face and red eyes. She turned her back to Nelle, wet her fingertip and flipped a page in her book without speaking. The cover of the book was gnarled and torn. The pages yellow and smelled of the dust and crumbs inside her mother's leather purse.

Nelle has secretly read from her mother's books before. There are always men and women on the covers in a tangle of silks and hair. Their mouths seem warm and speak to each other in crescendos of contours and shadows. Nelle likes how the books take her places, a departure from the mendacity of her parents' guarded conversations. These books fill her with language, history, and longing she never imagined existed between men and women, and even as a little girl she understands the purpose.

Nelle knows that her mom lives another life in the pages of those books, that in her mind she is participating and not observing. She is taken to other worlds. Escapism. The writing style of this genre allows her to smoothly transition to these other worlds. She is no voyeur, but the subject, the woman who is loved. She wishes that her father could love her mother like the stories in those books.

Nelle circled the boulder again running her palm along the crusted lichen. She stepped up on top of the boulder shuffling her rubber boots so she would not slip off. When she gained balance, she raised her head and viewed the meadow from this height. The clearing was a peaceful grass plain, the hill rolling out before her, steep and enticing. The highway jutted sharply in the background echoing of rubber car tires that connected with the asphalt. She turned slowly, putting her back against the highway and studying the forest. She could not penetrate the underbrush and knew that it would be foolish to clear a fort there.

The mound and striking tree resonated with such force Nelle felt hit when she came upon it. Her eyes explored the dips and bows of the tree. Excitement wrapped tightly around her spinal column, rushing adrenaline coursed up her torso prickling her cheeks.

I will build there.

She felt flight rise up and take hold of her arms as she ran through the clearing towards the bent trunk and towering branches. The hammer and nails knocked metallic against each other while she ascended the slope digging the toes of her boots into the earth and clawing her way upwards. She reached the top, panting, and leaned close against the trunk of the tree, beaming at her new vantage point.

The cusp of Moira Lake bled against the shoreline to her left, glinting through the trees to spread wide again like glass near her right. The highway curled between the two folds of the lake, knocking traffic along its cracks and corners. Her hill edged the highway and lake intimately but rose above this topography in an unnatural state of authority. Nelle eyed the roof of her house and thought of her family inside, rotating and shifting amongst each other.

Nelle could not know exactly that there were others who had settled their backs against the same tree staring out at Moira Lake just as she did. 1615 was a tumultuous year, and the hill remembers. It was winter and inhumanely cold. Champlain and his comrades were running from the Iroquois. They could not remain on the shores of the Bay of Quinte so they escaped inland, channelling the rocky bed of the Sagonashkokan until they found Moira and the hill. They built shelters out of pine branches and held blackened hands up to campfires. The pits remain, corroded faded circles with depths of moss and seared rock that Nelle does not notice. She does not realize how close she is to history.

The first peoples were also mound builders. Camouflaged with the brush and foliage, the white man did not know of the mounds at first. In August of 1859, T.C. Wallbridge opened five of the mounds located along the shores of the Bay of Quinte revealing burials. With his eye of expedition and tools of excavation, Wallbridge measured bone and skull. Angled fragments of fresh water shelled in the light and arced against his forehead. There were the lumps of iron ochre and sliver of an eagle breast bone. But these were the mounds by the Bay, not the one by Moira.

Nelle shrugged out of her backpack and impatiently lobbed the braid behind her shoulders. She peeled off her rubber boots and let them fall beside the bag. A small olive tan hand pushed stray hairs tickling her temples back, and she idled down against the tree. Nelle tapped her toes against a whitened rock nestled with several others in a vague circle and plumped her nostrils to the breeze coursing up from the shore amongst the crevices of the hill. She smelled the acid bitter of dandelion spit and the softening tar from the hardtop driveway, veneered in washed-ashore rotting fish carcasses and boat gasoline.

Cocooned against the tree she was not expecting a story. Connection. A conversation between a body, sacred and feminine, a tree, a spiritual well.

A foreign language without words. Vibrations. Like picking up a thread and following, spinning that thread around fingers and wrist until the source is found. All along that thread, like a live-wire, telephone, open and awakening. Body is conduit for spirit. Perspective is a gateway. Portal. Images. Communication before verbal behaviour. Feeling.

Tree showed her.

She heard footsteps. Breathe. Echo. A strange wind rushed through. Another woman, older and from another time trembled, picked up her feet and ran deeper into the brush. The night swelled around this woman as men in furs and hats probed the scarlet air ushering in low long mantras from this frightened woman squatting in the brush. This woman found refuge against the trunk of that tree.

Nelle's body had chilled. She rolled her shoulders and rubbed her palms rapidly together. The tree felt ancient now. She leaned farther back and embraced the crook of protruding roots like a cradle.

That other woman squatted there and locked down against the roots and trunk in hiding, rocking, child-like, quietly, listening to the forest around her body. The wind. The grasses arcing across a darkened meadow. A shallow quiet lake lapped against shores below her. This woman remained calm by breathing, deep, long, and slow. Her inhales and exhales coming in and out in tandem like thunder and lightning.

She is allusion.

Gaia ignored.

Eve cast out.

Isis forgotten.

White Calf Buffalo Medicine Woman rolling over and preparing to arrive.

Enheduanna wandering amongst thorns, writing holy laments inside her heart.

The Sacred Feminine in his story.

Reclaim. Storyteller. Reclaim.

There is a tree, it suspends an indigenous woman at the core of a garden.

A Tree of Life. Is feminine. Is a cosmic womb.

The wind picked up. The Moira lapped fiercely against her shore. Waves carved out time. White caps snapped like whips from the view on top of the hill. The squatting-rocking-woman willed silence, hoping her body would press against—into—the soil and that crushed leaves would not rustle. She didn't want the men to know she was there, and, if they sensed anything they would think she was merely an animal. She waited it out.

He neared. An expert nose, a hunter, one who survives exploration, picked up her scent instantly. The musk between her legs, the salt, her skin itched behind her knees from a thick fear-sweat. Chilled. This man of history smelled this Woman, and his mouth watered.

She saw his face easily in the moonlight. His pale skin glowed phantom, and she knew that his spirit was not there inside his body. He saw the whites of her eyes in the dark, framed by the backdrop of a tree. This pale explorer picked up on her fear like an animal, instinctual, he pounced through the underbrush trapping her to the ground beneath him, suspended.

His hands racked up her hides, snapping twine and showering the ground in a spattering of beads. His toxic breath, reeked, biting into her neck, fear knocked her into submission. For her culture, his act was the greatest shame. He forced a shriek down inside her with his hand and locked his thighs against hers, calves intertwined and strangling. He took her air and filled her lungs with earth.

She could look up through the girth of the tree, the branches crooning down stretching far to touch her. She wanted to resist him, to lash her arms out from her sides, pull the sharpened blade from her heel, push it between his ribs, but it was gone, she had lost that blade in the run. Now, she could only imagine reaching up, grasping a branch, pulling herself up and out from under him and this invasion, *up up up*, into the heights of the tree until she was safe, existing only between that invisible space where the tips of those branches touched the air in the sky.

She smelled the tears before they soaked her eyes and rivered down her temples. They welled, salt-falls, collected in pools in her ears to drown out the noise of him.

The soul will protect itself inside the prison of trauma. A going inside, digging deep. A lifting up, and this Woman could look down on her body, look down at her Self, retracing the thread of comfort in the mantras that came from the Big Turtle and the island on its back. She had left before he was done.

It was a coincidence that he dug down into the mound to hide her after he had conquered her landscape. He dropped her down and she curled naturally into the fetus embrace and grew cold. Her final breath, taken—the elders, ancestors, they had come forward and remained, carving out space around the taken woman. Her mother would have sung long and dropped shells into the grave, but he had only dropped dirt.

Nelle shot up, sweat glazing her skin. She balled her fists against her eyes and pushed hard. She could not fathom what she had just felt. What she thought she might know, and try to unknow. The flames of pain flashed white and orange, and she released her face, cringing. Nelle tongued her lips and placed her palms against the tree. The cool dirt at the base of the tree, relief, her feet sunk slightly and her shadow disappeared amongst the protruding roots. The safety of moss, blanket, the pungent fibrous stench of mushrooms, and dirt caked to bone. Nelle turned around and decided secrecy was best. That connection was something only for her. Her imagining.

Nelle caught sight of her mother on the boulder from her

vantage point at the suspending tree. Her mother tilted her face slightly against the fading light, licked her fingers and flipped a page. She read for several moments and then crooned her neck, checking for her daughter. Mother folds the book around itself cracking the spine wide. Nelle willed her to come with her, to rise up from the boulder and wipe the fear from her mind. This liberation won't happen. Not yet. Not right now.

What she wanted was impossible, so she bared her teeth in anger. She had knowledge, had gained an understanding of the hill and how the way was for the Women there. How it was the way for many women elsewhere who would have known worse. She knew, but she knew nothing, too.

Unsettled and agitated, Nelle slung her book bag over her shoulders and turned around to climb down the hill with her back to the openness.

She does not see her mother as she passes the boulder.

Grown up.

She does not look this time.

She does not hear the loon crying from the shore, or watch the shadow of the nearing sunset shift across the mound and bury the tree in darkness. Nelle will return and lean her back against the bark, but no longer would she feel that connection again.

Not until she learned connection was elsewhere too, with other things. Residue. Stories intertwined and empowering each other in reclaiming a knowing she gleans of a woman strong, loving herself despite the atrocities committed against her.

Sacred Feminine.

Not until Nelle learned to break from the confines of the compound, the house, could she walk the entirety of the planet. Opening to other connections, like prayers, like Father Sky and Mother Earth, too.

Not until she realized that Women are holders of another other-world, one unseen, but *felt*. Occult. Ethereal.

There were once priestesses and feminine oracles who ran temples.

There were once women who kept sacred fires lit and transferred teachings and spiritual insights to The People and the next seven generations.

Women who would be responsible for sacred discourse, the role taken, perpetuated and held only by the male hand thereafter. The feminine removed, fragmented through a masculine war mechanism.

Aggression. Conquer. Exploration. Invasion.

Religion. Politics. Military. Economy.

A Woman does not usually rape.

To each their own and their own situation.

Let the face of stereotype smile here.

But, acknowledge that it is sure—

A Woman has never started genocide.

STORYTELLER

Madoc grew up around Simon and Donald Mackenzie's saw and grist mills in the 1830s. The village was first known as Deer Creek, after the flowing river that ran like a thick vein through town, flooding in the springs at the bottom of the hill as a wide temporary lake. There were many names footnoted to our village's origins, the Upper and Lower Canada Directory of 1857 referred to Madoc as the "Village of Hastings." With a chicken-scratched note indicating that the growing town was also referred to as "Madoc Post Office" to some inhabitants.

The creek still bears the same name. The creek swells and bursts in the winter months, especially when the spring thaw floods. By summer the water has dried against the rocks and pools blot the rocky bottom throughout town. The creek, to me, my memory, is of extremes, either it is overflowing and dangerous, or, in the heat, it is stagnant and lifeless.

Water is alive, my Love. It communicates to you through movement, minute changes that speak more than language can hold. I watch water, how it breathes life into caverns, coming and going with the moon. Yes, water is living.

The way water spoke to me at Deer Creek was that of extremes. In retrospect, I see the currents of a family's life there.

An overflowing thaw. Other times, motionless algae growth. Fish carcass and dried stone.

The Mackenzie's encountered a vibrant creek that would power the mills two centuries before, not a fluctuating Nile creek. The mills do not function today along Deer Creek.

These are our colonial roots. A securing, a holding down by disrupting indigenous routes.

Projecting ideas through paper, or maps in a gradual simultaneous flux. Currents, thrashing and writhing after the ice melts, or puddling and drying in a baking summer sun.

Textual literacy was power.

Food. Shelter. Clothing. Yes.

But, to secure a village, language must be circulated. And like water, my Child, language is also living.

Language feeds the lines of communication, of ideas.

Madoc was established with the raising of a post office in 1836. Now, language was shipped out. The post office dictated literacy and shifted the tone of conversation from the warm mouth to the pen.

Know who holds the pen and how the writer, even myself, infuses their essence through language.

Words can propel bodies to shift landscape, reroute the course of water, and fuse the land with machinery.

That is what happened.

We forged inward with determination. On February 25, 1832 the incorporation of the Champlain and St. Lawrence Railroad from Dorchester, now St. Jean, to a location along the St. Lawrence River was Canada's first railway charter. This line was made public four years later, ushering in a current of expansion.

The people in Madoc did not feel this growth until the late 19th century. In 1877, citizens witnessed the expansion of the Grand Junction Railroad between Belleville and Stirling. The line reached Campbellford in June 1879 and on to Ashburnham, now Peterborough, in 1880. The Belleville and North Hastings Railway Company was integrated in 1874 extending a line from Madoc Junction to connect with the Central Ontario Railway just west of Eldorado.

Around this time, lumberman Edward Rathbun, who had personal investments with Marlbank's cement factory, oversaw the growth of the Bay of Quinte Railway which ran from Nappanee to Yarker, then northwest through Tweed, Actinolite, and Queensborough. This line intersected the Central Ontario Railway at Bannockburn. The Central Ontario Railway ran from Picton to Trenton, further on to Marmora and by 1900, the line reached Bancroft and Maynooth in 1907. These rail lines penetrated the most isolated and interior jungled pockets of our area. This penetration was how the colonizing society executed and maintained power. And, these communities were more connected, and perhaps more than physically, than now.

These transgressions into the belly of the northern wilderness were followed by the mapmakers. In 1858, Samuel M. Benson developed the first written plan of Madoc. Inhabitants and newly arrived immigrants knew him and remembered him as the public surveyor, but he was, essentially, a name-changer and land-shaper.

He designated the road from Marmora, the town halls and even the religious centers like the Presbyterian Church. He mapped frightfully straight lots through bending rivers, hills, and gullies. Roads of linearity, assured and levied in heavy pencil lead. In between the sketched lots, rectangular and perfect, he ignored landscape, rock that rooted deep in soil that would make life difficult for immigrants, nearly impossible to provide sustenance for their families. He also mapped civilization onto indigenous grounds. They were the first who flowed with the land. Existing prior, for thousands of years, not centuries, were sacred song-line maps that connected the Eastern and Western edges of Canada through the waterway system from the mouth of the St. Lawrence through the bellies of the freshwater Great Lakes. Along these navigational routes is sacred rock art. The nations comprising the Great League of Peace established by Hiawatha and Dekanawida hold specific territorial responsibilities. Gatekeepers. Ambassadors. And, Benson was one of many amongst that colonial fabric that wrote over these formations and currents. Two separate civilizations existing simultaneously on geography. Layered matrices. Horrifically, mutually, exclusive.

You see, our beginning here was about laying something else over, deliberately and gradually. Those pre-existing life formations that penetrated this New World far before rail lines and distribution postal routes, they thrived here. A quiet attempted genocide over generations. Degradation. A paper labyrinth suffocation.

Daughter, I specifically say "attempted" now because the People are still here and they are entering into an era of thriving, not surviving. We, the settler population, will see a turning of tables. Thriving to surviving. We are lucky if they will want to help.

We cared not to learn about how The People forged the waters with handmade canoes, or how much knowledge one needed to string a snowshoe or to set a trap before setting out on already named routes and places.

The ancient knowledge and wisdom of the petroglyphs was away and embedded deeper in memory. Undiscovered.

We ignored existing spiritual alliances, moved in diplomatic planes, carefully, and wrote over.

We wrote over The Way, the medicine wheel, the confederacy, and spiritual democracy, forcing a whole other life on this land. Their songs, spiritual and ceremonial, were perceived as savage and childish. We carried out this ideological package with expertise and bureaucracy. We took children and placed them in residential schools. We pushed culture down and stood upon ours, and we took land. The land that you will grow up on, was not ours first. And, Daughter, the story does not have to be about who "owned" it first. That is not our story.

We come from a people of material. Survival. Men of capitalism. Industrialization. Survival was tangible, something held. Survival was not orienting to that which could be felt.

My Daughter, you come from a setting that mirrored the

sparkle of antiquity, ribboned in myth and legend, you are born out of harsh existences. Extreme climates. Polarity. Flood and drought. Invasion and discovery.

Mrs. William Mumby, Sr., could not have foreseen the shift she would have on her rural life when she set out that morning to milk the cow. She needed to fill her bucket, relieve the poor beast from the pain swelling in the animal's swollen udders. That was all she was thinking of—the perfected routine to carry on through the day. She was living routine when she tripped over a rock, forcing her face and mouth into the dirt. Her cracked fingers dug into the earth staining her nails. She hissed from the burning itch thickening from her torn stockings and skinned knees. She dug. Intuitively, she dug. She did not know exactly what the nugget was when it glinted in the morning sunrise, gold and brown and shining.

Mrs. William Mumby, Sr., discovered the richest ore in Madoc Township.

The Madoc gold rush ushered in the advent of booming industrialization and those hopeful clinging to the back of the machinery beasts. There came two Americans, Mr. Carr and Mr. Johnston, who were drilling for oil in Sidney Township when their ears began burning from the gold rumours. They arrived in Madoc with determination, took an option on all of the adjacent land of the farm, offering the other farmers $30,000. Money talks loudly, and those farmers listened. The Americans dug deep, filling over 200 pork barrels with high-grade ore that was shipped south. They took over $100,000 worth of gold.

1866 was a year for fortune hunters and a following population boom. Village centres transformed from scarce shanties to "respectable" communities of progress. They named land after legends—Eldorado, the city of gold, was given to the centre north of Hastings where Mrs. Mumby, Sr., tripped. Ideologies stamped upon society through names and the stories that whispered of riches and power. They dug past the tip of the iceberg, surfacing other industries that fed the town. They found copper, lead, marble, talc, and lithographic stone that fueled the minds and made the hands busy. Survival.

Uriah Seymour gave everything and the shirt on his back to obtain a smelting furnace for his property and was the first to commence the manufacturing of iron. He employed 100 men to maintain this new industry for several years before the mill was shut down. He failed to show substantial profit, could only scrape along, back-bent and gasping. His yield was 90% pure metal, still not good enough. Survival.

The material could not keep pushing them through. Perseverance. I think, my Daughter, what pushed them was the idea, the premonition of endurance through ideas. They were religious people and had faith. Our mistakes lead us to our truths.

There is bias in my storytelling.

I am an unreliable narrator.

There is more.

Perhaps the farmer knocked into the 167.8 kilogram iron meteorite with his horse-drawn plough. The overarching narrative of this phenomenal discovery has stripped this farmer of an identity, and the story's precision of how he located the second largest meteorite in Canadian history.

I speak from a space of urgency, to not let this "writing over" keep happening here. I reclaim. Because, we are braiding memory with language.

The circumstances of the Madoc Meteorite have been lost in history. The retelling of events from those in power. One year after discovery, William Logan and Thomas Sterry Hunt of the Geological Survey of Canada gained possession of the meteorite, leaving any honor of the farmer in obscurity.

Amongst historical pages, Sir William Logan is a natural explorer, a man who had tramped thousands of kilometres through tangles of Canadian brush mapping the shield's geology, rewriting those that existed.

Be cautious, watch those figures who seek to own knowledge and dictate geography themselves. Mapmaking has always been subjective, rolled out with polemic.

Once in possession of the precious space matter, Madocians did not receive a chance to view and memorialize the meteorite for the heritage of the town. Instead, the Madoc Meteorite was sent across the Atlantic to Paris for the 1855 Universal Exposition. Madoc's treasure was viewed by over 5 million spectators, a startling number in comparison to the iron rock's origins of a mere several hundred inhabitants. Records do not indicate if the exhibition gave full credit to the spectacular natural terrain that housed the Meteorite for centuries, or the simple story of a farmer who stumbled across extraterrestrial material.

The narrative, however, Daughter, boasts of various exhibitions which are a strong indication of the ownership tagged to the Madoc Meteorite and exactly how the story of this finding was wrangled further from our own history of exploration. The meteorite was the first piece in the National Meteorite Collection of Canada, but presumably few from Madoc are aware of this honour. Let us change this.

The meteorite has literally drifted farther from the original territory of discovery. Displayed at the 1876 Philadelphia World's Fair. A slice has been contained in the Vatican Collection. In 1995, the meteorite was exhibited at the Planétarium de Montréal, in 1999 at the Montreal Museum of Fine Arts, and now can be viewed at the Canadian Museum of Nature. Only once has the meteorite been brought back to Madoc and that was in 2004. A vague internet source records that the iron matter was on display for the month of August at the Madoc Cultural Centre. My Love, I do not know where that is.

The story of the Madoc Meteorite is of ownership absent in our collective identity.

Water that evaporates in the summer months. The violent spring thaw forgotten.

Community members do not know this story. Perhaps, it was simple, a sliver of our local history not written into a public Canadian curriculum. Of course, a rural village did not have the capabilities to exhibit and allow access to the study of this meteorite, how could it stay? But, could a residual story stay?

The meteorite was purchased from a simple man who is only recorded as "unknown." The inhabitants of the very town were not given the authority to remember. Dictated memory loss by the delivery of power.

Reclaim. Rewrite. Birth creation.

We cannot own nature, much like we want to think we can own language and the way we want to persist and insist that we can control the way water goes.

River to rock.

RIPPLE

This place was the many rooms
of my childhood that I resided in,
chambers of a soul that rented.
Not eternally mine, perhaps,
never meant to be.
Figments, fabrications, stenciled
to a skin marked by scars.
Reality is expendable, and so is this land.
They will know when they discover
the faded plastic toys
I buried in my mind.

THE PAST

They were silent despite the chaos. The sweat-glazed bodies sponged with salt. The stench, bitter, clinging to their spent frames. Sophie inhaled the whirlpool of cotton and threadbare memories and exhaled into reality.

The walls of the train station shot back voices, echoes, shrill exclamations as they collapsed together muddling clarity. She had knuckled her brown suitcase against her side while they filed off the train. With her eyes locked forwards, she was hesitant to the mass of people and did not scan the crowd lining the train in an effort to locate him.

She listened to her father's watch and the family Bible knock together from inside the case. Her Mother's pearl necklace clicked along the strand coiling around thin yellow material with blazing black stars, without knowing. She had memorized the protruding ridges in the letters carefully folded inside the Bible, how his blue pencil crayon scratchings etched into the underside of the paper were like mountain ridges on a map. She felt destination sweep up from the leaves of the pages, journey, ascending her bone-cliffed wrists and arms, roping her heart from her soul in a secret mountain climb.

Wrapped around the book was her only pair of stockings and two flowing dresses Phillip had purchased for her. The case was lined with thick wool. She had sewn the wool in herself to fend off dampness. Layered between the wool was a collage of photographs, a faded miscellany of family lineage, of a tangible memory-line to preserve; the only semblance of her prior life that she wanted to carve within her memory—to pass on. The photographs, illustrative of aristocracy and luxury, contained pockets of bleakness too, if anyone examined them closely instead of merely accepting them for face-value.

There was the tattered photograph of her father, his body ravenous and hollow, shadowed behind barbed wire. She would tell her wide-eyed granddaughter about this photograph, letting her caress the furled edges in dismay.

He was captured in April 1915, during the encounter on Hill 60. It was a man-made hill, 60 meters above sea level in the locality of Zillebeke, south east of Ypres. The Germans held the highest ground of the hill, having captured the land from the French. From this elevation, the Germans made life hell in the Ypres Salient. Her Father was taken prisoner during this encounter and the switch of arms of the hill. He could not understand why they had not just killed him. The veteran had uttered to his stricken daughter verging on the brink of mature adolescence, decades later, that his survival was most likely because both sides of the army had been depleted.

"They needed bodies, and didn't care what their national affiliations were at this point. *La guerre touchait à sa fin.* The war was nearing a close. Neither side could feel secure about any possibility of winning. We could only see death. *Nous ne savions que la mort.* We only knew death." He had looked off at that point, for only a moment, unblinking. Shook himself out of that bleak stare and continued solemnly.

"They might have thought they could change me, keep me alive for a final reserve of fighting. I spat in their eyes, and what I despised the most of my incarceration, well," he cleared his throat. "The ability to see beyond the hill. The landscape was unnerving, nonetheless, and the tease of close freedom tested my composure. *Les salauds savaient ce qu'ils faisaient.* The bastards knew what they were doing."

He was saved by innovation and desperation. The British and French were determined to knock the Germans from the hill. They tunneled inwards, securing five mines around the core of the crest. On April 17th, 1915, they blew the top off the hill and regained their holdings.

"*Je devrais mort.* I should have died." He placidly spoke to Sophie one damp evening over a supper of cabbage, boiled potato, and homemade dinner loaves. She watched as he squeezed his eyes together, massaged the ridges and lines on his forehead and then thumbed the pulp of his eyelids before forcing them open.

"I don't know how I endured the hill, the explosion nearly cremated us. *Tu voyes ces cicatrices.* You see these scars." He pushed his cotton sleeve past his elbow revealing a snarl of tissue.

"I was seared black. You wouldn't have liked the smell. That scent of charcoaled flesh, sweet and pungent enough to rot your stomach." She shrank back at his explicitness.

"I clung onto that stench while burrowing through the bombed mud. It was the only thing that smelled alive and present. They didn't know whether I was an enemy or ally when my teeth knocked into the boot of a Brit. I tasted soil and bloodied leather. Panic. I begged for mercy. Thank God, I could utter French. I thought my tongue had melted from my skull."

Sophie coughed, felt the memory molt from her skin, she could almost blow the feathers along the floor of the train. The remnants inside her case were both bliss and burden. If anything, she depended on minute physical gestures of routine that planted her deep into the earth with haunches of sanity. She shuffled forward, gripping the case.

She had rolled her hair the night before, tucking white ripped material around the strands. That morning she tediously untied each, admiring the curls as they shuddered and fell against her jawline and shoulders. She unbound the coils with her mother's porcelain handled brush that was now pressing against the back of the case. She did not want to think about the hair she pulled from the bristles that morning, brown and straight. She dressed in brown, a tweed blazer buttoned tight over a pin skirt. Her square heels clicked down the train's car, out onto the steel stairs, and jarred down onto the pavement.

Sophie jutted away from the crowds, her knuckles white and puckered in the autumn wind. She puffed out her cheeks and planted her feet. She waited. She rooted.

She saw the tuft of blond hair part the people. His face was tan, his cheeks red leather, and eyes the bluest shade. She forgot how blue his eyes were. They bore two perfect holes in her chest as he neared her. His shoulders were rectangular against his buttoned shirt and leather bomber jacket, his legs muscular and elongated by dark lined trousers. A gold chain glinted around his neck with a charm of a racing horse skidding along the links.

She noted the new onyx stone bruising his thick pinky finger. His mouth was a rigid line against his wide jaw, the creases of his cheeks drawing jail bars down his face. He appeared tired and wallowed in the blue shadows sagging under his eyes. He stepped close to her, his face bowed slightly and he smelled the crown of her head, the warm earthy scent of brushed hair beaded with oil. They stood parallel for many moments, knees locked and hips aligned, hands hung lifeless at their sides. Post-war statues. A war bride greeted by her Canadian soldier. Husband and wife.

She nervously twisted her wedding band around her finger. He stooped, clutched the suitcase and guided her by the shoulder through the crowd. They needed space away from the mash of people. They would not share in front of them, or anyone.

"This way!" He muttered in a gruff drawl, his gaze lost amongst the congestion of bodies. She studied the back of his head and frowned from his fingers biting into her sleeve. She willed him to turn his body around and face her. She yearned for him to cup her face in his large hands and knead her temples lightly with the pads of his thumbs. She would have given anything for his eyes to connect with her, to say to her, I am relieved you are here. I don't want you to go again. That wasn't the way.

Instead, she fooled herself into believing that he was shy, that things were slightly different from their time in Brussels. They had not seen each other for six months, the circles under his eyes showed deeper incisions. Not hollows of grief, not because he had found out she was actually coming, but because he had missed her.

His aloofness impelled insecurity to rise bile-like in the back of her throat. She felt the walls of her stomach cramp and push darkness up into her mouth. Nausea plated by a viral mess of nerves knocked her into memory.

She could see the outline of her chocolate brown hair mirrored back at her—a shadow. Moist brown eyes, swollen and bitten lips. The ladies room was tight, forcing them to touch when they spoke. They had not been this close in months. Even their arms brushing together and the slight click of their eyelashes when blinking ignited a torrent of emotions between them. Reflection.

"What are you doing with that clout? *Il est barbare!* Why is that ring on your finger? What have you done, Amelié?" Sophie was invaded by the questions, the sound of her old name in the air. She felt the bullet of fear barrel through her arms, her ligaments tense and metallic. She could see Amy's profile on the tram from that day. How his arm was wrapped around her, their tongues wet and arching. Sophie said nothing, dared not lip the betrayal from her heart. It was easier to rely on normative definitions. Amy was enraged by Sophie's silence, the smell of cowardice twisting around her vertebrae spiraled out with flaring nostrils.

"It was meant to be that I saw you here tonight you know. You really put me through hell. *Vous m'a vraiment mis à l'enfer.* You never let me in. I could spit on your silence. Why did you not share your sorrow? For Christ's Sake, we were living in a war, nothing was normal. No, you wouldn't let me in, and I resented you because of that! Amelié, you are living a fantasy, it's a disgrace. Why are you starting your life this way, you won't like it in Canada. You do not have to leave. You love this country, our culture. What will you do overseas? *À quoi aurez-vous?* What purpose will you have? God, Amelié, open your eyes! Is he really going to be the rest of your life?"

Sophie felt her composure crack. She uncurled her fist, stretched out her fingers, and retaliated. Amy did not know of Eli, she did not know how they survived, the black market, his capture and return, the night he found the Romanian and knew she was with Germans. Amy could not know that Sophie was running away, surviving. Her hand of cards continued to be severely dealt, and she could only keep playing the game. The war machinery crunching into her life and decisions, eating away at the person she once was and could not be anymore. Amy did not know she was a name-changer. She spiraled out. Unhinged.

"Enough! *Assez!*" The shriek pierced the stall. Amy winced and fell backwards unraveling the toilet paper roll.

"It is what I must do. *C'est déjà fait.* It is already done. I am not the only one to move on. Forget me, forget our time together. We do not need each other and I will not have you attacking me. *C'est fini.*"

She remembers the trill clash as she slammed the door behind her. She cannot remember the look on Amy's face, or what she was wearing, for that matter. She felt sick and bent over suddenly and had vomited into the pot of a leafy plant. She felt the bars of an invisible cage press against her skin. Frigid and hard, she knew that she had created this life. It was of her own fabrications. She could hear a metallic clink in her head as she walked towards him. Her ears rang red and she tried to shrug the unceasing clatter. She envisioned her father in chains, shuffling awkwardly through a barbed wire fence.

Her memory slides and merges images in her head.

A silver chain necklace, delicate, and how it had rested on her chest while she hovered on top. The disparity of the memories, raw, they burned against the backs of her eyes. She focused on the breath hissing from her lips, the mechanical relapse of her heart pumping and her lungs filling and collapsing. She set her mind to these rhythms and badgered forward. He waited with an open palm ready to dance.

But, she could not shake the shadows fanning her peripheral thoughts as they pushed through the crowd of people in Belleville that morning. Her eyes stung from the cerulean brightness of the day, the blanket of clouds lifted. The laughter entwined with sturdy English felt like nails inside her head, clawing. The modern buildings, linear and crumbling from idle negligence, were grotesque and plain. She knew instantly, this would never be her culture. She could not fold easily into it. She would never become accustomed to the wretched winter cold, or the snow. This would not be home. In that moment, precisely, as if her life had become infused with the hands of a clock, she was now adrift, a virgin soul that had not mentally landed on Canadian soil, but rather bobbed the circumference of a boat and anchor.

They approached a glistening taupe automobile parked smartly amongst the line-up of other vehicles. The sheen of the car caught her off guard, clouded her head. She had not seen a vehicle this luxurious since before the war.

"C'est une belle voiture!" Sophie clamoured. The corners of her mouth, drawn up tight with exaggerated poise.

"Hmmf? What?" He did not look up but placed her case methodically in the back seat through the open window and pulled out a pack of cigarettes. His lips puckered around the filter while he cupped his hands against the wind. The cigarette flamed to life, rifling blue smoke through Sophie's bundled hair. She waved her hand in front of her nose, crinkling her eyes. Phillip laughed, and she smiled slightly.

"That is a beautiful car, I said!" She spoke slowly, each syllable awkwardly rolling from her tongue, she moved close to Phillip, plucking the smoldering cigarette from him and delicately placed it in her mouth. He arched his eyebrows and shook his head slightly, not expecting her sudden boldness. He smiled and finally looked at her. She coddled the gaze, inwardly relishing in her success.

For several moments, she let herself fall into the present, eye-watering relinquishing the weight of her days spent huddled on the steamer, or folded into a box car. The plane, she pushed the trauma of the plane and the social awkwardness of that new experience deep down. Exhaustion crept up her legs, pulling her shoulders down around her ribs, forcing her head to sink slightly. She did not want to see another train again. They took so much away. She felt a sarcastic boil of laughter clot her throat and swallowed hard at the irony. She had evaded knowledge of the devastating box car prisons throughout the war. She couldn't deny not hearing of the rumours, of the routed destinations to death. The bodies canistered like sardines in tin. Her face broke, and she nervously hulled on the cigarette, cradling the nicotine in her veins that rushed in shivers against her jaw line, she curled her lips inwards against her teeth in a dazed repose.

"What type of car is this?" She asked slowly. Her eyes lingered along the bullet-shaped fenders, her words compressed by a prolonged haul on the cigarette. She flicked the ashes and began circling the car. Phillip reached inside his jacket pulling out another cigarette and lit it. He sucked the smoke in through his teeth, flicking it back outwards with his tongue.

"It's from 1942, Cadillac Series 61 Coupe. They only built about 17,000 of these. Dad bought it while I was overseas. It's shit really, made during the war. They weren't keen on luxury obviously, although she is fully shiftless—automatic transmission, you know?" Sophie rolled the corners of her mouth down feigning understanding and crooned her chin towards her left shoulder. Phillip continued without noticing.

"She's got 150 horsepower too. Little bitch will fly. She's the first I've gotten to touch 80 km, didn't have to jam my foot on the gas all day either. She'll do for now!" He snickered and Sophie felt something sinister ache from the pit of her abdomen.

Phillip dropped his cigarette butt onto the gravel and

crushed it beneath his heel. Sophie bit into hers with the tip of her shoe and tightened the silk scarf around her chin that had come loose exposing her blonde curls. He had moved to the passenger door and theatrically swung it open slightly bowing for Sophie to crawl in. She subtly smiled and tucked herself into the interior. A sense of relief flooded her temples for the moment.

They drove north along Highway 62. Sophie watched silently from the passenger seat. Large Victorian houses with their manicured lawns lined the lazy streets and the traffic was free-flowing with many vehicles stopping to let others pass. As they continued North she observed the streets were not jammed with soldiers or shrieking crowds or shuffling refugees. Survivors.

The crowds here flocked downtown. These streets professed order, boxed yards, well-kept houses and fat red-faced children running circles in the grass. She did not look down the very nose at starvation. The gaunt lines of refugees with their bowls and spoons were unconceivable here. There were no crumbling foundations, no shrapnel. Sophie felt like a storyteller of this new movie—Canadian suburbia. Clean. Untouched. Maybe it was a good decision, to follow through. She had nowhere else safe to go. She fled.

Ce sera peut-être d'accord. Maybe it will be okay. Maybe he spoke truth of his wealth.

"I think I will get used to it here!" She shouted the words over the wind blowing in through the open windows and the traffic beyond their car. Phillip squinted and quickly turned his face to her.

"Why is that? No war here?" He laughed with a bared-tooth smile. His large hand swept forwards and he twisted a dial. Music flooded the car filling up the space. Sophie jumped. She contemplated and waited. Then, reaching forward swiftly she turned the music down. Phillip scowled.

"Well yes, I never thought I'd see a place not consumed by war." Carefully she picked through her words and hoped he understood. "Your buildings are not bombed, and the people are not starving."

He responded curtly, "Yeah, we don't have any of that bull-shit here. I'm relieved that I can walk through a back pasture without my eyes glued to the ground for mines. Europe's a mine field. It'll take years to clean that shit up. We might have had to ration, but I'd take that over ... well Belgium was shit ... I hated it ... I'm home." His words rushed through, and he jerked the volume back up.

Sophie watched him, puzzling over what he said. She did not probe, did not want to hear about more carnage, it didn't matter what he saw because that was over. It couldn't affect them here.

Sophie winced and turned her face towards the side window. She did not want him to see how his words stung.

This is what our allies think.

She thought of her mother, fingertips dancing while she created beautiful intricate lace shawls. She could hear her father turn the page of a book he was absorbed in, the wall behind him overflowing with titles. They were learned and intelligent. They loved and embraced their heritage, a history extending beyond Christ.

What do the Canadians have? They came from us, our land and culture, non? *What is Canadian?*

She said nothing more and rested her chin on her fist. She tucked her other hand between the folds of skirt for comfort. She studied her face in the side mirror. She cleaned up the line of her lipstick with the edge of a fingernail. She could see the contradictions, how her skin was pallid and pocketed with secrets, her hair windblown and large, but her fingers wrapped in gold, her neck chained with golden links and a diamond. She shrouded both luxury and depravity. She knew that Phillip refused to see both, only one, and that was the new Woman he brought to his land, his creation. He owned her.

Chattel.

She was soon distracted by the landscape as they navigated north along Highway 62. The sun beat down white rays that reflected like pools of water along the flat hardtop of the highway. She squinted, the pressure of her slanted eyes and the white brilliance of the sun made them water.

She searched for relief, dropped her gaze out the passenger window, tracing the tree line and thick underbrush. In this land, she would learn the difference between coniferous and deciduous. Would be able to smell the differences. Cradle the scent of pine needles and wet maple leaves in her mouth.

The forest was in transition, the conifers shot high up, their bark moist and their needles lucid green. Maple trees stained red and orange, blazing on fire, Sophie shook her head at colours. She felt both awe and unease at the rock cuts jagged and protruding from the sides of the road. If she ran her tongue along its puckered face she'd taste a plethora of salts and minerals. That rough inside feeling of tongue on unbrushed teeth.

She was unfamiliar with such organic beauty. Her eyes were accustomed to marble columns and rococo sedges. She was bred in the shadow of a gothic tower. She could only classify this beauty as something beyond human manipulation. It would be difficult to conquer this land, to dig your feet in the topsoil lined with rock, pounding fists against the shield. She wondered about the expanse of fields along the sides of the highway. The fields outlined in piled rocks.

She smelled what dawn could be like here, the purple light that bathed the fields, a wet mist coating every surface. The blurred silhouette of the settler, the pioneer farmer and his brood of children bent and retracting in the early morning shadows. They would live this repetitive motion, bending, clawing the ground in fist grips and retract, extending their chest to the open air and lumbering towards ox and cart. The oldest son would grip leather reigns and follow ox and cart, teeth clenched against the grinding inertia. Awkward wooden wheels, stiff, pushing through sludge, difficult and agitating. His spine would spit sweat until he reached the edge of the field. Sophie imagined little hands reaching inside the cart, their fingers scraping against unforgiving porous stone faces, blood mixed with dirt, they'd line the field with these rocks. Again and again, until they had defined the existence of an era, had encased their crops and animals in.

The people would dream of stones, they'd see their pale hands stained in red and dust, the muscles in their legs and back straining against the weight of the Canadian Shield. After several hours they would stop, raise the flat of their hand to their brow line, and tremble over the long mound of a fence line emerging. It was easier to focus on the birth of structure, slight control of nature, rather than assessing the virgin land left to surmount.

Sophie was warm from admiration. The courage of those who had immigrated to this land inspired and taunted her because she could neither see her own spine crooning against the bitterness of the earth, raising her skirts high to pocket stones, nor could she see herself emptying the sack of her skirts on top of the ever-growing rock fences. She knew that those who had come second were brave, a strong-willed culture that shouldered the demands of the Old World with the retaliation of the New Land.

They struck deep with the blow of a shovel, the glinting edge of a hoe. They felt they could hear the cries from the long grasses as the blade of the scythe slit through, severing the spit and guts of the grasses. They brought down the large weathered faces of trees, sheering them to silken logs for the walls of their shelters. The women rising before the sun, their fingers working the engorged teats of a cow, or plucking the feathers from the cold bird's skin. They were robust, their story one of resilience and grief. They showed up to the land, purchased uncleared lots, thick with the insanity-driving cloud of black flies and mosquitoes. Sophie borrowed from this strength, an immigrant thief, she knew that those who came earlier were originally like her, but had transformed altogether. She wavered, foresaw her strength emanating from a soul hardened, she'd crust over with a thick skin like the Canadian Shield. The only direction of her demise would come from the inside out, a slow uncoiling.

The car crested the edge of a mountainous ridge, Phillip

angled the vehicle into the wind. Sophie gripped the door handle and felt the cry connect with the air before she could swallow it. Phillip laughed and bit down on the gas pedal. The car reeled bending with the curve of the highway as it sailed down the sides of the hill. Fearless.

Once they dipped around the first sharp corner, the lake emerged, a mirror, resounding in her ethereal beauty. Moira Lake cradled the hollow of the highway as it dipped and rounded several rock cliffs before straightening. The reverberations of the rubber tires against the cut rock were clipped and repeating. They sped across a thick concrete bridge that ran parallel to the train tracks.

On either side of the highway, the lake swelled, shadowing a shoreline of thick trees that molded into a dense forest. Sophie said nothing. Her eyes connected with the lake, how it bled around the car, she felt insignificant. She immediately loved the lake, yet resented it with jealousy. She had not grown up around water like this and she saw how Phillip's eyes smiled at her.

"Moira," he purred as if she was a lover, "Moira Lake." Sophie warmed and took her in with sideways cat-slit-eyes.

They crested through the elevated tree line lofting up from the sides of the highway. She wondered if anyone lived on top of the hill beside the lake. She could not imagine that it would ever be her one day.

Phillip turned the car onto Seymour Street and made a sharp right onto Rollins Street after a small well in the road. The houses were smaller, some wooden, others stone, but Sophie could not get past the spacious yards that surrounded the houses. She eyed the look of the houses, how some were neglected while others were coated with fresh paint. The flowerbeds had been raked and weeded, the small shrubs and rose bushes were covered in potato sacks for the winter squalls.

He stopped the car in front of a red wood framed house at the top of the hill. A withered elm tree cast thin crooked shadows across the face of the house and fenced-in lawn. The house was two stories with perfect small windows and a screen door that clapped gently against the frame of the door in the wind.

Phillip shut off the engine, pulled the key from the ignition and with a long sigh, and leaned back against the seat. Without turning to Sophie, he spoke.

"This is it. I live here. You will meet my parents and sister. They live here too. My brother is not here, he and his wife live in Peterborough."

She instantly stiffened, she had not been prepared for this. This reality was not his story in Belgium.

My family is rich. I have my own house and you would love it there. I could give you anything you wanted.

She shrank back against the seat. He had finally spoken of his family and his home after the proposal. He was tight-lipped usually, only referring to his comrades, his officers. She thought he might have been orphaned. Memory. He had tilted his head back, the candlelight reflecting along the column of his throat while they ate. She watched his throat swell, swallowing the amber liquid from a crystal glass. He plunked the empty glass down onto the table top, a wet ring pushing out from under, staining the table. In a hazy tone, he began speaking, and she listened. He did not stop.

"You won't be disappointed with me. My family is well-established back home. Old money. Old name. My dad was the first licensed plumber in the town. He's built up a solid business around that. People like him well, he's a bit of a hard ass, but it will all be mine," he lifted a wine bottle and filled his glass without topping up hers. His lips wrapped around the rim of his glass and he drank deeply.

"We have a lot of property and I will build you a mansion," he paused, his eyes glazing over in a grin, "no, a ship. I'll build you a ship of a house." He cracked open in a loud laugh and finished another glass. Sophie left hers. She wanted to be sober to hear what he had to say tonight. He continued.

"I have one brother, he's also a plumber, but he's Union. My Dad and I ride him a lot, but he knows. He doesn't work too hard and gets sent all over Ontario. I don't want anyone telling me where to go anymore. No, those days are over!" He toasted himself. She bolted up uncomfortably, sat straight and rigid with wide eyes. His eyes slanted in a thin red line and he soaked his throat. Sophie picked apart her pork with her knife and gingerly scraped her cut buttered beans into her mouth. She said nothing and dared not look around them to see if anyone else was watching or listening.

Phillip ordered a whiskey. He picked up his drink when it arrived and sloshed the whiskey against the glass. He dipped his finger down and slowly bit down on the whiskey stained finger without speaking. Sophie watched how his shoulders sagged slightly. Rolling his head from side to side, loud pops and cracks from his neck rained out an uncomfortable crescendo. Without meeting her gaze, he continued once again.

"I have horses, too. I race them down in Belleville. I'll buy you a stylish hat, one of those big womanly things that knock us men around." He chuckled, ripped a chunk of steak off and bit into it with pearl-white teeth.

Phillip shoveled the beans in three large forkfuls after the steak, washing down with two gulps from his whiskey. His body arched slightly and circled around itself on the chair while he cleaned up the steak. Without pausing to look up at her, or to acknowledge that she was not finished eating, he loudly snapped his fingers and prompted for the bill.

Sophie sighed and followed him to the cloak room to fetch their coats before filtering out into the cold. Her plate was carried away by the waitress, the pork plump and bloody, the beans glossed in butter. The waitress handed the plate over to the young dishwasher. While the waitress turned her back and retreated, the boy dug his face into the meat and nearly gasped in pleasure as the beans slid down his throat. Sophie's stomach churned, and she pressed her palms against it as she followed him out into the street.

Now she sat rigidly, her face ashen as she took in the view of her new home.

"Their names, Phillip, you haven't told me their names." She arched an eyebrow and tilted her chin.

"Who?" He twisted to face her.

"Your family? What are their names?"

His eyes narrowed.

"My dad's name is Gregory and my mother is Magna. My brother is Alfred and my sister is Cassandra. Think you can remember that because they've seen us, look!"

Sophie swallowed hard.

THE PAST

In the car, Sophie's head shot up as she took in the figures emerging from the house. She met the eyes of an older woman, Magna, her light hair pulled back by a faded brown scarf. Her dress was plain and pulled taut by her thick middle. Deep-set wrinkles lined her face, a child's storybook, cracked back spine from comfort. She met Sophie's gaze with an expressionless face, her mouth and eyes set stone; Sophie swallowed and recoiled.

A younger, slightly thinner woman stepped out from behind her mother. She was tall, her skin was drawn, and Sophie could see the chapped skin of her hands as she rubbed them against her apron. Her hair was shoulder length, pallid, and straw-like bustling around her jutting chin. She smiled with her eyes.

But it was the aged man that held Sophie's attention. She baulked under his hard stare, refusing to let him see her nerves. She gritted her teeth, set her jaw tight and blinked tears away. He had been sitting the entire time in a sturdy rocking chair on the front verandah. His hands were massive, splayed thick fingers across the arms of the chair. His neck was like a tree trunk that branched out into a weathered face—the unblinking blue eyes that unnerved her bore into her. She felt fear, or intimidation, foil her cheeks and neck. The man met her wavering look and slowly rose from the chair. He pulled a red kerchief from his pocket and methodically wiped his nose. He tucked the material back into his pocket and nodded at them.

"Here goes nothing!" Phillip let the words fall like stones from his mouth landing into a still-water pond. He kicked open the car door and strolled across the street leaving Sophie melting to the car interior.

She inhaled quickly, forcing her hands to push open the car door, and stepped out onto the hill. Her knees nearly buckled while she made her way across the street. The family was huddled in a small circle. She could not understand what they were saying, her sparse English had left her as her tongue thickened into cement on the roof of her mouth. She prodded closer to the circle and shyly broke into the banter.

In a birdlike voice, wispy and clipped, she faltered in a short greeting. "I am Sophie. Pleased to meet with Phillip's family." Her broken English made her crimson with embarrassment.

Gregory narrowed his eyes over her broken English and Magna puffed her cheeks out as her dark eyes swelled, blinking tears down her cheeks.

Cassandra giggled. "I am Cassandra. Come in. I will show you the house."

The young woman led Sophie from the group and directed her around the side of the house.

"We didn't think you'd actually come." She half laughed. "Well, really, we didn't even know about you." Sophie felt the tears rise up and a knot snake in her stomach.

I want to go home.

As she passed, Sophie noted two maple wood trap doors that opened into a cavernous damp cellar from outside the kitchen door. She had not seen a cellar similar since her childhood stone house on the outskirts of Brussels—out in the countryside. She used to pretend that the trap doors were portals, once she passed through their dank threshold she would be beamed to another space or time. The cellar would become a cave ridden with tribal sketches, hieroglyphics, or even an apple seed. There were no limits to her imagination. This cellar, however, was where Magna stored the yields from her garden and where Gregory kept his moonshine. Sophie would later retreat to the cellar when demanded to fetch a jar, and there in the coldness she could press her forehead to the wall hiding the rivers of her tears like secrets.

She wondered why Cassandra had rushed her around to the back of the house instead of entering through the front. Perhaps it was because she was considered family already, not a guest that needed to be shown the house properly. She felt relieved, unnerved, and shaken by this unexpected intimacy that she had not anticipated.

The house was dark and stank of smoke when they ducked inside. Sophie could tell by the curl of flame and disarray of the room that this space was where the family dwelled when they were not busy with the day. The corner of the cramped kitchen bore a sturdy oven and brick fireplace. Magna lumbered in behind the girls and stirred the embers causing the fire to blister and hiss. Magna was the fire-keeper, she kept it lit and blazing each morning while she kneaded dough and watched her loaf rise with flour handprints dusting her apron. The iron oven would later be replaced with a streamlined propane stove that had been ordered from Belleville.

Often, the women would scrape the fireplace clean from charcoal and ash. Sophie loathed this task, grating her teeth when her hand would slip and her knuckles would scrape along the brick. Pin drops of blood swelled from her flesh and it stung bitterly. But the bricks needed to be clean because Magna would remove several bricks that were not cemented into the frame, wrapping them in cloth. She would tuck each brick at the bottom of their beds. Sophie relished the heat and wrapped her feet around the brick, waking in the morning with cramped feet. The warmth was worth the raw fingers.

The upstairs of the tiny house was frigid, the warmth of the fire lost through the outer walls not fully insulated, and the corners of their bedrooms would become laced in frost, a thin layer of ice in the pit of winter. Acclimating later, Sophie would cradle her puckering arms around her chest and bite down hard to stop her teeth from chattering. She was used to this, this cold, and it threw her back into the memory of surviving the war.

For many winters during the war she had lived this way. Cocooned under blankets, she endured bombings and cold in her bed, not desiring to move. She felt different with this house, it was not hers and she could not migrate through it set to her own rhythm. She had fled the cramped contours of domestic cages long before the war, she almost laughed at the irony that she had shackled herself back into such a prison. She thought they'd have their own house.

She was wrong.

Their bedroom was the only room upstairs. The house was built in sections and this addition was constructed hurriedly. The second story was added on for Phillip slightly before the war. He had shared a room with his sister downstairs beside their parents' room, but the war had repositioned the family. Phillip was now a man, and men needed their own territory. He helped his father build the loft and was ecstatic with the new space, but his father had sneezed into his red kerchief and informed him that it was temporary. He needed to find a wife and get out.

The bedroom was plain with a few pieces of furniture. Sophie eyed the bed, iron-wrought, it was no different than her bed in her own flat. Standing against the left wall of their bedroom was a small dress table with a porcelain wash basin, a sliver of lavender-scented lye soap. There was nothing else in the room except a shallow closet lined with Phillip's few shirts and pants. Sophie did not mind, she carried everything in the case resting in the car that could easily be slid under the bed.

Cassandra proudly tugged Sophie's arm and they retreated from the bedroom back downstairs. She turned sharply and pulled a small door open from underneath the stairway.

"We are one of two houses in Madoc that has one of these!" she extended her arm proudly while Sophie ducked into the small closet. "We have an outhouse against the fence in the back yard, but we use this one now."

She almost laughed out loud. She saw the toilet, its antique pull string and the tiny sink. Most flats had toilets in Brussels. The only house that did not have a toilet in her lifetime was the childhood country house. At least she would not have to fight the cold and trod out back to be relieved in the night.

"Very nice!" She feigned admiration as she closed the toilet door. She turned around and stepped back slightly in shock at the sight of the entire family circling around her. Cassandra sensed her forced feelings and stepped forward.

"Here, come along, let me help you settle into your bedroom."

THE PAST

Cassandra did not anticipate Sophie's reserved humor or how she was cloaked in mystery and secrets even when they were alone. Phillip brought her case to their room, laying it absently on top of the bed. He left the room without a word.

Sophie's heart jumped when Cassandra bounded over to the case and popped open the latches up ready to expose its contents. Sophie shot forward and smashed the case closed on Cassandra's hand.

"Ow! What did you do that for?" Cassandra moaned, while cradling her reddened wrist in her other palm. "I was going to help you unpack."

Sophie's discomfort spread across her face fanning down her neck in a red stain. She dared not explain anything to Cassandra, she was too young; had no idea what the meaning of her possessions meant to her. She could not have her fingering the yellow material, absently tracing the black lines of the star exclaiming how pretty the star was, not knowing the pain associated with the symbol. No, she yearned with every ounce of her being to keep that past shrouded. They could not know about him, she had not even told Phillip about him, no one could know.

"I apologize for your hand, but I would prefer to unpack my

288

case when I am alone, thank you." Cassandra tilted her head slightly and nodded in understanding.

Her mouth opened in a small tight circle but she closed it before she could speak. Sophie rose from her hunched position over the case and made her way to the wash basin. She dipped a cloth in the cool water and brought it back to Cassandra. The young woman looked up at Sophie and with a smile wrapped the cloth around her hand.

"Thank you! It doesn't hurt too badly. You just surprised me, that's all. It's not like you tried to murder me."

"What would possess you to say that? To jump to those conclusions?" Sophie asked with alarm. She was shocked at the shifting tone and turn of direction in their conversation. Then, she learned quickly that Cassandra was interested in indigenous history of the area before the Europeans came.

"It is what happened to Deganawidah, the Huron leader from Desoronto." Sophie was baffled, but intrigued. She'd never heard someone speak of indigenous history.

"Desoronto, where is that? And who is this Degan..." She was cut off.

"He is responsible for the Iroquois Confederacy, as legend has it. He was a peacemaker, but was almost murdered by his own family. It is a popular legend amongst the Huron. My father doesn't want me learning anything about the Indians, but I like them, their way of life makes sense to me. Sophie, please do not tell Phillip any of this he would not understand. He is the same as father and mother. I think you will understand because you are an immigrant and foreign to us." Cassandra shifted uncomfortably, crossing her arms against her chest.

Sophie felt for her new sister-in-law, her eyes were large and glistening, her hands fragile and thin. She hadn't felt this intimacy with anyone since Amy. She could snap easily, Sophie imagined. She was not malleable or weathered. She had not lived through war.

Sophie sighed and shifted to face Cassandra, interest piqued. "Tell me about him, this Huron leader."

Cassandra's eyes lit up, and she smiled wide. She leaned in closer to Sophie and began speaking in a hushed tone, her eyes shifting every so often to make sure that no one could hear.

"I read about this legend by an author named Wallace Havelock Robb, I believe that he was from Belleville. Deganawidah, was supposedly born in the middle of the fifteenth century on Eagle Hill about two miles west of Deseronto on the shores of the Bay of Quinte. He was born to a virgin mother, like Mary, of the Huron nation."

Cassandra met Sophie's gaze and blinked, "Well, Deganawidah was hated by his grandmother who tried desperately to kill him three times, by drowning him through a hole in the ice, by burying him in a snowbank, and by throwing him in a blazing bonfire. Each time the grandmother returned home, she found him there with his mother, safe.

"I really love this part. How he could keep returning, you know?" Cassandra's eyes widened, and she raised her hands dramatically. Sophie was amazed at how the story opened Cassandra.

"Imagine! Trying to kill your own family, treating them like your own worst enemy! That is what draws me to this story. And maybe this did happen here, on this land." Sophie winced, she saw lines of bodies, starving gaping rib cages and the biting sound of raining bullets silenced her. She thought the legend was simple—*family envy, that was normal, non?* She remained silent while Cassandra continued.

"The Great Spirit appeared to the grandmother one night and told her that he had sent Deganawidah to the Iroquois people with a purpose and that he was not to be harmed. The Spirit explained how later in life Deganawidah would do a deed that would not be forgotten." Cassandra paused to unwrap the cold cloth from her hand. "It's cold," she uttered.

"When he was in his early 20s, he was said to have built a canoe of white rock and to have paddled across Lake Ontario to what is now New York state. There he found several warring tribes whom he addressed courageously." Cassandra leaned her head forwards and puffed out her chest. Sophie smiled while Cassandra switched characterizations.

"I am Deganawidah and I come from the Creator to build the Great Peace and to give you the Great Law."

She broke character. "You see Sophie they would not have believed him had it not been for his stone canoe. They were amazed that the canoe was afloat, let alone had carried him there. When they saw that he had travelled in a stone canoe, they knew that he spoke for the creator. He was the catalyst that helped form the Iroquois Confederacy," she paused and looked up at Sophie.

"I'll explain the Confederacy later. Deganawidah laid down all of the laws for this Confederacy. He is very much honoured by the Iroquois people, though he thought it funny that his political enemies honoured him, but his family desired to murder him. I read that he had a speech impediment, so Hiawatha joined him to speak for him." She shifted her weight between her feet and suddenly seemed uncomfortable, as if she was caught doing something wrong.

"I don't know why I just told you all of that, I usually keep this stuff to myself. I'm not really allowed to talk about it."

"It is powerful. Your enemy is never who you suspect." Cassandra arched her left eyebrow and turned her head to gaze at Sophie from her profile.

Both women mused over the underlying tone of the story without knowing they were both thinking on the same current. Sophie felt weak and admonished the uncomfortable knot that pained her throat. In that moment, she felt so far removed from her presence as she was suddenly very aware of the reality of being perched on a metal bed in the middle of rural Ontario, far from Brussels. Chills.

She felt the cool metal of that public stall toilet, touching eyelashes, and smelled the vanilla aroma curling from her hair. Private tears.

She saw brown eyes and green eyes merge, detach. She felt warm hands around her waist that then brushed the inside of her knees like a feather. Sophie wanted to disappear from the room and not speak any more.

Like a warm wind of breath, a whisper that had only tickled the bottom lip, Cassandra rose from the bed, wished Sophie good night, bent slightly and kissed her cheek and then retreated.

Sophie remained transplanted on the bed, her hands curled tightly in her lap—drying leaves. She studied the wall, the indigo crack in the plaster that connected with the ceiling in a mass of dark lines. Delicately buttressed between the walls and ceiling was a plump black spider the size of a prune. It startled Sophie, but she dared not stand and swat at it.

She was in bed with Eli, tucked into his side with his warm arm draped around her. The room was balmy, coated in moisture and perfumed from arching bodies. It was the middle of July and the day was overly hot for Brussels. It was before the war, when they had taken days for granted and the feel of their bodies pressed close. Eli had spotted a dark blot in the furthest corner of the ceiling and pointed it out to her.

"Elles sont fascinantes." They are fascinating. "Humans, we do not appreciate their complexity, they have endured much more than our species, have adapted beautifully. They were originally water creatures, we all were, but when they evolved from the water to the land their bodies began producing silk to protect their bodies and their eggs. They were much smarter than that, however. They gradually began using the silk for hunting, first as guidelines and signal lines. They lived on the ground first, constructing bush webs, but it is the aerial webs that astound me. You see, they might look ugly and are killed fast enough in any house. I wish that we appreciated their intricacy, their beauty. You know they can produce different types of silk threads from various glands in their abdomen. They make safety lines that are not sticky so that they can balance upon them. They make sticky silk for trapping prey and fine silk threads to entomb their victims for preservation. *Magnifique!*"

His intelligence and knowledge of everything always

astounded and pulled her closer to him. Each time he spoke, she fell deeper in love.

"You must think me crazy, Amelié, but the structure of the web mesmerizes me."

Nervous, guilty heat rose up in her body, an anxious furnace. Looking discreetly down at her body, she saw a spider's body. She saw Eli on the web.

"They use their own body for measurement. First, they let out a fine adhesive thread that drifts through the air across the gap they are trying to forge. When the thread meets the other side, it sticks, the spider will carefully walk across it, strengthening the line by letting out a second thread." Amelié nestled closer. Eli continued.

"They do this until the thread is strong enough to support the entire web. Then, the spider makes the netting of the web. You see," he pointed his finger, Amelié studied where he pulled at dry cuticles, "the radials of points that the net spans across and meets with the support line. Once those radials are completed the spider fortifies the center of the web by weaving circular threads. Some are sticky, some not. Depends on how the spider wants to navigate their web. They know where the prey will land. They know where they will sleep." He paused and the silence cocooned them. He felt comfort in this silence, she felt angst.

"It is the perfect symmetry in nature. The web is always proportional to the spider's body," he held up a thumb and pointer finger, cleared his throat.

"Each spiral is congruent to the distance from the tip of the spider's back legs to its spinners. This is the way the spider will use its own body to space the threads."

She turned into his neck pressing her lips against the column of his throat. She turned back and they watched the spider twitch.

Sophie shook her head and eyed this New World spider. She was shaking, her skin cold and pale. She cupped her fingers around her mouth and puffed into them. She stood shaking the memory from her head. It shrank back and folded inside her, embedded with the other leaves of her memory. Shingles of her soul.

She hovered over the case, found comfort in the snap of the latches as she flicked them open. The case severed and split open. Sophie dug her hands into the case laying pieces ceremoniously on top of the antique quilt coverlet.

The bible was cold to the touch, the pages silky in her palms. The bed creaked, caved under her weight. She cracked open the book and let the letters fall into her.

In haloed lamplight, she read them over. Her eyelids, lead. She was not aware when they closed or when she laid back on the spring mattresses.

He found her this way, curled around herself on top of the covers, a made bed. Her hands cradled blue pencil crayon scratchings.

He found her this way.

The same sane woman
she was and
things were never the same,
the same sane again,
between them.

RIPPLE

"you are a horse running alone
and he tries to tame you.
compares you to an impossible highway,
to a burning house,
says you are blinding him,
that he could never leave you,
forget you,
want anything but you."

i am a white lotus flower,
open, fragile and moist.
cup me, shield me,
enable me the space
and safety to stay open.
ground me, memorize
my body with warm hands,
trusting-wanting-lips,
listen to my ideas,
let me write,
let me express my spirituality,
let me think,
let me love,

let me make mistakes, and,
to be imperfect.

i have stepped into my Divine Rights,
Sacred Feminine,
i am passion on that highway,
Ferocious cravings,
windows down, music blasting,
i am a rock, i am an island.

"you dizzy him, you are unbearable,
every woman before or after you
is doused in your name,
you fill his mouth,
his teeth ache with memory of taste,
his body just a long shadow seeking yours,"

"relationships are like this," she says,
splays open her right palm,
lifts it skyward, petalled,
"you're open, he's going to protect
you in that vulnerability,"
Juliet brings her left hand up,
duality, balled-gripping-energy,
Romeo will empower you,
"to bud and blossom, to stay open,
no matter where in the world you are,
if he's not open,"
she dangerously fists her left hand
and the lotus smashes,
sucks up, and wraps itself around
to protect the frightened fist,
"it's difficult for love to thrive like this,
two fists, well,
that's domestic violence, isn't it?"

"but you are always too intense
frightening in the way you want him
unashamed and sacrificial
he tells you that no man can live up to the one who
lives in your head"

it's brutally simple:
find the one in your head,
soul mate.

"and you tried to change, didn't you?
closed your mouth more
tried to be softer, prettier
less volatile, less awake"

that's what you do,
the white lotus flower
floats on water,
the water that erodes
stones, despite its
softness, its apparent
silence in certain
basins.

"but even when sleeping you could feel
him travelling away from you in his dreams
so what did you want to do love,
split his head open?"

he travelled far,
i journeyed too, went Away,
chest to chest,
nose to nose,
palm to palm,
we were that close,
wrist to wrist,

toes,
words we made,
crushed the rose.
we split and splayed
each other,

i cherish that story,
because young love was close
and desire burns,
we are both alive,
survived,
and will hold those memories
as secrets in our heads
in the years of aging.

"you can't make homes out of human beings
someone should have already told you that"

i am my own home,
alone, but not lonely,
i will give myself time to heal now,
but i keep moving my hands and feet,
spinning, weaving, rotating,
knitting another life, blanketed

"and if he wants to leave
then let him leave
you are terrifying
and strange and beautiful
something not everyone knows how to love."

now,
to learn the most difficult lesson,
how to let go,
the anger rises up in the pit of nights,
the double lives, perpetuated,

spear the severe and spit fire,
feng-shui-fiascos,

this lustrous polishing,
that fragmented domesticity that
sent me running from their confusion,
spiritual intervention,
profound rhapsody,

"you lacked me,
it was always me,
beautiful-destructive-creature,
injected with a divine madness,"
sacred breathe, planting roots,
it won't always hurt,
but then again,
this world wants to avoid the hurt,
when life is meant to feel alive from pain,
pain's ripe-rotting-fullness, once.

THE PAST

Phillip peeled the letter from her hand without waking her. He attempted to decipher the text, knew it was a missive from a transition camp, but did not understand why his wife would have brought this with her.

Who would have written this to her?

He could only see a list, things that this individual needed. He missed the encrypted meaning of St. Martin.

There was a moment in that miniscule bedroom when his eyes spotted the name childishly looped in blue pencil crayon. It read, Amélie Cyncad.

She was Sophie Anouk to him.

He realized, then, that he did not know exactly who she was, how she survived the war, or what her story was before geography exploded.

His mind had tiptoed towards the prodding earlier on in their courtship, but he had just assumed she was like the others, had survived by remaining alone, hiding in the right places, exposing herself in the right situations, not exposing herself in the wrong situations. He had not fathomed that she would huddle under names of pretence, was an expert at contriving identities.

Could she have worked for the Germans? Could she have

worked with them?

He did not expect the reaction he felt from the letter. She was cunning—deceiving him intentionally. He clenched his jaw and felt the throbbing ache of betrayal, and stupidity of assuming that because she was a woman and couldn't speak English, she wasn't dangerous. A scorching blush flushed his skin —humiliated, the war forced him to marry a woman he distinctly did not know. Worse yet, that she planned to live each day with him under this umbrella of a lie that her most secret craft was name-changing and identity-making.

He crumbled the letter in his fist and flung it on the floor. The paper ball rolled under the bed. Phillip stood for several moments watching her sleep. Her chest rose and fell with shallow breaths, the corners of her mouth twitched slightly while her closed eyelids fluttered. He felt anger, raw molten rage that he would never know exactly what she held captive inside her mind, what she thought, how she felt. He would not ask her and this formed the cusp of his resentment.

He sees them colliding by a streetcar. He remembers the confirmation that she was coming to Madoc.

His large hands rose and began to unbutton his shirt. He stepped out of his shoes. His belt buckle clinked as he dropped it to the floor. He leaned forward and forced her skirt up above her waist. She awoke to the callus of his palm suffocating her inside her skirt, him swollen and intimidatingly angry against her.

She could not see his face, his eyes, or know exactly how angry he was. She gasped loudly when he mounted her forcibly. Sophie's body stiffened and she cried out from the sudden intrusion. He grunted and forced himself further, bucking and rearing like a horse. She clawed his back and bit into his shoulder, which only sent his blood racing, coursing with rage and desire. She hovered in her pain, peering over his shoulder at the cracked indigo ceiling. Her eyes found the spider's web and stayed there, the radials that fanned across the ceiling and adjoining walls trapped her in the prism bending the light of realization and acceptance that this was her life now. A deep fissure ran behind the web extending up onto the ceiling collecting in a profusion of tangled swells and indents. She wept.

She focused. Her pupils shrank to pinholes, the muscles in her thighs tightened. She kept her eyes on the ceiling, the mass of cracks. She saw a leafless tree, bent forward and wilted. The branches were thin. Straining across plaster, her eyes fell into the motley of cracks. She smelled wet pavement and leaves. The musk of damp wood rose up and almost choked her. Her fingertips dug into his back. Phillip felt like leather, as if her gloves were pulled on and she was outside, pinned to the mud. His breath became ragged, a rhythm that flung her back into darkness, blood, and waking up underneath that tree.

Phillip stilled, the full weight of his body pressed down on her and she sunk into the bed. She did not thrash, she did not wipe the wetness from her face. She watched him with vehemence as he rose from her. He caught her look of contempt and balled his fist against it, but she only felt the blow of his tongue, hard and thick like a whip and clamped shut like a mussel.

"I do not love you and I do not want you, Amélie."

STORYTELLER

"Your children are not your children. They are the sons and daughters of Life's longing for itself."

-Khalil Gibran

There was a man from Deseronto, the same land that birthed Deganawidah and the Great Law. A man who lost his family.

Tuberculosis. A missing foot.

The man, taken away, not gone Away. He could not provide for family and keep them together.

War and the separation of family.

"They come through you, but not from you, and though they are with you, yet they belong not to you."

This man, much like the farmer who stumbled across the Madoc Meteorite is footnoted in family history, not national legacy. Names echo across time and keep us living. This family did not know his name. Perhaps the first name, but they did not know him and where he came from. His story is this: a man who lost his family, who fought a war and lost his family to sickness.

War disrupts family. Those who start wars do not care about

the family construct. They cut down and log trees, the trees of life; they kill children and women in war. Trees are people.

Daughter, I will tell the story this way to lay down a layer that could enable compassion. There is strength in the bruised aching membrane of this angle of knowing.

The man I speak of now is remembered for his sickness and how this sickness changed bloodlines, altered life currents that rippled beyond his own comprehension of influence, his own self-worth.

I wish I knew normal things about him. His favourite colour. Memories from his childhood. Where he exactly was from. The way he looked, and what his eyes did when he smiled.

The Sanatorium Age is whispered about, if it is even mentioned. In 1895 the anti-tuberculosis society built the first institution on Muskoka Lake near Gravenhurst: the Cottage Sanatorium. Most people stayed eight to ten years, and it completely uprooted patients from their family. In 1948 they introduced antimicrobials in treating tuberculosis, which short-ened the duration of the in-patient treatment. The average length of stay with treatment was seven to eight months. This concept of treatment was persistent until the 1970s.

He lived through a grim reality after the war, overlaid like a stencil on each other's lives—he and his wife alien to each other. They would be strangers, but they served each other like oxygen to humans and carbon dioxide to plants. While his wife rose and broke the ice in the wash basin to survive another day, he tucked blood coughs in his pockets.

The man from Deseronto was a sick man. His chest bucked, braying like a bull in coughing fits. His lungs buttered in a blood smear that chalked the inside of his lungs causing the most incessant itching at the back of his throat. He brought the tuberculosis back with him from the war like a good friend. Yoked to his sagging shoulders, he had spat in the eye of death, so death kicked him in the ass.

It was the same bacteria that plagued history, but this time it collided with our story.

Scientists traced the earliest strain of the disease, mycobacterium tuberculosis, in the remains of a bison from 18,000 years ago. Daughter, your great-grandfather was ancient.

He could not shake the tuberculosis from his life, and it latched on like a bloodsucker. It was his eventual ruin. There was nothing he could do.

We honour him for the best he did with what he had and what could be provided for him.

Before the industrial revolution, tuberculosis was regarded as vampirism because those infected eventually sucked the life from the family, one by one. When one family member perished, others would soon follow, a tidal wave into the grave. Folklore, tongued by magic, said the death and despair reigned from the diseased. Fear, that lonesome state, hooked the living in institutions. They leaned against isolation, the bones of quarantine. Sending the sick away was the only way.

Today, we repel the bacteria with immunizations; all he needed was the prick of a needle. But the sick man from Deseronto was forsaken by time, how in that era, during post-World War Two, and within the rural Canadian farm society, the sick man was taken from his family and placed in a sanatorium.

"You may give them your love but not your thoughts,
For they have their own thoughts.
You may house their bodies but not their souls,
For their souls dwell in the house of tomorrow,
Which you cannot visit, not even in your dreams.
You may strive to be like them,
But seek not to make them like you."

Daughter, you must know, we must acknowledge how much our lives were dictated by others and that they did not know, could not conceive of knowing, how placing that sick man from Deseronto in a sanatorium would coalesce in a generational unraveling and familial dislocation—policide.

This story haunches still at a beginning, unearthing our own paper trail. I've let textual residue come to me, rather than fully pursue it, as I typically do. Truths will be revealed as they need to be.

Archival record, your great-grandfather's name was Stanley Scruby. In 1949, he disowned his wife's debts. This record names her, Isabel Margaret.

Voter's lists shows in 1963 Stanley listed as living in Lonsdale, in Tyendinaga Township. Mrs. Scruby is not recorded. She was already gone.

She had been listed as living in Corbyville, Thurlow Township with him in 1957. The year my father was born.

The Scruby's emigration record from 1930 lists Henry, Maud, and Stanley embarking from Liverpool. Stanley's occupation, scholar. He was 14.

The florid whiteness of the facility demonstrated the value of rest, fresh air, good nutrition, and isolation to prevent the spread of infection. Institutionalization left no room for the darkness harboured in trauma from the war and desperation of being away from family. Sir William Gage, the founder of this sanatorium era, overlooked the drastic measure of isolation, how such dislocation would disrupt family lines.

What would have happened if these people had stayed home though?

Economics dictated the birth of the large centres that specialized in diagnosis and treatment.

All that depends on a needle and the swath of a cotton ball.

In 1938, alone, Canada boasted 61 sanatoriums with 9,000 beds growing to 19,000 beds in 1953.

He dwelled in one of those beds. Sunken and shaken, he mewled like a kitten for sustenance and matriarchy. Quietly, heroically.

Your great-grandfather was gone three years from his family. The government took him away and left his family with absence.

"For life goes not backward nor tarries with yesterday."

The War was over, but it continued to rage in more occult vibrations inside their hearts and heads, ripples in their lives that they could not live away from or avoid. She had six mouths to feed, and a wild tendency to abate. She pulled her fingers through her hair ravaging her cuticles. Her hair stood on end, her eyes bulged, and she counted the layers of the soap, calculating how many more bodies she could bathe with it.

They ate dust and bathed in tears.

He is buried in Shannonville, Hastings County, Ontario. Born 1915 and died 1992. 76 or 77 years old. His gravestone shows that he was a Sergeant.

His wife is there with him. Geraldine M. Scruby. Born 1924 and died 2000.

Either the records are wrong, or her name changes too.

Lest We Forget.

He took a stroll through the marsh along the levelled boardwalk and opened his mouth for three blue pills twice daily.

He sweated out the illness.

He dressed promptly the next morning.

Three years of waiting, and he was free.

He returned home to Hades.

The government had taken his babies and thrown them to the wind like dandelion wishes.

RIPPLE

The World War Two veteran
found the swastika drawn
on his Granddaughter's
hard plastic pencil case.

He gently brought the seven
Year old near
And offered her his only
Lecture, words from the wise,

For a curious mind, he assumed,
In a world marked by the pain
Of what that image meant for
A world recovering and healing
From Hitler's violence,

"This image is very bad
and if you keep it on your
pencil case you are going
to get into trouble."

She felt dirty, guilt, and shame

That it was so difficult to please
Her Elders, their stern vigor,
Not knowing that she simply
Was accessing ancient knowing,
A natural reclamation.
She blacked out the entire
Hooked black drawing firmly
With a thick black marker,
A line of burning tears
Etched a beautiful river
On her little cheeks.
The veteran was not schooled
To know that what the child
Had shown was a remarkable
Connection with intuition and
Spirit, that the symbol
Was unrotated and imprinted

In its pure state, ancient,
Peaceful vibration before
Hitler had manipulated and
Sunk angry teeth into it.

Hakenkreuz, gamma cross,
Gammadion, St. Brigid's cross,
Or fylfot cross, the oldest cross,
Perhaps the oldest emblem known
To human civilization,
Four arms, luck, light, love, and life,
On a Chinese coin dated 315 B.C.,
It was found by the mound builders,
The cliff dwellers of Mexico,
Central America, consider,

The universal reality of
The emblem, a charm to

Drive away evil and bring
Good luck, long life, prosperity,
The Greek's articulation was four Gammas,
In Hebrew, four Daleths, to the non-literate
It related to no letters, an equilateral cross
With four arms bent at right angles,
Hinduism, Buddhism, and Jainism,
A sacred symbol, Shakti,
Medicine wheel teachings,
How energy moves from and around
The Sacred Fire, the circle of life.

The Nazis stood it up diagonally
And placed it in a circle rather than
Running it four square, branded it,
A political logo,
Black, white, red,
A national seal of murder.

THE PAST

She walked alone. They would not go with her. The men left at day break each morning. The women remained, shouldering the cobwebs from the corners of the house, probing the deepest nooks for dirt and secrets. She was a pebble in the soles of their shoes. An object, hard and mute, they picked her from the bottom of their callused heels and tossed her lightly out the door muttering. She knew, but refused to admit it to herself, that she was useless in this new country, her language, folk knowledge, and experiences were irrelevant to the mechanics of the tiny household on the hill on Russel Street.

She felt the blow of the language gap, unraveling each day. Her tongue cupped vowels and pushed for assonance, her lips curled awkwardly, and she held much of the resonance of her voice in the back of her throat. Her attempts at English brought on the onslaught of discreet ridicule.

She heard more than she dared let on, understood much more than they thought. They could not know that she relished the solitude of her isolation, if anything it allowed her to live each day from the corners of her intellect, dwelling in the recesses of her imagination.

Sophie dressed early one morning, frozen on the upstairs landing, her toes hovering over the threshold when she caught some of Magna's words like hooks. Magna took it for granted that her new daughter-in-law could not speak strong English, because of this, she assumed that Sophie was not intellectually adept or socially aware.

She would never know that morning, while she pounded the dough and pushed it flat with her wooden roller, that the young woman was hovering on the brink of entering into their domestic cocoon. Cassandra, perched on a stool next to the oven, sat peeling potatoes. Her small knife glinted in the light, the tip of her tongue bitten and statued at the line of her mouth, the skin of the potatoes curling backwards spiraling into an aluminum bucket. When Magna spoke, Cassandra would raise her head and beam at her mother with transparent eyes. That was her look of assurance, that her mother was right.

"I don't know how he manages, with that broken tongue of hers. How'd he marry a stranger and why'd he bring her here. Do you not sense how cold she is, she is stone." Magna's eyes remained fixed on her hands, her knuckles dusted, her finger-nails chalked in flour. She cut the thick skin of dough into smaller squares, sprinkling them with ground cinnamon and nutmeg. She rolled the squares, her thick fingers peppering the dough in thumbprints that she did not smooth out when she curved the rolled squares onto a buttered baking sheet.

Sophie listened to the shrill clanking of the baking sheet as Magna maneuvered to the oven, sliding the tray along the rack. She gripped her stomach with her left arm and cradled the elbow of her left arm with the sweaty palm of her right.

She wanted to force her feet down the steps into the kitchen. She wanted to see the woman's eyes as she spoke of her, how they muddled in the corners with wet salt and dirt when she stretched her lips wide in gossip. She saw herself dropping the bag of flour on the floor, the sweeping white cloud dusting them in the center of chaos.

Then she could speak, and honed the words slowly in her mind. *If I stayed they would have axed me. I loved a Jew and let him go. I slept with a Romanian to survive. I even entertained a*

German. Women and war, they only survive if they know how to play their roles. I married your son to escape a country seeking out anyone who had trekked the enemy's side to survive. I changed my name so that they couldn't find me.

She pictured them growing smaller and sunken as she fluently conveyed to them her war bride story. She would force them to look her in the eyes as she knifed the last detail of her experience into their misunderstanding hearts, I was raped, and I cannot have children because of this. I wanted to die. When I lost Eli and tried to get his papers to him, I was raped for it; I wanted to die.

Instead she retreated, wretched, into the darkness of her bed and waited for the sun to rise before she emerged and abandoned them to their lantern lit lives.

That was the day she found the library. It was a small building tucked away behind the post office. She remembered his brown eyes flicking along the lines on the page while she memorized the movement of his lips mouthing the words. They read to avoid the war in the beginning; navigating through the pages, he was able to take her beyond the confines of the graying apartment and the bombs exploding around them.

She would press her palm to the face of his novels when he was not looking. The leather-bound holiness of their spines and how he cracked them, sending shivers down her hips and up inside her. She had loved books then, she loved how they fit in his hands.

Sophie said nothing to the elderly librarian who eyed her aggressively over the lenses of her reading glasses. She entered the library with conviction, a face of stone set deep enough that the librarian knew not to disturb her. The old crow knew of her, that this was the French woman that young Stone lad had brought back from the war.

She herself had unfurled her lips to let the bite of her words smear against her wine glass over a game of bridge. She flew with the elderly women who huddled around polished tabletops and wetted their tongues on others' lives.

"She must be pregnant. That's why he married her so fast and brought her here. No sane woman would leave without force." They were the words, the hard pebbles of their conversations that these women deliberately threw far into society. They crooned and laughed as the stories skipped across the surface of intellect, breaking the current, and eventually sinking in a cesspool of degradation. Their hands were not wet, nor their feet. Glass surfaces. Glass houses. Glass stones.

Sophie knew the narrative she wanted to fall into, thus ignoring the librarian's sideways look she disappeared amongst the stacks. She needed reassurance, something to pinion her quaking heart to the severity of her reality. She wanted to face herself, the emotions coursing through her, crackling like a livewire. Mostly, she wanted to be able to feel something tangible in her hands, and somehow, without knowing exactly, be able to mold that into another thing altogether.

She could not explain how she knew the volume was there. In that moment, she let her feet go, let the burn of mockery force her to pick up each foot and let it fall with precision. Her eyes followed the black font, the typewritten name, *Madoc*, by Robert Southey. She lingered in front of the shelf, her eyes mesmerized by the title. She remembered the first time she heard the word, had tested its sharpness inside the hollow above her tongue, her lips stretched. She drew comfort from the arc of her tongue, how it flattened slightly, and then quickly arched, clicking against the roof of her mouth. Her arm extended and her hand reached for the spine of the book.

The volume was heavy, the cover faded, and the edges of the pages yellowed. She hefted the sturdy volume from the shelf and locked it against her side.

Comprising two drafty rooms, one built in the mid 1800s the other after the First World War the library was small and cramped. The librarian's lumbering desk, centered in the middle of the first room, blocked the entrance. Books insulated the walls collecting dust and other fragments like red string and a child's black button sunk deep in recesses of the shelves and between the book's pages.

A bird's nest, woven with fingerprints and imagination, Sophie was ignited for the first time since leaving Brussels. She spotted several tables and armchairs littering the edges of the rooms, but journeyed to the deepest pocket of the library. She turned her back to the entrance and buried herself into the shadows.

The windows were narrow, small rectangles shaded by sturdy wooden blinds. Light rippled in between the upturned shades casting lined rays across a low pine table pushed against the window's peeling ledge. Sophie was drawn to the window and pulled the chair out from beneath the table and angled it so that her back was to the rest of the library and her face to the window. She sighed and sat down.

She anticipated opening books, the smell of paper and pressed ink massaged her nostrils, and she savored the minute earthy tones that always emanated from the pages. She traced the tips of her fingers along the inside cover page, her lips cradling the phonetic impression of the word against the crevices of her mouth. Gripping her fingers around the edges of the book she turned to the second page.

Sophie did not know, and would be surprised, that the book was an epic poem, the lines resting in a crib in the middle of the page. A classical eulogy for legend, she would take from this poem only the idea of reality, that the plot had unfolded in the lives of the past, and that she was somehow, however intimately and distantly, related to it.

She slowly made her way through the first sentence, not realizing her bottom had shifted to the very edge of her seat and was teetering in anticipation for clarity. A name stood out first, Owain Gwynedd, King of North Wales, and she knew that the writer was speaking of the king's death in 1169 A.D. She gathered that on the king's death his sons quarreled for power, slaying each other like strangers.

The second name caught her eye, and she understood then, her new village, diminutive and vast in one breath, existed in the shadow of a name of a Welsh prince, Madog ab Owain Gwynedd was Welsh and he sailed to America in 1170. Sophie calculated quickly that it was 300 years before Columbus, and she sensed the anticipation in her stomach begin to ball. Madoc had made the treacherous journey to the shores of the New World, embraced the New Land. He intermarried with local natives.

She wondered over the word "colony," and its similarity to colonie. Sophie thought of the word "settlement" and she could see the cut logs, lined together to form a wall, a component of the outside perimeter, the forest fortress where Madoc's men camped and conquered. She does not conjure up Moodie, "life in the clearings versus the bush," or that she was also "roughing it" in her own capacity for surviving the hard northern face of the Canadian Shield.

Sophie marveled at the bearing of the story, its daringness to challenge Columbus' foothold on the New World. The proximity of the story pulled, the lines absorbing through her with wonder, the enticement of strength and resilience—pure survival. She did not know of Erik the Red and the L'ans aux Meadows. How he had come only 169 years earlier. She conceptualized her story as only a speck of human dust in the wave of exploration, her forehead rested in her palm, a furrowed map, a constellation of skin cells and wrinkles that were both diminutive and a part of something larger. History hadn't yet contained the story of the Peterborough Petroglyphs, starships, and solar boats, even though Sophie sensed infinity in her veins. Sophie could only relate that she had also journeyed to the New World, endured the trek across the gut of the Atlantic, and bravely fell into a new existence. Her new home, Madoc.

The light shifted in between the window blinds and sunk towards the horizon. Sophie was lost, caught in the contours of Southey's poetics entranced by the new language she fell into. Eventually her tongue and intellect secured a firm grip, and she was able to navigate the classical lyrics with piqued ease. Reading the old language, it was how she practiced her English.

Warm bodies rotated around her, pulling the spines of books from the shelves, wetting their fingers, curling through pages. She was deaf to the living, the warm bodies baked beneath wool and hand knitted stockings. She did not see their eyes, the curious glances and the brave belligerent stares from the Madocians. She heard only her own internal scripting, the flush of her French accent braided with this new emerging language, comprehension pressing confidence. Time was abandoned and she savoured the escape.

It was nearing the moment when the librarian would clear her throat, reach forwards in anticipation, and prick the service bell mounted to her desk. Her voice, carrying to the intimate spaces of the library, cautioned the readers and seekers of closing time.

But Sophie had an epiphany before then. She had reached the fourth section of the volume, her pointer finger blotting out the page number. Southey was describing Madoc's voyage across the Atlantic, and Sophie noted how the poet delved into the cavernous alcoves of the narrative, the Welsh's very mind.

My days were days of fear; my hours of rest
Were like a tyrant's slumber.

Sophie dwelled on the line, testing her understanding with a toe in the water first, then plunging in without reserve or boundaries. There she was, a body and a baby rolling through the sea looking up at a woman holding the railing of a ship. She would write down the lines as she read to feel out the language.

Sullen looks,
Eyes turned on me, and whispers meant to meet
My ear, and loud despondency, and talk
Of home, now never to be seen again...

· · ·

Sophie's English convoluted the lines, but she felt the brevity of emotions, the sagging inside the heart. She also endured sullen looks with silence. There was talk of home, she could smell lavender and felt the cool metal of the ladies' lavatory, and embraced the impact of comprehension that splayed her open like a gutted fish on sun-baked drying racks.

Home, now never to be seen again...

Her fingers probed her face and worked the tension from her temples. She imagined a ship bracing turbulent waters, a crew tremulous and brave. They must have lined the deck during departure, saluting the shores of a home they had taken for granted, arriving on new shores, their bodies leavened, thick-skinned with calluses, for the fresh land. She looked over her shoulder impulsively and continued.

I sought my solitary cabin; there,
Confus'd with vague, tumultuous feelings, lay,
And, to remembrance and reflection lost,
Knew only I was wretched.

Sophie paused and leaned back in her chair. She snapped the book closed. Her mind unfolded, dictionary-like, unraveling the trail of words, like stitches in a crooked knit scarf, letting the emotions etch into her understanding. She knew wretched coils around sadness, that it meant miserable. She could only feel the tones of hardship, of the perception of living in an illusion of inadequacy and deprivation.

Years later when her mouth lipped English more fluidly and her French resided in the pit of her Old World happiness, Sophie would learn of etymology and elate in the fissures of understanding. She would think backwards from the state of wretched, to the very wretches themselves, and she would know and feel what it was like to have lived the meaning of "the other," stranger, *wrecca*, and *wrekkio*, an exile.

She will work through pain in each layer of understanding. It will take her years to accept the taste of vile in her throat—

acrid and suffocating—she will sense how they gravitated away from her and her conditions of dislocation and mistranslation. She does not blame them for this. The other Women who will come after her lifeline will not parallel Madoc's odyssey.

She will sink into her green leather armchair as an elder, roll a blanket around her stiff knees, and acknowledge that she is a person not understood. Those that rotate in her presence do so out of obligation and familial duty, they wish that, somehow, they could extend themselves as bridges, or locate the spaces between the shingles of her soul. She lets so few in, and that footing is unsure, constantly changing.

THE PAST

The boxed frame house atop the hill on Russel Street was full of family, and the nature of Sophie and Phillip's relationship was dictated by such residency. The Stone family rotated and shifted around each other for almost two years, most times with clenched jaws and grating teeth.

Sophie had gained weight, her hips clinging to the starch of homemade bread, thick butter, and milk from delivered bottles. The fresh air had stamped away the hollows in her cheeks, her pale skin now brushed with a slight pink blush, her blonde hair shone. She looked healthy, thick-skinned, and sturdy-boned on the outside, but inside … inside she kept how she felt private.

She learned how to shake the dark from her skeleton when he lay with her. His body, broad and heavy, sought the warmth of her pockets, the intimacy between her thighs, the thin skin splaying across an ankle bone with the callus of his heel. She rose to him awkwardly, offered her body, but turned her face to corners and shadows. They both, however, felt the edge of the disconnect, the hard ridge between her heart and his reality.

He felt the frost, layered upon itself deep within her cavity, and he struggled to connect. It was slight, like a ghost or curling snow drift. He would catch the shadow folded behind the retinas of her gaze. Her blue eyes polished and set against white, fluttered occasionally in a blink of shadow, the edge of a wrist, or the soft black tendril of hair. Phillip pieced them together slowly until he could slightly taste the outline of a man, a man of letters, the one with the yellow cloth and black daunting lines. Phillip only knew of the letter, had not read further with his fingers to touch the indents of longing on the underside of the paper, the dark spot where he had hovered, placing his lips to the cool surface of the page, yearning for warmth and a return home.

It occurred quickly once the men had deliberated. First, there was a conversation. Father and son planted like trees in the room while the women sucked in breath and rounded their chapped hands around the open face of potato peels and carrot skins.

"Phillip, it is time for you to build a house for your wife." Gregory spoke from masculine order and feminine concern, an understanding of familial structure, a hierarchy of residence, and his son would follow unyielding. A raising up, Sophie wondered why this conversation had to happen. Action wasn't faster.

"There is land by the lake, I have already arranged with the owners that you will purchase it from them." He leaned forward in his armchair, carefully spread open the newspaper in his calloused hands. Phillip looked at his father with trepidation and longing.

"Because I'm a veteran, they will help pay for the land. I only pay a certain percentage." Gregory momentarily looked up from his newspaper and beamed.

"So you thought about this. Good." Phillip nodded, his father did not see, and the young man left the house, his legs shaking subtly as he opened the car door and got in. The engine gunned to life. She watched from the upstairs window.

Land parceling was common for war vets. Language washed up on their lives later, the after-war recovery birthing another discourse to contain them.

Victim.

Alien.

Refugee.

Migrant.

Holocaust survivor.

Diaspora.

War bride.

Positions changed with conception.

Processes.

The Veterans Land Act, R.C. 1952, specified that "property'" was essentially land, goods, chattels, personal or movable property.

She was movable.

Sophie could not conceive that she was property—war bride property. War language created "refugee," and "displaced person." Constructs.

"Veteran," was deemed a person who was declared by "His Majesty on the 10th day of September 1939 against the German Reich," and those engaged in naval, army, or air force. A "veteran" was a resident of Canada and his duties were performed outside of the Western Hemisphere. The General Advisory Committee on Demobilization and Rehabilitation was mandated with preparing a comprehensive war benefits package: the Veterans' Land Act, the Education Benefit, the New Business Start up Benefit, and the Reestablishment Credits. When the Veterans' Land Act was created in 1942 the benefits were paid up to $3,600 for a parcel of land including improvements, equipment not exceeding value of $1,200, and, if he farmed, horses.

The first time he took her to the hill she was frightened and a helix of anxiety formed in the pit of her abdomen. The forest encased the construction site, full and bursting with noise, she wondered if there were animals lurking, perhaps a man with a dark face beneath a tree. She shivered and knew that she would spend many nights alone here.

The workers had cleared the top of the hill, their machines displacing jutting rocks that would become the driveway. From this vantage point they were able to see all of the Moira, how it wrapped westward around the land, transgressed by the highway and train tracks until it disappeared as a thick channel into the woods. The surface of the Moira glinted, was never the same sane surface, and this fluidity rippled Sophie's nerves.

She turned away from the workers and their growling machines, then gravitated towards a small clearing to the left of the property. Sophie nearly tripped over a bent metal fence lining the clearing and tangle of sumac. She fumbled over and pushed the powdery crimson branches of sumac out of her face. She fell into the quietness of the clearing.

There was a large boulder in the middle of the space coated in a thick carpet of lichen. A warm gust of wind swept up from the lake, across the expanse of the clearing, and down the neck of Sophie's blouse. She let the air pull her body down. She sat on the boulder for a moment, felt other women there, got up, and continued her walk. It took her several moments to shake the comfort from her skin and continue.

After twenty meters the clearing angled up in a steep incline. Sophie tilted her head, tracing the outline of trees high above her head with the tip of her finger. She moved towards the boulder and leaned against it. The rock's heat burned through her pants, and she quickly raised herself from its surface. She kicked her shoes through the long grasses, reveling in the scent of upturned mulch, wet and earthy. She gazed towards the lakefront, the wind tasting the back of her ears—burned red in the sun. She stopped where the hill began to level out towards a dirt road that ran along the back of the property. The decline was steep; if she fell there would be no relief from the stones in her back and gravel in her teeth.

She couldn't believe that she had not noticed the tree earlier. It extended black and snaked into the air. She stepped closer, placing the palm of her hand against a deep gash in the face of the tree. The gash had grown up with new bark, the light grey a severe contrast to the charcoal black scar arching up into the pit of the tree. She did not know, but assumed that the tree had been struck by lightning. The hit severed the trunk, causing it to sag under its heavy branches, eventually bracing itself with new growth. She pulled her hand from the tree placing it over her heart. She knew that there was a similar ridge that ran deep into her own secrets and knowledge. She felt the hollows under her eyes, like the grey bark, layers against the outside.

She walked away from the tree with a newly planted seed inside her, a garnish to her comprehension of how she oriented her new life, like the tree, expanding upon herself in rough stratums of preservation. She felt the current, womb vibrations, the chill that bled around the base of the tree, rising in waves of energy both electric and muting.

It might have been the wind, or a particle finger that pushed back the hair around her face to see who was visiting. She did not notice that the base of the tree, closest to the lake, swelled slightly, a trivial protrusion of soil, the hump of a shoulder blade, the curve of a hip bone, and then stone.

THE PAST

It took several weeks for the new house to take shape. She watched the crawl space cut into the rocky ground and smelled the cemented foundations, already reeking of mildew, mice skeletons, and leaves of milk-white snakeskins. She shivered and folded her arms over her chest. She was more accustomed to flats, she grew up several stories above the ground, and even now she wasn't ready to come down. She returned only when the framing of the house was complete and the roof had been secured.

The house was a long bungalow carving out space against the hill and forest line. She stood in the shadow of a birch tree, envisioning the life that would unfold here. She would no longer live pawing her way into the rotation of her mother-in-law's domestic subsistence. She smiled inwardly, sketchily, because no more would she set her jaw against the hushed tones of the woman, or endure the penetrating gaze from her azure eyes that were so rich in color Sophie often forgot about the perspective that looked out from behind them. She would miss Cassandra's storytelling, how she was able to weave fantasy into the harshness of reality. Her rooms would be silent throughout the days her mind reeled and her emotions congealed with 20th century rationality. The fogginess would settle and remain, drifting in the corners of her consciousness. She did not foreshadow sadness or isolation.

Phillip startled her when he stepped from the framing and strode towards the birch tree in three ample strides. His nearness unhinged her concentration. She smelled the musk of his sweat sponging the material tucked beneath his underarms, his mouth emanated in a sharp scent, the trace of alcohol constantly seeping from his pores. She feigned ignorance, said nothing of his scent. She pulled her left hand from the cradle of her right arm and swept it in the air before the house.

"It is nice. *C'est magnifique!*" She cleared her throat gently and angled her body slightly towards him. His stare remained fixed on the front of the house. His large hands hung by his sides. He did not look at her when he spoke. She watched his lips, noticed how thin they were.

"It's going to take about another week. We have to put in the plumbing, electricity, you know, before the walls are finished." He sucked his lips in. They disappeared, leaving a canvas of wet open pores. Sophie almost laughed, his mouth was gone, but she shifted her weight from her right foot to the left and continued to listen.

"What do you think of the embellishments? I thought they tied in well together?" He turned to her sharply and with vigor, she was startled. Her eyebrows arched, pulling the skintight. She shook her face.

"What's that? I didn't get you…"

He puffed out his cheeks impatiently and lumbered towards the house. Phillip didn't like his facial expressions, walked off for this. He stopped in front of the cramped cement niche that sheltered the entrance to the front door.

Supporting the angled roof was a dense black chain melded together forming an indissoluble foundation. The links were thick, the exact volume of a clenched fist, secured in the cement, extending to the beams of the roof. She found it ugly, but could not ascertain exactly why she felt this way. She knew the chain was cold without smoothing her fingers along its contours. She could smell its essence, the clipped metallic scent that snaked across her skin linking forcibly inside her.

She saw the chain biting into her skin, the delicate translucent skin of an ankle bone. It dragged behind her, groaning and scraping against the ground. She shuffled forwards, the chain pulling her muscles down, bruising the flesh around them, the tendons taut and strained, and she felt a tremor grow and pulsate in the meat of her wrist. Startled, she pushed her hand into the crevice of her bended arms. He did not notice.

"It's an anchor." He folded his fingers around one of the closest links while he spoke, his onyx stone camouflaged with the black paint. Sophie stared unblinking, her eyes drying and clicking against the thin membrane of her eyelids.

She missed the true weight of what he said initially. Rolling the word around in her head, anchor, the phonetics playing with her familiarity.

"*Ancre*, yes, I know that." She spoke slowly, her voice muffled by the wind gusting up over the face of the hill and coursing between them. He did not hear her, and, assuming that she would not return the dialogue, he disappeared into the chaos of the house, with the hammers blowing, the drills shrieking, leaving her alone with the anchor.

She thinks of the Mauretania and the massive anchor secured to the stern of the steamer. She is brought back to that grey day, how she gripped the railing, her feet planted on the wooden deck. She remembers the immense echo of the flowing current exploding over the rails into the tender curved shell of her ears both exhilarating and frightening. Her face glazed in salt water, the skin of her lips peeling and cracked. She cannot trace her fingers along lineage, the security of conjugal existences: marriage, children, death.

She cannot foresee that legacy yet. Not until the anchor is raised, the wetness glinting along the links, roped against the hull, scraping, metal against metal, an agonizing piercing noise, nails on a chalkboard. She does not clamp her palms against her ears, instead she leans forward, watches the chain rise from the surface of the water, splitting it open momentarily to glide through, solid and resilient, the water swallowing itself afterwards.

She does not know the term "anchor-rode," but has a more accurate understanding of the anchor composed of chain, cable, and rope straining to hook the vessel, to secure it to the seabed. To her, it does not matter, because she watches the crewmember heave the lever on board, how his back muscles swell and moisten under his clothes. The hook of the anchor detaches from sand and vegetation, rising against the hull of the boat, coiling around the large support that houses it when it's not in the water. She feels the anchor hit the deck of the ship; an immense vibration runs along the vessel. She feels the subtle, almost unnoticeable lightness of the hull. They are able to leave now.

She stands before her new house, the chain a dark blur against the grey cement, the dizzying stonework. The chain disappears in the large concrete block, ensuring that nothing moves or resists—a dead weight of the uncomplicated kind.

Simple and cheap, Phillip had created with ingenuity, tapping into his resources and aesthetic tastes of miniature ships in glass bottles. He could not conceive how his wife translated the anchor chain.

He knows that a dead weight mooring holds in a storm—maintains its position. There will be no drifting. This mooring is suited for rocky bottoms, where other mooring systems do not hold well. He knows that he is building strength and endurance into the structure. Sophie feels the bulk, heavy and awkward pressing into her soft skin.

If she knew what the term "aweigh" meant, she would use it now to describe herself and how she anticipates the completion of the house, the move, and the isolation. She is suspended, does not rest on the bottom. She will continue to drift although her foundations are permanent. He will not see her fall away into the unanchored realms inside of her.

STORYTELLER

"The face of the country is not hilly but rather rolling or undulating, abounding with never failing springs of the purest water."

-The Belleville Intelligencer, 1835

War moves bodies.

    From which we were uprooted.

    Where we are transplanted.

    When we plant roots.

    How we bud and blossom.

    Sun. Air. Water.

    We survive. We grow.

    Before the United Empire Loyalists arrived, the French were here.

    History forgot the indigenous.

    We remember.

    The Story Behind the Name Quinte, Kentio, concerns the French and the Iroquois. The village of Kentio was created in 1665. The Cayuga nation, members of the Iroquois confederacy fled to Lake Ontario's north shore from the south. Through the colonial pipeline, France, then Montreal, French missionaries were sent to bring Christianity to these peoples.

Extend farther, to the year 1615 when Samuel de Champlain encroached the Iroquois with a Huron war party.

Georgian Bay. Lake Simcoe. Rice Lake. Trent River. Bay of Quinte.

This land is history.

Champlain was wounded during an attack on the Onondaga nation. Know he recovered amongst the Algonquins and the Hurons, perhaps in the Bay of Quinte. Champlain's triangling of indigenous groups contributed to the destruction of the five nations and the Huron confederacy in 1649. The French colonial fist moved in quickly securing a foothold in the New World from the fragmentation of indigenous powers by bringing in more French bodies. The French married with the indigenous groups furthering assimilation and cultural appropriation; a generational genocide.

This word, "Francisation," Frenchifying, one stage in the process of assimilation. Ironic that the very land she felt alienated in because of her French roots was once the host of her Mother tongue. The indigenous groups farmed, pulled from nomadic formations and currents, they grew wheat and barley, not corn, agriculture grown overtop the Way, Mide, raised in French houses with hearths and chimneys, they learned other ways of living, trades, and specializations. Conversion was the ultimate agenda in order that the colony could carry out inter-marriage—cementing a French colony in the New World.

Kentio was abandoned around 1680 when the *coureurs de bois* took over for the missionaries. The Iroquois left for other hunting grounds. Facts and numbers keep the embers of an indigenous presence to eight souls left in Kentio.

THE PAST

She was a very sad woman. The war years had taken its toll on her nerves. She was a nurse and served as a nurse. Their move had severely displaced her mind and spirit. They came to Deseronto from Liverpool, England. The young English married couple bought a run-down farm along the highway. They lived there with their five young children.

This is the first layer of her story. Her memory.

He came back from the war diseased. Tuberculosis. He was taken away.

He was not there, and could not register the changing color of his English-immigrant-wife's eyes. Or the way she started to stare off into space, away. She went Away too. If he had known of his wife's dislocation, the no-man's-land between her spirit and mind. He could have the opportunity for concern, reacted on that, probed further into the depths of her. But, he was not there, and this probing did not happen. It needed to happen.

Each day her eyes grew over with shadows until the ochre brown pigment muddled into a midnight black. With the changing eye colour, her voice went too. Immigration severed the memory of her Self between the Old and New Worlds— suspended. She could not grow another life that could sustain her through the transplantation.

Darkness—it veined up and consumed her like roots growing through pipes. She could not stop those shadows creeping into her, fingering in, lattice-like, consuming her face from the inside out. Thought talons. She lost her soul this way. Those talons curled around her vocal chords, her throat chakra. She lost her voice this way too. Muteness protected her from ever speaking of how much the dark consumed and took up residence inside her traumatized body.

Her thoughts permeated her internal fabric in shrieks and blurred movements. She would lie in bed each morning, the curtain tightly drawn while her children murmured for sustenance and learned how to get it their own ways. The oldest one would manage the house while her mother remained in bed. The children carried out their day with the absence of a mother, not one child would ever have noticed that abnormality of this dysfunction because their father had been taken too. They were not old enough to compare their lives to others yet.

She'd lie, eyes achingly wide open staring up at the bubbles and blemishes in the plastered ceiling. The woman studied the ragged lines that ran along the walls until her eyes stung and her stomach churned in hunger. She remained statuesque, a gothic Madonna muted to the world around her. The walls were covered in faded peeling yellow wallpaper. There was a raging woman trapped behind it, an immigrant mother lying rigid, corpse-like on a wire-sagging-bed. She seldom rose.

One day her mind had come to a certain conclusion. The mother was silently sweeping the kitchen floor—that rare day—when she suddenly stopped, shuffled towards the closet and soundlessly propped the broom in the corner. This is not what happened, but that does not matter. She dusted her hands off on her apron and made her way outside into the sun. Her movements were ordinary, coordinated, but set to a more cryptic rhythm that remained hidden in sunlight luster.

She gripped the scythe from the shed and made her way to the field lining the yard. She raised the curved blade up into the light and then swung her arm steadily as the blade made a loud *swish* through the air. Heaps of cut grass circled her form as the mother continued rising and bending with the consistent movement of the scythe. She carried the cut grass to the edge of the house in strong arms. She carefully placed the grass against the sides of the house, lining the perimeter of the building. Without coherent meaning, her mind spoke words to her.

The green grass won't do. It is wet. Dry. Dry grass.

The mother turned her back to the wooden farmhouse and marched towards the sunken barn.

Her weary body—busy now—could be seen from the highway, the sun bending light over her hunched back, baking her in the afternoon heat. Like a determined soldier, she carried straw bale upon straw bale towards the house. She piled the bales like bricks around the foundations. Only when the entire house was rimmed with straw did she re-enter through the side door.

Her children had been oblivious to their mother. They'd gradually become used to her absence and ignored her for the most part when she did submerge, eyes blinking from the blackened bedroom. They lifted their faces to her when she entered the living room. It was odd for her to be in the same room as them.

"Come with me," she uttered in a monotone voice to her bewildered children. They had not heard her speak in days. They silently rejoiced at their mother's rebirth and blindly followed her into the bedroom.

Four sets of small brown eyes gazed up at their mother as she herded her children onto the bed and laid their three-month-old brother beside them.

"Stay here." The command was mothering, soft-spoken with an ambivalent tone of authority that the children would not question, but obey.

She left the house wiping itchy palms on her apron. Sweat droplets glistened around her mouth and hairline. She uttered a silent curse under her breath when she reached into her dress pockets to find them empty. She disappeared into the kitchen and returned wheezing. Elbows bent and angled into the air, she stood staring at the house with unblinking eyes. Her thick feet shuffled the perimeter of the house as she watched her veined hands closing and locking doors.

She forgot that she had already shut all the windows from inside. The woman came full circle again to the front of the house and reached into her pockets. Her tongue slid across blunt teeth, mesmerized. She sucked in saliva, her tongue pulled the wetness back in from the corners of chapped lips. This time, a steady hand withdrew a small box of matches.

The match made a sharp hiss as she struck it against the strip along the package and it sizzled into a flame. The arch of spine and set shoulders might appear as if she was lighting a fire in the woodstove, the mother sauntered towards the straw and carefully tossed the match onto the bales. Within minutes the hay was alight and blazing in the summer day, the house locked up tight like a prison.

She stood a respectable distance from the burning house, watching. Dark grey smoke billowed from the bales in clouds that rolled violently into the sky. The popping sounds of the flames licking against the windows drowned out the frightened cries of the children locked inside.

She was unnervingly calm as if she'd just peeled a bag full of potatoes and was waiting for the water to boil. She stood with her large farm hands balled against her hips, the back of her dress damp from summer sweat.

It did not look like a mother burning down a house filled with her babies.

Only a handful of moments passed before a truck along the highway noticed the smoke and saw the woman standing staring at the burning building. Brake-locked tires crunched in the laneway as the car stopped in front of the house. The sound of slamming car doors stirred the woman as two men came sprinting up the walkway.

"Are you okay? Hey, are you okay?" they frantically asked as they neared the blazing walls. The children's cries could be heard faintly, but were dying quickly as the roar of the flames intensified.

"There are people trapped in there!" One man screamed to the other, "we've got to get in there!" The men effortlessly kicked down the front door, and holding rags from the truck over their mouths and noses they found the children faltering, huddled together like kittens on the bed.

"Let's go! Holy shit! Let's go!" the one man hollered, securing a child under each arm as the other scooped the shrieking baby into his arms.

They emerged from the burning house coughing and gasping for air—the children suffering from smoke inhalation. The mother had not moved nor spoken. Her silence and apparent calm unnerved the strangers. Their eyes took in the scene in a growing sense of disgust as they saw the carefully placed straw bales around the house still smouldering. The placated woman, the barred house, and obedient children. It immediately dawned on the men that this fire had been deliberate. They had not merely saved these children from a burning house; they'd saved them from murder.

The police were called and squad cars quickly arrived. The children were hushed and placated from trauma, wrapped in blankets, and placed, eyes wet and gaping, into the back of an ambulance together. A paramedic cradled the still-shrieking baby against his chest and glared at the mother with fiery eyes. She was handcuffed and folded into the back of a cruiser as the ambulance sped away. She said nothing.

They took her straight to jail, and later after a complicated and lengthy trial she was sent to spend the rest of her life in an asylum in Ottawa. All of her children except the two oldest sons were put up for adoption. By the time their father returned home, with a stiff leg and a gnarled wooden cane, his children had been divided and separated, their lives shot in different directions.

His oldest son would remember the transformation of his father, how he had caved in around his skeleton, his skin jaundiced and bruised beneath his eyes. He limped through the door one unthought-of morning in a state of decay the son could not ignore, the sun pulling light around him in a blanket; as if the sky itself knew the man was cold. The boy knew, in that moment, that aside from his mother's absence and the separation of his siblings, he would now step in as the head of the household, the patriarch, and this would be something that would take his aged father years to acknowledge.

But on that morning, with the sun beating in on the eastern windows illuminating the most intimate crevices of the house, there was a transformation. The rooms that were bluntly stilled, collecting dust, witnessed movement. The old man shook dust from the furniture as he settled in awkwardly, anticipating loss. The cavern of the house was too quiet, the boy stood transfixed in the center of the stillness witnessing, watching as the old man fell into his favored rocking chair, looked around, and cleared his throat.

"Where are they? Why is this house so empty, boy?" His son coughed uncomfortably, and felt a heavy weight against his chest. Perspiration wetted his neck.

He could still see that fateful day, fresh—behind his eyes. The heat of the flames, molten and sickening, the cries from his younger siblings, the thrill of terror in their screams, he could never forget. Never forgive. He wondered what words he would use to describe his mother to his father. How her eyes were empty, dead, full of dark pigment, but empty. He remembered how she had cradled her hands. She had laid the back of her right hand against the palm of her left, folded in front of her, she was composed and steady. Her stance never wavering, this memory of his mother, statuesque, mute, and cold. He would—could— never forget.

"Dad, it wasn't good when you left. She wasn't happy with us. She wanted us to go away. Instead..." he pauses, "they came and took her away." He hoped that this would satisfy his father, that he would be able to visualize what happened because he didn't think he could articulate what he held inside his head, what he remembered.

It was almost immediate, his Father's eyes lined in red, bulged. He spoke deliberately and carefully.

"I know Son, I know what happened, and, I am sorry." He looked out the window and disappeared in his thoughts, "They are gone." He waited several more minutes and said again, "They are gone."

His father forced his hands against his cheeks. He could not stop the tears. They soaked the creases of his palms, which wetted the yellowed collar of his shirt. His elbow accidentally struck his cane, which cracked against the floor. His son shot forward, but hesitated on the threshold of an embrace.

He thought, bit his lip, and stepped backwards awkwardly. He gripped his neck with one hand, cracked the bones, and turned around to face the Western row of windows. The sun baked rays crimson of yellows and oranges into the grains of glass; they ran down the line of the aged windowpane. Glass grains, it was what he could focus on—it was easier, palpable. He did not turn back when his Father forced the devastating questions through his sharpened teeth.

"The other children, are they gone too?" His breath whistled slightly through the cracks in the words. The son hung his head.

"Yes Dad. They are gone. I don't know where."

"God dammit! God! God! God dammit!"

The boy winced with each curse, his face wet and his shoulders heaving. He heard his father beat the knuckles of his left fist in the palm of his right hand. Each thrust in his palm, the sharp slap of flesh, and the boy felt the murmur in his heartbeat, radiating, surrounding them both in a pulsating mass of despair.

A manifestation of distance in the blood, the bodies dispersed far across the country, their anatomy inside webs, their inward composites intimately real, and the same, painstakingly rendered—a forced alienation. They felt the hammer blow from those strangers, lucid illicitness, and a government that chiseled, crumbled bloodlines.

A cryptic rhythm, a political system set to an agenda of segmentation, officiated by black ink on white paper that dictated bodies to act. To bring the babies in from the cold and wrap their shaking fingers around steaming mugs. The baby cried and cried, until they pressed his tiny form to a hot neck and sighed around his slacking body.

They bound together by descent, and did not know this, for the simple memory that they were almost dead. Now, living dead, these vacant kin pushed through with emptiness pulling them back. They dwelled in the recesses of indecision, thresholds between themselves, their roots, and the faces in front of them.

Who they were, was not who they wanted to be.

THE PAST

"Alone again…
    I wish that someone would tell me what I have done wrong
    Why I have to stay chained up and left alone so long
    They seemed so glad to have me when I came here as a pup
    There were so my things we'd do while I was growing up
    They could not wait to train me as a companion and a friend
    And told me how they'd never fear being alone again
    The children said they would feed me and brush me
every day
    They would play with me and walk with me if I could only
stay.
    But now the family hasn't time. They often say I shed
    They do not even want me in the house not even to be fed
    The children never walk me. They always say not now.
    I wish I could please them.
    Won't someone tell me how?
    All I had, you see was love, I wish they would explain,
    Why they said they wanted me, then left me on a chain…"

They were both aware of time, dwelled within its dimensions, internally measuring the interval between events, corners of their lives, bookends, points of space in time, like a physics equation, precise and theoretically intimidating. They had lived on top of the hill for twelve years now. She wondered each day if this was the right length, it felt much longer, a whole other lifetime she considered. Hands cupped around an empty womb.

She gasps, clutches her arms around her heaving stomach, and she lets herself weep. She pulls in air, hiccups and sucks the tears through her teeth. She sinks to the floor, her knees burning, bruised.

She sinks further, lets her hips cool against the stone tiles, and stretches wide. Her fingertips meet shards of glass; she winces and retracts from the risk of a glass edge cutting into her skin. She can still hear the violent crashing, how Phillip's body flew through the house, a wretched tornado.

Sophie turns over away from the broken glass. She stretches wide again. Her knees fold against the broken legs of a dining room chair. She knows without seeing how the spindles are severed—white gashes and peeling splinters lay like matchsticks against the floor around her. She could strike one against the stone. Feel the fire hiss to life. She'd throw it into the tangle of their bed sheets, a bonfire. Testify to the pain going up in flames.

Sophie tries to ignore the atrocity of the reality of his vile stench, the ultimate demeaning link of his anger of this morbid chain-of-pain. Adjacent to the flattened table and kindling fractures of chairs, she knows the shallow puddle is there, pungent and acidic.

At least he relieved himself inside on the floor, this time, not her hunched back, a hunched shaking spine that blacked out and began convoluting memories. A gnarled black tree and wet pasting mud. A tree with letters, a coffee tin full of secrets, and manhood. Cauterized ego. A womb that could not be filled.

He had had enough.

This time he left her with emptiness, his black fingerprints rising on her bicep, the knot of her wrist. She can only see the oval contusion on her spine reflected backwards, with her profile straining over the arch of her shoulder blade. Wincing as her thumbs work over the pain, she arches her head back around refusing to know.

She embraces darkness while his taillights blaze red down the face of the hill, turning sharply onto asphalt. Her hand reached up inside the lampshades, flicking them off, melting into oblivion.

The hardness of the floor is a reprieve from the chasm in her womb. As the night sinks into itself, pushing shadows across the room, she is rocked from stillness from the blunt face of resolution.

Who says they need to know ... this will not be the way.

"He doesn't know that I know I can't." She utters the last thought out loud and feels relief in the abrupt sound against the hollow stillness of the room. Acceptance, finally, she can rise and begin sweeping the glass, can toss the broken furniture behind the garage, and can pull on long thick clothing to hide.

Yes! She wets her tongue and tries again. *Yes!* She forces the tears down and swallows.

"There will be a baby here."

STORYTELLER

That baby was my father.

THE PRESENT

"My body also changes, the creature in me, plant-animal, sends out filaments in me; I ferry it secure between death and life, I multiply."

-Margaret Atwood, Surfacing

Nelle fingers the stained creased papers, sets them face up in front of her, and takes a slow, long sip from her steaming cup of tea. She had returned from Queensborough the same day she found the gravestones with her last name engraved on them. Nelle tucked the sheets of paper with the gravestone rubbings in her office desk. So much had changed in two months. She sets the mug down lightly.

Seven and a half months pregnant now. Her body is swollen and bloated. She cycles through ruminations, mental loops. Her thoughts incessantly emerging, throughout the last two months, during listless moments when she should be mindful, enjoying the presence of her pregnancy. Breaking those moments—redirection—she's still learning how to be present.

Nelle wants a calm body, routine motions glazed over an

edge of anxiety and fear. That type of listless moment when she folds a bed sheet, or another one while she watches the neck of a spoon disappear in the dark wetness of a ceramic mug. But, no, Nelle continues to feel haunted. Quiet resonating mantras smoothed again and again against the roughness of her tongue encourage her through this wretchedness.

He was gone. Detachment rooted and wedged quietly as her body expanded with life. As they had tried to finish renovating the house, build their own lives, he had to go away. She knew now, in retrospect, they could not live their own lives because they let the past in like a lover, and that affair was a severe hammer blow, an iron wedge between them.

Nelle is getting used to being alone. She feels reprieve in the peacefulness of this reclaimed isolation. A gentle and yet ferocious coming-to-know, yet she doesn't know that she is stepping into her rites of Sacred Femininity.

She sets down the grave rubbings. She fans her hands across her protruding womb. These hands lift up from the womb, then fan across a citrus heart. Nelle rubs the space in the middle above her eyes.

Fifty-one days until my due date, that's close to thirteen weeks, two hundred and twenty-nine days in, seven and a half months on. Oh help me.

She implores a higher force, again and again, assurance through the simplicity of linguistic scripts inside her skull. Her prayers extend and lace with something bigger than she can ever imagine of herself.

Nelle catches herself counting down pregnancy days against her tongue. Like notches on a stick on a deserted island. She reaches down and cups the baby. She can feel the baby in each moment now, where her head is nestled, her tiny feet tucked; Nelle knows.

Nelle is fascinated that her child is now inhaling amniotic fluids to exercise her lungs. That practiced underwater breath— that sacred breath. The baby may have a few wisps of hair. She's also started to shed her downy protective hair, lanugo, and with

344

the exception of her still-developing lungs, her other major organs have completely formed. Nelle knows that the child sleeps ninety percent of the day, the stillness, and then a slight flutter, like the turning of a leaf, a wiggle of a tail, the flapping of hands, dog-paddling water. She's swimming in an otherworld ocean suspended in her own universe—that sacred space.

You are dreaming, hush, be still and do not thrash. We are okay. I love you. You are safe.

Thoughts are the currents of communication; umbilical chains, even when severed, keep mother and child attached, helix, forever.

She yearns to count tiny toes, fingers, strands of hair, everything. The baby's skin must be soft and smooth as she plumps in preparation for birth. The baby has completely turned, head downwards, she is ready to emerge and blink.

Her legs do not have enough space, the fish reels, Nelle gasps, wraps pyramid arms around the womb while the child draws her legs up, she is fully fetal.

Her little feet flay. She stretches and kicks, knocks against the ribs in an underwater grind. As well, the baby demands vitamins and minerals, sustenance, Nelle sucks in with a hiss when she feels the surge of energy being drawn down, a gentle, but powerful sucking.

Today, the baby is ravenous, riveting with energy. Nelle cannot think when the baby turns, roots for an engorged breast, submerges her face against the uterine lining, but she can only find relief with the minute arch of her thumb, and she places it deep inside her mouth, swallows and sucks in coordination. Nelle remembers the image during the last ultrasound, her child with the thumb embedded, innocent and primal. Yet, colourful like a hardcover coffee table book. She had wept and felt exposed; she willed the doctor from the room. He was not there, yet she did not feel alone.

The days have passed in a systematic whirl, and Nelle pinches the bridge of her nose with stress. Earlier that morning, in the purpling horizon she had pulled the canvas from the top of her bookshelf and placed it with anticipation on the surface of her desk.

She had pulled the drawer out slowly, listening to the scrape of wood against wood, the paper had not moved, remained fixed against the bottom of the drawer and she pulled it out too with heavy breath and laid it beside the canvas. It was time to continue. His absence, a tender wound, could not keep her from her Self any longer. Tired of rotating and shifting through the corridors of his memory, a young love lost, Nelle determined to stay strong for her Daughter.

She could make out the hush of the wind through the long grasses in the fields surrounding the house and that organic tidal currents soothed her. The window ajar, wisps of the cool morning wind sift through the papers on the desk like wind chimes. Nelle shivers and pulls a light blue fleece blanket around her shoulders while she covers the furling papers with splayed hands. Light glints across her hands, orange and puckering in the air, candlelight casts a halo of warmth near her face. She inhales, sets her teeth, and bends down.

The tree inks a straggling silhouette on the canvas, letters and names hooked to the black branches, names carved into bark. Nelle feels security in her mother's lineage, their names, full and trailing through the generations reassuring.

She twists slightly, pulls the paper from the desk and studies the names again.

Trees in her memory, reaching, stretching, laying claim, and carving out space. Nelle thinks of the generational grind, reproduction, how the bridges were laid jagged with adoption, contrived and strained pretenses of lineage, she accepts it then.

Women are trees. The circle of life, trees, women, the cosmic womb.

Nelle understands the severity of what it meant for a woman to lose her womb in the snow under a tree reaching for sustenance in a darkened Nazi sky.

I knew this pain from my mother, not her, not my Grandmother. Women and their secrets.

Family is also the soil that the roots dig themselves deep into and find foundation. Earth rhythms, the feminine forsaken.

Nelle breathes in the paper, curved against her palms, through open nostrils. The page, essence fresh as cut grass, fibrous, and earthy. She inhales the memory of the sun, the drive, that northern homeland, mother tongue, headstones, and the crazed screech of the crow.

Nelle acknowledges that women are the trees and also the very sky that those trees extend into, interconnected, sacred breath, water, light, and the intricate processes of photosynthesis, even metamorphosis. Oxygen cycles, photosynthesis, we breathe with Mother Earth. Underwater practices of expanding the lungs as an unborn. Women are not stagnant or permanent in face. They are eternally shifting, ebbing, and cresting—water currents contained in oceanic basins, divinely oriented to lunar rhythms, solar entrances and exits, waves against Gaia shores.

It is simple. Nelle holds the paper with her left hand, steady, copies the names to the top branches on the right side of the tree. She pulls back and examines the names once on the page; she sighs again and decides against copying names. The glue stick lid is popped open. Two pregnant hands work together to cover the back of the grave rubbings in glue, sticky as sap, and flip the pages over, placing them amongst the roots of that inked tree.

She tries to conjure faces, bodies with the names, but cannot, and pushes the prickling agitation down. She bites her bottom lip, ignores the branches underneath the names, and pens in names she heard in the shallows of cheeks, sucked in, and uttered in a hunch. She continues, tracing her fingers along the lower branches, to the names of her grandparents, the farmers from Tamworth, the hands she has touched and held. She cannot hold the stories of arson and violence there, yet she does, finding release by putting their story, their existence, somewhere else other than inside herself.

Nelle continues on down, to her father's name, to her brother and her Self. If only the heritage was that straightforward. She is startled by the abruptness of her exhale, the thick stream of agitation from her lips that ruffles the paper. She eyes her father's branch.

There is more. He is not the only one. Siblings. Lost childhoods.

She draws in five more limbs without reservation, her fingers sweating against the pen, the tip biting hard into the paper. She ignores the indents, forces the limbs beyond the diameter of the upper branches, disregarding balance. She can only pen in three of the five names with accuracy, the other two she has never known, does not know how to bring them into this world. Their dimensions are too vast for her storyline. The breaches, wide open, draw in like black holes, energy and understanding convoluted and almost lost. She perseveres, with a nagging voice of concern in the back of her head; she draws two thick branches awkwardly from the trunk of the tree near the base.

There is no longer symmetry to the tree, no equilibrium. If it were a real tree, it would fall over, creaking and groaning into the ground. Not only has she flipped the tree around so roots became branches, the limbs are bedrock pillars. Nelle smiles at the awkward beauty of it all.

This is Nelle's tree, and it exists on the page. She is assured by the reluctant inclusivity, the coveted accuracy and how her baby will be able to cup both the fullness and emptiness of her subsistence with strained acceptance.

Ladders and open windows.

I need to get back to them, the ones that immigrated as well, and those ones who lost their babies. I need to get back to my Nanny's side too, the ones from Toronto. This tree is not finished.

The handful of conversations, uttered against razor edges, inflictions of the tongue, the solitude behind eyelids, she attached these dialogues to her memory. An amalgamated identity, dictated by hands and faces she will never meet. Nelle will not know exactly because it was before her and above.

She cannot remember the first time she was told of her

father's adoption. She only knows it as if it were a mole on her skin, a rib bone tucked away, always there. Instead, she deifies the veins of understanding that flaked up around the word adoption. What they could not give her, straightforward, without contradiction, was why.

"Why did you adopt him?"

She blinks the buds of conversation into focus, their hands cupping tea around the table; she was naïve in her teenage adolescence.

"I had to adopt." Her Belgian grandmother looked down, quiet, and pushed the thick diamond ring around her finger. She paused, raised her blue grey eyes and continued.

"You do not know. It is very important. I will tell you."

Nelle knew then, everything the woman said was important, and urgent. It was difficult living in the warzone, that no-man's-land of urgency and wolf cries.

"You see, I went to the doctor, they told me there was something wrong." She swallowed hard and pursed her lips, leaned forward with a start and that younger Nelle wondered if this was truth or something else entirely.

"There ... there was something with my fallopian tubes, a blockage. I don't know…" She had trailed off, paused to sip her tea and craftily changed direction.

"I had a friend, you see, she worked for the CAS. I really cared for her and we spoke often. She knew I wanted a child, that it was difficult for me to have one. I was not expecting the call when it came, but a family had been collected, brought in to their office, she initiated the adoptions."

"What happened? Why was this family brought in? What did they tell you?" Nelle registered the calculated chaos that her probing unleashed amongst the elderly woman. Hinged-contrived-lives. Nelle forced the truth up. The older Nelle felt that she should go slowly, measuring her speech, but the younger Nelle did neither—instead letting the urgency filter through because her knowing was crucial. She was also tired of the lies.

"I, I, don't know. Their mother was very sick, she had, what do you call it, oh, she had, that depression,"

"Postpartum depression?"

"Yes, that. They both weren't very well."

"What was her name?" She hovered, anticipating clarity.

"I don't know. They never gave me her name, or his. It wasn't important." Nelle shrank. She wondered why there was simplicity in the advertisements for searching out ancestors when the reality of this story was exacerbating. Once, Nelle had plugged in a last name online, the only tangible fragment she was offered, she found death certificates, birth certificates, but no precision, because they were other certificates, other families. She felt her tongue flatten in a lucid surrender. She stopped searching in the same breath.

She had stopped searching because she had come across her blood cousin looking for information about the family too. They both searched for their life story that was not given to them. *I am looking for information about my grandmother...*

The twilight shifts, filters a thin stream through the window. Dawn. Nelle savors the subtle brilliance of the retreating night, the rising day. She feels transparent, in her nightgown draped around her crossed ankles, the empty mug now cold. The square of light slides into her focus, drops her into simplicity and the enigmatic memory of the woman she so wanted to know, the woman with the darkest of eyes, with a stone tongue and absence of intelligible language. She wishes that she could go back to that time, extending to that woman instead of retracting. If only that woman had spoken, if she had contained a language that could have carried their family story forward. If only she had not set fire to her babies.

Another Nelle was eight, new to the world of plurality. Her parents had divorced the summer before. Her Father had taken her for the weekend and she reluctantly went. He did not tell her where they were going. She had merely climbed into the truck, let the seatbelt click around her, and she rode. She watched the fields blur and fold into a Canadian Shield stone beyond the car windows. She did not track the path, the villages they pushed through, the name of their destination when they arrived. That day, she followed.

They walked into a hospital, a retirement home, an insane asylum; she does not know its name, or the name of the city it was in. Nelle can only remember the whiteness of the rooms, the murmur of words amongst the staff, his back as she followed him down a hallway. He approached the reception area, hovered awkwardly, nervously.

"Margaret?" he leaned back.

"Scruby?" the receptionist tilted her head to the left.

"Garland?" her maiden name.

"Yes," the woman paused, "she doesn't have visitors. You should have phoned ahead." She looked past my father to that eight-year-old Nelle, pressed against a wall in the background and narrowed her eyes. She didn't want her there, a young Nelle assumed it was because she was so young. The receptionist couldn't know how much they were each other's crutches, father and daughter. Age and generation couldn't dictate roles when a family was overcoming trauma together and alone.

They had first entered an elevator, a hospital escort with them. Nelle remembers the buttons, how the escort pressed one, and there was a woman knotted into a wheelchair in the corner. The woman hiccupped in gusts of shrieks and purrs. Nelle had followed every flutter, each jerk, with wide eyes. The worker gripped the handles and smiled, shyly. Nelle looked down. That was before they stepped into the hallway and she and her father were ushered into a room.

The room was sunny, spacious and cluttered with craft supplies and board game activities. There were ripped armchairs against the walls, a large circular table in the center with metal chairs. They sat at the table, yarn and glue and popsicle sticks scattered across its surface in a distracting cluster. There was a woman with dark eyes waiting at the table who did not know that she was waiting or that she had visitors.

Nelle is assured that the woman had thick shoulders, was short, and gazed upon her with unblinking eyes. There was no conversation, yet her father's awkward gestures, semblances of any familiarity held the only considerations of relatedness between them. The woman's eyebrows spoke in a flurry, rose and arched with trepidation. The creases under her eyes are dark, deep with longing, tired from life. Her forehead bruised from the blows, the connections she made with cold surfaces around her. A worker discreetly stood by.

It happened fast. Nelle remembers the boredom. She was not aware that she was sitting with her blood grandmother—the woman she would search forever-more in her head, in the Internet haze, but that she succumbed to boredom. She did not know that this was the first time her father ever had the courage to seek out his mother and visit her. He needed his daughter's strength with him.

Nelle does not know that the woman recognized them by their eyes—they had the same—and their pointed broad chins. The old woman knew without acknowledging in that moment that they were family, more so strangers, yet still the offspring of the children, babies she had locked in a farmhouse in Deseronto with straw bales and flames.

Nelle had focused on the yarn and tangle of craft supplies in front of her, unable later to recall its color even now in the rising morning light. But, she remembers the touch of it, how she pulled it around her fingers, impulsively unraveling the ball. This unraveling, or perhaps the gesture of her arm striking out from her lap to snatch the ball, was what triggered the old woman.

The woman shot up straight like an arrow and howled to a hidden moon. Nelle shrank back, felt the tears sting her eyes instantly. Her father was numbed in shock.

Over and over, she wonders why the woman shrieked, what it was about the yarn that sent her reeling.

Was it too much for her? Or, could she see herself in us?

The bodies, the dark eyes, the tilt of their heads to the left, how they curled their pointer fingers under their noses, supported blunt chins with right-handed thumbs and rested elbows slightly on the arms of chairs, tabletops, and car consuls. They shared each of these gestures, family residue, subtle ways the body flows, and this was too much for her. The babies from a burning straw bale farmhouse.

Older Nelle contemplates the severity of generational trauma. *She would have last seen that house aflame.*

Nelle has sketched dark eyes onto the canvas in place of a name during her reminiscing. She is satisfied and disturbed, but cannot penetrate this world further. She leans forward, her lungs expanding, and she blows a flame of candle out and sits in shadows.

A templed, empowered body anticipates the oncoming daylight.

THE PAST

"Pleasantly situated at the base of a large hill which shelters it from the west winds and is the most important village in the township."

—On Madoc, Belden's Country Atlas, 1878

The baby howled from his wooden playpen. His face was coated raw with tears and his screams faltered from strained chords; he'd been crying for a long time. His pudgy feet thrashed angrily. The rickety pen slanted in the living room.

They sat silently at the kitchen hutch eating. They faced each other from across the table, both gingerly hunched over their plates of tomato sauce and pasta noodles. Sophie's eyes did not meet Phillip's as she spiraled spaghetti noodles in a silver spoon and raised the perfect mound tentatively to her lips. She wasn't hungry, hadn't really been in weeks since the baby's arrival. A housefly landed on the table and began pacing back and forth, steadily, between the pair.

Sophie's heart thundered, and she jumped in her chair as Phillip's outstretched palm came crashing down on the table, smashing the fly into a small black paste. He wiped the guts off with his napkin and continued shoveling food into his mouth without a word.

The baby continued to cry, rolling his head violently from side to side. They did not rush to him. His skin burned, raw, alive like hot red ants.

The couple remained, poised on the wood of their seats, reflexively raising their hands to their faces, returning to their food. The baby's howls continued, until eventually the child settled, whimpering to itself, pushed a stuffed teddy bear across the bridge of his nose until he feigned a restless sleep.

She would find later, when she unclipped the metal pin and peeled back the cloth diaper, his bottom bleeding and broken in an angry rash, his skin contoured and bending in a pockmarked river where the dampness had collected and festered.

Mechanical hands worked petroleum jelly, thick and living on her fingers into the infant's skin, mesmerized more by the red glow of taillights descending down the hill between the trees. She saw the ghost light of the glint of a red flashing telephone tower kilometers away.

She kept her eyes on that flashing light.

Her baby whimpered and broke open in another fit of cries. Sophie winced, her ears popping from a fierce blood flow, her eyes never leaving that flashing light, hypnotized, she rocked that baby back and forth until he finally slept.

PRESENT

"This is the window I grew up inside."

—Stephanie Bolster, *Pavilion*

That octagonal window was wetted with my child fingerprints. I spent time there, waiting, wanting her to come home, hoping that whatever it was inside that house that contained me, that had, in fact, transcended generations, would not consume me. Tip-toed on my bed, palms fogging the windowpane, that port-hole, I learned that there was a separation between myself and my mother.

A little face was fixated, eyes searching out a ship window, pinpricks of light threaded with unlit forest, an immense building up before tearing down. Women in a drifting house, a rocking hull, atop that hill, eternally migrating. The soothing rhythm of that white-flashing light on a tower far away lulled me into a sleep-awake-trance, and eventually she would come home.

Scanning a horizon of subtle rolling hilltops and jutting tree limbs, that window cradled the fears of ghosts and crawling things.

"She won't come home," Father fearfully said. Lips curled in a weak young boy grimace, he'd seen many descend and pry away from that hill, that drifting house. Each time he watched one of them go, the fissures in his soul deepened. His fear that his children would go too. Fear protects itself. Fear is a way to endure pain.

"She doesn't want us. She's gone away." And he had retreated. I learned that what he said was not my reality, but a facet of his matrix of pain. Both could be leveled and something else entirely could grow up there instead.

A drawer with a secret has been buttressed with the forks and the cutting board that fit my miniature armchair just perfectly. I learned that I fit in secret places and I didn't have to absorb all that was pressed against my skin like tattoos—no—like heartbeats. The learning curve nourished a childish imagination of barefooted treks over moss and glass.

Expanses of water framed by this elevated state. A Moira that took her away and has kept me coming back, again and again, until my lips swept into the exodus of ecstasy and the trees, remembering how we stepped between them and found the man with a crow's feather.

The contours of my remembrance, the silhouette of my soul, stabs the deepest of nightmares into physicality.

I run my fingers over the slivered gash in the clapboard in which Father forced his mother down in despair. A red flag. They should have known that there was an immense sadness here that needed healing, and her presence, the Sacred Mother, we needed her to come home. Her bringing children into that house wouldn't make what happened before them go away.

Before I was me, this place shaped my destiny of indentured question marks that labored. It hooked my understanding and tossed me into a sharpened funneling of empowerment and self-actualization.

Pressure makes a diamond.

A silence they harbored, punctuated by ink-stained utterances in art and media, crossed the boundaries of appropriateness, so they say in that small town. It's difficult to face the truth when so many survived their own trauma. That lake holds other family's secrets.

I huddle in doorways that sever and extrapolate the goose-egged violence of siblings who anticipate the hierarchy of domestic violence and how it should be served.

The narrative of my childhood was dichotomized and pluralized amongst the glued tiles. Ceramic gray matter, our own brains pick-axed in a desolate mining town. Wind cries and crusted leaves rustle outside the octagonal glass, making me wonder if this house was built on someone else's land, a desecrated burial, and I hear the spirits that shriek about imperial injustices.

Eventually, that little girl Self lays herself down. Tucks herself in. Mother does return. Father stays.

I turn my cheek to the wall and let his story pin me to the mattress.

THE PAST

Wrapped in an abstract-patterned silk scarf, a thin cigarette poised between red lips, Sophie exuded European glamour as she raised her leather gloved hand and plucked the cigarette from her mouth and ground it under her heel. Her ice blue eyes scanned up and down the sidewalk, a carefully gleaned paranoia from that survey, and no one would have noticed, except for the boy. Sophie's sunglasses were dark, hid shadows under her eyes, swollen skin, the cat-like frames distracted, glittered with a diamond, she looked out of place in downtown Madoc.

The young boy, whom they called Aiden, Jared Aiden, a peculiar name of consonants, feigned ignorance that she was, once again, pretending that she was okay. Aiden straightened his shoulders and looked up at the woman, his eyebrows etched a deep crease between his eyes. He was tired.

Aiden pretended, too, and that was how he knew that his mother was uncomfortable and felt out of place. She shouldered a lineage and heritage she knew did not belong to her, perhaps was not intended for her. Anxiety. Mother and Father also forced the young boy to shoulder their pain quietly, adult constructs that eroded Aiden's confidence and assurance that the world was a place he could be happy in, that he felt safe in.

They walked, his naked hand tucked inside her gloved palm

past large picture windows carefully set with dishware displays and seasonal knick-knacks that he knew only collected dust, and were broken accidentally by children during play. They passed Johnston's drugstore, and he was surprised that his mother did not need anything there, or Stedman's where she loved to have the man put shoes on her. The storefronts reflected the pair, and he watched others around him on the sidewalks. Both sides of the streets were streaming with locals. These shopping trips were opportunities to see others as normally he was alone most of the time with his mother on the hill.

Aiden studied his reflection and that of his mother's, he pulled a finger along glass. The two pairs, one real, one reflection, connected by his finger—he delighted in the fantasy that both couples were real. Not one projection, but both, muscle and soul, a mirror replica of each other, and there might be other lives there, with siblings.

The window finger game made him sad, really, because he accepted, eventually, that there were just the two of them, that he was lonely, that this didn't feel enough and that he knew it wasn't going to change. Aiden felt empty—there was supposed to be something more for him, perhaps a house full of siblings, brothers and sisters with large brown eyes to play with. He didn't like to be alone.

He turned impulsively, suddenly, without a whisper, planted his two loafers on the sidewalk and forced her back.

"Why am I so dark, my hair, my eyes, and you are so light? Should I not have blond hair and blue eyes too?" She was startled, embarrassed, felt the heat of betrayal surge up her spine and stain her cheeks. The child's words flung her back into memory, into Eli, the dark hair, the green eyes, the hands that were slim and moist when he turned pages. Anger seethed, and an instinctive wanting for the child to be biologically hers made her wish she had created him with Eli. Aiden could not know where his mother's mind went. Sophie tilted her head, which appeared to her son that she was anticipating him with a jutting chin, he recoiled, and she spoke coolly to protect her pain.

"Somewhere, along the way, you inherited the dark pigment, those members of our family that we do not live close to." She nervously scanned the faces of the passersby entangled in their own tasks, but did not, or could not, notice the anxious thrill chipping away at her controlled exterior.

She stooped down to her son's eye level, tucked the scarf slightly away from the sides of her face and hovered close to him. She hissed in fear, and he did not miss the seriousness braided in her voice.

"I am your mother, you hear me, and your father and I do not have to look like you to be your parents. Okay?"

He gulped.

"Okay."

RIPPLE

"My father's body was a globe of fear
His body was a town we never knew
He hid that he had been where we were going...
...His early life was a terrifying comedy
and my mother divorced him again and again."

—Michael Ondaatje, Letters & Other Worlds

She broke open and came undone
   In that hallway, before the front
   Door of their one bedroom apartment.
   His face, his green probing eyes,
   Hands, gentle now, how they cradled
   Her swelling jaw and eyes, remorse,
   She imploded and ran,
   The image of his weeping face,
   Taking it all in, denying their internal
   Monsters, how, how
   Her face connected with the
   Neighbour's door like a mouse hitting a wall,

Commedia dell'arte, masks and broken addictions,
They had been crossing too many lines together,
She knew, he knew, this time, and the next, they
Couldn't come back from this no-man's-land
Able to be in love, able to move on and
Raise a baby safely together.

STORYTELLER

"But I bring with me from the distant past five nights ago the time-traveler, the primeval one who will have to learn, shape of a goldfish now in my belly, undergoing its watery changes. Word furrows potential already in its proto-brain, untraveled paths. No god and perhaps not real, even that is uncertain, I can't know yet, it's too early. But I assume it: if I die it dies, if I starve it starves with me. It might be the first one, the first true human, it must be born, allowed."

—Margaret Atwood, Surfacing

Daughter, this will be difficult for me—forgive me.

Let yourself fall away from it all, and then you can see yourself almost objectively. Bias does not leave us if we are alive and have a soul. This narrative, I hope, will prepare you to become proactive and set measures of safety in your own life so that you do not settle, that you know your worth and that you enjoy discovering the onion layers of your empowerment with that citrus heart. Reactive behavior is deadly; reactive behaviour is what permits genocide and military agendas. Long processes that conceal atrocity. Reactive behaviour makes us weak, vulnerable. But, the beauty of proactive behaviour versus reactive scrambling enables change to grow; we only need to plant it.

I thought that I could trust others readily, before I waited out for their authentic selves to come through. I was naïve and inside the living of that naivety, I got hurt. Ultimately, I had to learn how to trust myself first and be loyal to me, then, my vibrations attracted other strong people who did not hurt me.

Yet, there is unknowing and things are not certain, no matter how prepared or controlled you are. Balance. It is okay to not know and it is safe to not know. Be open to being shown something else altogether from what you expected because, in that shock of being shown something else altogether, you've grown and a valuable spiritual lesson was delivered. You will be tested; the presence of the tests only serves to affirm that you are on an empowerment road, and your purpose is perhaps bigger than the circumference of your singular life. Between that space of unknowing and knowing, love is there. Trust and let go of what you can't control. Ground. Plant roots. Grow branches. Mastering your Self inside that space is the difference between Good and Great. I want you to be your own Great.

It is both complex and intimidating, but most live in the fault lines of these intellectual currents; we cannot if we desire to thrive. Ideologies sever. Feigned understanding separates. Assumptions trap.

You do not really know them. I do not really know them. And in the larger picture, cliché yes, I know, it really does not matter because you have lived alongside them and around them, and that must be enough. Love them for their story. What they are able to share. Everything balances. What we perceive as a downfall is simply filling up something else that needs scaling. Pulleys, ropes, and weights. Scales. We glitter. We do. Learn to let them glow their way.

People will most often love you their way and not the way

you need to be loved. Love your Self the way you need to be loved. If you connect with others who love you the way you need, this connection is a gift: you found your tribe. But, no matter, love your Self the way you need to be loved.

My father and grandma were enigma, foiled identities, tethered to struggle. They knew themselves, but they did not know themselves either. There was closeness and distance around them. I grew and dwelled in the no-man's-land of these distances, remained close that way.

This is what is left to tell.

He knew that he had dark hair while they were fair. He knew that his mother's pride was always glossed in appearances, social acceptance. She wanted to belong as much as she wanted to honour her otherness first. Everyone, mostly, wants to be accepted and loved.

The crisp lines of an ironed suit, old world and aristocratic, the tress of French on his tongue, my Father grew into facets of her naturally. As is the way. He loved her and felt pain by her as he grew into his own. As is natural.

He perpetually loved his father, drew to him as a small magnet, his father the steel frame. The closer he drew, the more intensely he felt that he was also the repelling side of the magnet in his father's void. My father, as a young boy, and now as an adult, has not yet articulated, perhaps in his head secretly, but never outwards, that he could not mean anything vocal and tangible to his father while both men pushed out distance because their insides were fighting mental battles. It is unnatural to love what hurts you, yet we do that a lot, because we love people for them and not how they treat us. But, my Child, you will get hurt loving people for them and allowing them to hurt you.

Communication broke down completely between my father and grandfather for some time in his youth. But, let me tell you, everyone stayed and kept trying to love each other. They begrudged each other because they hurt each other.

My Father was given a comfortable childhood too—well-travelled as a young boy, schooled in cultures and thought. He hollowed himself out in this world because what he wanted and needed was for them to not hurt him. For them not to hurt each other. Pain outweighs material comfort.

I was a listener with burning red seashell ears. He couldn't stop it from leaking then, a deliberate verbal trickle for me to cup in my consciousness throughout the years. Confessions. Freudian slips. I came to know him this way, and also in the spaces of his being in the things he did not say, or left out. There might have been a casual story while tying up skates, a remark on a skinned knee, anything domestic and curtained with family. He was the only one who talked world politics with me. I kept trying to love. Anything that could be relayed briefly, an undercurrent of anxiety and proximity pushing the plotlines into me. It hurt, but it was connection, and what I wanted was connection. We grew into ourselves as interrupters because interruptions were both filling wants of connection and listening.

This was how I grew up with him, he grew too, pushing through leafs of memories, and we navigated both blunted and tipped emotional mountains. The shingles of his soul. He carried his child Self through this journey. I learned to enjoy the journey and not the destination.

The youth, those that live under the umbrella of domestic violence are usually the most tight-lipped or crazed in a storm of delirium—their opinions clipped and jarring. They assume that the forced pain, served on hands thick and marbled with personal history, bleeds a simple hierarchy and chronology. I was such a youth.

Imperfect and naïve, I viewed the pain served to me and the way it positioned me.

My skewed perspective. I was a victim, and the elders were perpetrators. There were no bystanders because of the privacy, the unspoken movements behind closed doors, yet, there were.

You have to be so very careful in a small town. But now, in

retrospect, I see we were accumulations of everything, an algorithm for domestic violence, singular and plural matrices, layered honeycombs. The make-up of our lives, our psychological constructs, were all fragments of a step-by-step procedure for the calculation of pain and self-pity, if we wanted it that way. Peace was a choice and required active practice. Double-edged swords. We lived in hopeless states, both outside and inside ourselves, and eventually, we manifested our own happiness and came to accept that only nothing is permanent.

I feel in retrospect and accept the reality that our identities were contingent on shifting perspectives.

He was both a victim and perpetrator.

He was both a victim and perpetrator.

She was both a victim and perpetrator.

She was both a victim and perpetrator.

I am both a victim and perpetrator.

We wanted to belong amongst the walls where the bystanders hung, like wallflowers.

We gripped white-knuckled fingers around victimization because that was where we wanted to be. Toes edging the cliffs, when we finally came down, we battled the forest of depression together, yet endured the pain separately.

I am the bystander-perpetrator-victim with incisive letters. Both perpetrating and witnessing with and without action. My discourse is barbed and biased. I speak only for me and only from my perspective. In polite circles, others tell their own stories; I know that I risk perpetration in writing others' stories here.

I am sorry.

I wanted to tell you my story.

You, Daughter, are everything and nothing as well. Distinguish this oneness as opportunity. You can choose how you want to be remembered. We are one, one on our own, apart from the whole, and one together, as a whole. Perspective. We are one.

We are the center and periphery of each other's lives. Family. Let us put family back at the center of the wheel of life. We love each other fiercely from the spokes of a wheel that will not stop spinning.

And, I learned, Daughter, there is not just the perpetrator, the victim, the bystander—no, we are missing someone.

Let this writing help reclaim, "The Healer."

THE PRESENT

"You have to protect yourself from sadness. Sadness is very close to hate. Let me tell you this. This is the thing I learned. If you take in someone else's poison—thinking you can cure them by sharing it—you will instead store it within you."

—Michael Ondaatje, The English Patient

Nelle sets the ceramic mug down with a quiet click on the countertop and pulls the carton of milk closer. The white stream slowly fills the mug.

She blinks, sees herself holding a clear plastic urine cup up to her body. Watches it fill, and anticipates the adrenaline rush.

She blinks, twists the plastic cap back on the milk carton. Glides to the fridge and sets the carton on the top shelf.

Haloed by the fridge light, she does not know that the outline of her pregnant body against the dark of the kitchen looks like a silver cloud lining. She does not know. She only knows that she feels anxious and alone. The baby turns over.

Cold, sweating fingers slide against the ceramic mug. She

blinks again. There she is, she catches the flash of her long child braids hanging down her back, she's huddled in the corner of her bedroom on top of that hill, the lake house, the boat house, the ship that the women of her family went away in, she is there, squatting.

There she goes, filling up plastic play cups intended for tea sets with her red bear and Barbies. She's too nervous to leave her room, to urinate in the toilet. One bathroom. One wretched family. Survival instinct. Coping mechanism. She's in the way. Filled plastic child's cups are left like Easter eggs on shelves.

The baby turns, Nelle leans her hip bones against the counter edge pushing them out, spreading and stretching like yoga. Her cold fingers warm against the swell of her stomach and she studies the residue of her nervous sweat against the mug. She blinks once more. Breathes in. Exhales.

She sees her pregnant Self enter that little bedroom atop the hill. Her child self turns suddenly, wide-eyed and teary. Nelle pulls her child Self out of that squat and leads her out of the room, fingers intertwined.

Nelle blinks, presses her open hands against the curve of her spine and deepens the stretch. Her spine pops and she feels the pressure release, energy deliciously coils and grounds.

Planting roots. Growing branches.

Her toes uncurl and splay inside her slippers and she lifts the mug of milk up to her lips. She sips long and slow. Licks the white film from her upper lip. Cups the mug to the center of her chest. Sighs.

She accepts that she's grown into the woman she is, rooted in the centre of her kitchen, steady as timber, she accepts it, she's weathered the storm, the bark of her tree has grown up and around the barbed-wire fences of her landscape.

No more. No fear here.

She refuses to suppress her body anymore, no longer feeling that she preserves and protects by pushing it down and ignoring her most primal needs.

She functions. She is free to move. She is safe to go with her flow. She is a river and she is coursing.

Nelle knows. She knows. Allostasis. Homeostasis. Brain retraining. Limbic system recovery. Pregnancy test pee. Pee on a shelf. She knows her family, essentially does not want her to live like that or live with the ghost of that memory haunting her.

She let go.

Turn. Float. Glow.

She found the yellow cloth star of David once, in a clay pot in her Grandma's basement. The frayed cloth, two stars, two J's, and two periods. She was confronted by the severity of history. Instant acceptance and realization, the women in her family hid things.

The residue of lives, remnants. The parts of ourselves we choose to hide. The parts of ourselves that we choose to share. The ways in which we tuck our most intimate selves into mundane domestic folds.

Nelle hid bodily fluids.

She is no longer afraid to take up space.

Milk in a mug.

A pregnancy test.

Pee in a cup.

She blinks, sips, cracks her fingers next, wringing each knuckle deliberately, slowly. The mug is half full.

A sheet of ice and snow breaks away and crashes from the roof. She jumps.

She jumps.

Emery is there, young, and they are laughing hysterically. She remembers, his smudged face, the interior of the car coated in yellow resin. Her heart thundered, a caged bird thrashing against her ribs. She screamed, closed her eyes, and forgot for a second that she was driving and they had fish tailed on the dirt road. His new paintball gun, why she had let him bring it out in the front seat, windows up, they exploded in laughter that he accidentally shot up the inside of her car.

"You're lucky that can wipe away." Nelle hears her younger self.

She empties the mug and sets it in the sink.

The laugh rises up deep inside her gut and she can't hold it in. She hasn't laughed in a long time since he went away, and the sound is a newborn infant to her ears. She had completely forgotten about that paintball car ride.

Emery survived the North Country of Marmora. Bike rides under the beating summer sun on dirt roads veining into Shanick country. He back flipped off train bridges. Crashed his dirt bike into a hydro pole smashing his collarbone. He was as wild as the jungle he grew up in.

Nelle had grown up just as north in a latitudinal dive east in Queensborough, but she felt Emery had arrived in an explosion of energy from a completely different world. Nelle was drawn to him.

His neighbor was Spider. Warren William "Spider" Hastings. Nelle never got to meet Spider, but when she recalls Emery in his youth, Spider is entwined with him. She knows—she remembers him this way because they were both a part of the North Country as much as they were exotic balls of energy erupting volcanically from it.

Spider was a punk rocker with rainbow dyed hair, body piercings, tattoos, and his own punk festival that essentially put Marmora on the map. Spiderland Acres. Emery grew up beside Spiderland Acres. Spider sent his father a Christmas card every year. The man was loving. He had a heart of gold.

As much as his lifestyle was a disruption to the orthodox conservative fabric of Marmorian society, the community knew that Spider contributed to the touristic flow of the international punk rock scene.

Punkfest. Held every year on Spider's birthday, July 13, the festival brought in more punk rockers than the entire population of Marmora. The residents were nervous at the throngs of youth that arrived from all over the world. Fearful of this punk culture —shaved heads, body piercings, rocker t-shirts, leather. The people were nervous of a wild culture, just as wild as the jungle growing up around them. There was once a roller coaster, a merry-go-round, stages, and trailers at Punkfest. The town succeeded in limiting the event to 50 guests unless Spider obtained a permit. The youth knew, everyone knew, no matter the legislation and collective fear of the exoticness of Punkfest, you couldn't stop it.

Emery didn't necessarily know, as he wove his way through the woods to Spiderland to buy some bud, Spider had once been a part of The Sex Pistols and earned his name "Spider" as an A&P stockboy when a woman had dropped her groceries for fear that there was a spider on her. He retrieved her groceries. They called him Spider. He also looked like one.

Names stick. Names make us eternal. Names are our legacy.

"Mopie."

She hears the name run through her.

Mopie meant "puppy" in Dutch. Or so she was taught. She carried the pet name back from her trips to Holland, and had tattooed their young love with it. They called each other "Mopie." Their own spelling. Their own naming. They created their own world in the midst of that North Country chaos and they survived for a decade this way.

Nelle reaches the end of the hallway and begins climbing the stairs, one step at a time. She shakes her head. Pauses for a moment.

"Mopie." She speaks to the house. The sound is as loud as the ice that fell from her roof, but as quiet as the click of a ceramic mug at the bottom of the sink.

She remembers. His face is twisted and he's weeping. She feels her heart harden and a molten lava globe encircles it. Her tongue has grown thorns and cuts the inside of her mouth.

"I am not Mopie."

She reclaimed. Nelle was now a Mother Wolf, no longer a puppy. There is pain from exposing double lives. Lies that had tidal waved and spiraled out from a dam, a decade of double lives. The choice was hard, but it was easy. It was too late, but it was on time. She strained to regroup and rope in the edges of her soul, pull her daughter down. The shingles of her soul. Her house. Her home.

Nelle wets her lips, tries her baby's name for the first time in the column of that house.

"Nevaeh."

She smiles and continues climbing the stairs.

THE PAST

The silhouette marched away in the tunneled light of the headlights. He learned desertion from this behaviour. He learned that parents do not always protect in a helix of fear. They showed him that parents were flawed humans battling themselves as much as they pushed their battles onto their children. He knew.

The shadow does not turn around, and the boy knows that his indifference is deliberate, intended to alienate both him and his mother. He listens to her sobs, and cannot determine whether they are natural or forced because he rarely sees such an edge of emotion in her—she too is reserved and barricaded.

The Cadillac was parked alongside the 510, the Trans-Labrador Highway, atop a steep incline running from the village of Forteau. Aiden knew that they are approximately 13 kilometers northeast of the Quebec border; he also knew that the name of the village means "Strong Water." He wondered whether it was irony or pure mockery that the village translates to "Strong Water." He did not feel strong; he wanted to sink to the floor of the car and sleep, when he woke up, perhaps then they will have worked things out, forgotten about fighting.

He tried to cloud his head, ingest it with useless knowledge to push the pain out. He remembered the tour that day and how the tour guide had spoken in a crisp voice about the history of

Forteau. The other families on the tour looked normal, with sun visors and maps, he wished his family could be like that.

The man had angled his hat and scanned the crowd.

"This town can owe its origins to a Jersey merchant named De Quetteville, who started a fishing business in 1774. In 1818, it was reported that Forteau was the largest British establishment in the Straits." He heard the confusion waft through the audience and he smiled with a finger poised before his puckered mouth.

"You'd assume this town was French because of the name. It's English because that is who settled it, simple enough. It was Guernseymen who settled on the western side of the bay and at Buckle's Point, while a group from Devonshire, England settled at English Point on the eastern side of the bay."

The guide paused, stabbed a long white finger in the air in the direction of a furred woman, and asked, "How do you think the English secured their roots here when settling?"

The woman stuttered, flicked her eyes towards the man standing to her left and answered unsurely, "They built houses?"

The guide straightened and boomed with authority, "No, no, they built a church! Bishop Field of the Anglican Church was appointed to Newfoundland in 1845, he was surprised to learn that Labrador was within his jurisdiction. He visited Forteau in 1848, and in 1849 the first church was built here. Folks, once there is a church, then it is known that the seed of a civilization has been planted."

Aiden would love to be inside the church at that moment, huddled against the hard back of a pew, the candlelight warm and flowing, anywhere really but inside the car, with his father slowly disappearing in the night, his mother weeping. Anger surged within him, detested how they ruined this trip with their fighting. He tasted the bitter fear in his mouth because he felt that his father disliked them, couldn't stand them, and in all actuality, was aggravated by their presence and the minute annoyances they caused him.

He knew that when his father spoke she did not listen, selective hearing packaged as language barrier, made them go crazy. The man could only repeat himself so many times before insanity festered. Aiden knew the stiffness in his father's shoulders when the white-hot blaze of anger took over, the rigid plane that jaunted from his veined neck, into the bulge of a bicep throb. It was not difficult for him to make his mouth disappear, his lips thin already were easily pulled inside, Aiden knew that his father would not speak when his lips were sucked in—his speech inside.

Except tonight it was different, the fighting terser, the anger more raw. It frightened him to see his father's hands shaking against the steering wheel, the shine of his forehead in the rearview mirror. Aiden wanted to reach forward and tug at his mother, who was sitting with her curled hair to him, her face fogging the passenger window. She would not see her husband's rage, could not trace it. Instead, she jumped when he hooked the car into the gravel lining the road and slammed the stick into park. He said nothing, but opened his car door, smashing it with one trembling left hand. That was it.

He left them there, on the side of the highway, in the dark, and he did not come back despite the boy's hope. It took Aiden slow deep breaths and two full hours before he budged. He said nothing to his mother as he climbed over the backrest of the front seat bench. Pushing his torso into the driver's seat, his right hand carefully adjusted the rearview mirror. Anxiety trilled a slight twitch below his right eye. He blinked hard.

Sophie said nothing as he shifted the car into drive and slowly pulled out onto the highway. They did not stop to eat, but only to fill up the gas tank, an awkward learning curve that he would recall every time he filled up his trucks in the future. He drove until his eyes burned and he had to pull over to relieve himself. She remained silent, not moving, not needing to relieve herself. Aiden knew she was in shock.

He forgot this memory until adulthood, his own vehicle packed for a ski trip and the incessant daughter's coughing from the back seat. The catalyst for an outburst he had kept inside of him since that trip back East. The coughing sent him into a delirium and he lost control.

The tables turned.

On this night, he would pull over to the side of the highway off of the Quebec and Ontario border. The children would cry and his wife, Eva-Marie, would fly from the van in a fit of tears.

And then, she will walk with her back to the headlights into the night. The silhouette of her ski jacket, haloed by the soft glow of her blonde hair. A wretched man who will drive beside his sobbing wife until she reluctantly gets back inside the van.

THE PAST

She watched him from across the room. His back bent slightly, his shoulders curled inwards towards his heart. Long dark hair blocked the sides of his face, she could not see his eyes. He nodded his head slightly to the plateaus and pitches of the music. Palms intimately cupped the notes, he pursed his lips and the muscles tightened around his jaw as his fingers plucked airily at a complicated melody.

If she were standing in front of him, with the piano graciously between them, she would know that at this moment, he was in his element.

Closed eyes, his pupils massaged an azure empty room while his expert fingers asserted themselves fully on the polished keyed surfaces, the steep crags of the black keys reprieves from reality.

He had memorized her surface, knew the measurements and lines, how far his fingers must splay across the scales, the edges of his fingernails gently, but assuredly, lipping the dips and valleys. He does not want to slip his grip, to plummet from the polished theatre of his playing, where his fingers could fumble, chunking the silkiness of the harmony into foolish obscurity.

Aiden broke a sweat in concentration. A crimson flush ardent and dictating along his neck and cheeks. Contradictorily, she gripped astonishment as the song erupted in a fit, the calculated climax followed by four long silent notes. She saw him hover, his shoulders suspended slightly as he inhaled, his body sank as he exhaled, his fingers resuming their endless tirade.

She cannot remember when she closed her eyes, let her body sag against the doorframe, his song speaking to her with intensity and clarity. In the chambered particles of her haze, she witnessed the slow passage across the room, a shadow of a soul hallowed against the cool light in the window glass, a slender manicured hand rose and cupped the crown of a mass of dark hair. The music continued, projecting beautiful sound throughout the house, the two figures suspended in linked silence. She smiled.

She was startled by the resonance and thunderous clap of wood and the keys died out in an ear-splitting twang. Her eyes flew open struggling to adjust to the room's white miasma aura. His torso turned unnaturally, his thighs and knees jutted forwards, the angle of his back completely bent against the keys, his face was taut and burned from anger.

Intrusion.

Their gazes locked in a breath, but he broke it by shifting his eyes and standing. Loud silence. Aiden disappeared into the back contours of the house. She knew he had retreated to his room. She pushed back the hair from her face with the wet plane of her hand and snapped her wrist.

Only the room could hear her pained sigh.

THE PAST

He was only eighteen. He told me this.

He can only remember that the blood caked between his fingers burned. The skin of his knuckles peeled raw to bone, white and fainting, cut as if a chain had whipped him, again and again, chained to pain, that chain was thrown overboard with an anchor attached to it. He went with it.

The glass shrieked in a tirade of sorrow and vengeance as he plunged his hands through the panes, one after the over. Sophie covered her ears from inside the imploding house and folded, weeping against the tiles; transplanted to a different geography, one of war and bombs and breaking windows, it took her several years to accept that the outline of the monster from beyond the windows had been her son.

The man beside him at the bar wood that night loved conversation; he soaked his mouth against it, released words from his drunken gut without thought, conscientiousness or consideration. To him, it was an offhand comment meant to stir and grind, he had no idea what he was about to unleash. He spoke from conjecture, not affirmation, though both pricked the boy's heartstrings, beveled to the knot of his born anger, jutting and imperfect; my father's chain; the man set free a cage beast.

For once Phillip was speechless. His feet stilled against the cool hardness of the floor tiles, his drink glowing amber in the lamplight. Triggered—shell shock triggered—he was the one to come after the battles to scavenge the wreckage. Phillip watched his son circle the house, a desperate shadow—exerting, sweating, wailing.

My house is wreckage.

Aiden smashed every single window in the house that night; the boathouse, the Moira lake house, the house on the hill, it all sank. Each punch with the blood, pain, and every shard of broken glass was a statement, his conjecture against the lies.

They did not know what he knew, and he never told them explicitly. The broken glass, one window after the other, systematic, left, right, left, right, was enough to leave them quaking.

While Aiden watched the pale sliver of his arm extend and crack into the transparent barrier of the house, he gained footing. If anything, he demonstrated how fierce his rage could be. That their lies could not contain a crafted story to be perpetuated on him as his life. They could not abate him.

The survey Self partakes in after atrocity, Self-perpetrated atrocity, the damage is engrossing and terrifying. Self under pressure.

I looked down at my own hands, knew that they too would have done the same thing and that above anything; we shared each other's rage. We were both angered, and because of this, we were defined.

He wrung his hands tersely. They pulsed and beat like hearts from his wrists. Blood pumped tidal waves up and down his extremities, chest heaving—he hadn't caught his breath yet.

Chaos hands. He raised these chaos hands in front of his eyes, flexing them in the light. Teeth clenched and veins popping in his throat, his skin burned. Aiden was enraged, livid.

Truth had come from a stranger. Truth did not come from familiarity. Resentment coiled up and threaded his skeleton, a tense fortress of muscle. Each blink cemented a brick in the walls rising up around him.

I remember how his voice fell flat in the pitch of the climax.

That he had snuck into the bar and found himself in glasses of draft and whiskey. They knew not of where he was, and he felt free. I wondered how he could control each inflection, the ripple of severe emotion within each widening ring while he spoke. He could control inflection—he could not control the intensity of emotions attached to memories. Emotions that he wanted to go away. She did not know her seashell ears were his healing space. Yet, she listened.

I felt both remorse and sympathy, because in that moment when he talked himself down into banality, I knew that he was exposing himself. Vulnerable and exposed. Sealed tight.

This was my father, and, in the crux of the eye of an aggressive generational storm, we did love each other.

RIPPLE

Like a cut earthworm,
A dropped lizard's tail,
The design sustains life,
Pain is the design.

Empathy is skill,
Staying open is practice,
The caterpillar gorges before
Cocooning.

Pushed down and against
The entirety of Self,
The process is individual,
Fast or slow,

Before empowerment,
A painful facing,
Knowing perpetration,
Rework behavior, thought roads.

It is painful to push from
The cocoon, chrysalis, womb,

Wings form under skin, inside,
The last shedding,

The butterfly pushes painfully,
Fluids pump from abdomen, core,
Without pressure, the wings
Cannot fill, harden for flight.

Carve out space for him,
Connect body and spirit,
For him to have heart,
Hands for loving, not hurting,

Stop making the Maternal cry,
Make the Maternal smile,
Let it be safe for her to laugh,
Let it be safe for her to want
To be.

THE PAST

She found his unconscious body in the kitchen, angled unnaturally against the floor. She shrieked, seeing his mouth and nose, submerged in vomit, his eyes fissures of bruised pain. His pallid complexion almost appeared angelic in lightness, the smooth glistening curve of his forehead, the shining bridge of his nose; she could see the broken halo resting on the crown of his head.

Sophie felt both guilt and fear from the drained Parsons Ammonia all-purpose cleaner on the countertop. She shook instantly, a severe quaking in her bones that rattled and spun her around. She had never encountered Death like this before, with its putrid dark scent clouding the corners, usually they ran from Him, avoiding the cool grip of unknowing, but now, His shock ceased her limbs, rendering her into stone in the kitchen, with her son poisoned on the floor.

She dropped the phone four times while dialing 911. The handle struck a resounding crack against the wood of the kitchen cupboards each time. When the operator answered her call, the woman had a difficult time understanding Sophie. Her despair had completely unraveled her language. She cried in French, the words were reassurances, but complete nonsense to the operator. She shook her head desperately as she heard the

French flood the phone and she knew that she was making the situation worse. The outline of his back against the white wall coiled around her throat, she gasped and retched into the receiver. The operator, urgent and slow, ushered Sophie into conversation, one of simplicity, the requisite credence of words, how, "fallen, poisoned, and still," could situate and propel bodies.

"Someone is on the way." A calm voice. The earpiece slipped against Sophie's sodden cheek.

The voice soldiered Sophie into action. She shook while she bent down beside the boy, his face red-raw from the acid of his vomit. She cupped his jaw-line, did not writhe from the thick wetness at the base of her thumbs. She pulled him from the vomit, exerting to flip him onto his back ensuring that while on his side there was no vomit caught inside his mouth and throat. She wept at the blueness of his closed eyes. She moaned and arched her body around the top of his head and shoulders in a desperate prayer.

Hovering over his inflamed face she pulled his jaw back and flattened her palm against his chin to force his mouth open. With his mouth gaping and seeping the foul Parsons lemon scent, deceptive in the sheer fragrance of supposed cleanliness, the odor made her insides crawl. Statuesque in a Mother's prayer, she waited.

There is a young man rolling in waves. His body is lulled and pulled by the vast waters.

She almost fainted when they rushed through the front door, persistent and systematic. She fell into their rhythm and coerced her palms together in prayer. She sweated and whimpered while they worked his heads and shoulders, encasing his swollen orifices in an oxygen mask.

The men shared discrete looks.

What a shame.

She would always be grateful for his life, yet fearful of her son, how he behaved from pain. He was capable of far more than her. He was outward and hidden like a landmine; one wrong step and she knew that everything would perish around them.

Her father was there again, telling a child Sophie the difference between landmines and hand grenades.

Sophie lived in the rubble of her son's mind, creeping over eggshells, huddled in his shadow, willing him to turn around and embrace her warmly. She wanted his eyes to look upon her and resonate with love. But they darkened, they looked at her unblinking, and she shouldered his stares with deliberate ignorance.

She learned to choose survival. She held onto emotions kept private. A grey cloud. A hovering grey cloud you watch, waiting to see it open and let the rain down.

Her son would try to kill himself several months later. She relived the darkness, a surreal and horrifying repetition. This time she purged the house of chemicals, locked away anything that was marked with the devastating skull and crossbones.

Foolish woman, she forgot the whiskey.

It remained, glinting from a shelf in the kitchen.

STORYTELLER

Daughter, as I hold you safe in my womb, I feed you the tremble of anger of the historical storylines that you will be born into. I am not sorry that you will know of it—no—I am sorry for those who perpetuated the toxicity of the physical and spiritual ripples in your world and what your generation will do with that knowledge. If anything, I sink back with my fingers splayed like fish around you, we will achieve peace.

People will rise to the occasion. I care about the plants and animals. I care about the environment. Peace to me is when Mother Nature and the Animal Kingdom are protected and have an honest chance to survive on this planet.

When we *all* have an honest chance to survive on this planet.

Daughter, I was one of the children who played in the forest of my homelands and witnessed the barbed-wire hellhole of a WWII landscape. Of the fences that went up, that kept us out, and caged us in.

Our family grew up around Young's Creek, the Moira River, and Moira Lake. The Black River. These water systems trace the hard-Precambrian edges of the Canadian Shield to the north of a space I want to speak of known as the notorious Deloro Mine Site.

This story continues to layer.

After they struck gold in Eldorado in 1866 and the gold rush tidal waved into this locale, twenty-five shafts were sunk in the area now known as the Deloro Mine Site. Deloro means, "valley of gold."

Daughter, this history is important to you, to your identity and self-worth, because I want you to look straight into the barrel of a gun that could lower you. The language that comprises a history and communal understanding of our worth as peoples in this geography echoes larger historical and national processes. I refuse to let my child remain a pawn.

In 2001, the Ontario Ministry put out a report entitled, "The Moira River Study Summary." Our environment and our river system is deemed "unproductive,"—"fish and benthic invertebrate populations are small and form communities of relatively low species of diversity."

Do not let what they have done in the past to our land, how they have taken for granted the richness of this wilderness, even what they did to the original inhabitants, dictate the structure in which you measure yourself. You are of worth, and I want you to speak with a mindful voice acknowledging this value.

The Canadian Consolidated Gold Mining Company was started in 1873. The Canadian Gold Fields Company purchased the site at Deloro in 1896. They constructed the first mill and utilized a cyanide process to extract gold, a harsh inorganic process that essentially left behind a poisoned landscape for others to attempt to clean up. My Child, pride yourself in taking out your own garbage and being conscientious of where that trash is going to end up on this planet and the impact it will have on the quality of life for others.

Cyanide is a compound containing both carbon and nitrogen that hardens metal ore. The Deloro gold was not pure, and the processes necessitated to attempt to remove impurities to achieve pure gold were not of economic benefit. The mill closed in 1903. The roasting furnaces remained, the skeleton of a mill remained, and the toxic resins of the treachery from this work waterlogged this sacred land like an unholy baptism—and remained.

The railroad complex penetrated the northern jungle, capitalist colonization pushed farther inland, and with the completion of the rail line to Deloro in 1904, the mill was reopened as a smelting and refining company for silver. The Deloro Mining and Reduction Company was established in 1906 changing its name to Deloro Smelting and Refining Company Limited. A man named Dr. Haynes produced the first commercial stellite globally, and Daughter, yes, that stellite was manufactured at Deloro. Stellite is a hard alloy that contains cobalt, chromium, molybdenum, and tungsten. Deloro, then, produced stellite, arsenic, silver, and cobalt until 1956. Silver ore was treated at Deloro until 1961.

The larger repercussions of the processes utilized in Deloro were products that contributed to death, not life. Arsenic based pesticides were created from arsenic by-products of smelting operations before organic pesticides were introduced in the 1950s. Know, Daughter, our history is enmeshed with a collective Canadian consciousness of military endeavors. We are not the polite peacekeepers that we project to be.

In 1938, Deloro was given contracts to supply stellite for the British aircraft industry. So, throughout WWII and the Korean War, Deloro contributed to a mining triangular trade of the Canadian and American governments that took resources from African mines to be processed in our locality and then sent back out into the world as aircraft that fueled war. Even after the end of WWII, Deloro continued to supply jet engine components. Deloro contributed to the waste of the Canadian Avro Arrow.

There was much waste with the Deloro Mine Site—the people and the environment have suffered from it.

Daughter, I want to teach you that in taking out your own trash, you are empowered and have a conscience to work through adversity. The men at the Deloro Mine Site, as much as a stereotype it is of domestic violence, regardless of a gender construct, just push aside and ignore the issue. What we do to our women, we have done to Mother Earth, Gaia.

What they did at Deloro was reckless and cowardly. The mine site was shut down in 1961 and almost one century of by-products and toxic residues remained. They buried the arsenite refuse. My love, they demolished the mine site and left behind tons of hazardous materials in Gaia like a murdered body wrapped in a stained ragged blanket.

Compounds.

Metals.

Cobalt.

Copper.

Nickel.

Uranium.

Low-level radioactive waste.

Slag and tailings.

Airborne pollutants.

Arsenic.

Cadmium. Cyanide. Lead.

Manganese Molybdenum.

Zinc.

Mercury.

In 1979 the property was abandoned. The Ministry of the Environment was obligated to take over. I can laugh awkwardly, Daughter, because, do you see, if they cannot make money, if it becomes too difficult, if it becomes ruin, they leave.

Oftentimes, I do not want to trip in my own traps of stereo-types and sexism, but most times—well, money dictates the movements of bodies. Remember, we stay. Our voice, our empowered voices, no matter the low volume or faintest of lights, our ripple in the vast waters, will carry on a memory of a time when they came, how they reaped, what they wasted, and why they left.

Our story makes them accountable.

Knowledge, the awareness of life processes and events, is first planted as a seed of an idea, these seeds sprout as mouths from the common folk pass this knowledge further. Conveyor belt factory line, Adam Smith's specialization of labour functions similarly. Before official reports are filed. Elite pockets. Barriers and isolation. Concentration camps.

People only knew their role, not the final solution.

Before those high up on pyramids are faced with the negligence of their own actions, if they are aware, knowledge of the actual happenings is passed on as an oral history, slippery as catching fish with bare hands. What is left is a gnarled tree growing up through the skeletons of lives, as blatant as the rising and setting of the sun. We carry that story with us into our future.

In the summer of 1958, a dozen cows died, others became sick after drinking from the Moira River. The Ontario Water Resources Commission filed a report for arsenic contamination. The anger and injustices felt by the inhabitants of Deloro and the Moira River—their realities—pushed down hard and were shelved with an impersonal and insensitive bureaucratic hand.

Policide.

It wasn't until 1997 that soil samples were taken. Arsenic, cobalt, nickel, silver, and other heavy metals were determined to remain at the mine site and beyond.

Careful, Daughter, watch how tricky language becomes in the Policide concentration camp. Seven gardens were used for testing the soil and vegetables. The samples showed that the poisonous contents tended to be at higher levels than others typically found in Ontario. However, vegetables were reported to not contain elevated contaminants.

Whatever that specifies—just laugh.

Every home, the library, the pump house, and the youth centre were tested. Remember, they only took samples of surface dust. Just laugh. Metals and radiological contaminants were similar to the study area of the mine site. Fifty-seven houses were tested for radon gas, and 10 of them were determined high compared to normative provincial guidelines. Whatever that specifies—just laugh. Vacuums were installed. Dirt floors were replaced with concrete ones.

But, Daughter, those efforts could not take back the damage that had been caused to nature, to the bodies and minds of the people living beyond the mine site.

Sorry doesn't bring life back.

In that same year—1997—a woman named Janet Fletcher and the Sierra Legal Defence Fund pushed for 8 charges against the Ontario government under the federal Fisheries Act and the Ontario Water Resources Act. The charges specified a protest against the government for allowing the mine site to contaminate the Moira River and Young's Creek. This event was the first act in Ontarian legal history of private citizens pressing charges against the province.

Policide persisted, court proceedings and paperwork slowed down the process of protecting the environment and the people. Four years later, the province was finally acquitted simply because they "planned" to clean up the site.

I shake my head, Daughter, because I yearn for the next seven generations to have a voice and power to protect home. I want language constructs to grow up around that word I use —policide.

The outcome of those court proceedings, despite the heroics of Janet Fletcher, was the posting of signs and a barbed-wire, chain-linked fence around the perimeter of the mine site.

Because signs and a fence can fix that.

We can only laugh sometimes, Daughter, at the ways they tried to exist on this land. Just laugh. Laughter is medicine. We've been forsaken by industrial process, economic elite pyramids—greed.

I remember the fence that went up and the talk amongst my school friends. No one knew we played in radioactive waste. Laugh. Sometimes you can only laugh at it. Our backyard, over there, before you arrive at the Peterborough Petroglyphs, that land, well, that dead zone became a beacon for pilots—who knew—to navigate to Toronto or Ottawa.

Look for the dead zone, they will find us there.

No fear, in December of 2004 the Ontario Ministry of the Environment projected cleanup costs between $30 and $40 million. Dump trucks appeared, at first empty, then pulling back onto Highway 7 full of contaminated fill. The total arsenic estimation carried out from the site is 100,000 tons. Seventy-five hundred tons of calcium arsenite were buried. The government planned to build basins to contain mass graves of "crushed radioactive slag."

Let me share the words from the doctor.

"Any member of the general public who spends 200 hours by the side of the fence south of the main gate will receive radiation dose equal to or in excess of one mSv, the proposed maximum annual exposure limit."

It gets better, Daughter.

"It is my considered opinion that radioactive material that is outside the fenced area, where I measured the ration field, presents a risk to the general public of deleterious health effects and an impairment to the safety of the general public. Furthermore, ongoing leaching of radium and other radionuclides from the plant site poses serious environmental problems that have not been addressed. These leachates probably drain into the Moira River basin."

Signs and fencing.

Our government took action.

Signs and fencing.

Never mind elevated arsenic levels in a child's urine. Never mind. Under the rug, the paperwork shelved and swept under legislative and legal rugs. Just laugh.

Policide talk:

"November 20, 1998, The informant says he believes on reasonable grounds that (1) Her Majesty the Queen in Right of Ontario between the 17th day of September, 1998 and the 14th day of November, 1998, inclusive, at a place near the western fence of the Deloro mine site in the Township of Marmora and Lake, in the County of Hastings, did commit the offence of:

unlawfully discharging or causing or permitting the discharge of a contaminant, namely, radiation, into the natural environment that caused or was likely to cause an adverse effect contrary to s. 14 (1) of the Environmental Protection Act, R.S.O. 1990, c. E.19, as amended and did thereby commit an offence contrary to s. 186 (1) of the Act."

Again: "On or about the 25th day of August, 1997, at the Deloro mine site, in the Township of Marmora and Lake and the Village of Deloro, in the County of Hastings did unlawfully deposit or permit the deposit of a deleterious substance, to wit, toxic liquid, from a seep on the east bank of the Moira River, in a place under conditions where the deleterious substance entered water frequented by fish, to wit, the Moira River, contrary to s. 36 (3) of the Fisheries Act, R.S.C., 1985, c. F-14, as amended, and did thereby commit an offence contrary to s. 40 (2) (a) of that Act."

We played there. We fished there. We hunted there. We drove by the fence and the signs, yet this story was hushed and uncomfortable for our government to process for us. Officials were insensitive to the actuality of the lives that lived daily with the knowledge that the mine site leaked toxins. Children were exposed. The environment and land were disrespected.

These locals showed up to meetings and conferences about the clean up and their voices were edged with anger, they speak up, almost appearing uneducated—innocent—as they make the entire room uncomfortable, and the government worker in front of the projector, well, he leers and pretends to live in a fantasy that these millions of dollars, containment basins, aqua barriers, dump trucks, fences, and signs will magically erase the damage.

Wrong, Daughter. All wrong.

It will never be fixed. Mother Nature—only Mother nature —can reclaim and heal it. Yet, the People will never forget how they were treated, more so, how they were mistreated.

Careful, Daughter, the water you drink, know where it comes from.

STORYTELLER

I am alter ego. I force you to face Self. I can also sever.

I drift between particles, internally and externally. I permeate everything.

Consider me the face in your mirrored reflection. Look me in my eyes. See the flaws and shining pearls passed down lines. I can make you smile. I can make you hurt yourself. Whichever.

My taunting could render you a troubled student—absences and bad reputations. Or I can help you rise up in your greatness.

I admire that no matter what I threw at you, this family was intelligent and mostly rose to the occasion. Mostly, you exceeded my expectations. Missed classes would not affect grade point averages or career foundations. You overcame addictions; put more life-sustaining things on the table.

Your decision in what you do with me can only determine how happy you will be.

I watched your family choose sadness, mostly, for a long time.

I am distinct, in the horror and awe, from the essential personality core.

Typecast.

Cliché.

You wore skins like gloves.

You risked falling into shallow-graved niches of dissociative identity disorders, living and breathing each other's stories. Remember, your stories are the past. I am here to push you to honour the present; to care about the future. If you want. Whichever.

It is an awful cycle, those souls plundering along chained to each other. It was a pleasure to watch you untangle those chains, unyoke yourselves and breathe. To forgive each other by accepting each other's wretchedness. You were sheep huddled together in your pain.

I wanted to lift the chains from your sheep-spent lives because I am also hope for those who have none. Ego does not want you to die a spiritual death. I need you.

I transcend, ghost-like upon you. Painstakingly piecing the nimbus of your existences.

An eyeball glazed with memories, clinking and rusted.

A heart shrunken, your family lay deflated upon my path gnawed, warped, and waning.

I forced you together and apart, splintering bone, ripping ligament, a fateful resurrection, vulgar and exposing.

Your rural society abhorred me, my interminable escalation; but they could not cope themselves that I would not leave your family alone.

Ego filled the numerous vacancies—empty spaces I heard screaming.

I testify to ruptured blood vessels, bruises, and chipped bones, the perpetual burns you lived with—endured.

I am the pilgrim with the most difficult task because failure always likes to rent souls. It gravitates there. It takes up residence in bodies that let their souls go.

I try, I do try, and that is the regiment of what I do.

I fail, I do fail, because success can only vine up and thrive when the house realizes that we are one. When you want your body back. When you acknowledge that you have a soul. I am there, particled between.

I am the voice you turned your backs on in childhood; when

you were newly open, before cruel societies closed you, locked you in.

I can only speak to you through gesture, by giving back the pieces of Self and memory you tossed out, pushed down, purposefully forgot along the way.

Today I found your mouth, now you can smile.

However, you can still not swallow.

THE PAST

The burgundy Grand Marquis SP, 1978, clipped along the 401 heading east. The cracked windows let in a torrent of wind that strung hair and words in the air. Sophie tilted her face against the window in relief for the coolness of the breeze. Her insides were molten and reeling. Driving was anxiety inducing, although she feigned confidence. She drove awkwardly, yet, she never had had an accident. Sophie was a European streetcar, she was not a backroad or a four hundred series highway. She stayed close to Madoc.

Sophie was now gracing her mid-sixties, but hid the lines around her eyes expertly with sunglasses and luxurious silk scarves in sharp patterns. On this day, her eyes were concealed behind a pair of dark, black, cat-eye sunglasses. A Burberry scarf wrapped around her hair, she radiated elegance. Her figure was trim, and she accentuated this vitality with tailored pants and pin skirts. Eva-Marie, Aiden's girlfriend admired the softness of her white blouse tucked into her skirt, how the fabric swam around the woman's shoulders freely, not sucked against her skin in a wet mass. Eva-Marie felt as though her clothes were stuck to her, a second skin. She repositioned her body, constantly attempting to evade the layer of nervous sweat gelling her body.

The women had to go and clean out Aiden's room that he

rented in Kingston, which was very close to where Eva-Marie's great-aunt lived. They could see the Kingston Penitentiary from there, on the same road as the hospital. The women had left the courthouse right after Aiden's trial as he went to jail in Napanee.

Eva-Marie felt numb, both from the pain of his conviction, and from the agonizing argument with her mother that lasted the entire night before. She was exhausted and clung to emotions. Red flags. Her mother wanted her to heed red flags.

Nevertheless, Aiden had spent three weeks in the Napanee Detention Center minimum security, and her mother took Eva-Marie to visit him. She didn't have her driver's license yet. Aiden was then moved to Kingston to a halfway house on Johnston Street. The place could still be there. Government-run. He spent six months there and was able to be released under good supervision and behaviour.

An older Eva-Marie would one day tell her own daughter the story, "then he came home to Madoc and was told never to do bad things again."

Sophie was rattled, gripping the steering wheel with hidden ferocity. She dug into her purse with one shaking hand, pulling out a pack of cigarettes. The filter tasted like wet cardboard as she bit down and lit the end with jarred fingers.

Eva-Marie said nothing and watched from the passenger seat; she knew that the woman had given up smoking years before. She herself hid the habit. But all that Sophie could think about was how the baby they brought to her at three months old, had come home and shattered the windows in the house, one by one, with vile anger and betrayal. She cursed, her lips pursed around the filter. That was the night he released the madness. She knew it. There was no going back.

He unraveled afterwards. There was a fire, arson, a moonshine beating, and theft. She wondered how he left the old man in blood, his back scalded, and painfully blistered. The bootlegger's house, aflame. A horrible transaction, in reality, the old man simply had been out.

Aiden was tried and sentenced to jail. Sophie pleaded with

lawyers for reprieve, for the courts to consider his age, his apprenticeship. His father did nothing but fill his glass, again, and again.

On this day, they were to release him on strict prohibitions in which he was to live at a boarding house for troubled youth. There he could complete his apprenticeship out of Kingston; he also was away from them, and could recuperate.

She was expecting the pain and shame that enveloped her, but not this unhinging. Sophie knew that once detached her mouth would fall open and swallow her entirely.

"I adopted Aiden, you know?" The words were alien inside the car, abrupt, and edged by the wind. The women had not yet spoken, and Eva-Marie was not ready for the impact of her words. She stiffened and listened.

"I have never told a soul about this, but I was in Belgium when the Germans occupied it." She shook her head, and Eva-Marie was mesmerized by the glassy surface of the woman's eyes. She looked hard trying to see behind the sunglasses hiding her future mother-in-law's face while wanting to know exactly what she looked like when she spoke of this. Sophie inhaled long from the cigarette letting the smoke coil inside, endorphins released—she relaxed.

"I hid Jews, Eva," she really had never gotten her name right. "I had to," she trailed off and pressed the cigarette butt into the interior ashtray. "I just needed to survive."

Eva-Marie was floored; she stared at the woman aghast. Heat rushed her face and she wiped a thick wet film from her forehead. She worried that silence would be rude and mustered to open her mouth.

"I did not know." She felt like a fool—inflated words fell on deaf ears. Sophie gave no acknowledgement of her comment, but continued.

"They found me." She struggled with "they," and Eva-Marie registered the pain in the woman's voice, how complicated "they" really was. She knew immediately that "they" were the Germans, and she could not deny the bitter sorrow that pulsed inside of her. She had never been so close to history before.

"They found me and now I cannot have children." The car filled with grim silence. Eva-Marie did not understand at first—how it had congealed, pushing any notion of rationality to dig through the complexity of her lover's life beyond her comprehension.

Families need women. Families also need the truth.

Eva-Marie realized, with trepid horror, that she knew more about her boyfriend than he knew of himself. She scowled at Sophie discreetly out of the corner of her eye, for the burden of knowing. She was only eighteen.

She did not want to possess this knowledge, to hold this dreadful secret inside of her. She felt the severance of the words, how they penetrated with such cruel force. She handled the remorse with copious guilt and conflict. Too bad Aiden did not share this side of his life with her intimately, wrapped between bed sheets away from a cruel world.

Eva-Marie wondered exactly why she was being told this, now, on their way to clean out his room. Perhaps to stay, not to run, to feel both pity and a part of something bigger and awe-inspiring of the woman's courage and sacrifice. She analyzed why the woman confided in her of all people, why not someone else? She sensed the budding loyalty for the woman and knew that she would do anything to help her with her son.

A young Eva-Marie did not want them to lose each other amongst such a snarl of degeneracy.

Completely baffled, Eva-Marie rolled her shoulders back, accepting a new resolution—they both needed her and she liked to be needed.

RIPPLE

We are fractal geometry,
Nature is physics,
We are nature,

2200 volts of electricity held against wood
Will trunk and arch out,
A surge of lightning bolts,
The pattern of a tree
With branches and leaves forms,

Currents that follow
Paths of least resistance,
Efficiency,

We are these energy trees,
This female body,

STORYTELLER

"He trembles and then I can feel my lost child surfacing within me, forgiving me, rising from the lake where it has been prisoned for so long, its eyes and teeth phosphorescent; the two halves clasp, interlocking like fingers, it buds, it sends out fronds. This time I will do it by myself, squatting, on old newspapers in a corner alone; or on leaves, dry leaves, a heap of them, that's cleaner. The baby will slip out easily as an egg, a kitten, and I'll lick it off and bite the cord, the blood returning to the ground where it belongs; the moon will be full, pulling. In the morning I will be able to see it: it will be covered with shining fur, a god, I will never teach it any words."

–Margaret Atwood, Surfacing

I am now in my last trimester, and you are almost ready. I can feel you. My body is uncomfortable. Daughter, I look forward to you being outside of me, it has been too long, too long. I am yearning for the time away from society to hold you, to be awake for you in the long winter hours.

You sleep now. You make faces. You even hiccup. My love, I

feel you nudging me. Weighing almost three pounds, you are almost fifteen inches long. The bone of elbow against the rib, the arch of knee against the wall of my stomach, sometimes I can only hold you fast and tight, press my back against the wall and wait for you to pull me down into your impulses, this will be the way for the rest of my life.

Your nervous system is regulating your body and your precious nerve fibers are now encased in myelin, your impulses travel faster. You are feeling now, Daughter, feeling the world in you and around you. Please, don't go numb, stay open, and let the universe hold you in this holy fold. Stay open. Impulses are okay. Feeling is strength. Emotions are valuable. There is a sacred flow orienting this way. Practice. Pain will remind you that you are alive and that you are human. Pain is temporary.

I feel more human with each blink of you turning— preparing to come down. This one has journeyed from heaven to hell. Back again. Contemplated the reality of this planet as a swamp, where the wild thrived, and in the grim, yet beautiful, reaping reality of that no-man's-land, I realized that I also dwelled in paradise with you.

Thank you for giving me Motherhood. Thank you for my femininity. Daughter, you make me human. You complete me as a Sacred Feminine. Thank you.

The incessant urination.

Swollen feet.

Agonizing back pain.

Acid reflux.

Insomnia.

The discomfort only serves to remind me of barriers, dichotomies. The spaces between the visible and the invisible. Mechanical and organic time. Permanence and the temporary. I've learnt that pain and pleasure are yin-yang. Attachment, though, is pain. Again, pain is temporary.

Daughter, your health and happiness are important.

At thirty-six weeks, you are growing at a rate of one ounce a day. I feel you carving out space, pressing hard against my inside soft contours. The hard outside pressing in on both of us. I remain hard and soft. Balance. As much as we crowd each other, this oneness is divine, and I hope we can carry the respect of this oneness the rest of our lives.

I know, oh how I know, this connection between a mother and her child is severed outside in patriarchy. I want to respect your boundaries and give you space to grow, but please, please do not forget where your first home was.

You are my inside secret. I choose to not let the outside sever us. But, when you come to the outside, Daughter, it will be difficult, we will be challenged and sometimes we will be bent, but not broken. That outside world will push up against us.

I want you to be empowered to be able to discern the power constructs around you, and feel that you can exercise the freedom to choose what you want to believe, how you will show love, more importantly, how you will love yourself. I want your behaviour to be a firm freewill fabric. Know I am beside you, in you, around you, under you, and above you throughout the journey of the rest of your life. It is time that the outside does not sever the power of the inside Sacred Feminine. That ancient priestess love between Mothers, Sisters, Grandmothers, Aunts, and Daughters.

Our love is powerful. Our love extends beyond space, time, and the physical. There is more to life than what meets the eye. What cannot be observed can be felt.

Feelings and thoughts matter.

Feelings and thoughts are matter.

Right now, your body is making the final preparations to bring you from the inside to the outside. You've shed your downy hair covering that coated you, my feline, and you've lost your vernix caseosa, the wax that glazed your skin and protected you as you were lifted in my amniotic bath. The vernix caseosa is a creamy biofilm containing water corneocytes embedded in an oil matrix. This cocoon will help you transition, the protection will act as a barrier to water loss, temperature regulation, and immunity. The intrauterine to extrauterine transition, Daughter, has evolved to keep you safe. Birth is a masterpiece, and you are a Divine Creation. I honour you as a sacred entity enjoying a human experience, because, Girl, I am learning about the exquisite intricacies of childbirth with you. Our bodies are gifts. Temples.

Know that you were created to swallow and come kicking out of the most grueling birth canal. A simple, yet complex flow of energy and substance. If your flow stops, you die. I want you to stay living, I want you to perceive your divinity and keep your energetic flow clear and open. Awaken. Be conduit for spirit and love yourself in the glory of that spiritual reality. You see, you swallow these substances and secretions in the womb, which will create a dark mixture inside of you, meconium, and this process is your first bowel movement.

The metaphor is so blatant, my Love, maintaining that organic flow, working through and processing, we let go just as much as we absorb. Water-drinking, sun-leafed trees. I remember how it was—the hardship—for my mother after her divorce. I witnessed her survive on her own, and from this struggle I also became strong. We sang out loud together while driving the backroads. Reclaim.

Turn. Float. Glow.

The shit, Child, yes the shit is integral and we process it. If you deny it, let it build up, back up, fester, we die.

Perspective saves us, Tesla.

Skin. Blood. Teeth. Nails. Hair. Air. Electricity.

I lived in a motel with my mother in the very same restaurant where she bartended. She went early and worked late. The poverty, the homelessness, well, my Love, I garnish some of the best memories from this time amongst the platter of the rest of my life. Poverty was temporary. Poverty meant liberty in other facets of our empowerment roads. Eyes in storms. Vortex. Tesla.

I was close to my mother, felt safe being in the same building, finishing my homework on restaurant tables, I was unashamed that my school bus picked me up outside. There were trails and paths behind the restaurant veining Moira Lake, and I took my bike and explored, Daughter, I found the most beautiful pieces of forest this way, right on the very lake I was raised on. So, essentially, I had never left home.

Home. My mother's side of the family carried home with them no matter the spaces. My grandparents had moved from Toronto after selling a family construction company. My grandmother had grown up in Toronto and my grandfather had farming roots. They purchased the Marysville Tavern and had run three businesses at once from this property: a tavern, a hairdressing shop, and, over time, the post office. My grandparents were hardworking people raising four children from upstairs in the tavern. The hotel was built by Patrick Culhane in the 1880s. John Fahey took over the hotel in the early 1890s; it was renamed the Headquarters Hotel. My grandparents then took over the hotel.

I have good memories of the hotel. There is one of calming gentle rain speckling a thin glass window in my grandmother's room. I am waking up in the morning, my grandmother already up and getting the day going. I knew even at that young age that the gentle song of those pebble-drips against that ancient glass and my warm body nestled in her bed, was peace. There were the tracks to the south of the village where freight trains lumbered past casting out metallic ghost-songs in the middle of the night that I found oddly comforting. Stories of train riders who stowed away on cars piqued my imagination as a kid, my aunt used to throw down socks to those riders when they found their way to the hotel as word-of-mouth spread that my grandparents would feed them. Another memory, falling asleep at night listening to the laughter and drinking downstairs while I was safe and tucked into bed. My grandfather never let anything get carried away in his bar. He didn't even allow dancing. Respect was fostered, boundaries were set.

The building of Highway 2 from York, then Toronto, to Montreal, opened up regions throughout the province to settlement and growth. With the introduction and surge of Highway

401, the communal hubs along Highway 2 were gradually abandoned.

Marysville is deemed a ghost town now. Sometimes, when I needed my Grandparents, I would park my SUV on the other side of the tracks and gaze down the phantom road. It's so quiet now. Just the thrum of grasshoppers and the banging of tires over the underpass. I'd ask for strength for my day. I'd thank my ancestors for walking with me. Standing near those tracks and the graffiti of an indigenous woman elder as a mural on concrete, I'd continue stronger.

This bloodline has been tried to be taken out several times. Our existence, survival, is a pinprick light in so many plotlines. There was the Navy ship my grandfather was supposed to go out on, but didn't, and was bombed. There is something more, darker, coming up that you will learn of. There was also the tragic fate of the hotel. The building was gutted by fire in February of 2005 when new owners took it over. Two tenants perished in that fire. The building is now leveled. When I drive by, I eye the corner slab of concrete that was the front step. I played on that front step.

We can't really care about what others think of us when they don't know what's going on inside of us. In gritting my teeth to severe societal regurgitations, I was shown other free matrices. I liked the knowledge of the existence of multiple matrices and in that knowing, I was free.

My mother and I finally moved into an apartment complex. I remember the night she sat on the stairs, hands draped over her knees, the large plastic portable phone at her feet, tear-streaked cheeks, she had been "let go." The owners of the restaurant claimed that there was a lack of hours, but my mother knew it was more, that her divorce and the ripple of independence in a conservative rural society was teetering us on the edge of white trash. My father's clan, despite their economic umbrella, could not keep my mother safe. She had "left" my father, and never said to have liberated herself and her daughter from domestic violence. Politics perpetuates the hierarchy of domestic violence because of allegiance. The economy splays loyalties, and you save your own family first, hope that others can make it through on their own.

I witnessed my Mother survive economic vulnerability and social hardship, she needed to get a job farther away, she left me earlier and came home later. I was alone. I was content in this solitude.

So, I cued my walks to school, memorizing the details of the street, when the neighbours' kids left, I would too. I followed them to school. I developed anxiety over separation and time management, but, Child, I persevered because I knew my mother had taken me away from the fighting and the absence of that fighting was motivation to master independence. I liked practicing independence. That practicing was an integral layer of my empowerment road. I mastered time management and overcame separation anxiety.

I was aware that my mother suffered from trauma after the divorce. Anxiety and depression were terms I didn't know, attached to certain behaviours. That's okay. We survived. Eyes in storms. Vortex. Tesla.

Turn. Float. Glow.

Cereal dinners, she slept, and needed to juggle schedules as a single mother to include me in extra-curricular activities, and time with my own friends. My father and brother were gone and away. It was my mother and me, the love and presence from Nanny, my mother's mother, got us through. I respected these women staying open, processing the shit around them, and continuing on. Life is a series of bowel movements.

My mother did not have a university degree or specialization. I helped her study for her school bus driver exam. It was peaceful serenity when she passed that exam and we knew she no longer had a job—she had a humble and respectable career. She could be home at a decent time at night. The fabric of normalcy settled into our lives.

Stability.

Social wellness. Buds and falling leaves.

Emotional wellness. Photosynthesis.

Spiritual wellness. Winds and upturned faces.

Environmental wellness. Roots that dig down. Nitrogen cycle.

Occupational wellness. We flowered, we grew fruit.

Intellectual wellness. The sapling that grows at the base of our trunk. Pineal gland mushroom cloud.

Physical wellness. Water we absorb. Chlorophyll.

Daughter, what we sought for as women in this chaotic world was wellness.

I make my life ready for your birth and entrance into this world. I balance the scales and try to embody a tree of wellbeing, for you, for us.

THE PAST

Sophie hunches, wide-eyed in the sacred hours, like a rabid dog, immersed mentally in the purple twilight fog outside of her head and body, she is the same as the trees hanging over the roof of the house. Her body folded, working underneath the wooden benches, the kitchen nook, a reprieve from the rocking hull of house carrying her away, again, on violent currents. A subtle swaying, she presses palms to cold tile and almost cranks her head back in the grotto of a howl.

He's really sent her reeling this time.

In this moment, the surface of the earth is neither completely lit nor completely dark and she feels relief here. She can be anything, or nothing, or both.

Sophie can exist. Sophie can pool into space without her container, the shaping has been wretched, and she yearns to be without form or mass.

The night has witnessed her eyes reddening, rolling back, drying into two vexed globes, requisite sleep feigned and beaten against the throbbing chambers of her lonely heart. She knows now she is a performer to the cool tones of the ambient light, *l'heure bleue*, her hour, she cracks her back to an empty theatre and believes that anything can exist here.

She has spent the last several hours gathering. An array of

pale colored paper clouds the table, layered with strips of newspaper and floral napkins, she took a pen between her fingers and did something she has never done—she dug the whispers out from underneath the shingles of her soul and hid them throughout the house.

Forgive me. A floral napkin in a sweater pocket.

Men and the bases of trees. A porcelain handled brush.

I did not deliver. Newspaper in a jewelry box.

My ruined womb. Tucked in with a birth certificate.

A puppet baby. Behind a picture in a frame.

Blue pencil crayon scratchings. A French coffee tin.

She bows her head. She leans back and slides out from underneath the table. Her slippers fold back and awkwardly drag along the tiled floor, her heels bitten from the cold. Her cream bathrobe hangs, unbelted, one shoulder exposed and goose pimpled.

It takes her several exacerbated attempts to pry the lid from the tin. Amelie says nothing, her fingers tangled in a nest of ink-stained utterances, a flash of blue pencil crayon scratchings, the soft yellow patches with that black star, before she snaps the tin shut. She returns the box to the back of her closet.

Sophie is distracted by the dressing table, her array of perfumes and lotions, the porcelain handled brush that unscrews at the base. She discovered this during the war after she had flung the brush and it shrieked against the wallpaper. She rotates the slim handle now, pries the patterned cap away and dips her index finger into its depths. She pulls her finger back and pinches two strands of hair. She cannot let them fall. She forgets if one strand is blonde, the other is darker and curled. In the bruised haze of the twilight hour they are both the same.

She cannot remember how she dragged herself to the books and runs her fingers along the spines regardless of clarity. She has one book open before she realizes that she has scribbled in the empty space on the underside of the front cover.

I knew of her. She pauses briefly, slaps the book closed and tucks it away. She blinks and retreats.

She might have laughed, but cannot remember.

He has seen her silhouette wander through the belly of the house for the last hour from the outside of the fish bowl. A slow meander, she moves without dipping her shoulders, her neck taut, her arms shot straight against her sides. Phillip can feel her tight niches, her lucid insides brimming. He spits.

He thought she'd be asleep, he could just slip into the house that way, nothing said but designed normalcy in the morning. Bile rises in his throat, and he leans heavily with his broad hands on his knees, his mouth gaping, a thick string of saliva webbed between him and the dirt. He vomits, wipes the back of his hand along the grease of his thin lips, and wavers. He places one boot in front of the other, begins the trek up the last steep incline of the property.

When he falls through the front door, his lumbering form crashes into the wooden island dividing the dining room and foyer. She jumps. The strip of napkin falls from her hands and glides under the large armoire in the dining room. The corners settle against grains of dirt and lint, peppering the surface with microscopic exclamation marks.

They are not dead. Her handwriting slanted and sure; she walks away.

"Where have you been?" She observed the iciness in her own voice. He looked down his nose at her with red feral eyes. She cowered slightly.

"Nowhere. Why are you awake … have … have you not slept yet?"

"No."

"Why?"

"Because you were gone. Like last night. And the night before. *J'en ai assez.* I've had enough. The town knows. They talk that you are out with other women. *Je suis pris au sérieux.* I'm laughed at."

She did not anticipate the shove; her feet gave out beneath her and she skidded backwards landing with a thud on her spine. Searing pain. Tears shot through, stung her eyes and she instinctively turned onto her side, shielding her face.

His shadow fell across the whites of her arms, and she felt the flight of her body from the floor into the air. Her body landed against the kitchen wall, her chin clamping, and jaw locking against the ground edges of her teeth. She lifted her face and met his eyes, blue and sinister now, and the redness blotting the skin around his nostrils.

She smiled.

He shrank from her.

She bit into her lips in a petrified grimace, her small square teeth glinting in the changing light. A Fleur-fanged-grimace.

He watched the shadows shift from her face, the soft blue glow lifting to pull a fiery orange veil across her cheeks and eyes. She felt the heat rushing along her body, penetrating her skin like a live wire of electricity, and she embraced the pulsations. Unground current. Conduit connection. She crooned her neck. Fixed two balled fists against the floor and pushed up. She rose before him, her face locked in an open-mouth snarl, teeth bared, she tipped her head back and laughed. She did not stop.

Her mirth threw him completely off, and a torrent of emotions unhinged his composure. Unbridled and raging, he flared his nostrils and lunged. His fist balled the terry cloth above her right shoulder and from this grip he forced her back onto the floor. She sank against the wall first, laughing and hiccupping. Her face flushed pink, and she let the tears run down her cheeks.

She itched.

"Shut up! I hate you!" He hollered, bent down over her, and clamped his hand across her lips and nostrils. He squeezed the flesh of her face until it burned and drained white, and she squirmed scratching and clawing at his thick iron-gripped fingers. She continued to laugh, wet gestations bubbled against his palm, and he imploded.

He fell away from her, and she dropped against the floor—a limp mannequin. She let her mouth shut into itself, tight and clammy, and swallowed the laugh to let beat against her ribs like a moth fluttering into a light bulb.

A suitcase opened on the bed and was rammed with clothing and documents. He swept the contents from the dresser top and stepped on her perfume bottles while retrieving stacks of his money from the safe he kept in the bedroom closet. The gold chain glinted around his neck in the rising morning light casting white speckled shadows against the walls.

He stepped over her body to reach outside, the front door was still open, banging in the wind. The lake smell, a pungent fish scent that saturated into everything—it never left, and she didn't acclimatize to it. A sharp loud burst of laughter slipped from her. He spat, shook his head, and retreated to the garage. She heard the engine of his Cadillac gun to life and knew she hovered on the brink of an ending. She glorified in the edge, the steep drop, and swallow of not knowing.

Aiden, who had been awakened by the commotion climbed out from his hiding place under the bed and watched his father's departure from the tiny manhole of his octagonal window. He cursed the retreating, the large hand gripping the suitcase. He swallowed and wondered why he hadn't woken earlier to be able to intervene. He heard the commotion, how her body connected with the wall as the bungalow shook. The sting of blame resonated in his mind, and he blamed her, the dislocation, her foreign awkwardness, the numbness of her tongue, and how detached she was from both of them. He assumed, conjectured that her otherness pushed the man away.

Her laughter was his hell. Aiden had drifted between waking and sleep throughout the night. He believed she was not aware of this little family, their constant spiraling words and mockery at her otherness. Like father, like son, he learned how to behave and treat women from his blueprint that he would later level and reprogram completely different for other women in his future. The men had tried everything to shake her, shock her from her otherness, but she bent and melded with their jesting, their instigations, and remained dislocated. He could not articulate that her indifference was a shield, a crafted fortress enabling her to endure, to wipe the sleep from her eyes, to eat, to breathe, and bathe herself.

Taillights flared red, and the exhaust billowed in the air. Aiden felt a tug inside him as the car reversed from the garage, nearing the house, then dipping down the driveway onto the highway. He stood until the highway was still again and he lay back onto the mattress.

Aiden was lulled into a fitful sleep from a crescendo of hysterics, her laughter and verbal self-talking gradually fluctuated painfully with bone-crushing moans and sobs. She did not stop until the wailing ripped the skin from her vocal chords, and her face stuck to the tile. He stayed in his room. She felt the cold from the crawl space seep into her burning cavity and for once that long night and early morning she felt relief from the pain take temporary residence in her body.

She rolled over and slept, smiling to the wall.

STORYTELLER

He was never fully gone because he always came back. That is the way with this family. We stayed close, yet we were separated.

It was normal, for me, as a young girl growing up to walk into my grandmother's house and find my grandfather and her sitting together.

He was a drop-in man, a door opener who would stick his head in, quickly relay information about the family, and be gone.

That was how he showed love. That was how he remained present.

Daughter, I've learned, and it was a hard lesson, it took many years of letting it sink in, people will show you their love their way.

Gratitude saves us.

Unconditional toleration is sometimes salvation. Honing and polishing an expansive perspective is redemption.

The idea of war is to protect something or someone we love. We need to be able to protect ourselves, when we lose that capacity of self-preservation, we turn into animals caged within reinstated borders.

He came back for conversation.

He came back for mothering.
He stayed because of guilt and shame, perhaps.
I know he stayed because of love.

THE PRESENT

"Alas! This frightful vice of drinking prevails throughout the colony to an alarming extent."

        —Susanna Moodie, Life in the Clearings versus the Bush

The book falls from her hands. It turns on its side, pulling the pages together like an accordion.

Dog-ears. Cracked spine. Highlighted lines. Margin narratives.

Her books are alive in her hands. Her reading, an intimate act, and she remembers each encounter with a book like the hands of a lover. Nelle gets up and paced around the room.

After several contemplative circles, she picks the book back up. She unclicks the lid of her highlighter, and lights up the line that planted her consciousness.

"If an appeal to the heart and conscience, and the fear of incurring the displeasure of an offended God, are not sufficient to deter a man from becoming an active instrument in the ruin of himself and family, no forcible restraint upon his animal desires will be likely to effect a real reformation."

The appeal works with us…I'm grateful. I like Moodie.

Nelle remembers stumbling across her memorial at Meyer's Pier in Belleville, the connection she felt that day knowing that her house was close by too.

Moodie survived the frontier of the Northern brush, in the wake of colonization, with a firm grip on the pen. Nelle respects her, despite Moodie's transparent dialogue of encountering the indigenous peoples. Her historical studies in University taught her to uphold a non-judgemental eye on past societies, the objective unbiased historian is to survey atrocity and move forwards. Nelle learned to write through tragedy. She does not always look back without judgment.

She speaks with Moodie through the currents of her own writing, and the value of an ongoing dialogue helps make the complexities of conquering the hard forest face of a Canadian jungle artistic, beautiful. Ethereal.

We are ethereal.

Nelle finishes the chapter with resolve. The edges of clarity assuaging her self-conception of the area's societal climate and the history of that fabric. She embraces this repositioning, the walls of perception shifting with a personally historical emplotment that she would settle into her life.

"We are not alone in this cohort of vulgarity!

Addictions and mental illnesses.

The self-medicators, the snorters and drinkers.

This colony was bred with weakness. We drank the holes up.

Not too far from the tree."

War did not solely breed topography of addiction taken away with the trauma of violence. Addiction modelled for the baby boomers to repeat and pass on to the next generations as learned behaviour. No! Cycling and fuelling a throwaway binge culture. No! Processes. Layers. To each their own, but in that contemplation, we let war disrupt family.

Her thoughts connect and fragment simultaneously, she appreciates when she encounters something, anything that will challenge her cemented ideals and her assumptions of existence.

I like to be wrong.
She likes to see her family work through tragedy, reclaim their minds, bodies and souls. Abate addictions. Substitute substance. Hammer away bad habits. Rise up. She watches them rise up and choose to walk the high road. They are walking single file, spaced out along the hanging live wire of the red and blue roads. The Way. Empowerment.

Moodie wants to put them in an asylum. Take the poison out and isolate it. We couldn't possibly take the poison out, cannot conceive of isolation. The luxury of distance dictates this. Intervention, AA, counselling. Nothing will work unless they want to remove the venom.

Empowerment.

They did this to us before, took him away to come back as one. He came back, yet we were scattered. She should know that we orient through patriarchy, when the central cog is removed, well, that leaves the family rootless.

So we learned. Picked ourselves out of the filth, washed our tears away, smoothed our hair and set the water to boil.

If you do not want to live with us, I mean really live with us; we have to learn to live without you. Even if you are beside me, clinking ice cubes against that glass.

She should have written it down, scratched through the lined pages with dexterity. Then she would have it for later—her men actually quit smoking and drinking.

We built houses inside of ourselves. We became our own homes.

THE PRESENT

"We began sending messages for some men that were a part of the underground." She looks up and stares straight into Nelle, tilts her head to the left and asks, "are you aware of the underground." Nelle coughs, and squints.

"Yes."

"Good." She looks down at her clasped hands on the table. Nelle thinks of pink silk and red lipstick.

"It was simple at first, sending names along with addresses, delivering conversations. I really felt good about what I was doing so I asked to do more. That's when it got tricky. I'd take clothes from my work and sew forged documentation into the fabric. I hid the papers pretty good, but I was always worried that I'd get sloppy." She looks up again and her eyes are wet.

"You become really good at what you do when you are afraid that you are going to die." Nelle bites her lips and presses her lids together hard, tears press into the corners of her eyes, and she is not ashamed to let them seep out.

"I honed my skills with sewing, but also that capacity to be a messenger." Nelle is floored and confused.

"I would meet Jews and direct them to places in which they would be hid. I'd arrange to send food to them and clothes. Sometimes, when I was brave, I'd venture back to their original homes and bring them some personal belongings. One assignment I was given was to bring a man by the name of Eli to his place of hiding. I met him at the *Au Bon Vieux Temps,* a really nice café I knew well. I tell you Nelle, he was handsome. I hadn't met someone like him before. I mean, I really liked him right off the bat! Maybe it was fate, I don't know, but when I took him to his place of hiding the street had been crawling with Nazis. They were searching high and low for Jews, and I almost dropped dead from fright right there. I had no choice, he couldn't stay there. But then, you know, Nelle, I took matters into my own hands."

RIPPLE

Was he your fiercest love?
The one you turn your back to, curved sharply,
dying around clicking black boots
polished raw amongst
the barbed-wire hellholes of that landscape.
Boot-kicked rotting cattle cars.

Or was he?
The one that was scavenging that place,
setting fires to the preservations.
You surrendered your shadow
and you collided into this land.

Canada.
Shielded from the old,
the battle raged inwards
mining the shingles of your soul.

I know.
I know.

THE PRESENT

She did not dream that night and wakes rested. Nelle wipes the sleep from her eyes and wonders if this will be the last full night of sleep before the baby comes.

Her bathrobe is a warm nook in the chill of the house. She did not get up in the early morning hours to add more wood to the fire. Her breath hangs around her jaw as she retrieves the steel prod and separates the charcoaled skeletal logs, ashes snap and hiss, and she rolls out several thick embers that fume to life. Nelle adds several kindling sticks and some twisted newspaper cones.

Her hands massage her lower back as she kneels slightly to blow on the tipi. The newspapers catch fire. She feels relief in her neck and shoulders when the kindling ignites and begins to snap. Her tongue slides across the wooly face of her teeth and she swallows. She places two thick logs in, collapsing the tipi, and blows again bringing the lick of flame up around the logs. The woodpile is high, lined against the walls, and she knows the shed outside is full with perfect rows of crossed ends, she is thankful he did this before he left.

He's still here, cutting the grass. He's still here, plowing the driveway.

She makes her way out of the basement in a pregnant

hobble. There is a thick blanket of snow encasing her car, she wraps her bathrobe tighter around her and turns away from the front door window. Her footprints from the day before are gone.

She enters the kitchen and pulls out the wet filter and cold grinds from yesterday's coffee.

It's okay.

She knows several other women who drank coffee throughout their pregnancy. She had asked them.

It's okay.

Nelle shovels several spoons into a newly pressed filter and inhales the earthy aroma. The coffee drips. The scrape of knife against the bread is soothing. Nelle spreads almond butter and slices a banana on top. The coffee cup from the night before is rinsed, cream poured one quarter up inside. She wraps her fingers around the mug, the coffee steams underneath her chin. The furnace kicks on, and she stands with her wool sock feet on the floor vent. She welcomes these mornings, these blizzard days, when she can write inside. Hibernation.

A blast of wind funnels up from the highway adding spiraling white clouds to the snowdrifts that have been collecting along the laneway and up against the north side of the house all night. Glass rattles quietly in the antique window frames, and she pushes down anxiety that she should have installed new windows back in the summer.

He is still there, going to fix them.

The snow is powder now, and she knows that as the temperatures continue to drop the mounds will compress, pack, and settle into themselves. Nelle is comforted by these sounds. Imprinted with the nature of that snow, how it behaves, and she hums slowly to the little life turning around inside of her.

Good morning, Baby.

The glass in the front bay window is laced with frost, and the heat from her breath blots a wet ring for her to look through.

A ghost niche from a past life kicks her back into memory and Nelle falls in.

Her ears prick. She hears him approach and encircles her

with his arms. He sighs, tucks his face in the hollow of her neck and right shoulder. They hover in silence, the rhythm of their breath pulls them away and into each other, their bodies arch and form as one. His hands hold her womb. Phantom. Nelle shakes her head. He is gone. It wasn't really like that in the end, and she's conjured up a phantom that would dare hold her womb. Poetry in motion.

we came back
back came we
Together

The poetry lifts up, and she aches at the beautiful haunting memorization. Her stacks of notebooks have consumed her evenings and early mornings lately, the time before she sits and writes through her current projects. Nostalgia. Nelle lets herself fall quietly back in to help move her baby through.

you opened the blankets and i slipped in,
a fish slicing white-capped frothing
waves. i fell in flight into your torso,
wrapped my every bits
round, round that soft skin i knew.

Round and round it went for a decade. A theatricality of emotions. Nelle couldn't identify the cyclical behaviour and volatile patterns that they translated as love inside of it. The comings and goings, arguments, and lovemaking. Betrayal and forgiveness. They had grasped and bound a chain of pain around each other, separation anxiety, they stayed close for fear of what would happen if they went out into the world on their own. Co-dependence. A generational grind. They crested and flung their young bodies over the edge of a learning curve.

i read between your lines, false pretense,
everyday. your absence, presence.

your lips, those whispers, the warmth
that had not engulfed this soul in months,
a yearning like no other rocked my bones,

Nelle and Emery carried the imprint of violent childhoods. Repetition. They almost had missed reliving it all over again. But, fingerprints and denial, it caught up, it caught up to them and they tripped.

i rattled and chattered with your jaw-snapping
motion, we plummeted over that
cliff's jagged edge.

i needed you back
with your spine curved
round my
Womb-womanly-circles

Mounted, sweat-glazed and finger-pressed. Nelle remembers how the writing etched out a time when she fell from reality— jaded. He was radiant, muscled, and contoured with a raw edge. He was hard to pull away from. A fraction of a second, tongue bound, she was caught up on the physicality, the comfort of him near, how he kept her away from a tortured family, for years, and she thought this theatrical physicality was forever.

I am a fish,
born into the wet of
these celestial turnings.
I swim in the waters of thought,
susceptible to thin sentiments,
the turn of cheek, furrow of brow.
Present but absent in earthen worlds,
he was a water shaper, plumber,

channeling currents,
constructing artificial piping
to keep the water coursing.
He brought water and took it away,
a liquid magician, he kept me living.

Nelle has found herself upstairs in her studio folding back notebook spines and working this painful narrative out of her, grinding, like her body arching and flowing over a yoga mat.

I keep me alive.

Her eyes flit back and forth across her cursive, the years of printing and handwriting, trekking worn paths in the forest of an otherworld life.

A wonderland.

A dream world.

She reads, lifts cold coffee up to her lips and sips. Her stomach shifts, erupts in a low hunger pain, the baby turns and she sips again.

She's discouraged, anchors her thoughts to shifting memories of an otherworld in which she's questioning having ever existed. She finds herself in an entirely other matrix of being now.

Her aching back. The baby growing restless and hungry inside her.

My Baby.

Nelle looks up and across the room into a mirror with a framed tile decor she had made with Emery in that past life. Her teeth come together in a halting grind, and she determines to put down the notebooks and return to the kitchen for some fruit and yoghurt.

She frowns at herself in the mirror. Sees her pregnant form, steps closer, holds a hand up, the other hand still clutching the turned back notebook, presses the hand against the mirror. She walks through.

There is water. She hears gentle lapping against stone, smells fish scale—a seagull shrieks, lands, the sound echoes across the surface of water.

She knows here, face upturned to a sky engulfed with swirling clouds, a sunset spiraling with the convex of horizon and hill ridge that she exists within multiple planes, dimensions. Double lives, synergy spirals, one life in real time, another life crouching on haunches on an otherworld island. She's counting the fingers and toes of her newborn.

Chaos and the womb of creation. Pentagram. The tree of life.

Nelle turns and searches the forest ridge. She knows where she is, and the Moira Lake House is perched now atop the hill. Inverted, she sees the tree that she had rested her back against as a little girl, had endeavored to build a treehouse in, she sees it now, in this world, and it is inverted.

The roots stretch and scrape the sky, carve out space, there are no leaves. She knows that the leaves are rolled taut in the hill like earthworms. This tree, she feels it out here, on the other side of that mirror, this tree was planted as a light seed, and the women before her had watered it with their tears. Watered it with their sweat. Watered it with their moontime blood.

There is song, it drifts and settles like fog down the hill collecting at the shoreline. That voice, she knows, is the voice of a lone spiritual warrior, the one in exile. Nelle cups the name lovingly in her mouth, she knows the story, Enheduanna's story. The song arcs through forest cresting the hill, touching down on the surface of water like dead brown maple leaves.

Ripples.

A woman holds the railing of the ship, *Mauretania*.

Restoration. Regeneration. Renewal.

Nelle pivots on her heels and turns to see the outline of an indigenous woman mounted, proud and stoic at the edge of water and earth. She stands atop a large rock and dips her chin, nods slightly at Nelle, and lifts up a deer hide bow. Her right hand reaches over her shoulder and from her back pulls down an arrow she crafted herself. She carved the spearhead point and arrow's body. A skilled fletcher. Gifted with feathers offered to her from spirit during her hunting treks on that hill.

Finding feathers. Synergy. Gaining knowledge.

She found each one along the path her feet pushed down from the lake to the inverted tree. She is the Lady of the Lake, a High Priestess, Nelle knows as the woman flexes the bow and releases the arrow in a perfect arc out into the water.

She calls in her energies, her spirit guides.

Sappho.

Inanna.

Enheduanna.

Lotus and lily.

Christ Sophia.

White Buffalo Calf Medicine Woman.

Isis.

Gaia.

Nelle is enthralled and enraptured. She feels the release with the flight of the arrow. She's faced a rage that had pummeled and forced her down inside the darkest recesses of her entity. She hears the winter winds of her reality tunnel through her ears and she grits, determines to stay with the woman mounted on stone.

Nelle cannot fully know in that sliver of time, tight roping between folded and overlapping worlds, that she's winning a psychic war that has haunted women for entire civilizations. She's breaking free from a false matrix. Standing her ground, carving out space against demonic forces, mind control, and attack. She's walking a road together with the women of that lake, the one on the stone, with her family, and the others that came before them, the ones buried under trees raped from colonialism, the ones that are yet to come. She walks back through the mirror, hands calmly palming circles against the life inside. The baby settles.

Nelle feels at peace inside that house entombed in snow, alone. She knows at that very moment that she is never alone, nor lonely, in that solitude.

She is safe.
She is loved.
She is held.
She is divine.
Goddess.

STORYTELLER

He is Sisyphus, the Greek king, punished and compelled to spend eternity pushing a rock uphill. Unavailing, the boulder hurdled backwards to the earth with each pained journey. Magnetism. Perpetual tortuous livelihood, a self-inflicted martyrdom, because, unlike legend, Sisyphus netted this pain, he harnessed this pain as fuel and identification. Definition. Yoked to the weight of that stone, the King neglected to see that his family would be snared as well in such a cycle. Locked together yet separate, their souls round and full, bursting with a want to put their love somewhere—deserving of the freshest air and brightest sun. They deserved laughter. They deserved the innocence of a smile.

Sisyphus lived for navigation and the forging of land. He pursued colonial encounters that enslaved species, entire populations. He carved out space from their struggles, the death of identities. Ironically, he perceived to place himself separate from the battlefield, the no-man's-land. Sisyphus promoted commerce, relished in the weight of coinage in his pockets, full and clinking, he slept soundly with this weight pulling him down and lifting him up.

THE PRESENT

"She spoke of herself gloomily in the third person, saying, 'Be careful, don't hurt Mother, don't sit on Mother's legs.' Every time she said Mother I felt chilled, and a kind of wretchedness and shame spread through me as it did at the name of Jesus. This Mother that my own real, warm-necked, irascible and comforting human mother set up between us was an everlasting wounded phantom, sorrowing like Him over all the wickedness."

–Alice Munro, "Images," in Dance of the Happy Shades

The stack of papers flood across the floor, tidal wave wallpaper.

Damn!

She squats down and begins retrieving each sheet of paper glowing white in the light. The pile of file folders on the corner of her desk were organized, but with the knock-over from her elbow, one particular file had exploded, and she frowns at synergy. Her slit cat-eyes roll over the lines of text on each sheet as she files them between her hands. Her body boils up, heated, and in pain.

I grew up thinking this communication was normal.

She had kept the emails, printed them out onto lined paper and filed them away. Rifling through the pages now between hot palms, the house shifting and popping in the cold around her, Nelle resents the pain and resents the anger she feels from these emails.

I forgot about these.

If only she could open herself completely to her grandmother, that it would be safe to open. That woman, she endured hell and back, survived purgatory. Their exchanges flopped between awkward disconnect and warm familiarity.

Her mood? Did our conversations depend on how she felt? The onset of dementia?

Family and strangers. Simple and complex.

I wish these exchanges had not happened.

She wets her fingers and picks carefully through the flurry of emails, tumultuous waves on rocky shores, there's a single white canoe drifting atop those whitecaps, and Nelle winces under the pressure crowning her head. Her body folds as she sinks into her armchair in the corner of the studio, and she begins reading each page carefully.

The emails stem from remorse, calculated deceit issued to protect, to preserve. But they cut into her deep, razor tongues and barbed-wire fences; her family was expert in setting traps that served to chain them to their own pain. Calculated movements dictated by fear, by shame. Calculated movements that gnashed deep rifts between bodies, between lives—their lives.

Nelle looks up and out the window. Her unhinge is quiet and private.

There is a tree, it suspends her.

A portrait of a hilltop moor, Eve's life tree, lost innocence, an indigenous turning, and a lightning bolt that shot right through and snapped that life tree open.

From the earth, back to the earth.

Without ending, without beginning,

Sacred spirals and hoops.

She continues to study the tree growing up from the

periphery of the backyard and forest edge. Charcoal seared fibers, others tried to carve history into it—her story—she knew and she forgot, healing would not happen until she extended, spoke story beyond the lightning storm, gave the next generations of backs leaning against the tree a language of planting roots, of grounding, clasped hands against wombs.

War, a searing lightning wound that lifted nostrils and forced them outside to look for the one that was hit, eyes glazed, roving, grass blades, and tumultuous skies. They find the hit ones struck split straight down the center. Learning curves, lengthening, shortening or replacing names, like the snake shedding her skin, memory can be as simple as a leaf falling, or the gnash that an entire entity grows around.

The same sane woman.

Same sane women.

Sane women.

Women.

A tree grows through and around barbed wire fences.

She lifts off from the tree, remembers the first time her little brother and father met, shivers, wraps her arms around herself and lets the tears fall. Encounters and exchanges. She wanted to advocate for transparency. The emails knocked her out and down.

Her grandmother wrote her down off the ledge.

December 9: *"...it is a serious matter belonging only to the people involved directly, and it happened many years ago, when they came up with a solution. Leave your writer skills and your imagination aside..."*

Nelle cradles her child in her womb and holds space. She knows that her elders were behaving within the constructs of a previous generation, another social space, and that it was a part of their capacity to hide truth and perpetuate perfection. However, they couldn't face that perfection was a construct, and the construct hurt the next seven generations.

Nelle sees a chain passed on to her, for her to hold in her hands like a peace pipe. No, she will not carry out this ceremony. Nelle sees herself dropping the chain. Nelle sees herself walking away from this chain.

I want us to love each other.

Healing is a process. Healing is not an artificial shift; humans are not cogs in machines. Growing up and orienting to a slow natural process, Nelle grew stronger having been snaked with a razor tongue.

A tree grows through and around barbed wire fences.

December 11: *"Although you have studied a lot you may have to live A LOT longer before you understand fully the mechanics of a disjointed family. You may not believe me but I always worked hard at keeping the family together...."*

Nelle puts the papers down, lifts up from the chair, and circles the perimeter of the room—her hand touches texture and edges. For some time, Nelle could not understand how established distances fit perfectly in their actions and composure.

We deliver stories to ourselves that we eventually think is the truth, to make us feel better.

Order within chaos.

A pregnant Nelle, a woman now flooding with new emotions and consciousness, a woman carrying another life, returns to her chair and continues to sift through the emails with gritted teeth. A Fleur-fanged-grimace.

December 15: *"While making fancy sandwiches for the Bazaar at the church this morning, something suddenly struck me. What are you doing here? And it suddenly dawned on me, what is an old Belgian woman, who had all of the kindness and love of Belgian parents and relatives, doing here? I was young, 24 like you, left all of my young friends, brother, nephew for a man who actually didn't want me (he said so a few months later.) But at that time, I possibly could not return, mostly a question of travelling, which was by ship, and also a question of pride. And every time I go to a function at that church, I feel as if I were coming from outer space. I still don't feel like I belong there, but such is my fate."*

Nelle understands now, only now, and only because of the brilliance of retrospective lenses that this intertwined loving and existing could not be fathomable within their lives in the moment. Poetry in motion. Each one of them lived to survive and to endure their own pain. Her grandmother was a stranger in this land, separated both intellectually and physically from the rural landscape. She was induced, into the life of the outsider, an alien.

Nelle sighs, lifts off again from her armchair, her back to the window, her baby curling and furling, she arrives at a decision then, feels the weight of it like the handle of a gun pressed against her ribs. She idles over to the canvas and picks up a pair of scissors from the desk.

The soft calming sound of shearing paper is melody ribboning around her. Nelle tongues her lips. Scraps of white flake around her. Snow globe. She bites down on her tongue and pops off the lid of a glue stick. The paper thickens and waves under her fingers as she spreads the glue pressing the margins flat. Nelle pinches the edges, flips the emails over, inhales and exhales deeply, then, she carefully and deliberately presses the papers underneath the roots of the tree.

STORYTELLER

Seeing you on the monitor for an ultrasound was like encountering a map, depths of lakes and bodies of water. I felt a little kick against the ultrasound roller, intrusion. A tiny ricochet, a bounce, a connecting.

Your little legs were wrapped up, bent, then you stretched out, there was a little bum, a frog kicking underwater. Your spine, an illuminated fossil. I saw four chambers that are your heart.

I took the printed pictures from the ultrasound home and sat them on top of my bookshelf in my closet. These pictures began attracting other objects, a coconut half and sage clippings for smudging. Feathers that had come to me over time. Two keys. The pink infant outfit I had worn home from the hospital when I was born. Two positive pregnancy tests.

Altar.

I was late for that ultrasound. My heart rate was up and I was rushing. I worried with you that you might take on my emotions while we share this body. You were moving too much at the beginning of the ultrasound to take pictures. But, as I calmed, you settled.

I don't connect to you with words or text. A photographic language, I imagine scenes in my mind and convey to you managing energy in moments, managing other people and presences coming into your space, to maintain vibration. And we calm and settle together.

Then, there are times I don't convey emotions or initiate internal dialogue at all. I have the whole rest of our lives to talk with you. Sometimes I just stay quiet. I rub you. I cup your bum and massage the side of your hip, humming and singing softly. Those little hard edges that push out against my skin. I don't smooth them over.

After dinner one evening, I stood from the table and suddenly felt heavier, you were taking up space side to side, weighing down differently, cradled against my hips and you were pulling down. Positional. You had moved from the right side to the left. With this move, I couldn't feel you as readily. I didn't feel you move for twenty-four hours. I fell into a rabbit hole of worry. An emotional process of the fear of losing you, that you had passed, and now lay heavy, asking why you were weighed down—why you were sinking away from me. After a full day of drinking cold water and not feeling you, going to the gym and using the elliptical and not feeling you, I reached out to the midwives. I waited for my appointment in the car, gently prodding and massaging my belly to feel you. To feel you move. To see where you were.

The relief of hearing your heartbeat during that emergency appointment lifted me. While the midwife listened, you had made eight movements in five minutes.

I could not feel you because you had shifted to the back, your hands and feet were not pressing against my belly, but were now dug in against my hips and spine. You had moved in deeper. Your umbilical cord was at the back of this pregnancy, growing from the rear of the placenta and not the front.

At the next appointment the midwife asked me if you were giving me any more grief.

"I just needed to feel her moving and know her heart was beating."

The midwife measures me, hands, the longitude and latitude

across me, length and width. You were traverse, cradled in my hips widthwise, not up and down.

"That's when I felt her move into that place the first time, she got heavy, and I couldn't feel movement below the surface but deeper."

"She wanted a check in, for us to know she is there."

The midwife hears the heartbeat, smiles at me, "she's happy."

The veins in my breasts are becoming a darkening indigo. Tree roots. November branches. My breasts are getting ready to let milk down. Oil now, over time changes to cream white. I massage coconut butter beside my breasts and under my belly for stretch marks. There is heartburn and frequent urination. I have not been able to lay on my back for some time. If I do, I feel vibrations and waves, movement from you that scratches against my spine. Subtle thrashing sensation below my navel. My hands and ankles swell. My ring is getting tight. My right hip aches, my sciatic nerve jolts in searing pain sometimes when standing or moving, I work through the pain in yoga flows. There is relief in cat and cow stretches. Tree pose.

I hone a sense of home in these pains because that means you are here, you are real, you are taking up space. Little sudden movements now. Frequent. I smile. There is a quiet thick hit against cartilage and bone. Sometimes you stretch and that extends my vertebrae. It feels good. We stretch together. Thank you.

I fainted once at work. I would get hot and feel dehydrated. My temperature would rise. Prickle. Black out. A custodian found me in the hallway and tried to get me to rest. I pushed up and out of fainting and went outside. The ice winter air hit my face and pooled down my body. I did one lap of the building and returned to my space.

I just have to keep drinking water.

There are moments I imagine I would share with your father. He would hum against my womb, sing to you, I would feel you settle then. We would lie together, and he would see you move for the first time. Stomach spam. A lifting up.

If we made love under a full moon, a super moon, and I got up on top of him, I would say, "I'm a full moon." His hands running over my body, belly, and breasts. Intimate and sensual. He would hold you from the outside. Your little body fitting into his one hand and along his wrist and arm. Your father stretches my body as I turn around and lay down on him, back to heart. Our bodies fit. He pulls out my hips, tucks his feet around and pulls below my shoulder blades up, stretches my hips, he opens me. He would find your heartbeat, a hand there, a hand on my heart, "there are two hearts here."

One night under a full moon, my body is pulled, neural, heart and breasts. Pain. It comes and goes in waves. I fell into yoga flow again. Cat and cow. Extended arms. Spinal twists. Super moon. Eventually, I put a heating blanket on my breasts and fell asleep.

I dreamt that I was able to hold your hands, fingers, and toes through my skin. Your father and I were holding you from each end. Hands to feet. Head to bum. Your hand furled gently against my womb. Then, your hand was up against mine. Palm to palm.

I got up fast one night to use the bathroom. The sudden rush must have startled you. You must have taken in fluid. I am sorry. You began to hiccup. Your little body convulsed every 3 seconds. I held you through my womb. The hiccups stopped after three to five minutes. Pain. I felt the pain of you being uncomfortable. Guilt. I know I needed to remember to move slower. Be gentle.

Then I had my first chest and head cold with you. I worried for you. Fear for the baby. I would catch myself turning on my stomach and back in sleep. Running my hands along my belly to feel you—your positioning—and wanting you to kick and move. You moved less when I was sick. Anticipating. Tucked up higher behind my belly button. Head down.

A lesson learned, I can go through weakness, and you are strong.

Untouchable.

And now, there is less room for you. You are almost ready to come out.

I acknowledge this, I don't want your life confined to my body.

I want you to outgrow me, physically, emotionally, and spiritually.

Do not ever let the perimeters of me define the space that you will carve out for yourself in this life.

STORYTELLER

"The Canadian storyteller's sense of entrapment is likely to be balanced by an equally strong sense of preservation: not self-preservation, but group preservation, Survival again. Families in Canadian fiction huddle together like sheep in a storm or chickens in a coop: miserable and crowded, but unwilling to leave because the alternative is seen as cold empty space."

–Margaret Atwood, Survival

This family, we are not huddling sheep.

Most times, we were the storm we created ourselves. Chaos.

We were not chickens in a coop.

We were not constantly miserable.

We learned how to walk in balance despite our idiosyncrasies.

We were not crowded.

We left.

We went out and circled the world and came home.

Some stayed, built nests, thrived. This family survives.

Yes, the weather is cold and the rural landscape is vast, but, my Daughter, life in the North Country, life on the cusp of the Canadian Shield is not empty. Life is full, overflowing.

We are brimming with life.

Our wretchedness is unearthly, and we are not alone in this wretchedness. War disrupts family. Domestic violence and intergenerational trauma are symptoms of war. Our perseverance in achieving self-preservation was an integral layer of our empowerment, on evolving and changing behavior after mistakes. Inside the pulp of that vulnerable acknowledgment of our wretchedness, flaws, Daughter, we are ethereal.

This life of mine sought spaces, comforting cavernous places to hide in and retreat to. The musk of an armpit, the concave cradle of his palm. A warm maternal niche to curve into. My story is no more linear than a window frame.

Each time I return home, I am different. Reality is fluid, and I know this simply by aligning this spine of mine along the earth, eyes roving over paper-craned leaves suspended from Sadako's ceiling. The air curls and furls their underbellies, lush and dark and living. There is so much we do not see with our eyes or smell with our noses. Do not assume the finite nature of flesh because matter is waves evolving and chemical reactions cooking. I had to learn first of the flows before I went with them.

Memory will plunder forward elephant-like.

Do not consume yourself with shadows from inside Plato's cave. Please do not let yourself be consumed by thoughts that this life is pointless and that you are not worthy. Negative thought flows sink you—they are anchors. People can be anchors. Circumstances and the consequences of decisions can be anchors, too. Drop painful chains. We are strong women. We are trees. Remember.

There is danger in sticking too close together, in huddling and fearing leaving. Be wary of huddling. Groupthink is soul-draining, magnetic like the moth to bulb. Mobs. Masses. Trees stand alone and together. They cannot grow in the shade of another.

Tree canopies do not touch.

Yet, do not overlook the immortality of the forest. Know, a tree prepares for death even though some trees survive centuries. See there, at the base of the tree, another vein of life is growing up, sapling. Our next generation, plantlets—they show us life is a sacred circle. Sacred spirals and hoops.

We do know where the dead go.

Child, they stay right here.

The language that detains the Canadian family to pens and fenced-in fields is essentially colonial drudgery. Baby Girl, let me take you back further, let me keep the sacred fire in you burning. We reclaim. The Sacred Feminine is known again.

The People loved this land. The People survived integrally on this land. The People formed clans, tribes, and behaved, walking in balance. Spiritual democracy existed and was respected. Matrilineal societies. Women and men were equal. The hard climate, the changing seasons, nomadic existences, a vibrant and thriving life, The Way, and they were one with the land. The People were happy and their quality of life was not low.

This land is something sacred. Something holy. The European man invaded and pressed depression, strife, and struggle upon it. Or, he brought all of this strife with him, laid it down.

Held down and away from knowing ourselves, anchored for generations, we could not lift up, we could not perceive. There was no space to exist with a heightened awareness. Treading heavy with military boots across the curve of Earth, barbed-wire fences and trenches laid lattice underneath us, we were enslaved. We were fury and flurry, locked inside the story of ourselves, it took aerial views taken from emphatic planes to throw us into perspective. We could look from outside ourselves, then look back in with love.

Birds eye view.

Houses on hills.

Mountain ski runs.

Flounder and flight.

Helicopter ride. Blueprint of our existences circling our stories like a bird. Wingspan. The curl of lake, and a jungle tree canopy. Forest floor plans.

Our lives are organic interactive maps. A map in our heads.

Our landscape, raw beauty. Our countryside, paradise.

I am grateful for ancestors and elders who offered us, despite flaws and fears, layered perspectives, a sensitivity that led us home.

This family, we are not huddling sheep. The women of this family reclaimed focus from distraction, severed anchors, and dropped painful chains.

Her empowerment was the act of her building her spiritual and emotional house.

Her empowerment built a home.

STORYTELLER

He reached out what felt—and feels—like lifetimes later. A first cousin from the oldest son on her father's side. He wanted to find family. He wanted to learn more.

He said his father came from England. His mom was native and she was born on a reserve.

I put down the phone.

RIPPLE

Her full story is unknown,
Knocked out and replaced by hearsay,

She could have been ashamed of
Her genetics,

Her family could have been
Displaced by larger historical processes,

Residential schools,
The harsh lines of the Indian Act,

Ghettoed reservations,
Boundaries drawn on colonial maps,

Attempted cultural genocide,
Penetrating legislative assimilation,

She might have wanted to kill
The 'Indian child' inside of her,

She might have been pushed to
Remove the children that came from her.

THE PRESENT

Painted canvases circle the two women. Northern Ontario shorelines. Forest tree ridges. Riverbanks. The places they retreated to. A North Country landscape. The O'Hara's Mill. A bridge entering Queensborough.

Nelle blinks. Smiles to herself. Epiphany.

She painted the places home anchored to.

Sophie had painted back through an Atlantic migration; the places her home anchored to. Lifting off from a raw-faced North Country canvas, past an Amish family, an Inuit child face, around the chalk drawing of a Jazz singer, and oil and canvas of an elderly woman, Sophie painted back to the Paris Opera House and La Grande Place. A physical path. A map in her head. The space between moving bodies and temporary residence on certain geographies. A cow path, her way, her way of braiding perspective with a living language. Enduring and surviving war. Recovery. Healing. Empowerment.

A painting of Starry Night.

A Parisian Street.

Oil and water colour. Pastel and chalk. Earthy peppering pigments, red blazing fall tree lines, lush green leaf scenes and soft pastel florals painted on silk pillows. Indigo and dark night scenes. Purpled and golden hues; a leaving behind of royalty and cosmopolitan metropolis, to a northern jungle. An otherworld to Nelle's studio, but with her new eyes, expectant eyes, she appreciates her grandmother's narrative that wasn't spoken into existence, but told through brushstroke.

Truth can be found inside things. When truth is outside, alone, it needs protection and security because then it is vulnerable. Truth is sensitive. Right now, in this world. See, watch truth dig its way inside and holds firm there until it is safe.

Nelle pictures the rolled canvas in her car, the tree concealed and private. Roots split, reconnect and sink down deeper. Leaves upwind and curling, anticipating rain.

Women are trees.

Nelle perceives layers. Process. Overlap. Wave and shore. Biology and nature. Roots and branches. Sacred spirals and hoops.

She closes her eyes, covers them with her hands and leans forward, elbows to knees, arched into herself, templed. She imagines her hands bringing out the tree, rolling it open for her grandmother to see. She could run her fingers over paper and names. Trace them back, up and around. She's pushed back, has caught the burn of fragments of text from printed emails pasted to the bottom. She inhales over tracing the wax crayon grave rubbings. Nelle waits while her grandmother studies the tree. Her grandmother palms the edges and smooths them over. She wants to ask questions then.

Did you put the papers in the tree?

Who do you write to on those photos of you during the war?

Why could he not know he was adopted?

Then, truth would be pulled up through and splayed between them. Sage smoke and feather. Palms in prayer to the third eye. Both women could recognize how her story ached down through, cracks in the fissures of memory, identity, for the next seven generations to hold on to and flow through. Nelle would truly understand what Sophie had to do to survive war.

Nelle uncovers her face, sighs, and lifts her hands from her face, takes her elbows off her knees, and stands. She faces her grandmother, arched against the couch, her hands tucked against her sides, one hand cupped a Kleenex, shoulders sunk back down, heaving chest, she inhaled trying to catch up to her breath, to slow it down. Exhausted from having pulled down and retrieved the canvases in the house—ceremoniously lined them around the living room and kitchen.

Nelle wants to know the truthful niches, the spaces in between the times of painting these canvases, the life events that motivated her grandmother to paint specific scenes. Some canvases could be more casual, some canvases extensions of hidden truths. Names. Context. Memory. Feeling and story.

"Grandma? Did you name your paintings? Did you put your signature on each one?"

Sophie tilts her head, pauses, closes her eyes. Smiles.

"You know, well, I have on most, but some I didn't. You know, I don't really know why I didn't do all of them."

Nelle inhales, lifts her shoulders and chin up to speak, but Sophie continues.

"I never really thought to give them names, titles, you could say." She pauses. "Or sign them." She opens her eyes smiling at Nelle. Her eyes glow, and Nelle returns her smile, eases back into the chair.

"Can we do that?" Nelle asks.

"What's that?" Sophie croons her ear.

"Can we do that? Can we sign your paintings?" She's accustomed to repeating her sentences now despite the repetition being physically exhausting.

Nelle takes initiative and stands from the chair reaching for the closest canvas. The women work through the paintings with ignited energy, Sophie carefully placing her name in corners and the names of the paintings on the backs of the canvases. She does not convey to Nelle how honoured she feels signing her own art.

Sophie smiles throughout this art signing and points to a painting she had done of Van Gogh's moving sky. Sunlight settles and lifts off from paint edges, the swipe of pastel knife and impressive oil brush contours, an emotional and honest application.

"He was put away," her voice is soft, continues, "Suffered from a love affair. Brilliant artist, misunderstood during his lifetime. I think he really felt a lot and expressed something very powerful that we didn't appreciate until after he died." Sophie waves her hand from the swirling sky to another painting of sunflowers.

"He cut a part of his ear off for love. He sold one painting while he was alive." Sophie goes quiet for a moment, Nelle waits, registering from her grandma's face she has more to share.

"We do things that look so funny to others…" She pauses.

They couldn't really know that it is a way to manage pain. How we behave in love, not acting like ourselves, but sacrificing —we become martyrs. Laying our bodies down.

Sophie continues, "I know, in my own way…" Her voice falls off, and she sinks into thought, both women hover close, unspeaking. The silence is comfortable. Nelle hears roots planting. She feels warm energy taking space.

"I left Phillip once, when your father was a boy. Yes, I did. I took your father to my friend in Toronto. She was the one who arranged the adoption through the CAS. Your father hated it there and did not want to go to a different school or be in the city. He wanted to be in Madoc with your grandfather. After three months we went back." Sophie purses her lips and sucks them inside between her teeth. Her chest expands and she breathes air out of her nose.

"She did stay in touch and knew what was going on. I was happy to be able to go to her." She stops, closes her translucent paper eyelids close and open. "I went back to him because my son was unhappy." Sophie sinks down into her padded kitchen chair. Nelle joins her at the table.

"Take that one," Sophie waves her hand towards the swirling sky after a comfortable prolonged gap in conversation.

When Nelle tucks the canvas between her arm and ribs, she descends the front stairs.

"Goodbye, I love you," she has to yell and pulls open the front door. Sophie's soft singing halts her over the threshold.

"Mais la vie sépare les amants, assez lentement, sans bruit, et la mer efface sur le sable, l'empreinte des amants séparés." But life separates lovers, pretty slowly, noiselessly, and the sea erases on the sand, the separated lovers' footprints. Nelle's breath fogs, cold air flows in. She knows she's letting the heat out. The French verses bring Sophie back to another time, peeling onion layers.

What is she singing? It sounds sad.

"Les feuilles tombées peuvent être ramassées par la pelletée, pouvez ainsi souvenirs et regrets. Et le vent du nord les prend dans la nuit froide de l'oubli." Fallen leaves can be picked up by the shovelful, so can memories and regrets. And the north wind takes them into the cold night of oblivion."

Nelle hangs her head and steps out into the falling snow.

STORYTELLER

We were not with her because she did not cross over at the hospital. She left during a private time during the night.

Your great-grandmother crossed over in her own bed, alone in her own home. She was not plugged into machines and fixed stationary with tubes. Her last breaths were not mechanically etched out nor supported artificially. Her crossing over was organic.

This tremendous Woman crossed over inside the womb of a solitary prayer. She was enshrined with the sacred remnants of her life. She was a living family tree. Her final resting was how it was meant to be, how we were supposed to discover her essence without curtains or veils.

Lifted.

Her right hand rested on the centre of her chest, her left hand cupped her womb. Held gently between her petal-curled fingers and the landscape of her chest was a picture of her great-grandchildren and a black and white photograph of a baby with round-dark-smiling eyes in her embrace.

Other photographs were carefully arranged around her and layered like shingles across her blanketed body. Most of the pictures depicted the baby boy with olive skin and a thick head of hair. I could tell, Daughter, that these pictures were set down in the grotto of story and that your great-grandmother had woven a sacred thread amongst these relics.

Picking up that thread and following it, I could see how this baby grew up.

A photograph capturing him on a train ride in the Swiss Alps, his little face turned out the window in awe and inspiration.

A photograph where he is seated as a young man at a white linen fine-dining table on a luxury steamer, toasting.

Again, at seventeen, he is resting his elbows against a blue Chevy truck in the North Country outback with an open plaid shirt and casual rolled sleeves.

He is cutting a wedding cake.

He is holding his baby daughter in his lap, fingers wrapped around the heels of her tiny feet, little legs outstretched—both smiling.

He is smiling with his wife at his surprise fiftieth birthday party.

He is standing proudly on a ski hill—his element.

He is holding his grandson at his baptism.

His granddaughter sleeps on his chest.

He is standing with his arms around his aged mother at her ninety-first birthday party.

He is living.

He is alive.

He lived.

Her left hand held a balled yellowed paper against her womb. French letters. Blue pencil crayon scratchings. *Bonjour á St. Martin.*

A thick gold wedding band glinted around her ring finger. She had put the ring back on after years of it being hidden in the contours of her bedroom.

A faded French coffee tin rested against her left hip.

Ribboned paper fragments of her cursive writing were woven like a nest amongst the shingled photographs. We discovered more of these ribbons when we organized her house before it was to be sold. With artifacts tucked carefully in between pages of books and inside pockets of sweaters, she continued speaking to us and letting us know who she was. A spider spinning a web, we discovered her threads. What we perceived as normalcy was pulled out from under us like a rug and we needed to accept our backs against the earth and acknowledge that we finally could know her essence.

"Depiction of Temperament and Character." Life residue.

"A simple time stripped away the superficial wrappings and let their souls shine through." Life residue.

What knocked her into inspiration? Which texts she had concentrated over, probing the realities of the characters she encountered? How did she make connections between text and life? Who did she think would find her written fragments? Did she want them to be found?

Her handwriting was absolutely perfect, the dips and dotted I's were symmetrical, the letters looped elegantly. The steady crossing of T's revealed the perfection of her calligraphy contrasted with the raw human imperfection of the texts' arrivals and entrances into our knowing.

Cursive fragments rippled out into our present, sometimes gentle like laps against a canoe on a foggy lake, sometimes these ripples came at us suddenly like salt-water waves that pulled us under and over ourselves.

I marveled her train of thought, what she left behind.

"Characters like fire and water:

1] Leaping from peaks of delight to depths of despair.

2] Running steady and even surviving from goals.

3] Peculiar blend can produce the strongest possible alloy for marriage."

This literary echo, that emotional trek inwards, she was not writing fiction, these fragments were her life, something pulsating and palpable that could be polished smooth in warm palms. She had melded brilliance with mundane realities. She had existed in a luminescent mendacity. Your great-grandmother crossed over from this terrain of thought, and perhaps, that is why she bore the wedding-ringed-petalled-fist with yellowed-blue-pencil-crayon scratchings kissing her womb.

There were no papers inside the coffee tin, just a rectangular piece of yellow material. The edges of the material frayed in yellow string. Emblazoned on the underside of the yellow fabric were two thick outlines of the Star of David. Positioned inside the middle of the star was a thick J. The material was designed to be cut down the middle, splitting the stars.

The material had not been cut.

The material had not been sewn onto a man's clothing.

The material had been hidden away.

The material had been saved.

I put this tin under a picture of a man from the Second World War.

RIPPLE

Our women went up, lifted, journeyed inside,
    they painted, they wrote, they read,
    they cut grass, they cut hair,
    they worked for a living,
    our men stayed on the ground
    where the money grew down, scrub, they
    grew like forests into work.

We orbited each other, pushes and pulls,
    unable to grasp the location of the pivot,
    gender divide amongst sequential phenomenon,
    for some time, we could not feel
    the cubed oneness of our collective existence.

We were actors and participants of
    the same story, perceiving it differently,
    but sensing, regardless, electro-chemical events,
    the ripple of our chaotic lives, blinks of solid frames

. . .

cut from an organic film strip, stacked neatly on top of
one another, I wrote into the sixth dimension,
looked up from my hands around the world
and conceptualized sequences of worlds existing
simultaneously and instantaneously.

I saw objects, worked through sequences,
witnessed the mechanism of a divine synergy
between human, technology, Mother Nature,
weather, time and space,
history, geography, science,
a rare circumference,
I realized the pin of many magical
turning wheels and I could
know much in an instant.

I was reassured by the soft rolling click
of ancient shoulder blades,
a rainbow tribe, hush, they're coming,
rising up, extending, awakening,
stirring the Egyptian graves, priestess backbends,
carrying the sacred fire, a putting in.

I wrote there, vessel, chalice,
filled my cup, pregnancy thereafter.
I wrote Away from a reality
of spaces that refused me to say, "No."
Heels dug in, our women weathered storms,
cuts on stones, scars in skin,
solitary midnight walks
in the halo of a full moon,
the dog followed and turned back around,
and the men of this family

set up camp, joined us before the
heat of a bonfire flame,
star gazers and sun wishers.

Dislocation and disorientation,
    we opened, awakened and learned
    just how powerful love is,
    sun wish, kiss of death, gift of life,
    when we relearned and reclaimed,
    relit the fire of the priestess.

THE PRESENT

She entered the house in prayer. Unafraid. Forging frontiers of rooms moving the energy through the house. First, she merely existed there, sharing space with the final residue of the old woman. Framed pictures of great-grandchildren on shelves. Magazines stacked against the wall. A rubbed raw green leather Lazy Boy. Empty. Tiny soldierlike penguin figurines on windowsills, on tables, on shelves—on guard.

Penguins mate for life.

STORYTELLER

For months I had dreams of my grandmother.

The first dream was the worst. She was trapped in the house, I was going back in. I hid from her. There was a dream scene of me running out the backdoor, much like I'd always done, quietly slipping out the back without detection. Goodbyes were prolonged and guilt-ridden. I was in my youth. I wanted to leave.

In dreams in between, she continued to be locked in the house. She would move from room to room. There was one dream scene with stained glass French doors. I would go through them. She would stay behind.

I would sometimes drive by the house on my way to work. The windows were dark. The backyard was cast in shadow. The house changed over time with the rapid entry and exits of new owners. A chain-linked fence boxed in the backyard. Her gardens grew over. They cut down her trees. I would think, *is she stuck there?*

In the last dream, her paintings lined the walls, I wandered through long corridors studying canvases like an art gallery. Hallways stretched out, rows and rows of frames infused with her spirit blended into each other. Water landscapes and Canadian Shield ridges. Thick Van Gogh brushstrokes and bleeding together Monet frames. A final testimony. Something beautiful left behind.

I would like to believe those hallways became a stairway, a ladder out. That she finally got out—was finally free.

I hung a landscape of O'Hara's mill above my mantle.

I sat an oil and paste frame of an elderly white-haired woman beside a picture of a man with sad eyes.

I still imagine there will be ghost stories told of an old woman in solitude who died in that house. What happens to a space when someone crosses over in it? *It is her house.* It is her house for our lifetime cycles or however long that house stands. It will never be theirs. I worry that it is now a tomb.

"I found empty bottles of Tylenol and sleeping pills beside her bed," my father had quietly told me.

And I know, she wanted to be buried on the property of the Lake House, underneath a Crabapple Tree.

There is no grave. No burial for me to go to.

Perhaps that is the best way for her, a diaspora soul, an uprooted spirit always longing for home. I picture taking her ashes to her father's grave in Belgium. I picture burying her with my father.

There will never fully be closure, but that it is the way.

The way it is meant to be.

RIPPLE

A short strand of yarn, wormy, hard from glue,
    a poem found, "Alone Again,"
    quotes from novels of Canadian writers
    strewn about,
    he sees it as a list,
    text from an email correspondence,
    wax-crayon grave rubbings,
    Elizabeth York,
    Daniel York,
    a black crow's feather,
    blue pencil crayon scratchings,
    a crumbled maple leaf between two shingled glass panes,
    an online chatroom request to know
    about a grandmother with yarn in an institution away,
    another one who sat up from sleep, fell over on her side,
    a ripped silk painted pillow cover thrown away,
    a tattered lotus flower.

He would take great pains with this project,
    not having come across such a creation before.

The pregnant woman had passed it across the counter to him,
    a stern look of determination emanating from within.
    He did not want to be the catalyst for disaster
    if she could somehow not master her past.

He spreads the canvas across his measuring table,
    stillness,
    a gentle probing of fingers through beard.
    He is mesmerized.

The sketched tree,
    rooted in the centre,
    black branches fanning across canvas,
    a beautiful arch.

He gently runs his fingers
    over scores of scraps and fragments
    adhered to branches,
    residue.

Touches warm fingertips to names.
    Hums dates along his chapped lips, places.
    Thick fingers pinch a bridge of nose,
    massages centre of forehead.

He knew of the yellow star,
    had never seen one in person before.
    The actuality of material,
    a tremor deep within his gut,
    his eyes watered.

A star uncut and sewn to clothes,
he wonders whose star this is,
whose clothes were they to be sewn to,
what happened to this person?

Torn letters,
elegant cursive writing,
absolutely perfect,
the dips and dotted I's,
symmetrical,
the letters slightly slanting to the right.
Black and white photographs of faces
angled precisely and solemnly in front of the camera lens.
Links in a chain,
Rings of the trunk of a tree.
Ripples,
Ripples growing out
From a skipped Stone.

He could have stood longer,
let the names and dates
pull him along into this past, but,
he sets his jaws, picks up his tape,
and begins recording measurements.

She had picked out the frame no one had wanted.
Handmade, carved out of maple, not pine,
peculiar for its misshaped way.
When he purchased it from the antique shop,
the man had been drawn to the barefaced pattern of the
wood.
"Wormy" from sporadic knots and flowing dark contours,
"Heartwood."

. . .

He knows she wants that frame
    precisely because of the imperfections.
    He saw the pregnant woman orient
    to the vibrations of that frame,
    knotted and gnarled.
    There was beauty and honesty in that alignment.

She had turned around to him,
    silently gazed.
    Stillness, a ripple sent out
    Changed the fabric of that stillness,

"This one is perfect.
    Do not change anything about it.
    Do not sand it,
    or stain it,
    or do anything to alter it.
    I want it just the way it is."

"As you wish,"
    he remembers hearing
    his own voice
    send out another
    ripple,
    from another throw
    that risked
    cancelling
    both out.

THE PRESENT

...and the thing was really inside
themselves
all the time
what they were searching for...

–Al Purdy, The North West Passage

Raw wrenching pain courses up and down her spine, a double helix livewire. Nelle bravely shoulders the nauseating waves with clenched teeth and flexing vocal chords. Deep coordinated inhalations and concentrated exhalations braid a tight hum through waxing and waning contractions. Swollen as a full moon, she knows, beyond the cusp of that livewire open-chakra pain, her calm and private new moon waits patiently.

"Nelle," the sound of her name gently tugs her hand from within her meditated moon mindset. Her glossy eyes follow the sound.

"You are ten centimetres now. Expect between two and a half to three-minute contractions." The midwife brings a cold wet compress to her forehead and sponges her brow line and jaw.

Nelle grips the edge of the birthing tub. Her tentacled fingers, pallid and phantom, thrum a melody against the inflatable edge. She opens herself to the room with a rasping throat-singing crescendo. Primal. She pushes up from her back onto her flat feet, squats sacred in the birthing tub, releases her grip on the edge, lowering her hands down between her thighs. She's ready.

The midwife thinks how haunting and grounding the song is, ancient roots pushing through from a woman's heart and womb, down through air into earth. A warm pulse of respect thrums between her temples as Nelle stops singing to breathe deep, pulling the noise privately inside of her.

The head begins to crest. Her daughter moves in and out, rocking, for several contractions, forging ahead, burrowing back in. The midwife immediately sinks her hands into the warm water, expertly guiding Nelle's hands, fitting them into position. They've practiced before and the prompt activates Nelle's memory, she rocks forward in certainty of movement. Eyes from two strong women connect and they nod.

Nelle is to lead.

A right-hand cups the emerging skull, that vulnerable fused peninsula, and Nelle knows she's holding a universe. She pulls up from her knees, stretching slightly, and sinks down deeper, opening herself more fully to the lapping water. The midwife supports her shoulders and helps keep her body steady in the water. Nelle gasps with the movement, sucks air in deeply between her teeth, hissing.

She closes her eyes. Another contraction rips through her, and Nelle swallows, the banshee wail echoes from deep inside a molten maternal core.

The midwife gently enters the closed-eyed internal banshee scream, "Open your eyes Nelle! Look! Watch her be born! Stay open!" The women lock eyes between blinks, Nelle's lips curl, a Fleur-fanged-grimace, the whitest teeth—her eyes drop down. Another private banshee wail, until, a discrete climax, the midwife catches the flash of white behind Nelle's pupils and immediately feels the release, the sublime funneling of downward energy.

Inside to outside.

Nelle catches her daughter's body in that moment. A fish in water.

The infant is pulled around and held beneath the water's surface for an inhale and exhale.

She is perfection.

Face to face. Mirror. Infinite regression.

Then, Nelle raises her baby into the air. The gentle swoop up onto her heart braids with the daughter's first noise, a rich fierce cry.

Her daughter's sound, that genesis of sound, connects and activates her mother, wet and balmy, glazed like a baptism in rain beside a tree or back pressed to earth, another woman turns the page with a tongue-wet fingertip on a boulder, on a hill, lifetimes ago, and Nelle cycles through, unfolds, a steady salt-water river.

The placenta births itself in a quiet release, Nelle digs deep against the side of the birthing tub letting the warm water guide her safely back into herself.

Quiet.

Sudden unexpected quiet.

Nelle kisses a tiny head crowned in a mass of dark hair, catches the glint of cat-slit cobalt eyes.

She sighs.

You are alive. We survived.

The infant suddenly forces the rubber of her arms underneath her chest pressed against her mother's chest—organic prism, sacred pyramids. Nelle's eyes split wide. Her baby locks her elbows and slowly, but with an otherworldly determination, raises her upper body off her Mother's citrus-heart chest.

The baby girl lifts her face and looks straight at Nelle.

ABOUT THE AUTHOR

Sara Hailstone's writing is born from navigating the raw and confronting connections that living in rurality projects by scouring domestic landscapes. She is an educator and writer from Madoc, Ontario, Canada who orients towards the ferocity and serenity of nature and what we can learn as humans from the face of forest in our own lives. A graduate of Guelph University (B.A.) and Queen's University (M.A. and B.Ed.), she has recently finished her Masters in English in Public Texts at Trent University. Sara is currently working as a book reviewer and managing editor. She teaches secondary school in English and Indigenous Studies.

Running Wild Press publishes stories that cross genres with great stories and writing. RIZE publishes great genre stories written by people of color and by authors who identify with other marginalized groups. Our team consists of:

Lisa Diane Kastner, Founder and Executive Editor
Cody Sisco, Acquisitions Editor, RIZE
Benjamin White, Acquisition Editor, Running Wild
Peter A. Wright, Acquisition Editor, Running Wild
Resa Alboher, Editor
Angela Andrews, Editor
Sandra Bush, Editor
Ashley Crantas, Editor
Rebecca Dimyan, Editor
Abigail Efird, Editor
Aimee Hardy, Editor
Henry L. Herz, Editor
Cecilia Kennedy, Editor
Barbara Lockwood, Editor
Scott Schultz, Editor
Rod Gilley, Editor

Evangeline Estropia, Product Manager
Kimberly Ligutan, Product Manager
Lara Macaione, Marketing Director
Joelle Mitchell, Licensing and Strategy Lead
Pulp Art Studios, Cover Design
Standout Books, Interior Design
Polgarus Studios, Interior Design

Learn more about us and our stories at www.runningwild-press.com

Loved these stories and want more? Follow us at runningwildpublishing.com, www.facebook.com/runningwild-press, on Twitter @lisadkastner @RunWildBooks